Observations & Nightmares:
The Complete
short fiction
of
JR Billingsley

The Rapps Barren Stories

MEN LIKE TREES

When the lunch whistle sounded, all but the main saw was shut off because it was too much a pain in the ass to get working again. Charlie walked into the office and wiped the sweat from his brow with a dust-covered palm. His fingers and nails were black with sap and bark flak. He pulled out his meatloaf sandwich (a slab of meatloaf shoved between a wedge of cornbread split like a gator's mouth) and ate his tomato. Papa Joe, seated behind the foreman's desk, dumped salt first on his meatloaf sandwich and then his tomato and jammed the whole slice of tomato into his mouth. Charlie took a swig of coffee from his mug.

"How's Alice coming along?" Papa Joe asked.
"Just fine."
"And my grandbabies?"
"Ornery as ever."
Charlie Cross hadn't been treated special after marrying the foreman's daughter. He had worked his way up from logger to bucker then drove the truck for a while, then decker and de-barker and on up to head saw. In the seven years at the mill so far he had edged and then had sweat at the kilns drying the trimmed and scaled pieces of long-leaf yellow pine, till he worked as scaler for six months while Pete Better was out with

a broken back when a thirty foot de-limbed piece of pine fell on him. When a professional scaler rode in on the Missouri/Pacific spur down from St. Louis and took up the position, Charlie was made assistant foreman.

What the other men didn't understand, what none of them could know unless they worked as assistant foreman and none of the men here had, was that the assistant didn't have it easy. When someone or another called in, it was the assistant foreman who filled in to get the job done, and on top of that he had to shadow the foreman and learn all he could about shipping and scaling and taking orders from all the companies that needed their lumber and he had to learn how to talk to the engineers and loaders and other men on the Missouri/Pacific. If you fell out with the railroad, Charlie learned, your business died. Then the yard's owner is visiting you, and then you're more than likely fired.

Charlie's father-in-law was on good terms with the railroad; he talked to them just right. That's how he got the job. He had been a scaler back in the day, third in line under the old foreman who was before Charlie's time and behind even that unruly alcoholic Fletcher. The foreman at the time—Brady—got into some argument with the railroad engineer running the spur. After he was fired, Papa Joe didn't have to wait too long before his promotion. Fletcher's liver swole and then he was retired and Papa Joe took over. And then he hired Charlie not six months later.

One of the men, a big ol' boy like most buckers were, named "Bucker" Nells, poked his head in with a knock and smirked down at Charlie before asking Papa Joe where the boys should head to after lunch. Everyone had called him Papa Joe, even before he became foreman.

"You done with that tract over by Wilson's place?"

"Yessir. Nothing left but some saplings."

"Go north, next quad. Start taping it off for us to hit tomorrow."

"Bucker" Nells said, "Yessir."

"A frost is coming," Charlie said. It was nearly October, and logging in those days was a seasonal venture, and while South Arkansas' winter climate was temperate, the mornings were still cold enough. Just after Christmas, in the dark months of January and February when there was always a real danger of ice, the mills shut down pretty regularly. The ice could seize up the motors or even worse, the logs could freeze and it was like cutting stone. They had learned a long time before Charlie ever came along that it was better to shut down for a day or a week rather than risk the saws.

"We'll be good another week or two." All summer they had been coming in just prior to daybreak and both men knew that once the frost settled in, they'd have to push back their start time to well after sunup to allow for the morning thaw.

Charlie opened his mug of coffee and drank. It was tepid and grainy, only a few hours removed from the morning's percolation.

"Come over tonight for dinner?" Papa Joe asked. "Listen to the game? Yankees won last night."

"Giants are terrible."

"This'll be a repeat of last year. Too bad the Cards ain't playing."

Charlie sighed. "Cain't. Me'an Alice got to ride in to El Dorado for her appointment."

"She's as stuffed as a tick," Papa Joe said with a laugh. "Gonna burst any day now."

"This summer was miserable for her." Charlie thought of how her feet had swelled and how she complained all the time of the heat and how she hogged the bed and sweat. This third child had been the hardest yet. Air conditioning like what the newer homes in El Dorado had would have helped immensely, but the electric company had yet to raise wires out their way. Papa Joe had misinterpreted his daughter's suffering for an indication of what she was having, and convinced she was going to pop out another boy, said they should name him Bobby Jo (and because they liked the name, when their daughter was born a couple of months later at Christmas they named *her* Bobbi Jo). Charlie thought of how small their place was. Some of the newer homes in El Dorado were bigger. Whole damn town was growing, not like Crossett, with its abandoned farms and barns and the old, dilapidated Quincy farmhouse with its rumors and history.

"Well, drop the other'n off before you leave. I want to see my grand-babies."

Martin was six and loved his Papa Joe. Petora was still toddling around and so never wanted to be too far from her parents. Charlie said it might be easier to have their neighbor Janie Wetzel watch the kids seeing as how it was twenty miles one way to El Dorado and it would be awfully late when they made it back. Papa Joe said whatever and reminded Charlie he was scaling the last load this afternoon.

"After work tomorrow we'll all stop by for dinner," Charlie said. "Tomorrow is Friday and we could listen to the game."

"Mama's gonna have some collard greens and a pot of beans and fatback. I'll get her to do up another pan of cornbread, even."

"That sounds fine," Charlie said.

He ambled home after work with his hands in the pockets of his dingy denim overalls. The road was dirt and narrow with deep divots and troughs worn into it, raised up above the swamp with no shoulder to speak of. He lived in the opposite direction as Papa Joe, and he never thought it would look good to the other men to hitch a ride from his boss who also happened to be his father-in-law. He saw the way the men acted around him, whether or not Papa Joe saw it or not.

He heard the horses before he saw their riders. "Bucker" Nell and "Bucker" Smith reigned back their mangy nags and smiled down at Charlie, allowing their horses to trot around him so as to try and impede his path. Looking at the two men was like looking at a broken mirror and its reflection. They were big men as most buckers had to be given the work they did, both men missing a tooth or two or three, both men perpetually dirty and both men just as stupid. Charlie was no scholar, but he had a brain compared to the two of them, and he had a future. These men were lucky to live out their days as buckers, when either should have been resigned to something less complicated, like a coal shoveler down at the paper mill.

Well if it ain't Junior Foreman." "How's it going, Junior Foreman?" It mattered not which one said what. If one man happened upon a thought the other expounded on it.

"What do you boys want?" Charlie asked.

"We just making nice, Junior Foreman," said "Bucker" Nell. And "Bucker" Smith echoed: "Yeah, nice." Charlie wondered if they had been to El Dorado to see one of those matinees like he had just taken Martin to, a gangster flick starring Spencer Tracy or something like that.

"You need to think about something, Junior Foreman," one or the other said, and the other echoed: "We need to know you are good for that job, and the best way for you to do that is to show you can be one of the guys. Now the best way you can do that, Plug, is take a ride with us tomorrow. Some of the niggers are coming back from the shanty towns on the Mississippi for their weekend furlough Saturday. Some of us boys are going to ride out to greet them, and you need to be with us."

"I ain't Klan," Charlie said, knowing full well it wasn't good for a white to ignore the Klan's call any more than it was for a black to ignore their presence. The Klan was notorious for demonizing whites as *nigger-lovers* and stringing them up right with the blacks or setting their homes ablaze if they didn't take up arms when called, but he wasn't ready to believe these two idiots were Klansmen.

"You got a wife and a couple of kids," one said, and the other reminded them all that Charlie's wife was expecting. "Big family." They grinned. "Getting bigger. It'd do well for you to remember the men. Not look so uppity. Show you belong. For your family's sake."

They rode off. If it was that western with Errol Flynn he'd seen with Martin a few weeks back, the bad guys would be riding off laughing. All Charlie heard was the screech of a distant crow, and in the underbrush to his right just off the road, something scurried and splashed into the South Arkansas swamp.

Ⅎℳ

Dinner was quick, more meatloaf and cornbread. Charlie didn't tell Alice about the men or about Papa Joe's request to drop the kids off. When Janie Wetzel showed up, Charlie and Alice kissed their kids and hopped in their '28 Model-A pickup.

Their doctor, a young man, had treated Janie Wetzel and some others out in those parts, and was used to late appointments. He introduced them to a wet-nurse who he said would come out when the time came. Just call if they had a phone. They had already told him the telephone lines, like the electric lines, didn't reach out to their parts yet, but he couldn't seem to remember that.

"You got family in town?" he asked.

"My sister Eudora," Charlie said.

"I'd think about staying with her," the doctor said.

"She got a phone," Alice said.

"I can get there a lot quicker," the wet nurse said.

On the ride home, Charlie and Alice talked around the subject.

"Janie Wetzel's brother works at the paper mill," Alice said. Charlie knew that; Janie had told them about his great job with great pay on a number of occasions. "They got a team. They need a short stop."

"I got a lot of time in at the mill," Charlie said. Neither acknowledged though they both thought about how Papa Joe was healthy and well-liked and Charlie wouldn't go no further. Not unless they found another mill that needed a foreman and there wasn't another mill for fifty miles. They'd have to move to Camden or maybe even up near Pine Bluff or even Little Rock.

"I ain't moving to no city," Alice said. She winced, rested her head against the window and rubbed her belly. "Besides, they'll recognize your time at the paper mill."

"I ain't shoveling coals," Charlie said.

"You wouldn't," Alice said. "You'd be up in the office. They need a merchant clerk."

She made him promise to go up and talk to Janie's brother and Charlie said, "We'll see," which of course meant that he would. They finished the ride home in silence.

 handbook

With the morning came a thicker frost than expected. Charlie was walking down the drive to the road when Papa Joe pulled up in his pickup. Charlie, clutching his thermos of coffee in both hands in an effort to keep them warm, only let go to hop in the cab. The interior of the truck cut the wind that had bored into Charlie while he waited but the cab was still cold, and Charlie nor Papa Joe talked on the ride up to the mill for their teeth chattering. Charlie sipped his coffee, but it was too grainy this morning and his stomach was already tore up, rolling and tumbling as if he was nervous about something. As the truck parked Charlie looked up to the saws. The trail of pine chips glistened in the early morning as though diamonds had been scattered over the path, twinkling in the shadowy blue of the predawn. They exited the truck and Papa Joe made it around the hood before he went down.

Charlie rushed to Papa Joe's side and found the old man sprawled out on the wood chips, eyes closed, lips parted. Charlie felt the back of the scalp for blood and found nothing. Papa Joe looked impossibly old. His face was ashen. His eyes flitted.

"Bumped my head," he managed. Charlie glanced instinctively to the steel bumper of the truck and wondered if Papa Joe had smacked his head on that or the grill with its sharp edges and decided no, if it were the grill there'd surely be blood.

"Just stay still," Charlie said, and called out for the guys who were already up getting the saws running. The buckers weren't there yet, wouldn't show for nearly another hour.

The scaler was the first to arrive. "Papa Joe," he said as the old man grumbled and shook off Charlie and sat up, wincing and grabbing for the back of his head. Charlie noticed fine beads of sweat on his father-in-law's forehead and upper lip. The color still had yet to return. Other men came down. One, Charlie didn't see who, had the foresight to turn off the main saw.

"Rest here a minute," one said, and when Papa Joe didn't get better, another suggested he get into town to the doctor. Papa Joe resisted. Charlie noticed he was slurring his words. They helped him to his feet but Papa Joe swayed. He braced himself on the pickup's hood.

"I'm taking you in," Charlie said, till one of the planers said he'd do it, that they could make do with one less planer but they couldn't afford to lose the woodsforeman and the assistant too. Papa Joe grumbled something about being all right and allowed the men to help him into the passenger side of his own truck. Charlie waited for the planer to drive him off before getting on the radio in the office to reach the mill's owner, and sent Black Mick up the road to Alice and her mother to tell them what had happened. Black Mick was the mill's mechanic and about the only other man Charlie could see to spare this frigid morning.

℞℟

The buckers hadn't wanted to listen when Charlie gave them orders. They were perfectly acceptable orders, right in line with the day's direction Papa Joe had laid out the day before, but from Charlie the orders were second-guessed and voices were raised and the entire mill saw Charlie loose his cool. He told them to get and slapped the office door with his palm and he ran his fingers through his hair before disappearing into the office. He calmed himself long enough to finally reach the mill's owner, Mr. Jacobson out of El Dorado. He was professional and spoke well, explained the accident as best he knew what happened and assured Mr. Jacobson all was running smoothly.

"I'm sure it is, boy, I'm sure it is. You hold down the fort and I got a few calls to make. I think I can have someone there by Monday, for sure."

"Someone? Monday?"

"Yessir. Papa Joe's replacement. Temporary prob'ly, but you're doing a fine job today."

"But I…" Charlie didn't know what to say. His voice trailed off and he turned off the radio and he sat back in the chair. He had actually thought he'd fill in for Papa Joe. He thought how relieved he was when he saw Papa Joe hauled away. Now it would be his time. But such ideas only made Charlie's stomach churn rotten and he felt sick and his head cooled and he sweated in the little office. He felt awful for thinking such things and felt awful that such thoughts were there.

Black Mick came back just before lunch. The planer returned on horseback just before the final whistle. He told Charlie he had driven up his wife and mother-in-law and kids in the truck and rode back on a friend's horse. They did that so Charlie could bring his own truck in after work. Charlie grumbled a thank you and shut the door. He blew the whistle and walked out of the sawmill and headed home.

☙❧

The buckers Nell and Smith rode up smiling still. They had been the instigators at the meeting. The other buckers and the gaggle of loggers were all content to do what Charlie had said. Now they smiled down on Charlie and their eyes squinted in the afternoon light to make their pudgy, dirty faces look mean. They were known around those parts for their meanness. They were big men and particularly stupid men and they were both mean men.

"You thought about what we said," one or the other asked.

"You boys know Papa Joe's in the hospital and the shock of it all might send my wife to labor," Charlie said. "You know I ain't going with you tonight."

"That ain't going to be best for your family," one or the other said.

Now each man outweighed Charlie by at least fifty pounds. Their arms were as big as one of his thighs, and Charlie was tall and stringy. But he was quick. He reached up and snatched "Bucker" Nell by the collar and pulled him off his nag, smashing his face in the dirt and rocks and divots and troughs of the old back road. "Bucker" Smith yelled something and strayed close enough to kick at Charlie, but Charlie grabbed his foot and pulled him and his worn saddle down and the horse scurried away a few steps. Then Charlie punched him twice in the nose, spraying blood across the road.

∾12∾

He turned. "Bucker" Nell was getting to his feet and Charlie hurried to him and punched him in the face with a broad haymaker that spun the man around twice before knocking him to the ground. Charlie scooped up some road and tossed it in "Bucker" Smith's eyes and pushed him backward through the undergrowth that lined the road into the swamp. The man thrashed in the water and screamed something about gators or bears and came staggering out.

"I ain't no Klansman," Charlie said. "You won't threaten my family again, or I'll make sure you don't walk out of the swamp. You sons of bitches get the hell out of here."

ರಠ

Each man staggered on their feet and eyed him narrowly. Charlie stood his ground. "Bucker" Nell found his horse and mounted it quick, but waited for "Bucker" Smith to throw his saddle up and mount before they trotted off. Once they got going, neither man looked back, and Charlie didn't move till they were out of sight.

ರಠ

At home he changed and washed his face. He wasn't particularly excited about getting up to the hospital. He had never liked hospitals, nor doctors, for that matter. Nothing personal, mind you. Dr. Greer served as deacon at their church and he was a nice enough old man, but beyond that Charlie was of the opinion that if an apple a day would work, then he'd eat two or three.

ರಠ

By the time he made his way into town, the sun had sunk beneath Daly Pond and El Dorado was pretty much quiet. Charlie had been thinking quite a bit on his ride up to the hospital. He was thankful the Mill's owner Mr. Jacobson was not there when he walked inside, into an unsteady quiet that had obviously just settled not long before his arrival. If he had been, Charlie couldn't have promised Jesus he'd have remained civil. But Mr. Jacobson wasn't there and Mama sat at Papa Joe's side, silently weeping, holding his hand. Papa Joe lay motionless. Charlie could see the young doctor talking to his nurses but Alice was the first to notice him and rushed to his arms and hugged him. She said they wanted to drill a hole in his skull. The doctor walked up to him.

"Mr. Cross. Your father-in-law hit his head something hard this morning. Pressure has been building steadily in his skull."

"What's this about a hole?" Charlie asked. Passion and surety that this wasn't real argued with the words the doctor spoke, with the scene playing out before him. Papa Joe wasn't unconscious. He ought to be sitting up, talking, joshing the nurses. He couldn't have hit his head that hard. He just slipped, is all. Anyone could have. Just slipped like that. He didn't hit that hard.

The door was open ajar to the room, and Charlie hadn't whispered like Alice had. Momma called out: "You ain't drilling no damn hole!"

The doctor sighed. He looked haggard, like he hadn't slept. Charlie thought dealing with Momma at her worst could do that to a man, and he fought back a devilish grin that was as much a response to the man's disposition as much as it was a reaction to the situation.

"It's called a Decompressive Craniectomy," the doctor said. "We do it when there's significant swelling to relieve pressure."

"But it's a hole?"

"Yes," the doctor said. "It could save his life."

"Could?" Charlie repeated.

The discussion ended there. The doctor retreated down the hall and did not return till morning. The nurses checked in sporadically for the briefest of visits, checking vitals, checking pupillary response.

"Mr. Jacobson was here a while ago," Alice said.

"Yeah."

"He said Papa's replacement would be in by Monday. Said you should take some time off. We'd need you here more and your job would be ready when you got back."

"Yeah." Then, "You know his name? Janie Wetzel's brother. I can't recall it. Only met him the one time."

"Yes," she said. "There's a nice house in town not too far off from his house. Good part of town, not a lot of colored folk. Got the A/C and a phone and 'lectricity."

That recalled to him the buckers, Nell and Smith. He winced as though he'd been punched in the gut. She clutched for his hand and saw the cuts, a bit of dried blood, but when Alice asked what happened Charlie just waved her off.

"I slipped on the walk home, stepped in a rut and caught myself going down face first."

That night, Charlie sat and hugged his kids and hugged his wife. The nurses brought in a couple of cots for the kids and they found an empty bed for Alice and Charlie sat with Mamma, watching over Papa Joe till he passed that morning.

ઍ઎

Charlie paid no mind to the service at the funeral home. He had seldom listened to Reverend Simms on Sunday, so a funeral made no difference for him. At the gravesite, Charlie stared at the trees. A northerly breeze chilled the day, and he watched the pinetops sway in sync. Charlie was only a little bothered by the cool, but he could feel Alice and the kids shiver at the gusts while he just swayed with the pines. He imagined coldly that Papa Joe wasn't bothered by the frost and wind no more, either.

Nearby four Bluff City Cemetery gravediggers leaned on shovels, slumped like willows, listening intently to the preacher. Three were black as coal and one was lighter, like cocoa; their foreheads and cheeks shined with sweat and their shirts were soaked transparent. Charlie couldn't imagine a worse job than grave-digging for any man, and wondered if it would be inappropriate to tip them for their troubles.

Charlie held his family and thought about how big things fell: how the buckers had fallen off their horses, how Papa Joe, larger than life, had fallen, how the pines fell effortlessly, as neat as you please, logs in a row. Big things fell hard and fast and easy and either recovered slowly (like the buckers) or not at all (like the lumber, like Papa Joe). The job at the paper mill would be more money, but Charlie would not be as big a man there. He wouldn't be a woodsforeman, but for Charlie Cross that was all right. He stood straight and tall for his wife and kids and gathered them close with his arms when the hymns started and the casket lowered. Tomorrow, Charlie thought, providing she felt like it, he'd drive Alice to El Dorado to talk to the bank and maybe look at some of those new houses over on Smith Street.

A STRANGER FOR THE SICK

Lance Cross lobbed another bale of hay off the bed of the Ford and leapt to the snow. Herferds and Angus raced around the side of the truck, trying to pull off loose hay. Black calves bounded across the pasture.

Lance let his right glove slip loose and smacked the head of a nearby yearling trying to eat off the tied bale, sending it bucking away. Ahead of him, like a chieftain, the Angus bull sauntered toward him. Its head held high, it did not run like the others when a human was near; Lance kept an eye on him as he cut the strings.

The bull took another step.

"Get back, Jack," Lance called—the name for the bull the name for each of his grandfather's bulls throughout the years. He threw a square and the bull stopped. Waiting till Jack began to eat, Lance scattered the hay and pulled four more bales down, sneering. When that was done he hopped into the truck and drove to the pond, pulled the axe from behind the seat and chopped holes at the edge so the cows could get a drink. He glanced at his watch, saw he was late, and thought: *Forget school.*

Two barns a ways off caught his eye, and further still he could see the farmhouse; not long ago it had a garage and a fourth bedroom added on. Behind him sat the truck with the implanted flatbed. Frank Smith had paid for all of this with hard work and owed for nothing. The new pole-barn built in the calf lot behind the house was his latest addition.

Three hernia operations in one year almost cost Frank everything he had worked for, however. The old man unable to tend to the cattle, Lance's brother had looked after the farm last winter. This past spring Lance's cousin cared for the old Smith homestead, and this time, it was Lance. He had been here three weeks so far, feeding every morning and afternoon; for Lance the minutes passed indolently whether in the house or in the field. That his tenure was half over came as a bittersweet revelation as he drove up the lane back to the yard.

Frank leaned on the corner post planted at the foot of the water trough, but that didn't surprise Lance. The thing to surprise the adolescent was that it had taken his grandfather this long after the operation to step out of the house. Lance knew the surgeon would have wanted Frank to wait longer than a week. Bundled with just his face visible, the stoic figure did not wince from the cold wind. But as Lance approached the gate he could see it. He knew the frigid gusts pulled at Frank's side. Lance could see the pain in the eyes as Frank tried to give a smile to his grandson.

Before the operations, Lance could not remember his grandfather ever looking … old. The once-leathery face was pallid. He had always been thin, but now he seemed like a shadow. "Did you check on the cow, John?" Like his bulls, Frank Smith had one name by which he referred all his grandsons. Lance cringed and lifted the gate over the snow, pushing it back.

In the timeworn barn between the calf lot and the main pasture, in a large stable, a debilitated heifer waited. "Yeah," Lance said. He trudged back to the truck and drove it through the gate and into the gravel drive.

Approaching his grandfather again, Lance noticed the old man's eyes turned longingly to the farm. "I took her two buckets of water," Lance said, "and fed her a fresh square. Also poured a couple more cups of grain."

"She finish all that you left before, did she?"

Lance shook his head. "No. Touched a little of it but I thought I better put fresh stuff out."

Frank sighed. "Well don't feed her no more grain or hay. We're only wasting it. I'll call the vet to come out and look at her when you get back from school. What time you get back?"

"Three, but I can come home for lunch and check on her if you want." Lance wanted to kick himself for volunteering.

"No, that's all right. Just get back here as soon as possible after school."

Lance studied the wrinkled face and read nothing. Frank's eyes darted over the landscape, surveying the cattle in the distance. Lance touched his shoulder and Frank sighed. "Town didn't use to be this big. Now it stretches out, and that new bypass they put in…"

"Right," said Lance. "What are you doing out here?" He didn't have to ask that, nor did Lance have to remind him the doctor's orders. He turned his grandfather, putting his arm around the hunched back. Frank leaned on him as Lance led him away from the fence, up the sloped yard toward the front porch.

CXEX

That afternoon, Lance fed the calves their grain as the cold reminded him of where he was—the last place he wanted to be: sloshing through frozen mud and steaming cow dung, pushing his way through the hungry yearlings that tried to run him over to get to the food. Lance bundled up and walked toward the ancient barn. He noticed the vet's truck parked by the entrance and figured the vet must have slipped in while he was feeding.

He opened the barn door and found the vet standing beside the ailing cow. Her coat was red and white, as was the cow's. Lance watched the woman. Her dark hair fell naturally curly to the middle of her back. She wore thin-rimmed glasses over her brown eyes. Her features were angular, her face tan. Lance allowed his eyes to roam over her body. She was in her early thirties. Slowly she stroked the fur along the top of the bovine neck. Lance watched in silence. "She's sick," the vet said.

Lance thought of his grandfather. "So what will we do?" Glancing at his watch, he realized he had fed the grain too soon.

"I'll have to talk to Frank about that," she answered.

"Paw is still sick."

"Well, you'll have to be the one to do it, but since it's his cow, I've got to talk to him."

They rode in her truck to the house, only to find his grandfather in his pajamas in the living room, slippers on his feet, nestled in his recliner, gooseflesh on his forearms though the fireplace put out enough heat to cause Lance to sweat. The vet started abruptly before Frank could get underway with the small talk. "She's going to have to be put down."

"That bad, is she?"

She stepped further into the living room, allowing Lance to move between them by the fireplace. "She's got pneumonia in both lungs. Her foot's so torn up we can't do anything for it. She's got to be put down."

Lance noticed she turned on a twang to speak to the elder. Frank nodded, then looked at his grandson. "Guess I can get my .357 and shoot her."

The vet shook her head. "You need to rest, Frank. Let the boy here do it. He's going to have learn it someday."

Lance grew flushed. "Why he can't do it. He's never shot a gun in his life. Nope. I gotta do it."

"Now, Frank!" she said. "You need to rest. Let the boy take your gun down there. He can do this."

Frank sighed and regarded Lance. "Can you do it?" he asked the vet.

She shook her head. "I got a bunch of calls this afternoon. I'm sure Lance here can take care of it."

Without saying another word, she left. Frank's eyes settled on his grandson. "Bring the gun, John."

Lance walked to the gun rack and pulled out the .357 revolver, carried it to the living room and handed it over. "You know where I keep the shells?" Frank asked. "I need two .357 shells."

Lance nodded and retrieved them. As Frank loaded the shells into his gun, Lance watched obediently. "Now this gun can hold either .38 shells or .357 shells. The .357's are more powerful, and that is what I put in here for you. The cow's skull is tough, so you got to hit her in the right place."

"I know how to hit something."

"Now listen to me boy. You gotta hit her in the right spot in order to kill her. You got to imagine horns on her and draw a diagonal line from that horn to the opposite eye. Where those lines intersect is where you gotta hit her." Lance nodded again and looked at the gun. As Frank handed it to him, Lance noticed the weight. *Mom should be here soon*, he thought. He held the gun in both hands, the heaviness of the weapon drawing down on him. "Now be careful, John," Frank cautioned. "That's a loaded weapon you got there."

Lance entered the bedroom of his grandparents and pulled a pair of protective earmuffs from his grandfather's chest of drawers. He reentered the living room holding them out. "It's way too cold," Lance said. "Got to make sure my ears are warm."

"Can you do this?"

"Yeah," Lance offered after a pregnant hesitation.

"Well be sure and lead her up to the double-doors. Otherwise the back-hoe won't be able to drag her out."

Lance said nothing but forced a smile, pulled the door open and stepped onto the porch. Snow drifted to the ground; he sighed, watching his breath rise up before taking his first step. Too innumerable to count, his footfalls ultimately brought him to the door of the barn. But he could not look at the door; he couldn't even raise his fingers to the handle. He turned away, first to the house but he couldn't focus on that, so he turned around and stared past the barn to the field. The calves still played in the snow. The cows grazed on the remnants of the sunrise feeding. *Just one more minute*, he thought.

Climbing the gate leading into the pasture, Lance walked into the shed where the tractor once sat. He put the earmuffs on then stared at the gun. It was heavy. In the silence, Lance could hear his rapid heartbeat echo into the hard plastic of the muffs. He wanted the vet to be wrong— he could march right in there and tell his grandfather the cow *IS* doing better and he didn't have to put her down. But thoughts that the cow would be healed couldn't linger though they tried, so he thrust these fancies aside, left the shed, and climbed back over the gate. Taking a quick look back to the house, he entered the barn.

The cow stood by the trough next to the door he entered. She looked at him then looked straight ahead. Lance knew he was going to have to get her to the other end. He pushed on her and she didn't move. He pushed again and she all but fell over. He put the gun in his coat pocket and used one hand to nudge her while the other stroked her back.

"C'mon girl," he said, muted. She looked at him, her brown eyes staring into him. She seemed to respond to his voice. "C'mon girl," he said again. "C'mon let's go up there."

Slowly, painfully and with deep sighs, she began to walk toward the double doors. About two-thirds of the way there she stopped. Lance knew she couldn't go any further. "We'll just have to drag her out later," he said out loud.

His voice sounded odd when heard through the earmuffs, but he continued talking as he struggled to turn her toward the door. Facing him, she watched as he moved to stand by the double doors, then watched him as he looked around the barn. The bleak day crept in through the cracks in the walls, allowing him enough light to see. "It's amazing this place hasn't fallen down yet," Lance said to the cow. Frank had made some repairs to it and put a new tin roof on not too long ago, but the barn's wood was cracked, filled with holes, and termite ridden. In the hayloft above, Lance knew there were places you could step and fall straight through.

She looked around haltingly then back at him as he removed the gun from his pocket and held it in two shaky hands. Again her sorrowful eyes met his. He raised the gun; his trigger finger on the outside of the guard, he pulled the hammer back. The revolver clicked over. Using the sight, he drew the imaginary lines and found the intersection point. All was silent, except for the echo of his heart in his muffled ears.

His finger rested on the trigger. Holding the gun in place, he took a few deep breaths that only came out as sighs. Then, slowly, he began to squeeze.

The noise was muffled, as he had hoped. A bright flash went off in front of him and smoke wafted from the barrel. He had felt the gun kick, hard enough he thought the bullet had missed its mark. But there she was, on the floor.

There was a trickle of blood on her forehead; her ribcage rose and fell with effort. Her eyes seemed duller. He had been off slightly. Lance debated kneeling closer for a better shot, opted to stand and so raised the gun again and re-drew the lines. It kicked again, and again he questioned whether he had jerked it prematurely, and now wished he had taken the time to screw in the 60 watt for what little it could have illuminated.

Blood and gray water poured forth from her nostrils and mouth. Her leaden tongue flopped out and the ribcage settled. Her eyes were lifeless now. Lance took the earmuffs off and discharged the empty casings from the revolver, returned the gun—now strangely lighter—back into his coat pocket. His eyes would not tear from her body.

☙❧

The walk back through the calf lot to his grandfather's house was slow by design. Several of the calves had run to the barn, probably wondering what the noise was. They called to him as he passed but he kept his eyes on the ground. He sidestepped a few piles only looking up when he neared the gate. His mother's car was in the drive.

He walked in to find his mother and grandmother sitting in the living room with Frank. He handed the revolver to his grandmother and asked her to put it up.

"Are you okay?" his mother asked.

Lance took a seat away from them. "Why?"

"You're all pale."

His grandfather smirked. "Well, John, did you get it done?"

"Yeah. She's dead." Lance tried to ignore the look in his grandfather's eye. His grandmother returned to her seat and the three of them resumed their conversation. Lance sat there in silence.

☙❧

Two days later the sun had warmed things a bit. The vet returned with some toothless yokel pulling a backhoe behind his truck, and after some polite chitchat between Frank, the vet, and the yokel, she and Lance walked to the barn while the man drove the rig. Lance opened the gates for him, saying little to his two companions. They pried the double-doors open; the snow had melted enough that mud blocked the door's path.

He shuddered at the body ten feet from the door as he stepped inside—recoiled slightly from the smell—the vet and the yokel backhoe driver on either side. "Good shooting boy," the driver said.

The vet looked at Lance and placed a hand on his shoulder. His face had grown pale again. "You okay?" she asked.

"Took two shots."

The backhoe driver knelt down at the head. "You probably got her on the first one."

"I just wanted to be sure. Rather than let her suffer."

"We'll have to drag her out," the backhoe driver said.

"I got her as close as I could. But she was weak."

"You did the right thing," the vet said.

Lance nodded.

They wrapped a chain around the forequarter legs and wrapped the other end around the base of the backhoe. The driver climbed aboard and began to pull. The chains came loose twice and the cow didn't seem to scoot well. Still they had gotten her closer.

The driver turned the backhoe around and used the arm and shovel to rake her out. Lance and the vet held their breaths then braced the cow's back, their gloved hands ruffling the fur. As the bucket scooped the cow into its teeth, the boy could only think of the times he had tried to pet a cow only to have it bolt away in fear. This one had just pleaded with him with her eyes.

The backhoe carried her into the open air and Lance and the vet shut the doors and followed as he drove to the designated spot. From behind, the herd raced around them. Lance watched as they gathered, fearful he and the vet would be trampled. She seemed to pay no attention, however, and kept her head down, watching where she stepped.

"Thanks for coming today," he said as ahead of them, the backhoe dropped the body and began to dig. The cows formed a semi-circle and began to moo loudly.

"You're welcome." She looked at him and studied his face. "He's proud of you, your grandfather."

They watched the backhoe drag the corpse into the hole. The cries of the herd grew louder; a calf bawled not five feet from Lance. The backhoe raked the rocks and dirt, filling in the hole.

When the cow was buried the herd proceeded up the field, still mooing a sound like sobs and dirges as they filed away slowly. The backhoe stopped to pick up the vet and Lance and headed on to the house. Frank Smith paid both the driver and the vet by check and remarked that it might snow that afternoon. The vet said she thought there was a good chance of it.

After the vet and the backhoe driver left, Lance stoked the fire. Shutting the fireplace doors, he turned and stood on the hearth and looked around the living room. His grandmother wouldn't be home for another hour. His mother had made no plans to stop in today. He and his grandfather were alone.

Lance huffed and sat down. Heat from the fireplace stung his back.

"Well, she's buried," Lance said. He didn't want to leave his grandfather's side yet. He looked up and saw Frank staring at him.

"That old boy said you got her on the first shot."

"I took two. Wanted to be sure is all."

His grandfather's stare penetrated and the fire stung. He even imagined the glass angels were watching him. He knew it was Frank's turn to speak and entertained the thought that they were going to be sitting here in silence for the rest of the afternoon.

His legs, without thought, began to stretch, but before Lance could stand and walk out of the room his grandfather cleared his throat. Lance looked the old man right in the eye.

"You did good, Lance."

The boy shifted to the loveseat. He decided then he could sit in that living room all afternoon, just he and his grandfather, in silence or not.

G1 BAD

I tried to flick a ladybug off the hood of a canary yellow Mustang and ended up smearing it in a long red streak that came out orange, so since that didn't alleviate my boredom or my own worries about starting high school that upcoming fall, I resolved to following my brother around the lot, the vehicles washed and waxed like those women out near Beale Street the last time we went to Memphis, and much like some of the hookers, the vehicles here looked appealing on first glance but hid God only knew what inside. My brother read the sheets on the passenger windows and pressed his nose to peer into the interior, spoke of horse power and torque as he held his hands to either side like blinders against the glare.

A red-permed man in a short-sleeve polo approached us with a grin too wide for his freckled face. He extended a spotted hand, offered his forgettable name, and beamed at the '95 Camaro alongside my brother.

"So tell me about your financials," the red-haired salesman said, and my brother omitted his life as a college student, and said he had a secure job at Baxter Labs making dialysis equipment on third shift. It was just a summer job he'd taken after his last semester at Ole Miss. It was a Saturday in late May, and I found myself sweating as we walked through the lot.

"How are you going to pay for this when you go back to school?" I asked during the test drive.

"I don't know," he said, and gripped the wheel and never once looked at me. He steered the white muscle car over the stripes of the road and depressed the accelerator as Pearl Jam played over the radio. He was lost in the moment and as the sun set in the west, we drove southeast toward Norfolk so the golden rays of dusk splashed across the windshield and hood.

"It handled nice," I offered as we pulled back in and he whipped the vehicle into a tight space between an Explorer and a soft-top Jeep. I instinctively searched for an Oh-Jesus-Bar that had never been installed.

"Yeah," he smiled. I watched him walk in to talk to the salesman, hoping beyond hope he'd come back out and we'd climb back into his Honda Civic and we'd go our merry way. As cheesy as it may sound, I've always looked up to my brother. Not many people escaped this small town in North Arkansas after graduation unless they enlisted. He was one of the few to go off to college. Most went to work in a factory job or started farming or worse, just floated around from job to job and trailer to apartment to trailer, getting some girl or another pregnant, drinking and smoking cigarettes and some others got hooked on other things. High school graduation held little promise for most of the people here, and that dim outlook was part of the reason I wasn't looking forward to going in the fall.

John came out twirling the Camaro's keys on his index finger, a shit-eating grin spread across his lips, like he'd solved whatever problems he thought he had.

⊂℈⊃

It only took a month for the night shift to wear on my brother, who paled despite the summer sun and our frequent family trips out on the pontoon. His eyes darkened and his mind grew unfocused: He'd forget daily chores like gathering trash on trash day or loading the dishwasher or putting away his clothes, which became a massive pile on one side of his king-sized bed; everything save for the car, which he'd polish to a shine every Saturday and sit in and stare at in the quiet moments when he was too exhausted to drive or the day delivered summer showers and rain drops that beaded on the wax.

One morning after Dad cooked creamed eggs, I rapped softly on the ajar bedroom door and watched it swing open. John lay sprawled across the king, his legs and torso entangled in wadded sheets. When he raised his head, his hair was a sculpture of tumultuous brown, and his cheeks were scarred like dried creek beds flushed with draught.

"We're supposed to go to Paw's," I said.

He thrashed till he was free of the sheets, and sat on the side of the bed, hanging his head and legs over the side. He hadn't been in bed more than three hours. I'd watched him stagger through the door just a bit ago and plod toward his room.

He had lost nearly twenty pounds, it looked like, since he'd started the job, and now he wore the profile of a skeleton. He said something that sounded like "car" and "tags come?" and I said that we could take his car. He shook his head like he was shaking off a nightmare and said, "What?" He looked equal parts angry and bemused, but this lasted only a moment, and he dressed and we were on our way to our grandfather's house.

γαω

What charm the car had maintained wore off relatively quickly once we noticed the smell.

At first we thought it was something with the exhaust, the emissions. A friend of our cousin owned a garage, and with one look under the hood quelled that theory. We thought it was something else with the car, to the point that John took the Camaro back to the dealer and yelled at the salesman with the red hair and the freckles. He printed off the Carfax and slapped the paperwork down in front of my brother.

"Take a look. Ain't nothing there about smells! But if you want to return it no harm no foul, I'll fish out another'n who might buy it."

My brother stared at the sheet, and I believed he considered it for a moment. I found my own hopes rise, imagining that he would cast off this cursed monstrosity and return to reason, slough off this debt and return to college to finish his degree. Instead, John shoved the paperwork back toward the dealer and looked to the floor.

"It's turkey litter," John said as we drove through town along the strip the kids cruised, between Dairy Queen and Pizza Hut, a half mile of Business 62 –the main route through the town that hadn't been other-wise renamed. It was evening and cooler at sundown, but the smell had only diminished a little.

"Papaw said farmers spread turkey litter in the spring," I reminded him.

John grimaced and drove us on to our parent's house. He'd barely time to shut off the engine before he was bursting through the door, catching our mom and dad in the living room and calling them out to the garage.

"Damn son," our dad said. "It's like something crawled up in your car and died."

A memory then dawned across his face that shifted quickly to a furious spark in his eye; John stormed to the hatchback trunk and popped the lock. There was a pause, a moment of silence that, now in recalling this event, I can relish for its tranquility, the calm before the storm, before John let loose a litany of profanity that would make any sailor blush.

Our dad entered the garage and slapped on gloves that reached to his elbows, and I unfurled several large black trash bags. Our mother asked if he wanted some gloves but John was already reaching into the trunk.

The errand we'd run to our grandfather's a few weeks earlier was to fetch meat for our parent's Labs who now congregated at the Camaro trunk, eager for the smell that had thus far eluded us. He was preparing to slaughter another corn-fed steer and had some freezer-burned meat that he thought the dogs might enjoy.

After festering in the summer heat, the paper bags which held the meat were rotten, and the various packages writhed and wriggled. Maggots squirmed over the trunk carpet and through John's bare fingers. He raised masses of putrefied flesh out of the trunk and tossed them into the bags and when our father approached, he helped after stifling a squelch of laughter behind a gloved hand.

☙❧

The solution was not a simple one. My brother and parents shampooed the carpet and we bleached the metal frame, then washed it with Lysol, then bleached again. We allowed it all to air dry, gave the carpet another shampoo and let that dry before soaking it with Febreeze and returning it to the car.

I would love to tell you this solved the problem with the putrescence, but it was still there, lingering like a phantom, haunting us, not permitting us to forget.

In mid-August, I rode with my brother to Ole Miss. We had found through trial and error which fragrances best masked the smell. New Car was not a good bouquet to accompany rotten meat. Blossoming smells were better. Strawberry provided the right amount of sweetness to counterbalance the festering fumes in the trunk. Lilac proved a little too weak. So, after dousing the cloth seats with strawberry fragrance spray and hanging a few freshly opened strawberry fresheners on the rearview mirror, we began the four-hour drive south.

We didn't talk much on the way down. Once, around Jonesboro, John told me how much he spent on the car.

"What are your payments?"

"About two-fifty," he said. "And insurance, and gas."

"They pay you good at that job."

"Shit," he sneered.

We rode on. The sun beat through the windshield, working on the stench and against the strawberry and the A/C. Ahead of us, the highway jiggled through the heat. The A/C at full blast could not deflect the sun's unobstructed rays.

"Tint would've been nice," I said, but I knew that tint was the least of his problems.

As we skirted West Memphis, John said, "The plates came today." He turned down the radio and hitched a thumb to the backseat. I turned in the seat and saw the plate he'd ordered, an Arkansas plate with the letters: JNS CAR.

"You should get your money back, or see if they'll change the name," I said, and rattled off the number and letters, one after another for him. "1-S-H-T-T-E-R."

We both laughed.

Just after Memphis, we pulled off the highway, grabbed a drink, and topped off the tank. I told John I had to go to the bathroom and he took my Mountain Dew from me and walked to the counter. I entered the tiny room and instantly decided against sitting on the toilet. I pissed and read the names of the condom labels on the machine on the wall over the tank. Various pen-marks and scratches illustrated crude pictures and vile messages. One message signed BAREBACK promised that whomever called the number scrawled wouldn't need or want a condom. I didn't even touch the faucet to wash my hands.

John stood just outside the gas station, holding the bag of our goods, staring at his car. The bell jingled overhead as I emerged. I took a deep breath and sighed and we climbed in to stagnant, superheated air from our short detour that had allowed the stench from the trunk to gain some ground, enough that we had to crack the windows and turn the vents on full blast until the smell had retreated some. I opened the lid of my Mountain Dew and sniffed the bottle as though I was a wine connoisseur relishing a '43 Chavagne Blanc.

"Give a spritz," John said as we pulled back onto Interstate 55 South. I reached into the glove compartment and fished out the Strawberry fragrance spray and aimed a few blasts to the rear, as though I were returning mortar fire to an entrenched enemy.

"It's not too late," I said later, as we took the Batesville, Mississippi exit and headed east. It was only then I realized that John had never turned up the radio.

"I like Ole Miss well enough," he said. "I don't think I want to come back here."

"You should go to ASU," I said.

"Jonesboro is ghetto," he said.

"The U of A, then. I bet you can get in."

"I got this," he said, stroking the top of the steering wheel.

He had been out on a number of dates since signing for the car, but the girls weren't anything to be proud of. The highest level of education achieved by most was twelfth grade and that was only because they had to go. I had seen John with some of the girls. He never seemed to talk much with them. They didn't have a lot to say, I imagined. He studied literature and writing and had taken some physics and calculus at Ole Miss. His idea of a good time was swimming in the lake for an hour and then sunning on the boat dock, reading Tolstoy or Faulkner or Flannery O'Connor or Anton Chekov's short stories. The words that rolled around in his brain, I'm sure, were too advanced for most of his conquests, but they were cute girls and probably good fucks and they liked his car. I knew, though, that keeping this up, even if he could succeed in vanquishing the smell, would only get one of those girls pregnant and then he'd end up in a double-wide if he was fortunate, the goddamn car rusting on either flat tires or cinder blocks, and my brother's great mind would be extinguished from overnights at the factory and shitty diapers and a wife that, as soon as she snagged him, would work hard to let herself go.

I thought DING DNG might make a better personalized plate. That's what this future trailer wife would get fat on, and that's what he would be. We met his friends at their apartment, and I kept my opinions to myself, only responding when John told them my idea for 1SHTTER and we all laughed and his buddy, a barrel-chested guy with high sculpted hair and wire-frame glasses and a booming voice and a goatee, said that he could get one that read 1PCASHT. His laugh was infectious and loud and overbearing. His girlfriend smiled demurely, a pretty Texas blonde a bit on the chunky side but nice enough.

Φ

John and I hung out by the grill with his buddy, who was lording over the sizzling chicken and telling us about this salvage yard on the way to Tupelo and that we should all visit it. Back when we had arrived, he had stuck his head near the trunk when John said the smell wasn't as bad and recoiled quickly.

"The fuck you say," his friend said and laughed.

We ate grilled fajitas and John drank a couple of Coronas with his friend. I learned that while it looked like apartment buildings when we pulled up, his friend and girlfriend actually lived in a two-bedroom townhouse. One bed and bath with a shower was downstairs and upstairs housed one bedroom and a full bath. They had a queen-sized mattress in the guest room downstairs and John and I were fine for a few nights.

Φ

The next morning, we rode out to the auto salvage. Tucked away in the deepest woods of Mississippi down a paved two lane county road that twisted and turned and meandered through oak and pine laced paths, John's friend drove and John rode in the front with me and his friend's girlfriend crammed in the back. That was the closest I had been to the smell and found it ten times worse. Prior to leaving, they had thrown out the old carpet and bleached and cleaned the metal again. Even with the carpet gone, the smell was noxious like it had seeped into the metal and I regretted eating the eggs and sausage they had offered me that morning, good as they'd been at the time.

The salvage place had been fenced off with rusted tin panels standing seven feet tall and nailed to newel posts or great wooden fence posts and across the top two rolls of barbed wire had been strung. The old man that ran the place wore overalls and had flecks of red in his silver beard. He shook John's hand and called his friend by name and directed us to the salvage yard.

Great piles of Camaros and Firebirds, as well as their parts, lay strewn over a field sparsely seeded with Kentucky bluegrass. A great maple smothered in creeping moss shaded a couple of trashed Mustangs and a rusted Hyundai. We walked toward a collection of Camaros in various states of disrepair as the old man talked.

"If it weren't so goddamned hot, my ass crack is sweaty, mind your step, got some rattlers out here, and just last week I found a nest of copperheads or some such, now I got tons of parts to choose from but we want to find a body style close to yourn, what is it, a '93?"

"'95," John corrected.

There was a red one with a black stripe over the hood and the top of the car. The interior was gray but in good condition. The man said he'd part with the trunk carpet for twenty-five dollars. John's friend was examining the car with the shrewd eye of a businessman.

"How much for this muffler," he asked. It had twin pipes and wasn't rusted or holy.

"Another twenty-five."

John's friend had his leather wallet in his hand. "I'll give you fifteen."

"Alright," the man obliged.

⊂⊃⊂⊃

On the ride back, John asked his friend what he needed with a muffler that had come from a Camaro. His friend had vocally shared his love for the cars but at present didn't own one. He smiled at John and winked and said "Happy early birthday, buddy."

John thanked him, but the smile he returned seemed strained.

When we got back to the townhouse John optimistically said the smell was better.

His friend laughed. "No!"

They put the carpet in and the next day we drove to a local mechanic. He installed the new muffler in just under an hour and new glass-pack twin tips that John's buddy had ordered off the Internet as another little surprise. When those were added, we rode back to the townhouse and ate dinner and then he and I drove up to campus. The car was deafeningly loud, now, and the strawberry was actually winning out.

John pointed out a few of the more interesting buildings to me. He showed me the bullet holes still in the columns of the Lyceum from the Civil War and Civil Rights Attacks of the fifties. We walked around the Grove and walked most everywhere on campus. We only got back in the car to drive over to Rowan Oak. After our brief respite from the vehicle, we had returned with fresh noses to discover the lingering wretch of the visitant still haunting from the rear.

He parked at the base of the drive on a gravel turnabout on this side of a metal cable that blocked off the dirt path that led up between the grand oaks to Faulkner's mansion, and ushered me to hop the wire cable and hike up the path, the shadows deep and long already. The place was old and abandoned at twilight and made me uneasy. John didn't tease me with ghost stories, but I was sure a place as old as this had a few.

"I used to come here," John said as we approached the old home. "You know the plot of one of Faulkner's novels is written on the wall of his office."

"Which novel?" I didn't know what else to ask; it wasn't like I'd read any of them.

"*A Fable*," he said absently, and laughed a little at a joke he didn't offer to share with me.

"What are those buildings over there," I asked him.

"Slave quarters, stable for horses, an old barn."

"Doesn't look like Papaw's barn," I said.

He walked up on the porch and breathed in deep the redolent pine and quickly cooling Mississippi night. I waited for him to speak as a sweet peace settled over the residence.

"We won't stay long," he said. He waited till later to tell me that the University owned the land and we were technically trespassing. "It still smells," he said.

"What are you going to do?" I asked.

He shrugged. "Arkansas has a good writing program, a good journalism program too."

"Fayetteville's not that far," I added.

We looked off the porch down the path between the ancient, knotted oaks to the car shining white, perched at the other end. I wanted to ask him what he intended to do.

"They won't take it with that damn smell, he said. Not freely. The new carpet will help."

"We matched it good," I said as though I had a hand in it. John didn't correct me, grammatically or otherwise.

"I didn't send in last month's payment," he said casually.

"Oh," I said. It was dark now but I could see him on the porch, smiling, his teeth shining bright in the moonlight. His eyes, normally blue-gray, seemed black with a spark deep in the pupil that might've been a tiny reflection of the car.

"I don't think I'll send this month's payment either," he said.

"How long do you think they'll let you get away with that."

"Hopefully not long," he said, grinning like the Cheshire cat. "Classes are starting soon."

ჵ

We said goodbye to his friends and roared back home the next morning, talking about what classes he'd already signed up for and when he planned to tell mom and dad that he'd quit his job at the factory and where he was going to live in Fayetteville. We turned the radio up loud to drown out the new muffler and stopped at that same gas station in Southaven to buy another three-pack of strawberry air fresheners.

"Your buddy was a nice guy."

"Yep."

"Loud."

"Yeah."

"He spent a lot of money on your birthday."

"It wasn't a lot for him."

"Still."

"I told him last night, when we got back." I believed this. I was tired and had gone to bed a lot earlier than they did.

"Was he mad?"

John smiled. "He laughed. Said I was a dumbass for leaving school."

We rode on, and a week and a half later John moved to Fayetteville hitching a ride from our folks, and the Camaro stayed parked in our drive till a guy from the bank showed up to reclaim it three weeks later – my first day of tenth grade. He came with a tow-truck driver and a lady with high hair and too much makeup who was hired for the repo and the red-headed salesman from the dealership, and they all looked stern and the tow-truck driver and the lady looked like they expected resistance, but when my mother opened the door before they could even knock and handed over the keys, all the hot air stored up in them kind of deflated and they looked disappointed that they'd take the car with such little fuss. We watched them from the kitchen window, not a one of them looking back to us. The lady snatched up the keys from the bank guy and started to get in the car, but jumped back like she was snake-bit. "Jesus, the smell," we heard her say.

"Breakfast is ready," Mom said.

I was hungry and nervous about the first day of class, so I sat down to polish off my eggs and bacon. I glanced over my shoulder to see the car round the corner and for a moment, caught a phantom whiff, and thought it's their problem now. That's when Mom sat a package down in front of me, thin and of cardboard, like a book or something. I saw it was from John and it had no mailing address, and when she said he'd left it for me, I ripped it open to find a personalized license plate. It took me a minute to get it, but when I did I hung it on my wall and the thought of high school no longer scared me.

2TRIAGN

QUITTING

On Monday I decide at work I'm going to quit smoking. That evening, as I wait for my soon-to-be ex-wife to carry her stuff out the door, I read the box the patches came in. The warning reads not to put on more than one patch at a time; it also says one should wait thirty minutes after removing the patch before lighting up a cigarette. I feel a little woozy, swoon a bit, and sit in my leather recliner. I take another drag and pull the patch of my left bicep as Mandy slams her suitcase on the kitchen linoleum. I don't hear the door open.

"It's real easy," I say, not looking over at her. "You grab the knob, turn and open, pick up your shit and walk outside."

After about thirty seconds, she does just that. Maybe it doesn't take her thirty seconds, maybe I'm still high from the patch/cigarette combo.

On Tuesday Mandy calls. Her number is blocked. When the phone rings I'm in my office, chewing my third piece of gum. The gum also comes with a warning, waiting to smoke or whatever, could cause gum disease. I spit it out and light up a cigarette.

"Look," I say. "I've got a lot of work to do, make it fast." I'm an executive for Wal-Mart, a district manager and my office—half the time—is in my apartment. I supposedly have an office in the store, but it's more like a desk and open to whoever wants to walk in."

"It was just one time."

"In my fucking bed! Your name isn't even on the lease." I don't know why I'm so angry; we weren't married long. I feel betrayed more than anything. She was hot and she was mine and I know how that makes me sound.

"I just wanted a house, I would have…"

"You know I can't. This fucking company, the way it moves us around. I could be in New Mexico tomorrow. Worse than the military."

I could afford a big house. I have a small apartment in north Houston, directly in the middle of my district of Vision Centers. She is a pretty little half-Hispanic girl. She can turn on the accent whenever she wants, but she can't speak a lick of Spanish. I find that funny.

I stub out the smoke and light another. She goes on and on about how miserable the company makes me. I agree, then I hang up. Rubbing my temple, my eyes closed, I try to determine what set off the migraine: her voice or the nicotine.

⊂⊃

On Wednesday, I think cold turkey could work. I read on the Internet some old school way, start the morning fresh and brush your teeth and my dad once said he kept an unopened pack nearby as kind of a crutch. He was able to go longer just seeing it there, it built his will power. I have to visit my stores today, so I drive the company car—a new 2011 Malibu. I put my coffee in one cup holder and the unopened box of cigarettes in the other cup holder. Traffic is bad this morning. I don't even make it to first store before I'm opening the pack of cigarettes.

⊂⊃

On Thursday, Mandy calls my work cell. I'm in with one of my Vision Center managers. He's bitching about lab orders and the time it's taking the Nikon poly lenses to get back. Dallas is our only lab that handles Nikon, I remind him, and he reminds me we're in Houston. "They service the whole country," I say.

"And tints," he says. "We got problems with tinting out of the Fayetteville lab. I just ordered a ½ rose tint and had to drive across the city to the Sugarland store because they are the only store left in the area with a tint machine."

Our meeting goes on for almost an hour.

He's old. I know he doesn't like me. I'm twenty-eight and I wear a suit every day. Other than the cigarette smoke I try to maintain a well-groomed appearance. I even try to mask the smell with chewing gum and good cologne. Today it's Armani Code. I make more money in one year than he has in five years of work. He's been stuck in this position for fifteen years. He's too old to promote and he knows it.

☦

On Friday, at 9:00 in the morning, it is ninety degrees outside and we aren't even in the hottest part of the summer. The heat is moist, Houston's built over wetlands, and the humidity makes your clothes cling to you, smothering. I am reclined in an air conditioned room, my phones are off. My eyes are closed and a sleep mask is over my eyes. A man is talking, slowly, his voice deep and smooth. He has been talking for a half hour like that.

"Every time you see a cigarette, you will get violently ill. You will picture sewage, and the smell of smoke will make you violently ill. When I count to three, you will sit up and remove the mask."

I pay him one hundred dollars.

At five that afternoon, I realize just how good I've done. I think maybe there is something to this hypnosis thing, after all. My air is on high in the car, but I can still feel the heat. The sun is smiling down on me, unencumbered by a cloud, magnified by the windshield. I can barely hear Mandy on the other end.

"You never call my work cell! Understand?"

"You didn't yell at me like this yesterday."

"I was in the stores all day yesterday. We're done. Get it. I'll see you in court in a month."

What I get for marrying a hostess at Hooters. I throw the phone in the floorboard of the passenger side. I pull into a gas station, buy a pack, smoke two on the way home. I pull into a parking space but I don't get out of the car. I lean over and pick up the personal cell off the floor and dial. A buddy of mine has a practice, sees mostly families, but he's treated me on the side. Perks of knowing a doctor, and he's nicer knowing that I'm not one of those people who comes to him with every pain and asks for a free diagnosis.

"We on this weekend?" he asks.

"I'm ready to quit."

"Tell me where to call it in. A script for Wellbutrin."

"Isn't that an anti-depressant?"

"Which is why I'm prescribing it, your insurance will take care of it. Start taking it tonight. One dose a day. Take it for two weeks while you smoke. Then put the cigarettes down and keep taking it for two more weeks. We tee off at nine."

☙❧

Two weeks more and I had to fire someone today. The old Vision Center Manager who doesn't like me as his boss sits in a back office across from me.

"You stepped on her glasses," I said.

"I was adjusting them," he said.

"You called her a pretentious bitch."

"I'm copasetic today," he said with a smile. "I was in a good mood."

Our conversation went on for over an hour. It ends with a finger from him and he storms out the door. I fill out the green sheet and walk outside. It's after twelve-thirty and I haven't had a smoke all day. Now my stomach is turning. My hands are shaking and I feel the beginning of a rush of breath as I get dizzy. I see a kid, a cart pusher, puffing away, leaning up against the building. I walk up to him.

"Can I bum one?"

He says sure, hands me a smoke. I take two long drags, then I look at the cigarette. The ash is long and ready to fall way. I walk away still staring at the cigarette. At my car, without having taken another puff, I drop it on the ground and drive off.

☙❧

Two weeks later, the divorce is finalized. I walk out of the courthouse smiling. It is hotter today. I think about that last cigarette, half-smoked, dropped on the ground. The sun gleams off the surrounding glass and concrete, it's so blinding even shutting my eyes doesn't help. My friend said it's all chemical, what the anti-depressant does. He described it a little but he lost me. I put on my polarized sunglasses and start to drive. The sun is hot and burning and my A/C is loud, but this is my own car and I am ready to do what I want. I drive out of Houston, away from Wal-Mart, away from that crappy little apartment and Mandy and cigarettes. I don't look back.

SEASONS

arly spring, a drift of a cold front, the grass is green but all the trees are still bare except the Dogwoods, the wind is from the north and it is cold, your eyes just opened a few days ago and you fit snuggly into the palms of my cupped hands. As the weather warms you follow us outdoors, exploring the grass, the trails. You don't stray too far. The world frightens you, surprises you: the noise of the vacuum, the splash in your water bowl, the screech of the bald eagle as it returns to rest on a cliff-side oak's limb below the house, your voice so high-pitched, but you use the bark more and you explore.

ʘʘ

Summer brings heat and presents you leave in the dark corners because you don't know yet to bark to be let outside. You leave them indoors for us when the world is your shitter. It takes us a few months to teach you that. The wet carpet, the little stinking logs, but soon you take your refuge outside and we take you to the lake.

You swim naturally. We try to teach you how to climb the pontoon's ladder but you are young, so we grab you by the scruff of your neck and pull you back on the deck. You stay less and less on the pontoon as you become stronger in the water, taking your own initiative and diving off the deck and splashing, swimming for the Nerf football. You whine and bark for your turn on the Sea Doo, so I cradle you on the saddle in front of me and drive slow, turning in wide arcs.

⌘

In the fall you play outdoors with us. You are lanky and your coat has darkened, all of you is black save a patch of white on your chest, you're knob-kneed and scrawny legged, your head large and your body not yet muscular. One day around Halloween your voice changes. You sniff eagerly at Thanksgiving and are denied.

⌘

In the winter, my sons and I take turns wheeling the wheelbarrow out to the woodpile. When I'm out one day you follow. I pick up green logs and dead split wood, you assume it's time to play. You pick up a stick you can easily handle, a foot long and two inches thick. I throw it as far as I can and you chase after it down the hill. We do this every few minutes as I load the wheelbarrow, playing fetch, till the wheelbarrow is loaded and we enter the house. You watch me, your stick in your mouth, sitting calmly on your haunches. I throw a few dead pieces on the infant fire and you watch me load the wood-box, saving the green log for before bed so it can burn through the night. When all that's left are a few pieces of bark and some twigs and dust, you drop your stick into the wheelbarrow and look up at me and then you walk away. This is the first time you help me bring in wood but it isn't the last by any means.

Your fur thickens. At the New Year's Party you sit upstairs with John who's drunk on wine. When the fireworks go off, you prefer it there, inside, watching him, licking his hand. You are as nervous with the fireworks as you are in a thunderstorm, chest-thumping booms ricocheting off the walls, rattling the windows. I come upstairs and see you're with him. He's trying to go outside and you keep bumping his chest, walking under foot, licking his face and hands. I say, "You keep a close eye on him, Bear," and you look up at me and wag your tail and then turn your attention back to him. He says he loves you and I know my son does. You lick his face.

You fill out in the spring, you shed the winter coat and cut a more lean, muscular figure. You aren't knob-kneed anymore and your head isn't too large. I take you to the lake often after the last thaw, it's still too cold for us but you can't stay out of the water. You come swaggering out of the surf, the white diamond on your chest like an emblem, the waterlog thick and slimy, clamped tight in your jaws. When Bates brings his Husky down you bristle and bare teeth. The dog is a reflection of the man and Bates is an asshole drunk—a bully. Bates' Husky outweighs you by fifty pounds. It snarls and barks and I tell old Bates to get his dog out of here. He tells me I should fuck off. His dog—don't know the Husky's name, it's Bates' Dog, is what we call it—circles you. You fight. Fur flies. I notice black and then gray, and white, and silver, the color of Bates' Dog. You've got him pinned, you're snarling, looming over him. He fights to get back on his feet and you grab him by the scruff of his neck and you pull him down into the lake, the two of you still in the shallow, but with your front paws and your strong jaws you shove Bates' Dog underwater over and over again, till either he glimpses freedom or you get bored. Cowering, he hurries inland. Again you swagger out of the lake, water dripping off your black oily fur, beading on your back and head. Your brown eyes unblinking, staring resolutely, the Husky crawls away. This isn't the only time you'll face Bates' Dog. I call you Bear, Black Labrador, Alfa Male.

☦

This second summer you sail off the front deck of the pontoon. You are stubborn though; you don't know when to quit swimming. You nearly drown a couple of times. You're heavier this year and to try and lug you on board takes a Herculean effort. When you can you climb up the ladder, when you haven't worn yourself to a tether. Other times we have to forcibly hold you on the boat until you get enough water in you and your breathing calms. You are excited. You are strong and proud. You whine for your turn on the Sea Doo but now you straddle the seat behind me, front paws on one side and rear on the other. I still go slow with you.

☦

That fall we welcome a third son. John is off at college. Lance has his own children, and this third child is a late in life surprise, not an accident but we never thought possible—so, a miracle. I watch you around the infant, you are always around him. Your ears perk when he cries out or even laughs or coos. The only time you leave his side is during the Thanksgiving holiday. He's sleeping in his crib, a midmorning nap. You wait for my wife to leave and for me to get into the shower. I thought the pies were pushed back far enough on the counter and besides, I never dreamed you would leave the baby's side. You are his guardian and have taken up that title proudly. So when I get out of the shower and see that you've managed to pull the pies off the counter I'm surprised. You lower your head and look up at me. I yell at you. I say you might as well eat it now. You wait to see if I'll change my mind and chance a quick lash of the tongue to a bit of pumpkin pie on the tile. I walk out of the room and you enjoy your Thanksgiving. We learn to put you outside every big meal after that.

CREO

You stand with the youngest when he learns to walk and you stay near. He hugs you and enjoys it when you lick his face. His first word is "Bear." For his birthday three autumns later, you give him a friend, your son.

CREO

The new puppy comes to our house in winter. We remember your hidden surprises and crate-train your son. It works, he house-trains faster than you. But you are still the Alfa Male. Once when the boys are in the yard, during a few days of uncharacteristic warmth, the little one in the swing, Bates' Dog comes sauntering up. He forgot about the other times. You remind him. He cowers and you stand between my three sons and your one as he retreats. We play fetch and gather wood, and then the Thundersnow hits. You sit beside me, watching the lightning, watching our tracks disappear in the falling snow.

You lay as the puppy tugs at your ears, climbs on your back, growls and snarls. Once in a while you take a paw and effortlessly flip him on his back, remind him you're playing but also reminding him who's the father.

CREO

That spring I see you teach your son. He follows you into the under-growth as you lead us on our hikes through the back forty. He's more skittish of the water than you, though. One day I can't find you. But my youngest says it looks like your son got into a fight and lost. I get a call from Bates' widow then, calling me to come get you. I drive over, find blood. The Husky cowers in the corner of the garage and a couple of other medium-sized dogs have backed off too. You stand against all of them. You aren't growling or snarling or barking. You are silent and your eyes are narrow slits and you look to each dog. I call you but you stand there. I walk up and tug at your collar. You don't budge. I tug again and you nip at me. You don't break the skin but you let me know you don't cower down. None of the dogs are badly hurt, I find out later. You don't have to fight Bates' Dog again that I ever know of.

╬╮

You get older, your son gets older, my sons get older, I get older. I see more gray around your muzzle, about as much around mine. Damn kids do that. You and I start hobbling about the same time. Mine is my hip. Yours starts out like something in your foot. I check for bristle and thorns and find nothing. Yours is arthritis, a few other complications. Our trips to the vet increase from just checkups to repairs. We fix you late in life and that fixes you for a while. A few years later you need hip surgery, common with Labs, the Vet says.

You slow. Your boy is lethargic, we've fixed him too, he fattens like a steer. I start noticing little presents again and occasionally puddles of bloody piss. I blame the ancient Tabby at first, then even the son who is as big as the father. My wife says she knows.

Your trips to the vet come more and more frequently; you venture from the house less and less. You can't make it down the hill like you used to and you can barely make it up and down the stairs without help. You sleep a lot. The vet tries his best. You always feel better after you see him, for a while. At the lake you barely get wet. You shiver. We don't take you out on the pontoon anymore. It's hard enough for me, with my hip, to man the pontoon. I can't make it up and down the ladder myself anymore. The last time we went out, John and Lance had to drag you up the ladder. That was two years ago.

╬╮

It's fall again and you're at my feet as I sit at my computer. I email John then I call Lance. When my three sons are home we assist you upstairs. I help you up onto the back of the four-wheeler and we take you down to the lake. I've spent the last week watching you at night, talking with my wife about what we had to do. I held on for the two eldest boys to come home, but they almost didn't make it.

At the lake you limp after the stick and tire easily. We all gather round and pet you. Your son walks up and nuzzles you. We help you back on the four-wheeler and carry you back up to the house.

As we creep up the hill, I catch your reflection in the mirror. Your head is on John's lap. His hand strokes your fur back from your head, his fingers deep into your pelt. Your muzzle is white, you close your eyes with each pat.

∿47∿

❧

The vet administers the first shot. You look to each of us. You yawn. You manage to lick our hands, nuzzle us as we hug you. My wife sits down by the wall and you lay your head on her lap. The vet is readying the second syringe. I cry silently. It's harder for you to keep your eyes open, so I kneel with great pain and pat your head till your eyes stay closed. The boys have left the room. My fingers interlace with my wife's and we massage your pelt, your back.

The vet says at sixteen, you are well beyond your years for a Lab. We have spared no expense in treating you and he says this has allowed you a good long life. Downstairs by my studio on a wall of family portraits one painting hangs of you, above a shelf with a few knickknacks that will be cleared away for your ashes.

When we return that day, your son and the cat meet us in the kitchen. Their nostrils flare, they study us. Then they lower their heads and turn and walk away. John heads back to Fayetteville. Lance leaves for his family. My youngest—now almost old enough for a learner's permit—retreats to the Playstation in his room. My wife goes to bed. I go downstairs and sit at the computer, staring at a blank screen. I see neither the cat nor your son for the rest of the evening. We have each resigned this autumn night to mourn you privately.

MONOLITHS OF ASH

The bar stuffy with smokers, permitting me a headache when all I came in for was a couple of beers as the patron next to me, a scruffy guy with a salt-and-pepper coif wearing flannel and drinking Chivas Regal, puffs away inconsiderate of my sinuses. Whether by design or happenstance his smoke congregates over my space, and as it perpetuates the inflammation in my sinuses, the familiar smell of tobacco conjures not unpleasant memories. If you don't count situations like this, in bars, I'm ten years smoke-free. By and large I don't miss it, but every now and then...

I click on a news story on my phone and think back when I was an undergraduate at Ole Miss, to a particular day when it was raining and I stood under the portico of a red brick building where I took a creative writing class, my breath pluming even before I lit the cigarette, the cold and soupy day where a thick mist hung like a shroud over everything. *Visibility less than a hundred feet,* I think and smile and the patron next to me shoots me a dirty look as tendrils of smoke coil toward me; my thought a quip inspired by the biographical sketch the instructor had given us at the start of the semester.

"Thanks for the smoke," my instructor said. He was short and rotund, with cropped gray hair, his face as round as his spectacles, a gravelly voice. He was the in-house author and instructor at Ole Miss. This day he hadn't brought enough cigarettes to our weekly three-hour class for our mid-class break.

"Good story today, John." I was surprised he knew my name, what with thirty students and I always managed to unobtrusively park it in a desk against the back wall.

I had inserted a saxophone into that story. He had smiled and said that a saxophone reminded him of a human voice, and he liked to hear good alto or tenor. In another life he was a pilot. Duality, like me. At Ole Miss I was a student in a creative writing class and I smoked. Nowadays I'm a journalist and I run three miles a day. I'm also married with a kid.

"Thanks, sir," I said.

"Barry," he said with a wave like he was casting a spell. He wore a tweed jacket that day with leather elbow patches. "Writing's like being a pilot," he said, exhaling smoke. "It's like a nicotine high."

I wouldn't have pegged him as one who wanted to talk shop while on a smoke break. I told him I always enjoyed writing. I enjoyed it more than reading, even.

"Why do you think that is?" he asked.

I shrugged. "I just haven't gotten into the reading lists at school."

When he asked what specifically, I told him I was reading *The Faerie Queen* in one class and stuff by Joyce in another. He said no wonder. I told him I did enjoy a book by Harry Crews and Thomas Pynchon's *The Crying of Lot 49* and Graham Swift's *Last Orders*.

"Which Crews' book?"

"*A Feast of Snakes.*"

He nodded. He stubbed out his cigarette and I looked at my watch. We still had five more minutes before he had told us to be back in class. I handed him another and started one for myself.

"Gracias," he said.

"I can't get into Spanish, either."

"Keep your lighter even when you give up smoking. As long as you're single keep the lighter."

"How do you know I'll quit smoking?"

He chuckled. "They make you take a lot of crap as an undergrad. Wait till grad school. You'll read more of what you want and what you like.

You a Lit major?"

"That or journalism."

He made a face like he'd just been punched. "That's the factory work of writing."

"I thought that was technical writing."

He laughed again. "You know about the lighter?"

"For girls. Even if I don't need a smoke they will."

He gave me a smile like I would have given my younger brother when I had just trusted him with some piece of *The Man-Code*. We stubbed out our second cigarettes and walked back into the red brick building.

❧

I pay the tab and walk out into the fresh air and pop a piece of gum into my mouth, knowing full well the effects of the bar extend beyond my breath; the smoke threads through the fabric of my shirt and pants and salts my hair and scalp. I can smell its stubborn refusal to relinquish me when I climb into my car and I'm sure, like a virus, it has begun to weave in and out of the threads of the seat. I lower the windows and open the sunroof. It is a nice day, an affront to my mood.

❧

It was by chance I found the article at all. It came as an attachment to an email I never read, an alumni newsletter that I somehow qualified for even though I hadn't finished my undergrad at Ole Miss.

When I read the email at work, I sat at my desk stunned, then rushed to finish up the story I was working on. I sent it to my editor via email then rapped on her door and said I was taking off as her inbox pinged, alerting her to my message and attached file. She waved me away dismissively and I thought about rushing home to my wife and little boy. But Ole Miss is not theirs. It's mine.

❧

Rather than turn onto my street, I head to a White Oak a mile away, park and enter. I stare up to the racks behind the attendant, who stares at me jaw agape, a fat and pimply woman with short hair who addresses me as sugar lasciviously when she asks what I'd like. I point to my old brand and snatch up a lighter, and back in my car I cradle the pack, turning it over and over in my hands. The cellophane tag with the gold thread wants me to tear it away, and then there is the foil, easy to detach, and then I'm reunited with my twenty closest friends.

I toss the pack – still tightly shrouded in the plastic – into my glove compartment and say "Sayonara, sucker" and put the lighter in the center console. At home I park and see that my wife's SUV is not in the drive-way. I enter to a quiet house and the ghost of the bar smoke still clinging to me, threatening to disperse through the air vents and my movements. I strip down to my skivvies and tuck the wad of clothes tightly like a running back and make the laundry room behind the kitchen, depositing my wad in the washer after assuring myself my pockets were empty. I shower and wrap myself in my robe and view the email once more, not on the circumscribed screen of my cell, but on the wide flat screen of my desktop. I click on the hyperlink and reread the article, thinking about the pack of smokes in my glove compartment.

The article is short. The school—particularly the English Depart-ment—gathered this year to commiserate the anniversary of the passing of one of their long-standing faculty, who had died of a heart attack. His death occurred just days before the annual Oxford Conference for the Book where his work was to be featured.

That day when he borrowed the smokes plays over and over in my mind, and though I haven't thought about that semester, that class in years, now I can taste the cigarettes. I haven't craved a cigarette in I don't know how long but I crave one now, reading this article, this snippet, this blurb on a man's life. I can taste the burning tobacco. I can smell the rain and hear it on the tiles of that portico, hear it slap feebly against the red brick. I can hear his voice and see what the shroud of mist allows me to see, his tweed blazer with the leather elbow patches, and the two of us loitering under the covered porch of the red-brick building.

The distant crinkling of a paper bag and my son's plaintive call for me lull me from the hypnotic swirling of my screen saver. I toggle the mouse to wake the monitor and hear more crinkling and my wife say, "Let's find Daddy" and "I smell smoke" and her feet on the stairs as my boy says "Smoke!" like he's learned a new and important word.

"What's wrong?" she asks, walking into my office.

I take him from her and tell her as he stares at the computer screen. "Oh John, I'm sorry. What do you need?"

⊂⊰⊱⊃

After a seven-hour drive, I find the Oxford cemetery with Google Maps and some patient driving. I find the tombstone with a little more patience. My trip down was silent save for the radio and my thoughts, a juxtaposition of ideas: temptations for the smokes only a few feet away; memories of how I quit, a lonely, angry several weeks. The first two weeks were always the most difficult; my time at Ole Miss; our class – I was an undergrad the following semester still, but he overrode me into his graduate level creative writing course. I consider my cell as I kneel over the patch of grass bearing his name on a concrete monument. There are phone calls I could make but I don't.

"I'm sorry I dropped out," I say, unwrapping the cellophane and tearing away the foil under the lid. They're packed in there, and I trace a finger over the white butts perversely. "I wasn't ready then."

I tell him about being ready now, about all I've accomplished. I try not to think about the email I received after I dropped his graduate course, asking me to come to his office, nor of how I never went. Right before I left school a couple of semesters later, I bumped into him at the student union. We were in line both ordering cheeseburgers; I glanced back to see him with a tray right behind me.

"How are you, John?" It always surprised me that he remembered my name. How many other students had he, that he'd recall their faces but that was all, and here I stood, and here I kneel.

I pinch a butt and pull till it gives, close the pack and lay it by a vase of fresh irises adorning his stone. I take a puff, careful not to inhale, as I light the smoke, and stick the butt into the dirt till it burns like a torch leaving a mini monolith of ash down to the filter. I consider the seven-hour trip back and I don't feel like driving more. I consider friends and acquaintances still in the area and call no one, but check into a hotel that wasn't here the last time I visited. Oxford has changed, though Mississippi is still the same by and large, flat and piney and poor.

The next morning, in the time leading up to check-out, I consider returning to the grave and retrieving the rest of the pack and the lighter. That's all it is, though – a consideration. Well, that, and my last thought for a long time about cigarettes.

THE LIES WE TELL

ohn Cross kissed his wife goodbye then kissed his son and drove
off, but when he should have arrived at XNA's long-term parking
twenty minutes north of his house, he was south on I-49, having
just passed under the Bobby Hopper Tunnel, speeding on toward Fort
Smith. He muted the radio and called from his cell, opting to not use
the blue tooth in his car because it sounded different, and his wife could
always tell. She would know he should be passing through security.

"Just passed through security," he said. The southern stretch of road
extended before him; pretty soon he'd be heading east towards Little
Rock on I-40, and then onward to Memphis. "I'm shutting the phone off
for the battery. I forgot my charger. I can use the USB port on the laptop
but I won't be able to do that till I get to New York. Yeah, I'll call you
when I land. I love you too."

After crossing the Mississippi River, he snaked through the Memphis
interchanges to the exit for 55 South and crossed the state line, taking the
familiar exit to Southaven, Mississippi and its landlocked ports of call—a
few houses, a Walmart, a gas station, a few fast-food places, a Best Western—unchanged. He got gas and contemplated calling her back. No, it
was too soon. She'd know he should still be in the air.

He bought a coffee and headed south. Last year for this trip he told his wife that his mother was sick, and she did not call his mother's house. His mother would have covered for him, though.

Just outside of Oxford he found another gas station and pulled in and dialed. His wife answered on the third ring. He glanced at the dashboard where the clock read "4:30."

"Yeah, almost six here," he said. "We just landed. Well, I'm going to get my bag and try and hail a taxi and get to my hotel. Thanks. I think it'll go smooth. The editor my agent recommended is someone he's known for years. They work well together."

This was true. A month ago, he had skyped with his agent and an editor. His agent handled some of his journalism articles and some of his short stories and was helping him write a nonfiction book about growing up in the South. John had considered a novel.

"But you're a white guy and a straight guy," his agent had said, and John had said: "And that counts against me?" He had not told his wife about the conference call or about this line of dialogue because he was saving it for details about this trip when he got back. He needed a touch of the specific like this.

He thought about his son. Last year the boy was three and John was learning that the terrible two's lasted longer than just twelve months. He felt bad about leaving them last year and felt worse this year.

John pulled into a row of apartments on the north end of Oxford near the campus. She had moved twice since last year, she'd written in the email. She was still alone, she'd written, and he knew she wasn't coping well.

He knocked on her door and hugged her completely when she answered it. Neither of them spoke for the longest time, just held each other tightly on the landing. When she invited him in, he dropped his bag by her sofa and slumped onto the couch.

"Are you hungry?" She was cooking something on the stove that smelled nice. He watched her, her matted hair, her clothes and affect … dirty, the best word he could come up with, then edited that to unkempt. She had no one to care for and no one to care for her, and such isolation begged neglect.

"Yeah," he said out of obligation, and snatched her remote off the coffee table and flipped absently through the channels.

"Did you want to go tonight?"

"I'm tired of being in the car," he said. "I need to stretch my legs."

"I go every weekend," she said. "Sometimes two or three times a week."

This didn't surprise him, and they ate in silence. They had known each other so long there was little left to say between forkfuls, just nips and snarky bites, was all.

"Your wife still doesn't know you come?"

"She has no idea," John said, as if this were a secret on the level of a private alcoholic, or an affair. She stood and fished a bottle of beer out of the fridge and popped the cap and handed it to him. He hadn't the heart to tell her he'd switched brands five years ago, that this brand now tasted like panther piss.

"Sam," he said, but had no idea what was going to come after that.

"How's your son?" Sam asked. He looked at her and she looked at her food. Her hair was dirty and greasy and stringy and he thought if her longer strands touched what remained on her plate he might throw up. He looked at his own plate and inspected it for stray hairs. He sipped his beer and allowed himself to remember how beautiful she once was. She had sharp features and bright eyes and her skin shined like polished marble. That was then. Now he could see the pores on her nose and her cheeks were pockmarked and her eyes were gray and sunken and rimmed with heavy black bags.

"Are you working?" he asked.

"I get by. I don't need any of your goddamn money," she said, but she didn't raise her voice or her eyes. She said this simply and calmly, like she had just told a waiter no more pepper. He knew if he offered a check, she'd deposit it first thing tomorrow.

He nodded and finished his beer. Dutifully she rose and tossed the empty bottle and got him another. She sat the plates and silverware in the sink and said she was going to clean up. He did the dishes while she was in the shower, grabbed another beer, and noticed there was a fresh eighteen pack with only three missing. He finished that bottle by the time she emerged from the bathroom. He didn't drink this much at home and supposed this was insight to what his life might have been like: dirty like her and drunk all the time.

She had retained her figure, which was nice. She had combed her hair and applied some makeup and resembled the girl he'd met in college, though there was a sadness about her older eyes.

"Do you want to…?" she asked.

He rose and led her into the bedroom and not much later they were asleep on opposite sides of the bed, a great chasm of mattress between them. When she moved in the night he awoke to overwhelming guilt and moved out to the sofa. Sleep came in fits throughout the rest of the night, and his eyes opened for good when he heard her piddling around the bathroom just after eight o'clock.

He showered and changed his clothes and followed her to her car, a faded blue sedan filled with empty fast-food containers and other assorted trash. He picked up a receipt from the day before showing her account was overdrawn and tossed it in the back and sat silent as she drove them through the town.

At the cemetery they approached the tombstone and stood silent, as if they were praying. They intertwined their fingers and let the autumn wind sway them. John knew things were never clear cut. He imagined a different life, finishing up in the ROTC as Sam had wanted. He imagined forgoing the writing career and serving on a ship six months out of the year. Sam had joked (only partly, John realized) that she had come to Ole Miss for an M-R-S degree. When she realized she was pregnant she was ecstatic, and he'd been happy, too.

"So, you've moved on," she said, not for the first time. "Good for you. Good for you." He could hear the anger in her voice, just under the surface.

"You can move on," he said.

She knelt and ran her fingers over the tombstone. She was in the third trimester when they awoke to blood on the mattress. She said her gut felt knotted like the baby was playing hopscotch with her small intestine and they tried to laugh as they made it to the car. Looming over her, his shadow a long cast over the stone, he realized she couldn't move on even if she wanted to.

"Sam," he knew what he wanted to say, but didn't have to finish because she knew too.

"This is your last trip."

"It has to be," he said.

"Fuck you."

"I can't keep watching you wallow in self-pity," he said. He didn't care how harsh that sounded. The town of Oxford had profited little from Ole Miss' success, and Sam hadn't profited, not at all.

She said nothing, her arms crossed like a child. Sam and this whole goddamn town refused to change. That was the problem.

"Christ, Sam, people lose babies all the time." He knew that was easy for him to say. He had his second chance waiting for him back in Arkansas, but her lower lip quivered.

"Not anymore, Sam. I can't caudle you anymore." He swept his arms over the expanse of the earth that surrounded the tombstone, as though this were the load he carried. "It's not fair to my wife or my son!"

"Your son," she snickered, her lips twisting into a snarl, her eyes rolled.

"You could've come with me!" He didn't care who heard. He wasn't going to share the blame for an accident any longer.

"You hated me before that," she said, turning on him.

"Bullshit." He couldn't remember when he started hating her.

"It's like you knew but you lied to yourself," she said. He could feel how she despised him, how she saw him as weak and stupid. "It's like you're still lying to yourself. So you can pity me."

Tears welled up. Christ, this wouldn't work anymore.

"Maybe I do," he said. "It's been about 'us' and parents and kids, but I didn't lose the kid. It … he was in you."

"I didn't lose him the night we went to the hospital," she said. She was sobbing. She hid her face in her hands and he knew it was from shame.

"What?"

"I didn't want it and I didn't want you!" she screamed.

He took a step back. "Oh God," he said, though he wasn't sure if he was calling for a plea or a curse.

"I'm a fucking monster," she said, and pulling her hands away, she revealed her face: a tangled mess of hair, wild black and red eyes, red-inflamed flaring nostrils ready to puff smoke matched by lips eager to spit licks of fire, red-rash cheeks scarred by drying trails of acidic tears.

"You should have told me," he said.

"When? Back then? I've been crucified enough by the strangers in this town and by my friends and family, thank you very much."

"This town?" Was he the last to know?

"C'mon John. We know what it means to be a Southern Christian."

"Why didn't you just leave?"

"Where would I go? Who would I stay with, when no one I've known wants to associate with a morally bankrupt pariah? Think your wife will let me sleep on the couch?"

"So when we went to the hospital …?"

She hung her head and dropped her eyes. Slumped her shoulders. "A complication from the process, or karma. I don't know, maybe both."

Silence passed, a great divide as impassable as the sea of time that separated who they were when they were in love and who stood over the grave of a boy that had never breathed. John looked at the tombstone and wondered if the carved name was a ruse for his benefit or remorse on her behalf. He didn't know what to say.

◌≈◌

They rode back to her apartment. When he exited, he stood by his car looking north and west and squinting because the afternoon sun was ready for the day to be over.

"Would you like something to eat?" she asked.

"I'm good." He allowed himself to take her in once more. She lurched forward and wrapped her arms around his shoulders, but she was decent enough not to let any other part touch.

◌≈◌

He found a motel in Southaven and found that the gas station where he liked to stop now served beer. He drank and thought about how much his life had changed. Maybe Sam was right. Maybe he'd been as tired of this as she was, and maybe for just as long, and perhaps he had known what she'd done, what she'd stolen from him. Halfway through his binge he pulled out his laptop and wrote a bit.

Realizing creative nonfiction was like small town gossip, better with a bit of fiction weaved in, he read over the story twice for revision and once for errors, then emailed it to his agent. He had three beers left when his agent skyped and said it was bloody brilliant like he was British and not from Hoboken, originally.

John closed the laptop and turned out his lights and dreamed of two sons. One was covered in blood and mangled and half formed and spoke eloquently and articulately despite the fact that he hadn't a fully formed tongue. He spoke of Socrates and how John could better understand Shakespeare now and how he so would have liked to go fishing. His other son sat on the other side, looking out off the porch-swing to the expanse of field and a pond nearby, quietly content in his father's arms. A grove of oaks lined a single lane gravel road in the distance.

"Is this Rowan Oak, Papa?" the articulate baby asked.

John nodded and he knew this was supposed to be, but it wasn't right, and he knew then he was dreaming. He awoke before checkout with enough time to shave and shower and put on his only pair of clean clothes left, and after getting coffee from the Southhaven gas station, he drove home.

ℚ℠

"How was your trip?" his wife asked as John played in the floor with his son.

"Yeah, Daddy how was twip?"

John smiled. "Good," he said and told them about the conversation, the one he had on that teleconferencing call last month that he had held back until now. He said he was a boring heterosexual white male who came from a family that hadn't been rich enough to own slaves and would not consider the Klan as an option, when he discussed himself as a viable Southern writer.

"Well you're a good writer," John's wife said, though she had never read a lick of what he wrote so she was saying this with only his word to go on.

"I have other stories," John said.

"Tell me a story, Daddy," his son said and John bounced him on his knee. There was only one story on his mind right now.

"Later," he said. It wasn't an appropriate story for a three-year-old.

"What stories?" his wife asked, a playful smile on her lips, an eyebrow arched. She was sitting next to him and ran her fingers through his hair.

"I have no stories," he whispered and blew her a kiss, which she returned. She should probably hear the story first, but he had no intention of telling her this night and he had no intention of really telling her anytime soon.

THE SMELL OF THE PINES

The day is hot and seeps in through the cracked caulking and weather-stripping around the window of the den. She looks up to the thermostat but she can't see the numbers and decides it's too dim in the room and her son is too cheap to turn it down. On the television an old show. Not too old, not black and white, but grainy like the film was worn with age. A show from the eighties, she decides, and feels like one she's seen before, but she knows she can't trust that feeling.

An old man enters the den and kisses her head and calls her mom. Was Martin so old, now? What did that say about her? He said her great-grandson was coming and she said which one and he said, "John," her oldest and she hears the door open. She expects a little boy to run around the corner and give her a big old hug but instead a man enters: tall and lean, he hugs her neck. There is a sadness about his eyes and she thinks her grandson is far too young for the realization that life isn't an adventure but a responsibility.

She says: "My uncle was engineer 'n he ran the spur from the logging camp up to the Missouri/Pacific Line. He let me ride next to him in the cab of the locomotive when I was little…We had the bluing water—rinse water 'n Mama always had me bathe in it. I was Wee Willie, as a young 'un."

He looks over at her, his great-grandmother, she who gave birth to his father's father. She sees herself in his eyes, because she sees her husband in the features of his face, in the furrowed brow, the curve of his jaw line. She sits withered in the loveseat, her shoulders hunched, her eyes sunken and listless. She is small and thin—she has always been small and thin—and there are more times than not when her mind is no longer her own. Still, moments of clarity peek through. It's up to her to decide which is which.

◈

Reeder, Arkansas, the turn of the century, long-leaf yellow pines protruded from the barrow pits, a town of wooden shanties on dirt lawns, a town risen above the swampland due to the recent oil boom and its logging industry. In the backyard of a house, a black iron pot that had just recently held clothes stewed over a smoldering fire, a broom handle jutting out the top. Next to it a tub of soap-filled cleaning water and in it—now that the clothes were done—two toddlers bathed and splashed each other, a white girl named Alice and a little Black girl named Ditty. A thin white woman worked the clothes in a third tub; a squat Black woman hung sheets on a line. The sky above was clear through the pines and a warm breeze wound its way amid the trees and barely eased the heat of the summer.

The backdoor opened and Alice's uncle strolled outside, dressed in his engineer's uniform. Stepping past his sister, he stopped at the tub and squatted.

"Wee Willie," he ruffled Alice's wet hair then wiped his palm on his pant's leg. "Wanna ride with me over Crossett way?"

Alice clapped and smiled. Her mother, drying her hands on her apron, walked over, a frown wrinkling her brow, pulling her whole face tight around her broad nose. "Papa Joe will be home in an hour or so," she said to her brother. "You have her back by then, hear?"

Alice's uncle lifted his niece out of the tub. "I'll take her over to the logging camp and let him bring her back. She'll be all right."

◈

She says: "In my room's a picture sitting there on my bedside table, right under the lampshade. Bring it to me."

John brings the picture. "It's you," he says, and it sounds more like a question. In the black and white there is a short girl, wafer thin, dressed in mud-stained knickers and a T-shirt with a number eleven on it, her light hair a bob, squinting through the sunlight to the camera, despite the brim of her ball cap, caked cleats, the ball bat slung over her shoulder, spearing an outfielder's mitt where normally her hand would go.

𐆑

Fifteen-year-old Alice swung the bat and connected; the softball pop-flied. She watched it, scurried a few steps, and glanced to the first base-men then to the outfielder. The girl in the outfield sprinted under it but the afternoon sun blinded her, the ball dropped to the ground. Alice took off. She rounded first and pressed on. She glanced to the outfield, the girl picked up the ball, searched the field. She picked out Alice and hurled the ball toward the short stop. Alice slid.

She led off from second as the dust settled, and she could feel every-one in the stand watching her. Maybe fifty people were up there including her parents and a seventeen-year-old whose own baseball uniform was soaked from the combination of dust and sweat.

The gray, cracked wood of the bleacher risers gave a little with each footstep, just enough to make Alice's mother nervous. Papa Joe sat down to watch the game and Mama found she had to talk around him to the young man in the muddy baseball uniform.

"She can't date yet," Mama said to the boy. He was tall and lanky and just a few years older.

"There's a hayride Saturday night," he said. "I'm going with Susie Mae down the road, but maybe Alice could tag along if she liked."

"Where's this hayride?"

"Goes to the square…a dance," he said. "We'll keep an eye on her."

Alice's mother looked to her husband. "What do you think about that, Papa Joe?"

Papa Joe frowned. "She keeps stopping like that to watch the ball and they'll tag her out for sure." He cupped a hand to the side of his mouth to yell: "You run when you hit it! Make them do all the work!"

"No, about Charlie Cross taking her to the hayride?"

"I'm going with Susie Mae," Charlie said. "We'll keep an eye on her."

"Old Plug?" Papa Joe took his eyes off the game and studied the boy. "You watch her, Plug. Watch her good."

The evening of the hayride, Alice rode with Charlie and Susie Mae after the wagon appeared. The pines were stiff, the early September evening humid, still carrying with it the heat of the late summer afternoon. Sweat beaded on Alice's neck and rolled down her back. Straw needles clung to her dress and stuck in her hair, scratched and poked at her arms and legs. She tried to ignore how uncomfortable she felt.

Charlie—her friend for a long time—sat next to her. He was a good ball player and a good talker and seemed to enjoy having Alice around, the only person who refused to call him Plug.

"Will you buy me a drink, Plug, when we get to the dance?" Susie Mae asked, running her fingers through her blonde hair as she batted long eyelashes at him, her hand dropping to the side and searching for his.

How could Charlie bring her anyway? Too bad he never saw the way Susie Mae and her friends treated Alice and the other freshmen girls, always laughing and snorting and saying real girls didn't play ball. "Leave that to the boys," they'd say. "Maybe they want to be boys," they'd say. Susie Mae and her friends were even worse than that, sometimes. The only peace Alice and her friends got came when Charlie and the other older boys were around. Then Susie Mae and her friends were too busy flirting to pay attention to the likes of Alice.

"What are we going to do next weekend, Plug?"

Alice sat forward and cleared her throat. "Charlie promised me we'd go fishing next weekend. Right, Charlie?"

He smiled at her. "Daly Pond bright and early. But first me'an your uncle got to stop off at that old slough on the creek behind, seine for some bait."

"Do you like my hair, Plug? I fixed it up right just for you."

He shrugged.

Alice didn't like these new ideas she was having about Charlie. He was a good ball player and a good fisher and that was that. But other stuff kept getting in the way, saying *that* wasn't just *that*. As the ride went on, she lost herself in silly ideas. She could be as pretty as Susie Mae. She could let her hair grow out, start wearing make-up, spend all her time sewing dresses and brushing her hair and batting her eye lashes. She could forget all about baseball and basketball and being the fastest girl in Quachita County. She could just be a girl. Charlie would be out of high school this year, and in two years she would be out of high school, and he could work for Papa Joe at the lumberyard. They even had a baseball team for the yard, and Charlie made a great short-stop.

But Susie Mae was already pretty. Alice watched the older girl give Charlie a peck on the cheek. He was smiling and for the moment, he wasn't paying attention to Alice. Charlie wouldn't have to wait as long on Susie Mae to get out of school because Susie Mae was a year behind him.

The ride ended at the town square near four men on a stage with guitars and a banjo. Alice meandered to the back of the crowd and sat down, watching. Boys gathered sticks and limbs in a large pile. They poured gasoline. There was an explosion that started with a sucking of air. Fire spat forth, flames spread quickly over the pile. Nearby a statue of Brigadier General John S. Marmaduke faced the bonfire astride his steed. The boys brought larger limbs; three boys carried one log.

"Band's playing."

Charlie sat down next to her, knees folded up under his chin and arms crossed.

"I don't feel like dancing," she said.

"Then neither do I."

She asked where Susie Mae was about the time Susie Mae walked up with a couple of mugs of apple cider. She handed him one and he gave it to Alice.

Susie Mae reached down and snatched Charlie's hand: "Dance with me."

Charlie cast a sideways glance to Alice, smirking.

"Dance with me!" Some of the playfulness had left Susie Mae's voice, and while she was still smiling, and still batting her lashes, there was something else rearing up, green and flickering, staring down on him. Charlie allowed her to drag him away, but the song was still playing when he returned, Susie Mae following close behind.

There were fewer stars in the sky because the full moon hung low, just above the pine tree line. Still Alice tried to count what stars she could see. The moon lit the path well, a dry dirt road with hard divots and troughs. The smell of the pine mingled with the smell of the swamp. One was sweet and fresh; the other reeked of dried mud and stagnant water. If not for the smell of the pine, the smell of the swamp would be unbearable. Cicadas and grasshoppers sang their chirpy songs out of rhythm. In the darkness something hissed and rattled. Alice stepped a little closer to Charlie and felt for his hand. Not too far away an owl screeched and she jumped. Susie Mae saw, made a face, and mimed a laugh behind Charlie's back, and Alice wondered what fresh gossip Susie Mae would invent to spread through the school come Monday.

They arrived at Susie Mae's house first. Her father was a farmer with over a hundred acres. They had passed by a small, unfenced lot he owned, uncut gold fescue, white in the moonlight. His house was bigger than most in the area, nicer too. Alice waited at the edge of the yard under a lone oak smothered in Spanish creeping moss while Charlie walked Susie Mae to the door. Alice turned her back to them, looked up over the pines to the stars and the moon. She felt a tap on her shoulder and Charlie motioned her on toward her house.

There was still a ways to go, if they were to follow the road. Few houses lined their way, a few shacks and a couple of farmhouses. Across Ms. McSpadden's old place, Charlie said, they could cut through the pine and save some time. Just overgrown farmland, he said. "No swamp, no quicksand." He squeezed her hand and guided her safely between the barbed wires of the fence and led her into the overgrowth. The night closed in on them. Alien sounds echoed through the shadows.

"Did you have fun?" Charlie asked. His head was down, his feet shuffled over the worn dirt path.

"If you want to see Susie Mae next weekend I understand." He didn't live much beyond her house, except that he was further east, closer to town, so this was kind of out of his way. There weren't many kids out this way. All the kids they went to school with were scattered thin throughout the South Arkansas pine country. In these parts it was just Alice and her two older sisters and her brother, and Charlie and his little brother, and Susie Mae, and a couple of them Flint kids a mile or so further down, who didn't ever bother with anyone and didn't even bother with school.

"The thing is, her daddy said this would be about the last hayride she'd take here, and didn't want her to go alone," Charley said, dipping his head, stuffing his hands in his pockets and shuffling his feet. Was he blushing also, under the moonlight? "Told me he wants to move the family to El Dorado to a better school so she can go on off to college. She won't be happy till she can find some lawyer or banker or something. That's what she says I should do."

"So you better spend some time with her then."

"I promised you."

Up ahead a kerosene lantern illuminated her porch and she could hear the slow creak of Papa Joe's rocker as they passed under a canopy of limbs dancing in a soft wind, hiding them from the moon and stars.

"Still, you like Susie Mae, I know."

"I've known you since you were a little girl," Charlie said.

"She's real pretty."

His arm braced her shoulder. He kissed her.

"We're gonna remember this night forever, Alice."

He began to walk again. His head lowered, his feet shuffled. He stuffed his hands into his pockets. He was ten feet in front of her, but Alice still saw him just smiling down on her, a hand on her shoulder.

When they reached the porch, Charlie waved to Papa Joe, said goodnight to Alice and walked on, not changing his gait. She went in and washed her ears and face and ate a bite of pork and some beans, a roll with butter, and told her folks most of what happened that night. When she went to bed, she didn't sleep right away.

❦

"You and Plug were married sixty-six years," John says.

"We were."

She gives her great-grandson a smile then she settles in to another television show. The minutes tick by, measured by the far-off drip of a slightly leaking faucet. Alice wonders when her son will be back. John offers to get her another cup of coffee and she says she wants a little something to munch on, so he leads her into the kitchen. The transient ischemic strokes have shortened her stride to shuffles. He holds one of her hands in his and braces her back as they walk, her eyes cast downward as her feet slide over the hardwood floor, then over the linoleum. In the kitchen they find oatmeal-raisin cookies and he pours himself another cup of coffee, her a glass of water, and holding all of this he lets her walk by herself back to the den.

She lowers herself onto the couch; only then does he hand her drink and cookies to her. Back home she would have the TV tray in front of him before setting down the plate of cookies and glass of milk. He was a lot smaller then. Back then. My how times have changed.

Her son Martin's heavy footfalls echo up from the basement steps and then his wife's car pulls into the garage. They complain about the heat and talk about their days and hug John, thanking their grandson for staying the afternoon. He pats his great-grandmother's shoulder and says he enjoyed himself.

"Things haven't changed much," she says. "Gotten bigger is all."

On the television an old episode of *In the Heat of the Night* begins, and she says it looks like home. John reaches down and pats her hand.

"You come visit me when I go back home, John."

"Sure," he says.

"You know where you from?" She squints, a crook in her mouth, and her grip on his hand is surprisingly strong.

He wears an incredulous smile and blinks at her. "I was born here. I've lived all over, but yeah, I think so."

She shakes her head.

John's grandfather leads him down the hall. Alice follows them till they disappear into another room, then turns away, and half a minute later can't remember who she was looking at and only sees Martin's wife sitting in the nearby loveseat.

"You should know where you from," she mumbles, pretty sure that's what she'd wanted to say.

Martin says, "So what did the two of you talk about."

John tells him the story as told to him, about how Granny and Plug met and how Susie Mae tried to intervene, all the while Martin is searching through drawers in his dresser until he comes to a couple of old photo albums and lays them out on the bed. He smiles and asks John leading questions like "What did Susie Mae look like?" and "Who all went to the hayride?" and "Who used to drive her up to Crossett on the engine?"

"Her uncle," John answers to the last question.

Martin flips a page and points to an engineer in a faded black and white.

"I never met him. He died long before I was born."

"How'd he die?"

"Train accident. Boiled to death when a train derailed and he couldn't get out of the engine in time."

There are a few pictures on the opposite page. In one two girls: one he recognizes as Alice at when she was younger and the other a pretty blonde in a dress. John points to the pic.

"That's my mother when she was a little girl and her cousin, Susie Mae Faircoat."

Martin flips another page. John recognizes Alice by her facial features, but she appears a touch older and more resembles her cousin in the previous photograph. John frowns.

"You remember the old paper mill on the outskirts of El Dorado? How it smelled when we drove into town. You used to say you always knew when we were close to Grannie's and Plug's because you smelled that paper mill."

John reflexively wrinkles his nose.

"Memories are like smells. Sometimes they're fresh and good, like how the pines smell down by Daly Pond. Other times they're like that paper mill. Nowadays, she's got more memories like that than fresh. Her mind, to compensate, mushes things."

John nods. "You guys need me tomorrow? I can sit with her again."

His grandfather sighs and smiles. "Come on over. The three of us will visit."

Alice tries, as the sun sets, to remember. There are so many stories, but as the night stretches from the east, her memories fade a little more. Before bed she prays to a God so engrained in her she will never forget Him that she may hold onto the memories she's already struggling to recall. Maybe when she wakes she'll remember more again.

THE ROUNDS

On the gravel drive, John Cross checked his cell phone for messages that had not come yet. With a sigh he hoisted himself out of the Camaro and padded up the steps to the porch. Wind chimes at the end of the porch caught his attention, hanging from one of two hooks that, back when he was a kid, supported a bench swing. How many Saturday mornings had he spent on that swing, his grandmother rocking, rocking, singing sweet Southern hymns till his grandfather walked out dressed in his shit- and mud-stained coveralls and thick rubber boots and kissed her and ruffled John's hair before heading off to the pasture.

The spring hinge of the screen door creaked and the door opened inward easily, the old familiar smells of his grandparents' house returning him to his childhood. It was too warm for the fire in the fireplace. Back then, a good log fire warmed the living room in those cold winter months. Frank Smith would set a new log and empty out the ash in a large plastic bucket and stoke the fire and open the flue. Now John's cousin stood at the hearth, punching at the burning log with a brass poker.

"It's hot," John said.

"It's what he wants," John's cousin said.

"Round bales!" Frank Smith barked from the recliner, an afghan wadded up in his lap.

John, already exhausted, rubbed his temple. "We have too much to do today anyway before this afternoon."

His cousin was younger, but a bull of a man with the intelligence of the registered Angus their grandfather used to keep to stud out to the herd. He turned ferociously on John and slurred his words in his thick Ozark accent. "It's what he wants."

"Now you boys quit your fussing and sit."

"Pa," John said.

"I need some good twenty or thirty bales. Now you boys take my truck and go down to McGregor's and see what he's got."

John and his cousin exchanged a knowing glance. "John, you drive. Buddy Drayton, you know what I want. Fescue, or some good *Bermudi*, but make sure it ain't that thorny shit like he got me last time."

"How about we let Buddy Drayton get the hay and I stay here with you, Pa," John said.

"Yeah, Pa. I can manage."

He looked at them fiercely, his eyes narrowed, and he pointed at them each in turn. "You do as I say, now. We got to get it ready for when it turns cold. This afternoon I want you to go get about fifteen hundred pounds of grain."

Outside, John's mother picked up on the third ring. John said, "He's sending us out on this damned fool's errand." He paused before the passenger side of the truck, tossing the keys to his cousin. He walked around the garage to look out to the pasture behind the house. The wheat stood tall and golden and swayed in the warm August breeze. The barn still stood in the distance, still gray and sagging, but seemed to sag even more, the field haunted and empty. Dirt clumps and long dried mud ruts scarred the lot behind the house. The pole barn door stood open, revealing the old blue John Deere.

John stuffed the cell back into his pocket then climbed in the passenger seat. The truck was already running and the A/C was turned on high. "Told you it was hot," John said.

"It's what he wanted," Buddy Drayton said.

"She's sending Uncle Crawl over till we get back."

They began driving. "Where the hell are we supposed to go, anyhow?" Buddy Drayton asked.

John gave the directions by pointing and motioning, talking on his cell, first to his wife and then to his boss. He assured both he'd be back in Fayetteville by the next morning.

"You better hurry," his wife said. "Your son is pitching a fit without you."

"We're in a bit of a crunch," his boss reminded him. The story about the delay on the widening of the interstate corridor to three lanes had been promised to him, but John knew it wouldn't hang around forever.

He texted a couple of people while Buddy Drayton drove, Conway Twitty on the radio.

They pulled into the drive of an A-Frame house, and the boys walked in, receiving hugs from John's paternal grandfather and grandmother. The talk meandered like an Ozark hog trail till the topic came up of what they were out doing.

"Pa wants round bales," Buddy Drayton said.

"I guess we better go," John said.

"Be careful," the paternal grandparents said. "We'll see you this afternoon."

They drove, this time Buddy Drayton guided them. John talked to the highway foreman on the contentious stretch of road. The man promised to be in his office the next afternoon. John hung up.

"Where we headed?" John asked.

"You remember Kyle Freedmont, dad was Kevin? Lived out on 201? You used to run with him and them Crenshaw boys for a time."

"What's Kyle been up to?"

Buddy Drayton shrugged. "Don't know. Called me up the other day. Said he needed to talk and I said you was coming to town and he said that was good and asked if we could stop in."

This reminded John of when they were teenagers. It was so easy to con Frank out of his truck and then the night belonged to the boys and to whatever wild hair Buddy Drayton got. The roads wound dark and cold through the hollows of the hills, and Buddy Drayton had led them at a minute's notice to many a place with booze and girls and pot. From what John remembered, Kyle lived out at some reclusive place where anything could happen.

"We got three hours till we got to get him into town," John said.

"What's the point," Buddy said. "He won't remember."

"He will eventually."

Kyle's trailer was a singlewide with only half the under-skirting, and what tin panels remained were discolored with rust. The boards of the wood front porch seemed to give too much, especially under Buddy Drayton's weight. Their friend Kyle opened the door. The interior was surprisingly clean, the sofa and big furniture was still out but boxes had been stacked about, labeled with a permanent marker in block lettering: LIVING ROOM; BATH; BEDROOM; KITCHEN.

Kyle smoked a cigarette and sat nervously on the couch, hunched over and trembling. Buddy and John waited as patiently as they could, which for Buddy was not very long. He tucked a plug of snuff into his lower lip and regarded his friends.

John said," Hey Buddy, why don't you go check in with my mom, make sure our uncle made it over."

" 'Kay," he said, rising, his knees creaking under the weight, he pivoted on one hip and sauntered out the door.

"What's this about?" John asked.

"She left," Kyle said. "And I can't take this town anymore. I can't stay here."

"Where you going?"

"Little Rock maybe. I heard Eureka Springs was nice. Maybe some place that don't give a shit about what one guy does or thinks about and won't judge him for what he wants."

"You didn't want her?" John asked.

"Not for a time," Kyle said.

Outside Buddy waited by the driver's side door, leaning against it, head down, arms across his chest, legs straight and crossed at the ankles, his substantial gut distorting what otherwise would have been the profile of a lean cowboy. Buddy spat into the dirt brown bits of saliva and chew.

As they drove away, Buddy asked, "What in hell was that about?"

"His marriage is ending," John said. "He's gay and worried what people will think of him."

"Shit," Buddy said, shaking his head. "Hate to hear it about his marriage. What he does in his own place makes no never mind to me, though. Long as I ain't got to hear about it."

Buddy's cell rang. He leaned on the opened window and spat and talked on the cell while his right hand guided the wheel, his thumb drumming in time with Randy Travis. John, exposed to so much country music, was pretty sure his ears were going to bleed any minute.

Buddy's words were noncommittal and ambiguous. "Huh huh …. Sure, sure … chicken maybe … I ain't got a fucking clue … well you should … well don't ask me … yeah, I'll see you later … I don't know, after this thing … after dinner, we put the kids to bed and she'll crash not long after … yeah we got to get Frank … kay, love ya. Bye."

John cocked an eye at him. Buddy Drayton didn't feel the need to explain his conversation to John any more than John had explained his own. They stopped at Sonic and Buddy Drayton grabbed a cheeseburger and a coke and John got a coffee. The drove to a local ball field and watched some little league baseball.

"You don't like coming around here much, do you?" Buddy Drayton asked.

John watched the pitcher. He wasn't very good. "There's nothing in this town for me."

Buddy Drayton snorted in derision. "I been taking care of him. Me and your mom comes over and we watch over them."

"I've been coming around more and more." A weak argument that brought another scoff from his cousin. "I didn't ever fit in here. You and Pa would have your own language out in the field. I felt like I was running to catch up."

"You were his oldest, John. He always knew how smart you was and he was quick to point it out."

"You were his favorite," John said. "I always felt like I was looking in."

"Nope. You were. He was proud of you. Of your brain."

"He never told me," John said.

They got back in the truck and took the long route through the small town of Rapps Barren back to Frank Smith's farm. They didn't speak. Buddy Drayton found the only rock station broadcasting in the area, 93.1 out of Batesville. Aerosmith's "Dream On" guided them home.

In the living room, Frank Smith stood still while their uncle struggled with the necktie. John took over and successfully completed a half Windsor around Frank's neck. Frank's eyes were listless and seemed foggy to all he saw. Pale clouds had dimmed the pupils.

"Well I haven't seen you in a while," Frank said. "How you been, boy?"

"I'm fine, Pa," John said.

They helped him into the front seat of the sedan. John's cousin and uncle climbed in the back, and John behind the wheel, all four men as cleaned up and dressed as the progenitor of their family.

"You look spiffy," Frank said. He laughed and slapped John's knee.

John drove them through town, turned by the hospital and found the brick building down the slope of the hill, centered on a green lawn that had been dotted with monuments of all shapes and sizes and colors. John parked in a handicapped spot near the door and the four men walked in. Presciently silent, Frank walked behind his grandson, holding his hand. John's other grandparents stood near. John's mother came up and hugged her father. Frank hugged her and kissed the top of her head.

The visitation room held a lot of people. Frank approached the coffin alone, stood with his hands on the lid, staring down. John stood back by his mother. This was time Frank needed by himself.

"We have a place picked out," John's mother said.

"He won't go quietly," John said. He'd wanted to bring his wife, his little boy, but at two he was still too much of a handful for situations like this.

"I can't stay with him and I can't hire someone to stay with him."

"I know," John said.

When he finally tired of standing, Frank took a seat and John sat next to him. People came for hours on end, shaking Frank's hand, expressing condolences. He smiled and nodded, barely cognizant of their offerings. John wondered as the afternoon wore on if Frank even remembered who lay at the front of the room.

After the sun set, John drove Frank back to his house. They pulled into the garage, the old man silent for most of the afternoon and silent on the ride back. They walked into a dark house and Frank looked around, befuddled, frowning.

"Where's your Ma?" he asked.

Such quaint old titles the eldest had ascribed to the new grandparents. But John had been prodded by this duo in their insistence to be referred to as Ma and Pa. Still, he didn't know how to answer that question now.

In time, Frank either forgot he'd even asked the question or remembered the answer. Either option brought only a lonely house.

THERE IS A RIVER

The man -- almost forty, and dressed in a polo and some khakis -- descended the loose gravel of the bank and bent to place his fingers to the surface of the perpetually cold water that lapped at the shore. Downstream families splashed, some swimming, some in canoes, some floating on oversized tubes. He'd floated another river once on a tube. Once, never again. Too damn hot and after eight hours, he had to peel the burnt flesh of his back off the rubber.

He walked the bank further upstream and knelt again. On the other side, a turtle basked on a toppled log, and he spied the head of a water moccasin as it cut a wake toward the other shore. He found a flat stone and skipped it across the surface of the water toward the turtle who'd had enough and flopped into the water. The man stood, ignorant of the time.

❧

The seven-year-old boy stood plaintively on the rocky shore, his brow wrinkled with distrust and his mouth drawn into a tight frown. Next to him stood his grandfather, holding out a paddle for the boy to take.

"I'll do all the work," his grandfather said. "You'll sit up front and whenever I tell you, you put the paddle in the water and stroke, like this," and he demonstrated with his own paddle. "It'll be fun."

"Okay, Papa," the boy said, his brow still wrinkled.

"There's our canoe. Now just remember, if you drop anything over the side, don't reach over to try and get it. You'll end up toppling us over." He sat the cooler in the center and steadied the boat for the boy to climb in. When he pushed off from the shore, the boy's heart leapt. The river bent around some low hanging trees, concealing the rushing sound that startled the boy, and bent around the canoe so that its drift dipped into the water.

"What is that Papa?"

"Rapids," the grandfather said. "You'll enjoy this."

❧

The ten-year-old boy crawled up the shoreline, ringing out the tail of his shirt as his aunt, young herself as she was still in college, laughed from her own perch, safe and dry in her own canoe. He hoisted the front end of his boat up far enough so it wouldn't float away as his grandfather sat the cooler down and dumped the water out of the belly of their canoe. He was laughing also. The boy didn't see what was funny. The sandwiches were ruined, and he was sopping wet, and his grandfather had broken his own cardinal rule about reaching for something that had fallen overboard. *We'll take the lunch*, he'd told his daughter and her college friend, some boy she'd brought home for the weekend. *You'll flip*, he'd told her.

"Don't be so sour, John," the grandfather said. His aunt and her friend paddled up to the shoreline and helped sort the edible from the ruined. In defiance of her father, she'd opted to carry their sandwiches, and she took hers and split it almost in half and gave the boy one portion. The chips weren't ruined, but the cookies hadn't been wrapped tightly in the cellophane. Still, they had their bottles of water.

"Want us to carry the cooler with the rest of the drinks, Dad?" the girl said and laughed. Her friend offered up smiles. She could get away with it. The friend couldn't.

"We can carry the cooler, right Papa. It won't happen again."

"Right, John."

❧

The twelve-year-old boy shouted, "Look!" and his seven-year-old brother screamed, "Snake!" and their grandfather said, "Keep paddling."

The grandfather took his paddle and splashed at the moccasin swimming toward them. It turned nonchalantly and swam the other direction.

He said, "Now boys, he won't bother us if we don't bother him."

They quieted and floated down. Afar but unseen, they could hear a sluice in the river.

"Like I told you, Lance, you got to watch up in the trees for snakes cause they're bound to drop right in the boat."

"Shut up, John. That's not true. Papa, is that true?"

Sounds like a trickle whispered the river melody to them, as the trees on the shoreline blocked out the harshest sunshine. It was cool still, this early morning. John, now an expert at canoeing, knew the hottest part of the day was yet to come. But for now a breeze sliced down the length of the river like a knife opening a scar, dropping the temperature ten degrees and shivering them.

John used his paddle to nudge them a bit faster. "Now they drop at any time, and sometimes when they drop, they just go ahead and bite."

"Shut up, John."

John looked back. Papa was grinning but still he shook his head.

John said: "Lance! What's that?"

"It's not funny, John. Papa!"

A bird in a tree rustled the leaves off to their left, to the nearer of the two shorelines. A few leaves fell flat to the water and drifted down, caught in the current.

"You got to make sure you know the difference between poisonous snakes and nonpoisonous snakes. Water moccasins are poisonous. Can you spot one?"

John looked back. His brother's eyes darted first to one shore then the opposite, his fists clenched under his chin. When he saw nothing, he screwed his face up to his older brother and screamed.

"JOHN!"

"John, don't torment your little brother. Lance, don't be so gullible. That almost never happens."

"See John!"

"He said *almost*," John said. He paddled up in the front. Lance sat in the middle, his job to guard the cooler. John knew he couldn't see him grin. Their grandfather still steered the canoe from the back, slow j-strokes piloting the canoe downstream.

"Papa, when are you going to teach me how to steer," John asked.

"Yeah, me too," Lance said.

"When you get a little bigger, Lance. John, we'll practice a bit a little downstream. There's a shallow pool with no current around where we normally stop for lunch, on that little island. We'll practice a bit there."

Inverted J's proved a bit trickier to master for the boy.

☙❧

John dragged the canoe up the shoreline with Lance towing the front, both boys sopping wet. At least he'd agreed to let his aunt and her friends take the food. They paddled up behind him and she said, "Now let me look at that," and examined his arm. He'd been trying the inverted J to steer the canoe and caught a small shoal that drove them sideways into a mess of limbs hanging out over the river. His right arm and his back were scraped up pretty good, but he wasn't bleeding. They'd flipped almost instantly.

He'd thought, when his grandfather suggested this trip, that it felt wrong to go without him. The float trips were always his and Papa's, no matter who else tagged along. He'd said briefly that he didn't want to go.

His grandfather had ushered him down to the basement garage and they walked out back underneath the covered porch where the johnboat had been dry-docked, and as they took off the cover and began sweeping away the cobwebs with the old broom kept there for just such a purpose, John's grandfather instructed him again on how to use the paddle as a rudder to guide the canoe, and illustrated with the broom.

"It's not going to be the same, Papa, without you there."

His grandfather smiled that easy smile. "You'll do fine."

"Can't you just take the day off?" John asked.

"I wish I could," his grandfather had said. "I wish I could."

☙❧

Maple and oak and pine held the secrets of the wilderness and shielded the floaters from all signs of civilization. John and Lance stuck to the middle, for the most part, drifting to the outer bend of the meander when they wanted deeper, faster water, and to the inside if they wanted to stay shallow and let the idle current drag them along. Once or twice they managed to misjudge the depth and dragged along the alluvium with that grating sound. They avoided the few eddies they saw and marveled at the river cliffs and slip-off slopes, this middle-course that ran relatively flat through the Ozarks.

They heard the crunch on the abrasion banks and spied a deer bending her neck at the water's edge, her tongue lapping at the river while her black eyes seemed to register the canoes with caution. Overhead birds chirped and sang, camouflaged by the various trees and shade, and for a brief moment all that could be heard was the river run and the far off echo of the rumbling rapids, until some redneck in a rounding canoe called out, "Wish I had my shotgun!"

But that was one of the few glitches in the day. Really they floated alone, letting the others get way ahead and drift lazily through the current in near silence, becoming one with the river.

۞

The seven-year-old boy heard his grandfather say, "Look!" Ahead of them the river widened, and the rapids sounded louder. This was the waterfall his grandfather had told him about. There was one spot in the middle, his grandfather had said, that you can go down the shoot, but there are three large boulders in the river that you have to navigate just so in order to hit that shoot. If you don't, you'll have to get out and carry the canoe down by hand.

As if to make his words prescient, there was the rocky ledge ahead, but the boy couldn't see the boulders. Floaters all around were waist deep in the water, lifting and carrying their canoes down the rock embankment. A canoe holding two teenage girls seemed anchored in place right in front of them, the back of their canoe spinning, spinning, so that the boy thought they'd hit them until right before they were to crash, the girls drifted off and started down toward the shallow falls backward, giggling and laughing.

To a seven-year-old, the falls seemed huge, and the shoot nearly vertical, but his grandfather navigated the boulders and angled through the shoot and it was over before the boy could even think to scream, and looking back downstream he saw that it wasn't that deep, and that people could walk over the falls and most had to because to do what his grandfather did was too hard.

۞

They navigated the boulders and shot down the falls smoothly and turned and the ten-year-old pointed and laughed at the college girl and her friend as his grandfather guided the canoe around to face upstream.

They were lifting the canoe over the rock wall and struggling for footing on the slippery rocks, as most others were. One boy was lifting his inner tube over the wall when he slipped, and the tube went sailing downstream. The grandfather paddled to intercept it, and they held the tube till the boy – just a few years older than John – could retrieve it. Only when the college girl and her friend were back in their canoe did they resume the float.

⟡

The year had been particularly dry and the river, while still floatable in most parts, was too low. There wasn't enough current, so the grandfather helped Lance down the rock embankment and then he and John carried the canoe down the wall. John felt a tinge of disappointment as they floated on. He'd built up the waterfall for his little brother, something mythical like Niagara, much as John had envisioned, and John had longed to see the fear in his little brother before their grandfather deftly whipped around the boulders and lead them heroically down the only safe passage. But the drought had robbed him of the joke.

⟡

Lance said, "Just pull off to the right. Papa said it would be easiest to carry it over there."

It was what a lot of people were doing. Their aunt and her friends had drifted to the left and were trying to lift the canoe over that steeper ridge. John noticed the river was up. It had rained a lot this year, and since their accident at the start of the float, he'd gotten a lot better at guiding the canoe.

"No," he said. "When I tell you to, paddle. We're going for it."

"Are you sure?" Lance asked, but he really didn't have time to ask the question. They whipped around the boulders and the shoot lined up in front of them, and Lance cheered as they shot down the middle. Downstream, waiting for their aunt, John guided the canoe through a wide victory circle in the eddies, catching shallow flows and letting the river do the rest. When his aunt and her friends caught up, Lance said, "Did you see, did you see?"

She smiled and said yes. John was sure to tell Papa all about it when they got home.

⟡

Another van pulled up, loaded with people and pulled a trailer with at least a dozen canoes strapped down. The sign on the van read: WHITE RIVER FLOATS and looked familiar to the forty-year-old man. He watched the people climb out and the guides offload the canoes and paddles and life jackets. He couldn't remember having to wear life jackets when he floated down the river, and figured that in the years since, some poor schmuck must have gone and ruined it for everyone else by getting himself drowned.

"Don't be so sour." He smiled at the words.

He watched the people load up their canoes. Overprotective parents secured their kids in life jackets and positioned their ice chests just so. Father figures pontificated to bored wives and doe-eyed little kids and teens wishing to be elsewhere the dire importance of listening to them on the river.

The man struggled to remember if his own father had accompanied them once. On the river where he burned himself, sure. They were in Texas, where they were living, and his father was sure he could give him the same kind of experience as he'd received on this Ozark river.

But the thought was fleeting. A trio of teen boys hopped in their canoe after pushing it off the shore, nearly toppling it save for the last instant. Upstream, two women in one-pieces carefully steadied their canoe in a shoal as they readied to push off.

When the last of the canoes rounded the bend, he walked up to one of the workers and asked if they had pricing information. They gave him a card with a website address. He walked down to the water's edge and knelt yet again. The sun was hot and, standing in it so long, the ice-cold of the water felt good to his palm. Some wildflowers grew up the ways from the shore and so he picked them and shook the roots. They smelled like nothing and yet they smelled like the river, so they were perfect.

ದದದ

The cool of the river didn't transcend to the town. Here there were cars and brick and mortar, and though it was a small town, it felt hot. It was summer, after all. The two lane roads were black and wavered under the heat. He stopped to buy a batch of greenhouse grown wildflowers and mixed the ones he'd picked in with the bunch and noticed how slack the ones he picked looked by comparison. Crossing through town, the man walked across the manicured lawn and noticed the stone that had finally been placed. It was a flat plaque that, he thought cynically, would be buried by overgrowth and erosion after a few decades, the new name-plate a polished bronze and glaring the afternoon sun. He knelt and placed the flowers in the vase and said, "Here, Papa," though the stone didn't suggest that name – just Martin Cross, and there was just enough room for the dates of birth and death and a short Psalm.

BUDDY'S IRIS

When the sheriff got the call he best get out to Buddy Drayton's place, in that the county didn't pay him enough to keep a regular deputized force, he asked a bunch us old boys to accompany him. Given the nature of old Buddy, we weren't sure what we'd find out there. Buddy Drayton Smith was a big man, slow to cool, and as Buddy's wife Iris wasn't specific as to the nature of the call, the sheriff felt it prudent not to show up alone to handle the man. For those of us that rode along, we were more curious than scared. Not that Buddy Drayton wasn't someone we'd each want to go up against one-on-one, or even two- or three-on one; everyone in the county was wary of crossing him, but there was fifteen of us what rode along with a various and sundry catalogue of shotguns and pistols, and it had been ages since we'd been out by Buddy Drayton's place, and we was all itching to see what he'd been up to.

Buddy Drayton hadn't been a recluse all his life, but he'd always been a big man in the county, efficacious in temperament and physically preponderant. He was out there every summer when Pete Wessler hired a bunch of us to load up hay. Pete was pretty regular about squaring up bales at close to seventy pounds a bale, and a bunch of us boys would get out there with Buddy Drayton leading the charge, and while we all rotated between driving the flatbeds and stacking on the truck and tossing up the squares as we drove through the field, Buddy Drayton lumbered on in the pasture, tossing up the bales and not losing pace no matter how high the temperature climbed nor how high the stack got on the back of the flatbed. He'd sip from his cans of Pepsi and spit chew in the empties and toss and toss, and he'd only ride in the truck once the loads were done and we'd deliver them to one or another farmer who regularly bought from Pete each year. We talked privately, marveling at the strength and stamina of the old boy, even as we wondered how his substantial gut didn't slow him down any. But he had a way of throwing around the lobe of a gut using his arms and his shoulders and his back.

He climbed up in the truck once we reached the farmer's barn and he'd just as easy toss the stack, bale by bale, into the hay loft faster than the two boys in the loft could stack it tight against the wall. We'd do the job twice a month from April to September, each time taking all day from sunup to sundown.

❦

But Buddy Drayton and his family had been larger than life in the community for years before that. Folks 'round here like parrots with the gossip. His dad had been well known through the community – a womanizer and a drunk forever, but what happened inside their home no one was for certain. Buddy wouldn't talk about his father, and he wasn't much older than five or six when his pa up and left his ma for this mess of a waitress two towns over who already had three kids. Buddy Drayton's ma did her best with the boy and tried to instill in him the value of an education, but Buddy Drayton preferred his time in the field with the hay and the cattle and in the woods with his shotgun. He muddled through high school with the help of the girls he enchanted, with his thick drawl and his physical prowess, and for years we thought Buddy Drayton would succumb to his father's fate, leaving bastard children and broken hearts strung across the Ozark countryside.

But then Iris came along – a church-going gal who'd placed third in the Bluff County Fair's Beauty Pageant, a pretty little blonde thing who'd run in different circles for years than ol' Buddy. He'd seen her, he told us at the bar one cool September night, at the fair with her sash and in her bikini answering questions about kids and how to improve the school and hospital or some such – and confided he wasn't really listening – and he interrupted Pete's story about dodging a deer and running his granpa's old '57 Chevy pickup into that big oak out on Bulberry Road to ask us if we knew anything about this girl.

"You didn't want the girl what got first place?" Pete jibed him.

"You a dumbass," Buddy Drayton said and downed his ice-crusted mug of beer in one gulp, and we all laughed, even Pete, because everyone had better sense than to contradict Buddy Drayton, who went on to clarify that Pete shouldn't have dodged that deer but hit it dead on and then the truck wouldn't be as wrecked and he'd have a slab of deer meat in his freezer.

∁

When Buddy Drayton and Iris got married the next spring, the whole county turned out, and we all waited to see if he'd turn out like his father still because we weren't totally convinced that Iris could tame the hard-drinking, rebel-rousing bull of a man. When Buddy Drayton announced she was pregnant, we all hoped that a baby might calm the meanness out of him, remembering that time he crossed a couple of old boys at the Back Forty Bar and put them in the hospital just because one of them said something about his ma. But then five kids went missing a year after his first child's birth, and, with his wife pregnant with what would come out as twins, Buddy Drayton joined the sheriff and led the community on each and every search that summer till we found each child in various spots in Wilkins' woods, in various states of decomposition. Five kids over five months, and we all sat back and marveled at how Buddy Drayton had jumped to take charge. When the sheriff finally caught the stranger what had been seen in town, some homosexual living out at McBride's Adult Trailer Park, it took five of us to hold Buddy Drayton back from going into that interrogation room and beating that man to a pulp. We realized that his meanness had been focused on protecting those who couldn't protect themselves, its half-life not yet expired.

For his part, the suspect was crying, fearing Buddy Drayton would break through us and come get him, and blubbering that he had nothing to do with them kids' murders, but he didn't even go to church and he'd just moved to town and we just knew, back then, that given his lifestyle, he had to be our guy. Buddy Drayton would just say, "Them kids need saving from men like that."

❦

We later learned that the homosexual was killed in the county lockup, but Buddy Drayton was out in the deer woods with us when the news came. No one suspected him directly, but we all knew he had lots of people what owed him favors and others he called friends. Still, nothing was investigated and none of the men locked up in the general population would own up to the death or snitch on the actual killer, so we all just assumed justice had been served.

Things stayed quiet for a few years. Iris brought the kids to town daily for school and church and visits with friends and family, and Buddy Drayton was seen working on his ma's old place on the outskirts of town. He'd go out into the deer woods with us and he'd still help haul hay, but he didn't hang out at the bars as much and he didn't attend the school functions that his kids were in, and he didn't go to church. We all figured the deaths of those kids had messed him up badly, and he relegated himself to caring for his ailing mother and his wife and his own children. They fixed up his ma's house so that she could have her room and the family moved in and Buddy Drayton got himself a few head of Angus and a young stud bull to put on his ma's forty acres.

❦

It came to pass that the cows and his ma and his kids and Iris took up all his time, so the only way we'd see Buddy Drayton was if we drove out to his place, and even then he wouldn't hardly talk to no-one. So, by degrees we quit going by. There for a while, our only connection to Buddy Drayton Smith was the comings and goings of his wife and kids, and an occasional passerby near the farm. One such old boy said he didn't see Buddy Drayton nowheres, but he saw his ma gallivanting on the screened-in porch, dressed in her sundress. He said he didn't get a real good look at her, but he saw her hair and he saw her dress, and as Iris was a petite thing, he was sure it was his ma.

Then even Iris quit coming to town. That was just a few months ago, at the start of summer, and we knowed Buddy Drayton had sectioned off a plot of land near the house and he was trying his hand at growing some crops and we thought what better summertime activity for them kids than to learn some farming. It would certainly be better than loitering or playing their video games all day.

So, we thought nothing of it, and Buddy Drayton Smith and his kids and his ma and Iris were in the backs of our minds, though reminders of him were everywhere. Still, we felt a shift in the town that we couldn't quite put our finger on. Like a cloud or something had settled over us, and then the sheriff got the phone call from Iris.

Some of us talked as we rode out with the sheriff and said it was like them days when those kids were killed. The fathers of those kids were with us and they agreed that whatever we were about to find harkened back to them days.

ಲಠ

The house was a single-story ranch – the lawn grown over. Buddy Drayton's truck sat on cinder blocks with a rusted-over look, like it'd just given up. The sheriff led the way and we decided that some of us would wait in the yard and the rest would follow the sheriff with our shotguns and pistols. The sheriff took the lead, knocking, and didn't have to wait long for Iris to answer. The few months since we'd seen her last had erased all vestiges of the beauty queen. Her once blond hair coiled bronzed and greasy from her skull and a cigarette dangled lewdly from her lips and the pink robe she wrapped herself in was tattered and stained brown in places. She eyed us all and stepped aside so we could gain entrance into a house that smelled of the staled air of an unopened attic.

The sheriff didn't proceed no further into the house than where Iris retreated, to the kitchen where she sat at the table with a cup of coffee that smelled of whiskey. We looked around nervously, not sure where Buddy Drayton was, or the kids were or his ma.

Iris said, "I found the pictures. Dumb shit forgot to erase them from his phone."

"Where's Buddy Drayton, Iris?" the sheriff asked, his voice soft and easy like calm waves on the pond at dawn.

She lifted her left hand over the table and we saw it held a pistol and she motioned down the hall with a shrug and the barrel of the gun, then laid it casually on the table. We parceled off again so some of us could stay with her as the sheriff took a few with him, and it wasn't till we heard a frantic call that we all raced down to join him. By then she was laughing and said that he was crazy and didn't want to tell no one even when his ma died cause he kept ranting about all of us finding out, and she said that his ma was buried out back where the garden was to go, and we asked her when she died and Iris said three years ago.

We were about to ask then who that old boy saw parading around the house, because in the shape she was in, Iris would still not be confused with Buddy Drayton's ma, when we rounded the corner and saw Buddy Drayton himself laying in his bed. He wore a wig like his mother's hair and a sundress and laid in full makeup – he looked just like her. The sheriff asked her the whereabouts of the children right as the kids walked in calling for her. Seems they'd been out playing when they heard the gunshot, and we could see she got him right between the eyes.

"Y'uns never figured it, he was the one," she said, handing her phone to the sheriff. As it passed through our hands we saw the selfies of him all dolled up and other pictures, and we remembered that Buddy Drayton had led the search for them kids, and it had been him or someone in his party that had been the one to find them. We knew now it was because he knew where to look.

"He said to me that them kids needed saving from adults like that," Iris said, "because his own mother couldn't save him – his dad had just got bored with him and left." And to that, not a one of us had anything to say, but we hung our heads. Each one of us felt the weight of the transgressions that had been laid at our feet.

The Nightmares

Matt studied the sketch in the back of the minivan, oblivious to the talk of his parents. His dad smiled into the rearview mirror; his mom saw but Matt didn't. Matt had his sketch pad on his lap, folded open to the latest penciling to which he was adding the finishing touches. It was a portrait of the family dog—the black lab—Frazzle. Frazzle had posed for a headshot, sitting down. From that shot Matt had sketched this portrait.

"It's dead on," Matt's father said, glancing again into the rearview mirror. Turning around in the passenger's side captain's chair, Matt's mother—smiling—examined the picture. It was obvious that she had missed the enthusiasm in her husband's voice, because her jaw dropped, her expression changed from a complacent *That's nice, dear* countenance, to one of awe. If she could speak, she would have said the same thing.

"What's that mean, Dad?" Matt asked. He was a bright kid for ten, but that was a new one on him. He maybe had heard his father use a similar phrase before, but it hadn't caught his attention until now.

"It means it looks exactly like Frazzle."

Matt frowned for a moment, and then perked up. "If I stay with you guys for the summer then maybe I could do more pictures of Frazzle. And of the house and of the yard and of the street and of the neighborhood and of the …"

His mother faced front again. "Nope."

"Your mom's right, pal. Your grandfather wants to see you."

Matt slumped down in the seat, frowning, arms folded across his chest, nostrils flaring. This had been the source of nightmares for some time. His grandfather was an outdoorsman, loved nature, didn't own a television—just a radio he kept on the oldies station. He was vocal about the waste of time of books, so, Matt figured, his grandfather wouldn't be too keen on drawings, either.

"You can still draw them, honey," his mom said. "Just imagine them."

"I can't!"

His father's eyes went to straight to the mirror and his mom spun in her seat, a look of shock on both their faces. Matt's eyes welled up; he looked frightened, and only after he took a few breaths did he explain. "I only draw what I know is real, and I only know something is real if I see it. I'm scared to draw something if I can't see it."

"Everything will be okay, honey," his mother said. Her hand touched his quivering knee; she looked to his dad with worry.

"I don't want to leave you guys," Matt said, staring into his mother's eyes.

"Your grandfather will take care of you," his father said. But for a while, that wasn't good enough.

They drove. They stopped for gas and the parents found that the simplest way to turn him from his fears was, surprisingly, to draw them away. They pointed out a cow in the field and Matt drew the whole scene. They rounded a bend to a breathtaking view of the Ozark hills and Matt sketched it. And always was the touch of realism, the shading, the layering and texturing—you could feel the bark on the trees and almost hear the leaves fluttering in the breeze. Matt was on a roll, and as the light faded, his dad flicked on the interior light and asked Matt to sketch what he saw. His human profiles were accurate. There his mother turned around in her seat, smiling at him. There his father behind the wheel— we see the back of his head and in the mirror, the reflection of his eyes. The seats and dash were detailed, the glass of the windows held the glare at the right angles, and everything seemed normal and in place. Outside (the van had stopped at a country four-way, as Matt included the finishing touches) trees and brush and hills were there, but silhouetted against a deep purple sky. Stars were luminescent, amassing around a crescent moon, jaundice and hanging just above the tree line.

Matt frowned as he drew the last detail—cat-like eyes peering out from the underbrush, eyes devoid of irises or pupils or detail of any sort, except that they were a deeper shade of the pencil's gray than, say the moon. It was no stretch of the imagination to know that these eyes were red, even in this black and white picture.

His mother commented on them and Matt just shrugged them off; he stared out the window to his right, to just past the stop sign where a big oak stood against that barbed wire fence. He turned in his seat and espied the area for as long as he could, until they topped a hill and he lost sight, and then they were there.

Gravel popped under the tires. The house was one-story, ranch-style, brick and siding with a brick fireplace. The porch light came on and Matt's grandfather stepped out, waving to them. And as at the end of any long trek, the last leg began, the scramble to exit the car with all baggage and all the drama of releasing what once was confined.

Matt's father pulled the grandfather aside, while Matt's mom helped Matt get ready. Presently all were inside, and the grandfather approached Matt gravely. The boy was seated in the loveseat in the living room—quiet and timid—clutching his sketchpad. Matt was small for his age.

"Can I see your drawings?" the old man asked.

He had only met his grandfather a handful of times. He stared up at the stranger looming over him, nearly every inch of his body quivering. Finally, timidly, he handed his sketches over. Then he watched a smile creep to Arthur Cornell's lips.

"Very good," Arthur said, but in his eyes was the same awe Matt's mother and father had shown.

☘

It took Arthur several days to prove that he was not going to hinder his grandson's creative spark. Realizing the task needed work and compromise, Arthur started by leading Matt outside—much to Matt's chagrin—to draw. Arthur introduced Matt to a whole natural world full of rocks and flowers and fields of hay and streams and brush and trees and hills and plains and ponds, of cows and deer and fish and squirrels, of birds. And Arthur spurred the boy on. He reminded Matt to grab his sketchpad and pencils when the two were set for their walks.

Never did the boy disappoint; he drew what his grandfather showed him. They walked longer and longer, and Matt began to see the value of outside. Arthur's lessons came after his grandson went to bed, and he began to thumb through the sketchpads, looking at all the drawings.

CREO

By the end of the first week, Matt actually smiled when Arthur suggested they go for a walk. It was just after breakfast when he gathered his freshest sketchpad and pouch of pencils, but a sudden thought stopped him. It was one of those worrisome thoughts that are ever so important to boys, incessantly asked until they had an adequate answer.

"But we walked everywhere," was the best way his question could be posed.

To which Arthur laughed.

"I got lots of land, boy. I got nearly two hundred acres, and only eighty in pasture. We ain't touched the surface yet."

Arthur walked and Matt followed. He asked his grandfather if they could walk to the end and happily, Arthur obliged. Matt watched Arthur stare at the canopy of limbs and cock his head toward the chirping birds of various species.

They walked up and down the woven path, under the trees, as forest undergrowth began to bloom. Stretching vines tried to trip them up as their feet stepped on saggy leaves and the moist dirt floor. Cedars were spaced intermittent among the oaks, the silver-leafed maples. Hints at a blue sky and sun spotlighted irregular points on the forest floor. There was a lot to draw here, but still they kept moving.

"Draw me a stream," Arthur said. He sat upon a stump, smoking a cigarette; Matt stood dutifully beside him. "It rambles through some gentle hills."

Matt began to draw. It took him twenty minutes, and in that time Arthur rested, smoking his cigarettes as the boy brought something he imagined to life.

They walked and for Matt, it seemed to take forever. They followed more of a dirt path and more of the same scene. It was worthy of a picture, but it was commonplace. Matt found himself sweating and wondering how far they had to go, until they topped another hill, and found the path blocked by a single strand of barbed wire. But it lent a hell of a view—as his dad might have said.

To their left and their right, the bluff and the wire continued. In front their path continued down a very steep path that all but vanished before them. The path down the hill was surrounded by rocks and shrub, a few pines smattered on the vertical terrain, little growth; impeded by the single strand of barbed wire.

To look at the fencing, one would think it was of little value. It was a single strand of barbed wire and the barbs weren't evenly spaced. Arthur did not seem amazed that Matt noticed this eccentricity.

"Why do you think it's like that?"

Matt looked downhill. Down the hill, even the bright green of the cedars and pines seemed scarce. Everything was gray, like spring had yet to hit. What green there was seemed an accident. Rocks were more appropriate. Dead trees were more appropriate.

"You're trying to keep something out," Matt said finally.

Despite himself, Arthur smiled. From his pocket he pulled another cigarette and lit it, took a puff and sighed with smoke, curling from his lips. He closed his eyes in ecstasy.

"Do you remember the picture of the stream and the hills?" Arthur asked.

Matt nodded.

"Do you think you could add a cave?"

Matt immediately sat upon a flattened rock and flipped his pad to an empty page. Again he began to sketch the stream, the hills, and Arthur had to stop him, a bemused look upon the grandfather's face.

"The last picture was done," the boy said. "This is a new picture, is all."

And he drew. He recaptured accurately the original picture of this Ozark stream passing through some gently sloping hills, and then as naturally as Monet, he incorporated a cave's opening.

☙

All through dinner Matt stared at his new picture, particularly at the mouth of the cave. There was something missing, he was sure, but he didn't know what. He studied, taking a bite only when his grandfather reminded him there was food on his plate. He missed Arthur's sad gaze to his own plate.

Matt waited, after the entire house was dark, and the evening news had been muffled. His blanket tucked under his neck, he was warm and secure in the covers. But his mind was working; Matt would not sleep tonight. He had to know what was beyond the barbed wire. Whatever it was, he knew it was linked to the cave in his drawing.

Matt waited until the sounds of his grandfather had quieted down, and then he folded back the covers. His feet touched carpet and he waited--eyes unblinking—until his vision adjusted. He could make out shapes and obstacles, tints and shades, just enough to maneuver quietly. Nervous but confident, the ten-year-old boy dressed in relative silence.

He opened his door a crack and listened into the darkness. No sound. No light. The darkness was as inviting as it was unnerving. Matt stepped into the hall and pulled the door too behind him.

The latching door stopped him. It would almost be reassuring if his grandfather opened the door, Matt realized then. Then whatever was lurking in the cave wouldn't be after him.

Not just in the cave, a little voice in his mind said—it sounded like his own but not really. Thinking back, Matt remembered the eyes. He had drawn them into the picture of the interior of the van. Even then it was watching him.

He had to get to the barbed wire.

Every floorboard creaked with every step he took, and Matt wasn't sure until he pulled the front door too—and paused to wait as no light came on and no sound was made—that he had escaped. As he walked across the yard, the butterflies settled. As he climbed over the corner post of the fence that separated yard from field, and he walked briskly past the sleeping heifers in the pasture, he gazed back intermittently to see a darkened house, and so felt a little better.

Matt walked down the hill sloping toward the pond, saw a cow— perhaps searching for a midnight drink—lowering its lips to the water's surface. It watched him as he walked past. He met the cow's eyes.

Don't go!

But cows don't speak, he scolded himself.

Matt reached the southwest corner of his grandfather's pasture, stopped to catch a breath and looked back. The field was dark. Silhouettes and shades and shadows overwhelmed Matt, and thinking about the eyes, the boy again came unnerved. He was visibly shaking, but the urge to mount the fence was something primeval. He had to know what was beyond. He had to see the barbed wire, and what it could possibly restrain. Consumed by the eyes, he climbed the fence, and began down the moonlit path into the wilderness. He was oblivious to the two forces stalking him: one with a flashlight whose beam focused on a certain point; one guided by smell and a keen sense of night vision.

The land traversed was familiar even in the night, and Matt didn't even have to get his bearings. He saw but he didn't see. He walked, knowing where he was going, but not conscious of it. He was lost between sleepwalking and somnolence. He recognized where his grandfather had paused in reflection, trees and shrubs and such landscape points. He followed the trail onward, until his chest smacked against something sharp. It was a pointed jab; Matt could feel the blood instantly.

His hand reached up first, tugging at whatever invisible thing snagged his shirt in the darkness. It was a wrinkle in his line of sight, a simple snap that made Matt realize he had reached the threshold. The barbed wire had snagged him, as it was supposed to do. His eyes adjusting again, Matt saw the hill fall away, the winteriness below. Everywhere else spring was in full bloom. The season had birthed with the bloom of the dogwoods, leading quickly into the Easter season. Overnight, the grass had greened and more trees had bloomed. Aside from a few late bloomers, nature had recognized spring. Except down the hill where Matt could still see the gray. Nothing was blooming.

The moon broke through the clouds and illuminated everything, painting the scene in navy. Uphill, color struggled to break through. Downhill was bare—the dark, the gray seemed to fit. Matt listened to the scuffling of things in the underbrush, things unseen, and it happened, that as he fully awoke, he became afraid. His imagination kicked in and he could imagine some pretty wild things sneaking around out there.

"But none of it's real," he whispered, and the sound of his own voice calmed him.

Then from down the hill came a sound unlike anything the boy had ever heard. Looking that direction he saw the eyes, millions of red eyes, highlighted and bright and sanguine and not tainted by the navy. He blinked and backed away, and imagined some of the eyes nearing. And then something strange happened. Most of the eyes blinked out. They were gone, and only a single pair stared up at him. He couldn't tell if they were moving, but he would have been surprised if they weren't. They were featureless, as all the eyes had been, and the same shade of red as all the others, but still he recognized them. These were the eyes he had seen the night his parents brought him up, and these were the eyes he imagined in the picture he had drawn.

He took another step back.

Long fingers wrapped about his shoulder blade; he was yanked nearly off his feet.

Spun around before he could scream, his imagination told him that he was going to face the rest of the eyes. They had ambushed him, blinked out and snuck around and now they were here, ready to eat him up. No, not eat him up, but play with him until the other one arrived. It would eat him up. It … was his grandfather.

Arthur stared down at the boy, frowning, his face grave. The old man tore his eyes from Matt as he raised his left arm, a pistol in his hand. Glaring down the hill, the old man pulled the trigger. Matt looked down the hill, but he didn't see the eyes.

"Come on," Arthur said. "We still need to go."

And so they left, and didn't speak again until they were sitting in the living room, Arthur standing by the fireplace, frowning, looking at the ground.

"We've always called it *The Aminal,*" he said to start. "The kids in town named it, years ago, when the first disappearances happened. Now we all just know. A child goes missing, *The Aminal.*

"*The Aminal* takes children. It has taken many children, over the years. It looks kind of like a wolf, but it is the size of a cow. Your Aunt Shelly saw it. She isn't like most people though. Most people who see it become obsessed with it. And then they disappear. We've had a few adults, but most have been children."

The two locked eyes and stayed silent. This lasted a moment.

"Now get back to bed," Arthur said.

Matt rushed to him; hugged him. Arthur hugged back. Matt returned to his room.

He undressed and put on his pajamas quickly, and laid down in bed. Pulling the covers up, he could hear his grandfather through the wall, coughing, shuffling about—probably undressing and going to bed himself—and stared straight out the window.

The curtains were pulled back; the blinds were drawn up. Blackness stared in at him, framed like a portrait, though a portrait missing something.

Red eyes.

Throwing the covers back, hopping out of bed, Matt rushed to the cord that controlled the blinds and yanked it. The blinds crashed to the windowsill. Unhooking the satin cords, the curtains fell and closed, and the blackness was gone.

Matt laid back down and pulled the covers up. He felt safe under the covers. He believed, as most children believe, that the monster can't get you if you are covered up. So he tucked himself in nice and tight. He forced his eyes shut, took a few deep breaths, and then settled into the mattress.

☙❧

Arthur laid in bed in the dark, thinking. *The Aminal* had taken many children. He had watched it over the years, watched each of his friends fall into mourning. Frank Cross lost a son, some thirty years ago. Barry Levi lost a daughter five years after that. For some it skipped a generation. Kelly O'Roarke from Chicago had his grandkid to visit one summer about ten years ago—just a toddler—and the boy went missing one early June morning while they were getting ready to go fishing. And when Arthur was a kid, he remembered stories. He had friends that went missing.

The Aminal, always *The Aminal.*

Even at seventy-five, the mere thought of the thing sent shivers down his spine. Still, the one questioned remained, and to it, Arthur had no answer.

Why? He loved his grandson. He relished in the boy's talent. So why even introduce it? They had hunted it, once. It had taken the mayor's nephew, back in '77. Still a younger man, Arthur—then a volunteer fireman and a deputy for Sheriff Larsen (Godresthissoul)—led the hunt. It was never a question for any of these people in this rural community if this creature ever existed.

Some twenty men tracked *The Aminal* in the wee hours of the morning, in separate packs of five. No Dogs. They followed tracks. They found first a stream, ambling through a gently sloping series of hills.

They found a cave. Four went in. Arthur and the others heard a cry—"Red Eyes! Red Eyes!"—and then they heard gunshots. They heard a growl and then all went silent. When the smoke wafting out the mouth of the cave evaporated, and no one came out, Arthur called. When no one answered, Arthur motioned and five guys inched forward behind him, gripping their guns like aimed teddy bears, quivering.

The four lay in the semi-darkness, mauled. The official report said missing. As the darkness enclosed the six-armed men, as they pressed together, the heat wafted up from below. In front of them, as near as they could tell, the cave fell gradually; the wind softly rising from the depths was that of a furnace, not cool, as most Ozark caves. That was about all Arthur had time to notice before the eyes blinked and stared, and all six men opened fire.

The eyes were red, feline in shape, featureless. There was a growl, a guttural rumble emanating from this thing, and it didn't take long for the order. Shotguns and rifles fired at Arthur's command. The eyes stared. They unloaded their casings into the darkness, at the eyes, but the eyes remained unmoving, and when the guns stopped and the echoes faded, just below the ringing in their ears, Arthur and the men could hear it. It growled louder.

And then other eyes opened. Further back and further down, other red, almond-shaped, featureless eyes opened. The six backed out of the cave.

"Plan B" Arthur called out, and eight more guys carried up bundles of dynamite, wired to one charger. The bundles were set inside the mouth of the cave, even as one guy asked about the first group that went in.

Arthur didn't answer.

The charges were set. When the living stepped back—no barrel left the mouth of the cave, and nothing emerged into the sunlight—the charges were ignited, and the mouth of the cave and half the hillside fell in, burying the mauled men and the red eyes.

Tonight Arthur had seen all the eyes.

Sniffling broke his concentration. The sound came from an adjacent room. Walking down a u-shaped hall, opening a door, Arthur found Matt laying in the fetal position in bed.

The grandfather sat on the side of the bed, pulled back the covers, stroked the boy's back. After a moment, the boy spoke.

"I don't like to pretend things, when I draw."

The grandfather realized his mistake immediately.

"The last time I used my imagination, Mommy got hurt. I didn't pretend in a good way."

"What happened?" Arthur asked; he did the best he could to mask the concern.

"Mommy and Daddy were fighting, and I wasn't happy. They told me to stay in my room, but I could still hear them. I imagined Mommy got hurt, and I wanted to draw, and I started to draw. I drawed Mommy and Daddy fighting. I didn't really want to, but I could hear them. I drawed Mommy getting hurt. And Daddy hurt her."

"I'm here," Arthur said. He rubbed the boy's back and hovered over until Matt drifted back to sleep. He stayed a while longer, looking at his grandson, thanking his lucky stars that the curse that had struck his friends had avoided him. And he felt lucky, that the draw of *The Aminal* had not enthralled his family.

ಋಠ

Two days before the birthday party, Arthur pulled a large tarp out of the shed and tied it to limbs of four trees, some fifteen feet overhead. Matt steadied the ladder for his grandfather. Then Arthur contacted an old friend at the school, and he and Matt drove the old pickup into town, returning with a truckload of metal folding chairs and three eight-foot tables.

Through this the phone kept ringing.

As they put the finishing touches on a banner reading CANTRELL FAMILY REUNION—incorporating Matt's special talent—Arthur found his grandson frowning.

"But it's my birthday," Matt said.

"We are using the occasion of your birthday to bring the whole family together."

Matt scratched his head with the end of his pencil. "You mean all our family is coming for my birthday?"

"Yep."

ಠಋ

With all this preparation, there still wasn't enough seating. The house was full. Kids ran around with balloons and cap guns they won in the pin-the-tail-on-the-donkey game. Others sucked on lollipops and ate Tootsie Rolls and Sugar Daddies they won out of the busted piñata. The garage door was opened. Lawn chairs were placed on the concrete slab between the garage and the gravel drive. There was just enough concrete for the kids to draw a hop-scotch game in chalk.

Relatives Matt had never heard of—but he recognized from his drawings of their headshots on the banner—congratulated him on turning eleven, while those same people hugged Arthur. Arthur had come to believe he would never see some of them again, it had been so long. The cake was brought out and the audience focused on Matt, who walked to the table as nervous as a freshman politician at his first debate. His smile frozen, his eyes unblinking, Matt stood behind the flickering candles, as the wind threatened to blow them out. To his left stood Arthur. To his right stood his parents. In front of him the nameless horde that swore they were his family.

They all sang. And when they finished, expectant eyes were upon him. For a flicker of a second Matt swore the eyes were red, but he took a deep breath. The eyes were normal; Matt blew.

The candles flickered, but the wind and breath were too much. The candles all went out.

The cheer sent the birds in haste from the trees; flutter of wings as thunderous as the applause that this child's wish had come true. Only when the moment of truth had come, and the wish had sprung to life in his own mind, did Matt realize what it was he truly wanted, and the notion that it was going to happen completely shocked him. He saw sanguine eyes again in his family, and after the blowout felt as though he had collapsed.

His parents ushered him toward the living room, along with his grandfather and Aunt Shelly, and Matt obliged. He walked and was cognizant of everything, but responded to nothing. Like a zombie Matt sat on the marble hearth, his body framed by the brick fireplace. Aunt Shelly sat in a recliner, as did Arthur. Matt's parents took the loveseat adjacent to the couch—all were situated in a very conversational way—and old times were discussed. To Matt it felt inevitable that the conversation turned to *The Aminal.*

"I saw it," Aunt Shelly said, "and I wasn't a child."

They had disclosed—without Matt's participation—the midnight sojourn he had taken to the brink of *The Aminal's* lair, and how Grandpa Arthur had arrived just in time. Of course Matt's dad laughed it all away, but Arthur remained ardent in his narrative, and Matt only listened, occasionally nodded.

"I was driving one night, back home, when I still lived off County Road 314. I had just hit the gravel when I glanced over to the ditch and saw the eyes, those red eyes. I thought wolf at first, but it was standing as tall as a cow. It seemed to take notice of me, and it howled. Or it growled. I couldn't tell, but the neck tilted back and some sound came out.

"I slammed on the gas and spun the back tires and fishtailed just about in order to escape, and that thing watched me. And then it followed." She laughed, a humorless joke to herself.

"I was doing seventy on gravel and it was keeping pace. I could see it out my passenger-side window. It had human features. I looked into its eyes.

Matt kept silent. There were lots of kids that went missing, due to *The Aminal.* They probably saw its real eyes, too, he thought. They probably saw its real eyes, before—

಍ರಠ

They had laughed, Matt thought, as he crawled out of bed. He was quiet. It was still dark, and he was sure that no one was awake. His parents and his aunt and his grandfather had laughed at his aunt's story. Only his grandfather had looked at him, with a kind of serious look that replaced the laugh. But it was only for a second; Matt had tried to smile.

He felt like an experienced dresser in the dark. He walked through the halls, and imagined the old black and white movies his dad watched, about the prisoner, spread-eagle across the wall, dressed in pinstripes and wearing a burglar's mask, inching along the brick wall and freezing when the spotlight danced across. The spotlight danced across when he came to the archway of the kitchen, the light still on.

His grandfather sat with his back to him, alone in the kitchen. Arthur seemed sad, or deep in thought. Matt didn't stick around to find out which. He returned to his room, flicked on the light, and noticed all the pictures he had drawn over the summer, stacked neatly on his dresser.

Seated on the edge of his bed, the pictures on his lap, he began to sort through them. They were loose, and as he viewed each, he laid it face down beside him on the mattress. The last picture was not completed—Matt knew—as he stared at it.

There was a stream, and some gently rolling hills, and a cave, and stepping stones leading across the stream. There was barbed wire stretched across the nearest side of the stream, and flowers by the mouth's cave. But something was missing.

∾∾∾

Wind slapped at the eaves with a screech; the house moaned in response. Albert tried to remember if the weather forecast called for a storm, even as he caught the faint sounds of rattling somewhere deep within the house. He stood, took a step toward the living room, then stopped and turned. Just behind the kitchen a crooked hall bent to the back set of bedrooms. Arthur stepped into the darkness and heard the strange sound more clearly. Like cards shuffling.

Like flapping, he thought, as he followed the sound—no cards, wait. It's a whipping noise. From behind he heard Matt's dad groggily ask what the noise was. Seeing Matt's parents triggered a spark in Arthur. Not enough to connect all the pieces, yet, but more a sick sense that he knew what was coming, he just didn't want to admit it. In that instant, Arthur understood what the sound was.

Despite the wind, the door opened easily enough, gaining them access.

All of Matt's drawings flapped and fluttered about the room. The screeching wind had found an entrance into the old house via a window in Matt's room. Where Matt should have been laying on the bed, however, lay only a single picture atop the covers. It was undisturbed by the wind.

The parents called for the child; Arthur sank to his knees and pulled the picture close.

The picture was of a familiar scene, a stream or a brook, ambling down a gently sloping hill, a series of stepping stones leading across the water, and a cave on the opposite side. On this side of the stream, a single strand of barbed wire, and in the cave, a pair of eyes. Just stepping across to the other side, a little boy.

Arthur cried.

FIDDLEBACKS

The duplex was a rundown building with a wide cracked cement drive, siding that exhibited wood rot. It was good for the impoverished that could afford nothing else, the trash and the youth that spent what money they had on going to college. Two such youths stood in the drive now, the young man was a grad student and his pretty brunette girlfriend was studying dietetics. The day was cloudless, an autumn bright day that seemed dim in this part of town. Chuck slammed the cell phone shut, glanced to Carol, rolled his eyes and kicked gravel. He dropped the phone into his jean's pocket and put his hands behind his head, began to pace.

"Bitch hung up on me!"

"What did she say?"

"I could barely get a word in edgewise. She was swearing she cleaned the carpets, said she was a good landlord, said she didn't need this aggravation."

"What aggravation?"

Carol looked in the palm of her hand, to the lone key.

"She said leave the door unlocked and she'd get the keys, and that's when I said I wasn't about to leave the door unlocked because I'm not going to risk someone else getting in there and tearing the place up and we get blamed for it, and that's when she said she didn't need this aggravation and I reminded her we only wanted to do the walk through, as per the lease, and she tried to tell me what the lease said and…"

From her purse Carol pulled a folded yellow piece of carbon paper, unfolded the elongated page with a snap of her wrist and held it up.

"My mom knows a lawyer," Carol said. "Down on the square. Said it wouldn't cost anything if we go talk to him. Said he'd place a friendly phone call to Harold and Betty."

"She tried to tell me she didn't have to send us the security deposit back, but she would because she's so nice."

"Bull!"

"Bull right."

Chuck walked down the drive to the mailbox which dangled from its frame, its side dented in. He sat the mailbox upright with a creak, opened it and looked in, saw nothing. He shut it, steadied it and walked away, only to hear it fall. It dangled from the post by a solitary bent screw.

"Ghetto," Chuck said as they got in the car. He had never been so happy to move.

⚭

Several nights passed, another house across town, an old single story ranch style, sat quiet and dark at three am. An older man and an older woman lived there, but for the past few days, no one had seen hide nor hair of the older woman. Left to his own devices, the older man ate out and drank beer. On the second day, he filed a police report. He kept up his daily routine, came home and went to bed easily enough.

On the third night, at three in the morning, Harold's eyes opened. Darkness, the plush mattress, face depressed into the pillow, the room cool. He had been sleeping soundly under the circumstances and was at first confused as to what could have awakened him. He was usually a sound sleeper. For all his sixty-five years, this had been an alien time of night. But here now, faced with the anti-hour, Harold lifted his head.

Maybe Betty's come home, he thought. But the house wasn't that big, and his eyes, just opened enough, like a cracked door, could see no light from any of the other rooms. He heard no footsteps. Rather, he felt the prickly points of pressure alternating as they moved across his temple.

He wasn't used to life without her and it wasn't like her to not call.

He entertained the thought that she had run off, but quickly pushed that aside. He knew her too well. She hadn't been out of north Arkansas her whole life and she wasn't exactly something a younger boy would pine after. Plus she didn't have a lot of money. She ran the rentals, but Harold handled the accounts.

Whatever Harold felt on his temple now scurried across his forehead. He screamed and jumped out of bed, scrambled for the lamp but heard it fall. He fumbled, eyes darting about, adjusting now to the dark room—there the edge of the mattress, the wardrobe, the jewelry armoire and her closet door, the dresser, the mirror, reflecting the moonlight through the blinds. He felt the brass knob, shaped like a key, clicked it once, then again, the light came on. He looked down to the mangled lampshade, the lamp had a big chunk broken off.

Nothing. Nothing on the mattress, on the sheets. But the sheets were dark and it was hard to see—nothing on the pillow, and nothing on him. He stood, watching the bed, felt the sting on his right heel and cussed again, looked down, saw blood on the shard and on the carpet.

He tossed the sheets back, snatched up the lamp, held the bulb toward the bed.

"Where are you, you little bastard," he said with a thick Ozark accent.

Silence and stillness but Harold found no comfort in that. He knew it was there, scurrying about, sending him a message.

☧

Betty was still quite capable of screaming, and would have if a ball of webbing hadn't been crammed down her throat. The same covered her eyes, bound her in the corner, on her butt, hands behind her back. She had never been a strong woman, but this was just spider webs and she should have been able to break out of this. Wrapped head to foot in the silk strands, bound tight, legs straight out in front of her, holes had been intentionally left around her nostrils, which flared. She squirmed but had long since discovered she had been robbed of any grand movements. The only sound she made was a soft mewling noise, pleading and weak like a kitten. The deaf fiddlebacks scurried over her, taking little nibbles here and there, injecting their venom to deaden the skin just under the cocoon. Take a little bite and then move on. Never enough to kill her, but she could feel it all. She could feel the flesh inflame underneath the bite, and then more—Wolf Spiders and Black Widows—would swarm in, spin more web, trap in the heat, the infection. She could feel the necrosis, the black rot swelling, could smell the older bites, felt the sepsis in her blood. She made the sound again, what was meant to be a cry out for God.

ᔕ৶৹

At dawn, Harold pulled his truck up slowly to the four way stop, braked, and looked about. None of the neighbors were outside. Their windows, near as he could tell, were dark. It was Saturday, overcast, the start of the cooler months. Early October in the Ozarks was cool, the nights people kept their windows open and snuggled under a warm blanket, and the days, even the sunny days, required long sleeves or a light jacket. This weather suited Harold. He couldn't take the heat like he could back in his younger days. He couldn't breathe in the heat and when he thought about it, didn't much like winter, either. The real cold hurt his joints. He liked the fall and he liked the spring, and the rest he could take it or leave it.

Glancing to his left, he saw the duplex, its wide drive empty of cars. That couple wasn't here. Probably sleeping still, young kids today, can't appreciate the early morning hours, probably sleeping off hangovers and sex and whatnot. Empty and still, the windows dark, the duplex seemed more like a tomb. Seeing it like this made Harold sad and he suddenly got the impression that things weren't like they used to be. The feeling hit him, as it does most people in times of nostalgia, that the times had irreversibly changed and left him behind. Harold, faced with the future, decided he didn't want to move forward.

He got out of the truck and walked up the drive to the front door where that guy and girl had just rented. They had been good kids. They paid their rent on time. They were clean and cordial the few times he spoke to them. But damn it they acted like they were the only renters, and now, hassling them like this, when he and Betty had other concerns. He reached in his pocket for the keys and that's when he heard her voice, like it was just over his shoulder.

"I had to, Harold. I can't let them take my car."

"You should have talked to me first," he said. They had been sitting at the dinner table over a plate of spaghetti she had made. Back when the kids first told them they were moving out.

It wasn't just a pride thing with Harold. She had really put them in a bind. He had given her car allowance money and money for the refund.

"They don't get it, anyway," she said, and shoveled another fork-load of twisted noodles into her mouth. "They didn't clean the carpets, and they got a mouse in there, and they tore up their own mailbox."

Harold knew the neighborhood, the people living next to those kids. Some punks were playing mailbox baseball, was all, but he wasn't about to tell Betty that. And the mouse, he shook his head, thought-- screwed into the plaster, like he was disappointed in himself. He should have secured that light over the dining area better, is all.

"Yes, dear," he said.

Harold snapped back to the present at the sound of a voice.

"We just wanted to do the walk through with you."

Harold spun around, eyes wide. Chuck stood behind him, alone, staring at him, a young man not quite thirty and in good shape.

"What do you want?" Harold shoved his hands deep inside his coveralls.

"We just wanted to do the walk through, like in the lease agreement. Why wouldn't you meet us?"

"Stay the hell away from me!"

"I'm here now," Chuck said. "Why don't we do it, now? Then I can give you the keys and you can give me my deposit and we can part ways."

Yes, Harold thought. We can go in and we can take a look around. Maybe we can even look up in the attic. Got a little surprise for you up there. Harold nodded. With his left hand, he pulled the key out of his pocket, smiled, his lips quivering, turned slowly and unlocked the door.

They stepped inside. The air was cool.

"We already shut off the utilities in our name. We're out of here. See, we swept and mopped the kitchen and dining area, and we vacuumed the rug. I got pictures, Mr. Swiggert, and Betty didn't have this cleaned. There are date and time stamps, taken with my digital camera. This place was filthy when we first moved in. I had to work, took Carol two days to clean this so it was liveable, so we aren't paying for cleaning the rugs now."

Harold spun, caught the boy off guard, the barrel of the pistol slapped Chuck's temple, knocked him to the ground. Harold took hold of the gun with both hands and stood over Chuck as blood trickled from just above his ear.

"You got a mouse, you snot-nosed little punk."

"Listen!" and Chuck stared up at the older man, up to the barrel of the gun with defiance. "You got the fucking rats, you asshole. You hear them, scampering behind the walls, up in the ceiling. I'm not paying for your goddamn rats!"

"You want to see what that is?" Harold asked, and shoved the gun almost up Chuck's nose. "Get up."

Chuck rose and raised his hands above his head.

"You wouldn't leave well enough alone. Just had to have your money."

"You're a slum lord."

Harold cackled, ushered the gun toward the hall and so that's where Chuck walked. Harold took the moment to lock and deadbolt the front door, in case anyone else, including Chuck's pretty little thing, wanted to bust in to save the day.

"Stop," Harold said.

Chuck stopped, his back to Harold. Just in front of the younger man, a rope dangled down from a panel in the plaster ceiling.

"Grab the rope," and Chuck did as he was told. He kept his other hand up.

"Why didn't anyone tell us? I don't understand that. This town isn't that big, but surely someone would have warned us."

"They know what kind of people we rent to but they don't know about us. Pull."

Chuck pulled down on the rope. The panel came down and wooden stairs unfolded nearly to the floor. Chuck caught the bottom rung and guided the staircase down, then stared up to the blackness.

"I'm just a college kid," Chuck said. "The town knows us. I'm studying to be an entomologist-arachnologist. Do you know what that is?"

"Walk."

Chuck walked up the stairs and Harold followed closely behind. The old man stepped twice to his right, reached up with his free hand and pulled as soft light broke some of the dimness of the attic.

"Every creature has its own language," Chuck said. "I study that language. I study how they communicate with each other and the environment."

"You hear that?" Harold asked. He shifted the gun to his left hand and looked at Chuck's back. Even with his stroke last year, Harold was confident he could still pull the trigger with his left index finger if the boy even thought of turning around. With his right hand, Harold began searching the pockets on the right side of his coveralls for the flashlight he kept on him all times.

"God put us on this earth to take care of the animals," Chuck said. "Wanted Adam to name them. It's in the Bible. All of them. Even the ones I study. I've named a lot of them."

"Like a cry," Harold said, and turned his flashlight on. "Oh."

The flashlight didn't illuminate the mass completely. Most of it was still in heavy shadow. What the two men could see was a large lump of white webbing, pregnant with something that wriggled. They were robbed of translucency and only saw the faintest of shadows underneath.

Harold raced to her, dropping the gun, began clawing at the webs. Tears streamed down his face. He said the word "no," and the word "oh," a lot, rambled on with unintelligible things as he pulled the webbing away. He saw where she was, the gangrene bites, the infected areas, how they smelled, covering her body with red welts, the rotten places, her eyes rolled to the back of her head.

"Do you think she suspected the rats?" came the voice from behind Harold, but he didn't spin around. "Or do you think, when she heard the scurrying in the walls, in the ceiling, she knew it was the Brown Recluses?"

Harold looked at her, stroked her puffed out cheek, black in the center. "You knew what was up here. Why'd you come up here?"

"Because I wanted to do a walk through," Chuck said.

Harold rose and spun around. Chuck was smiling.

"I was checking the mail the other day and Betty pulled in. She offered then, much like you did today, thinking your dirty little secret was safe between the two of you. Too stupid to realize Carol and I lived here nearly two years. You think we wouldn't know what scurried behind the walls?"

Harold stooped, reached toward the shadows. He heard the cock of the hammer and looked up, the pistol in Chuck's hand. Chuck, so big, so broad, smiling. His eyes were wild and shined red in the beam of the flashlight.

"Sit!"

Harold sat next to Betty, staring only at the gun. He reached down and felt her hand, interlaced their fingers. She was still a little warm. He looked over at her frozen features, her jaw agape, a brown recluse crawled out from between her lips, stopped on her cheek, seemed to regard him.

"I fed you," he mumbled, and the spider sidestepped, then stared at him some more.

"Help me," Betty whispered.

Harold and Chuck jumped. She didn't move, her eyes stayed vacant. Harold clinched her hand. Hail began to rain above them , pounding on the tin roof, only they knew it wasn't hailing. From the shadows they came, all brand of arachnid, scurrying about Betty, spinning their webs. A black widow climbed over the steel toe of Harold's boot, began her web at his foot.

"I fed you all."

"You should have just paid us back our security deposit."

The webs covered both of Harold's feet. Beside him he heard a gasp of air and felt Betty's hand go limp. He clutched her fingers, pressed her hand to his thigh, the webbing spun over them. Harold didn't fight.

"I know how they communicate. I know their behaviors," Chuck said as he moved closer. "That's what I study at the university."

The arachnids had worked fast. Webbing now mummified all of Betty and nearly covered Harold up to his chest. He found he could bare-ly move his shoulders. He flexed his biceps but found the strands too strong. Looking down, he saw them, the fiddlebacks—the brown reclus-es—scurrying about his waist, his thighs, a few moving up, staring into his eyes. Wolf spiders and black widows spun their webs, and from above tarantulas crept down, one on Harold's shoulder, then up his neck, into his gray hair, across his scalp.

"They're coming for you, Harold," Chuck said, in the most ghoulish voice he could muster.

Fiddlebacks began to crawl over Harold's thighs; he tried to block out Chuck's voice, watched as one crawled into the web and bit; a sting, that was all for now.

"You know why they're called fiddlebacks? Because they have a fiddle shape on their head, pointing to the rear of their body."

"That's the black widow," Harold said, looking up to the barrel of the gun.

Chuck shook his head. "No. The black widow has a red hourglass on its belly, the brown recluse has a black violin shape, or if you're from the South, a fiddle. Also, one could argue they fiddle around, toiling in your warm spots, your cozy spots. But you know, they don't like to bite. In fact, a brown recluse will go out of its way to avoid confrontation, to avoid a bite. They have very distinct behaviors for running away and escaping harm. They generally only bite when they are pressed against skin, like when you pick up a load of laundry. And even then, their fangs are so miniscule that if you have any kind of cloth on, their fangs can't penetrate."

A few of the other fiddlebacks slid under the webbing, began to bite. Harold saw one crawl in just about his waist, felt it trail down, under his pants, against his skin. He gave a yelp when it bit, the sting in his pecker. The other spiders were up to his neck. Suddenly his throat was tight, Harold found it hard to swallow, to breathe. He tried to move his arms but the webbing held tight, stuck to him. His chest hurt. Probably having a heart attack, a thought which was a pleasant alternative to this.

A brown recluse crawled slowly up his chest, over the webbing, up his neck. Harold struggled more but could not move. Watching it edge closer, he tried to thrash, to tear out of the webbing. It crept upward and Chuck began to laugh.

"You know Betty pulled a pearl-handle pistol on me. You must have given that to her. What, a gift for her to use on those degenerates you normally rent to?"

Harold felt their prickly feet on his lips, on his cheek, tickling the little hairs on the back of his neck. He couldn't even part his lips. The brown recluse edged upward. Harold could feel it on his cheek. He could still shake his head. He didn't fight when his eyes welled up with tears.

"The tarantulas fell on her first, but that was just to freak her out, make her drop the gun. I picked it up and held it to her. A few of the fiddle backs came then, placed a few bites to keep her seated, then the others came, spinning webs. When they were done, all the fiddle backs swarmed, just like they're about to do to you."

"I'll give you the damn money!"

"It's the principal."

Harold could feel the webbing tickle his lower eyelids, and just as he prepared himself for blindness, the spiders crept away. The solitary brown recluse began nibbling on his cheek, stinging. Chuck knelt before him, gun resting on his thigh.

"Carol wanted to call a lawyer. I told her I had a better way. Aren't you glad I spared you all that courtroom B.S.?"

Harold felt them, crawling, stinging. He knew he had a while. As thousands of fiddles covered his body, he imagined the pain to come. He knew Betty had suffered, and that he was about to suffer. He knew she died slowly, always aware, always in pain, and that was about to be his also.

"Don't worry," Chuck said, and stepped into the shadows, back to the ladder, then took the first steps down from the attic. He waited to speak again when only his head was visible. "They left the webbing loose about your neck, so you can turn your head and see Betty. I'll leave the keys on the counter, but I must lock the door. I can't chance someone coming in here and vandalizing the place, and me and Carol getting blamed for it."

Chuck left, chuckling to himself.

Stings began, thousands of them.

Harold glanced over to Betty. The webbing was too strong. He settled in, closed his eyes, he didn't scream. He refused to scream. He let the fiddle backs bite, exhaled though his nostrils as the door slammed shut, locked. It had always been the two of them. No one else. Only now Betty was gone now, and Harold was alone, left here in the dark rafters entombed in this web, alone with the fiddle backs and their stings.

SUCH A PROMISING DAD

Perry wasn't sure he was ready for marriage. He was almost positive he wasn't ready for fatherhood. Standing in a McDonald's on a Saturday afternoon, the day bright and the sky cloudless, Perry wondered what he was doing. How could he be responsible for a kid? What if he gave her too much sugar or gave her the wrong advise? What if he lost her. Cassie stood barely a head taller than Perry's waist, prim and proper with the palms of her hands placed flat on the counter, she stared at the girl behind the register.

"On my double cheeseburger," Cassie said, "I want only pickles and ketchup. I do not want onion and I do not want cheese, despite the fact that one can only order this particular meal as a double cheeseburger, as strict as we must adhere to the chain vernacular. To hell with the notion of 'Have it our way.'"

"Cassie!"

She turned sky-blue eyes up toward Perry. Her fine blonde hair fell away from her face, and an air of innocence and maturity came over her ten-year-old features.

"Well am I wrong?"

Perry shook his head. "No, dear, you aren't wrong."

Their food came; they filled their empty cups and sat at one of those colorful booths, one across from the other. She peeked between the buns of her hamburger and sure the order was correct, she took gargantuan bites of the burger, but chewed slowly and spaced them between the fries and drink.

"There is a difference in weight as muscle and weight as fat," he said as she pushed half of the burger away, frowning at the sandwich. "You're in gymnastics now and as your muscles grow, you are going to gain weight. Muscle is denser than fat. That won't make you overweight in the least, just because you gain weight like that."

She picked up a fry and nibbled on it. He understood how parents got their gray hairs, with all the worry that could be out there. What if she continues and becomes anorexic? What if she gets knocked up in high school, or fails out of college, or what if they had another child and that child had autism, or Down's Syndrome, or what if Cassie was raped, or kidnapped, or murdered, or was in a car accident, or…

"How's your food?"

Cassie shrugged and averted her eyes. "You love my mom?"

Perry muttered a yes and his mind began to wander. Cassie's mother could be spiteful, degrading at times, and was in constant need of verification of her self-worth: But on the plus side, she was gorgeous. She was bad with money yet wanted to control their checkbook, like she had something to prove. But she wasn't trying to prove it to him. Perry wasn't sure what the demons were that haunted her. He knew only that she had passed her demons on to her daughter. It wasn't a far stretch to imagine that Cassie would waste away from some eating disorder that she was already birthing.

"I want to play."

Perry blinked. She was looking to the playroom encased in a two-story glass patio. Plastic piping twisted around, just large enough for a child to crawl through. He saw two brothers, their silhouettes faint as ghosts behind the red and yellow plastic wall about ten feet above the ground; netting let the kids climb up from a tub filled of plastic balls to the pipes and slides that brought them back to earth. There was a sign at the entrance that said no kid could wear shoes into the play-station. A redheaded freckled boy chased his older brother ecstatically, though the redheaded freckled boy's older brother was faster.

Cassie was just fast enough to cut in between them.

Perry reached the door as she darted up the netting. He watched their silhouettes in the pipes, lost sight of them around the bend, and then saw them return. The elder brother slid down first, followed by Cassie and then the baby brother. Making the laps, they disappeared and emerged like clockwork. Laughing, always laughing, and at first Perry didn't even notice.

The brothers chased and laughed, younger after the older. They made two laps before Perry really caught on. There was only one set of piping, one slide. He walked to the bend, looked up, saw no silhouette.

Faintly he heard her. Amid the laughter of the brothers and the idle chatter of the parents, he could barely make her out. She was giggling and then he heard her whimper. Then he heard her plead. Then he heard her scream. All just as faint—right around that bend.

His eyes wide, staring. She was fading fast. He turned in place. His vision began to blur.

Around him the brothers raced, and for one wild moment Perry knew his impending marriage was a dream. But that idea faded as Perry caught sight of the shoe rack by the glass doors leading back into the restaurant. It could hold forty-eight pair. It currently held three. Cassie's pink shoes waited to be put back on.

AT THE STROKE OF MIDNIGHT

September 13, 2004

Dear Timothy,

*I*t was good hearing from you. I must say, from the pictures you sent, the Burmese mosquitoes look gargantuan. I can only imagine the effect of the panoply of God's creation there on that mountain, with the jungles flowing to the ocean and beyond. Truly I can say you were galvanized when you found Christ in our humble church, and that we could send you on this journey was a blessing. Yes, hardships befell you during your misspent youth in foster care, but those trespasses have secured your relationship with our Father, and I can say fervently that it is such an honor to call you my best friend and confidant.

Now as much as I can praise your efforts and commend you on the turnaround you have accomplished, you are still a tad flighty. This is something which I have the luxury to jibe you, surely. I can understand that there is no tower available so that your cell phone is not a necessity, but sir—your laptop? *Ye who liveth and die by the electronic connection to the rest of the world?* So I am forced to send parcel mail, when even this old-school Baptist has grown accustomed to the advantages of the Internet. There is something antiquated in all of this and thus, I suppose, befitting my manner of speech as you would undoubtedly say. How did you put it?—the *eloquence* of my words. That I was blessed with a gilded tongue—as you so affectionately refer to it—is as much a gift from God as the work you are doing.

As to why you wrote me: I could tell by your letter that you knew how I would answer. You were seeking a sensible head that would either validate or argue against these matters of the heart. I should caution you that in situations like the one you described to me, the head and the heart rarely agree. Their ways on that island are not our ways, and you should take heed to what you told me, that their rituals and traditions scare you. Her family is already opposed to the idea. So allow me now to disclose the first chapter in what is to be an undoubtedly strange story. This will validate my answer to you.

The story concerns Mr. Bufort Clemenson. You remember him, of course. A lifelong bachelor and Sunday School teacher for our advanced age class, Bufort went to live at Pine Crest Retirement Village last fall and is now wheelchair bound. Well, we know Bufort has never talked much of his life, especially after he was saved.

But others of the area alive then and still alive now, still fuel rumors like wildfire about him. It seems our Bufort was—in his early years—a rapscallion and real ladies man, before meeting and settling with a young woman here in town.

Annabelle was her name, and specifics aren't generally given, except that her grandmother was a feeble woman who owned that house up on Charles Lane—you know the one. Annabelle was taking care of her grandmother and it was widely assumed that after her grandmother passed on, she and Bufort would get married. Well, Annabelle's grand-mother finally did lay to rest, and the strangest thing happened.

Annabelle up and left. Nobody was sure where. Bufort was distraught for many days. They say he called up the sheriff at the time and orga-nized a search party to go looking for her, and nothing was seen or heard of her for nigh a week, until Bufort received a letter in the mail in her handwriting. She gave no return address, and only wrote one sentence, three times.

I can't have you.

It was signed with her name, just below the words "I love you," and everyone—including Bufort—took it to mean she had called off the engagement. He tried contacting some family she was known to have back east, but none of them would return his calls, and eventually, Bufort gave up. It took me forever to get out of him what little I could. Since those days, the house in which she lived has stood empty, and is now in such a state of disrepair that I can't imagine anyone ever buying it. But someone did.

A married couple, he a carpenter and she an interior decorator, had apparently seen the house, fallen in love with it, and said they could restore it to its former glory. They told Selma Dodge of Dodge Realty that they would like to spend the night in the house. They offered her some earnest money. She agreed, never once telling them anything about the place.

The next day they called from the road, talking a lot of gibberish and saying she could keep the down payment, but they didn't want the house. The story they told her sent her to Detective Bullocks of the Bluff County Sheriff's Investigator's Unit, which in turn sent both the detective and Selma to me.

From there I went to talk to Bufort, and now I am writing you. Not that you may give me a response in time, because I have to have a decision soon. You see, my dear friend, Bufort, the detective, the real estate agent and the couple that were to buy the house are thoroughly convinced that the house is haunted. And to that, they have called upon me to stay at the home and, for lack of a better word, *exorcise* the disquiet spirits.

I can almost see you chuckling now as you read this, thinking what I am thinking—my reputation proceeds me. Well, my congregation and obligation to God proceed me as well, and it is here I must again leave you, with a promise that more will be sent your way as I experience it.

Read this, if you must, as a morality tale. I'm sure that's why God sought for you to contact me, before making what would have been a rash decision. Allow me to resolve this issue with the house, and I will keep you informed. Promise me only that you will do nothing before I'm done and this story is complete.

Yours,
Pastor Wallace

༄

Dear Timothy,

I am spending the night in the house and all is well, so far. It was once a marvelous home, I'm sure you remember its less debilitated days, but it has fallen into such a state. The two-story Victorian home sits on the ridge of a hill in southern Missouri, the once beautiful home is now falling apart. I cannot ascertain the validity of Bufort's story as to why the home originally fell vacant, but I can tell you now that it is uninhabited because it is uninhabitable. The cupola has all but caved in on one side, and the gabled roof is crumbling, and the turret over the sitting room had fallen in almost completely. An oak has grown through the window in the living room, and the flue has been clogged with hardened soot and ash, a hazard for anyone wishing to start a fire. It would be cheaper for someone to tear down the once grand home and start again. Except the well won't perk—it has long since dried up—and a tangle of brambles and copse block the drive, the yard, and have engulfed the house, making it nearly impossible to find even now. Poison Ivy and Oak scale three sides of the house. All I could wonder, as I parked my car, and as much as I am in love with the architecture, is why anyone would want to buy this property.

I gained entrance to the house through the kitchen door. The kitchen was small and covered in a layer of mildew, reeking of the stale odor of buildup. I took to open a door to the rest of the house and had to catch myself on the knob, pulling at the weak hinges that supported the door. I had opened to a vacuous cellar whose steps had crumpled from the moisture of the unsealed passage, a dampness I could feel rise upon a cool breeze and caress my face. But it wasn't a good feeling, my friend, and I could feel my flesh crawl over my back and neck and arms. Indeed as I glanced at my trembling right hand, reaching into the void to pull the door too, I could see the goose-flesh on my arm, the hairs jutting on end, and I could only take a deep breath as the door closed.

I found the correct passage into the remainder of the house, through which I could pass easily and safely enough, and found in the library a tremendous view. I found myself rapt at the view of the lake some two-hundred feet below, at the bottom of the steep drop from the short backyard. For a moment I forgot why I was here.

The sounds of the scurrying rats roaming through the walls gave me pause; reminded me of my task. I tore my gaze away and proceeded back into the hallway to finish my survey of the aging home. I walked into the parlor, then to the living room where the potential buyers had spent their solitary night. Their story rang in my ears, and though I consider myself a sound man, a rational man, grounded in faith, I could not help but feel chilled, now that I stood where they had, and imagined what they had seen.

Around midnight, they had said, they were resting in the living room together, nearly dozing, when both woke with a start, sitting straight up. What aroused them was not a knocking or boom, but the gentle creak of stairs that were no more, resounding from the kitchen. They heard the cellar door give its unique cry as it opened, the rusted knob twisting coupled with the brush of air as the hinges squeaked. It was not an over-whelming sound, but—like the footsteps—whispers that should not be. Their ears focused, they said, and they waited, as footsteps echoed slowly from the hall, drawing closer, until the door opened from the parlor—

Well that's as far as I can get in recounting their story, seeing as how I am still in this living room, writing this letter to you, I can permit myself to go no further at the present time. Suffice it to say I cannot bring my-self to imagine what it was they said opened the parlor door and entered. I can say, however, that he promised to send the detective the shirt he had been wearing at the time, its ruffled collar scorched and hole-ridden from where he had been grabbed by two hands.

September 24, 2004

Last night I willed myself as midnight drew nearer to return from investigating the upstairs and reenter the kitchen, where I sat objectively with my sermon notes in an old dining chair, facing the cellar door.

I heard no footsteps. I saw no door open. And by dawn, my fears were somewhat alleviated. Still in the efforts of science I had not duplicated the experiment precisely.

I have returned to the house this night, to give myself tonight to sit and wait, perched in this living room, to see what I can hear or see.

To help pass the time I should maybe explain a few things that I haven't even told you. Did you know that Bufort came and visited me, not long before he had gone to the retirement community? It was during our fall festival at the church last year. Bufort had been one of the chaperones assigned for the lock-in and I was another, and after the kids were secured away in sleeping bags in the youth center, I walked down the hall to my office, aware immediately of the shuffling gait of Bufort Clemenson. I stopped, turned and watched him, a small round man, hunchbacked, his white hair thin, his eyes nearly sealed shut from the puffiness of his wrinkled face. He hobbled after me so I approached him, offered him a hand, and walked with him as he said he wished to talk to me. I inquired as to what was bothering him, but he would only say that the night seemed fitting, and he didn't want me to laugh at him, but to hear him out.

"What was it Paul said about those that already died?" he asked, once we had taken our seats in my office.

I saw immediately why he had been cautious about broaching this subject on that Halloween night, and so I smiled and took my Bible off my desk, and read to him the words of Paul. "In First Thessolonians 4:14, Paul writes, 'For if we believe that Jesus died and rose again, even so them also which sleep in Christ will God bring with Him.'"

He considered this for a moment, then looked at me earnestly, and with a voice akin to a little child, asked, "What of those who don't sleep in Christ?"

My smile waned. Up until this point I had considered him concerned with his own mortality, and approaching the subject on such a reputed night gave a sense of foreboding. But I felt quite sure of the faith of the man, and so my pleasant countenance gave way to a bemused expression, and I shook my head a little, and prodded him to clarify.

"Do nonbelievers sleep? Do they roam? I got to know."

And honestly I had no answer for him. I know only what awaits them after the Day of Judgement, but of what becomes of them, how they wait, I found myself at a loss. Finally I had to tell him, as much an assurance for him as it was for me, that I believed all who passed slept in

Christ until they were called to their final destination.

Bufort dropped his eyes and shook his head. "I don't believe it. Doesn't it say in John or one of the Gospels that some are given work by God?"

I racked my own memory and yes, I remembered that, and so I told him.

"Well," he continued, "If God can put those to work what who believed in Him, then can't Satan put those others to work also?"

I told him that Satan had no power over life and death, and he reminded me of the works of Job. I recounted and said yes, sometimes the devil can make you ill, and be permitted to hurt you, but he could not bring someone back to life once they died.

"I ain't talking about that," he snapped, and I saw the look in his eyes of a man trying to work something out, something that was beyond his grasp, and I had the sudden impression that it could be beyond mine as well. Christ did say there were more things in heaven and earth than we are meant to understand. "I'm talking about spirits. I'm talking about ghosts."

I gave a chuckle despite myself to which he only shot me a forlorn gaze. "I knew you wouldn't take me seriously," he said, and rose to leave.

I tried to protest but he waved me off, said thanks anyway, and if I could find out for him, then that would be great. I apologized and he said that it was all right, if he had been in my shoes he'd have done the same thing. But he stopped before he left, his hand on the open door's knob, his back to me as he stared down the darkened hall.

"What if they ain't dead?" he said, like it was an epiphany. "What if they're kept from death?"

All that has returned to me now, and even as I glance at my watch, sitting here in this living room, I see there is but a minute till the hour at hand, when even the Devil seems unrestrained. I watch the second hand as it ticks. It seems to be slowing its pace, but I am also very tired. I think after disproving this final trial, I will sleep like the…

October 8, 2004

Dear Timothy

How shall I begin this? I mouth the words of my story, and know what I want to say, but the pen in my hand seems to procrastinate once it touches the paper. I shall therefore force it and myself to face the horror of that night. Mind you, I have no explanation for what transpired, and as soon as I come to a conclusion, I will gladly offer you a rational explanation.

First, as to why my last letter ended so abruptly, is simply because I was scared to finish it. At the time I rediscovered it in my coat pocket, in my home, I was still shaken to the very core of my soul. Though I began to read the words in the sanctuary of daylight and my own living room—as one who stumbled across a piece of forgotten writing by some unknown author—the memories began to overwhelm me. I realized that while I wanted you—my best friend from childhood and complete confidant—to read this, I could not end it, just yet. Still having left you hanging on the previous installment, I could not *not* send it, for fear that it would worry you. So I sealed it in an envelope, addressed and stamped it, and sent it as it was, so that you could see the very act of me having it delivered to you proved I had not come to harm, though the finality of the letter might have left you perplexed.

As to what happened that night: I do not know.

Words fail me, my old friend. The pen yet again delays my unsteady hand. If you could see how I tremble, at the very thought. I can only promise that if the writing starts to become illegible, then I will give pause long enough to regain my senses, until you are caught up.

I heard the noises, much as they were described by the prospective buyers. First the creak of stairs that were no longer there; that it was coming from the cellar there could be no mistake. Along with it flowed the most secret whispers that intensified as the cellar door gave its audible creak. But I know the difference in a low voice, mumbling as one in prayer in church, and the scurrying of rats in the walls. This didn't come from the walls, my friend; it was not rats.

As the first steps touched the cracked and worn linoleum of the kitchen, I could not help but perk. The sounds of footsteps increased some, but they were muffled from the beat of my own heart. As afraid as I was, I wanted more my heart to quiet, so I could hear better; as such I was angered with my own cowardice. I could follow the steps as they moved from the kitchen down the hall, slowly, methodically, as though whoever it was knew exactly where I was. Could they hear the thud of my heart? Could they smell the sweat drenching me? Could they sense my trepidation? I do not know. But that they knew my location became ever more obvious with each footfall, until I heard them crossing the parlor, then gripping the door.

It swung open slowly, as though only prodded, but when I closed it earlier, I had heard the latch take hold. Shadows rolled in from the darkened parlor, and the pool of light spilling from my lamp seemed to recede a little, as my eyes, transfixed on the one spot, found they could no more blink than the rest of me could move. Save my hand, I should add, which found its way drug by my crawling fingers, to the cover of my Bible that lay on the end table by the dusty high back chair in which I sat.

The footsteps echoed first into the room, followed by the dim figure, who still in the shadows seemed a transparent, pale beauty that inspired lustful thoughts for which I am deeply ashamed. At another step my lantern's light held firm, and I could see her then; her pallid face and glassy eyes, her arms outstretched and reaching for me, a wide, toothy maw dripping with saliva. Her steps were uneven, as though she had forgotten how to walk, her eyes so glazed over that I couldn't imagine her seeing, her whole countenance frozen in that horrid, famished grin.

She neared, and with courage summoned I stood, held the Bible aloft, and shouted, in a voice not my own, "What in the name of the Lord do you want?"

The very mention of our Father forced her to recoil. As she took a step back, her face changing to a pained look, she clenched her teeth then…disappeared isn't the right word. She…*evanesced*, as though she were made of a million bats that retreated to the shadows at once.

I stood in my spot gasping for breath, still holding the book high, unable to move, unable to blink. Then comprehension returned to my mind; I rationalized what I had just seen. I fainted, and didn't awake till the morning, to bright sunlight pouring in through the windows, revealing all the alien shadows from the night before. I left the house and came straight home.

I wish there was more, Timothy, but now all that is left is to wonder at my next move, for even as I reread this letter and contemplate my own memories, I must come to terms with the fact that this was indeed a demon. How I shall proceed, however, I do not know.

Yours in faith,
Pastor Wallace

☙❧

October 15, 2004

Dear Timothy,

A few days and nights of thought and prayer have cleared my head of superstition, and I have a firmer grasp on what is happening. I went to see Bufort the day I mailed my last letter to you and spoke at length with him on what had so far transpired. He said nothing as I told my story but handed me a picture even as his face grew longer. He didn't have to point Annabelle out to me; I recognized her immediately, pretty in the picture as she had been in the shadows before she stepped into the light.

I went afterward to the detective's office, saw the shirt she had gripped while still on the husband's back, and the holes produced. I told him what I had learned and then returned to my office, pensive. I should tell you that our associate pastor filled in for me the Sunday after this had transpired. Today I knelt before the cross over the dais in the sanctuary, my head bowed to my knee, and fervently a prayer rolled from my lips, asking for guidance.

Let me tell you, I heard no voice. The cross did not gleam with light and no thunderous choir of angels appeared. But I did feel a tug within my heart and knew the answer even as I pleaded for His will be done.

I am going to have to go back to the house and try and reach her again.

I will tell you more when I can.

Yours,
Pastor Wallace

☙❧

October 16, 2004

Dear Timothy,

I have been blinded by lies, and I only hope that I can wrong the right, even after all these years. I did go back to the house last night.

I waited in the living room for midnight.

As I waited, a sort of drowsiness came over me. It got to where I thought I was sleeping. This mindset led to rational ideas, like I had dreamed the whole experience. The knocking on the invisible stairs didn't rouse me; I was so lost in fantasy.

But I raised my head at the echoes down the hall and froze. Gliding footsteps on linoleum jolted me to total consciousness. I waited, my breathing intensifying as she moved, until the knob turned, and her erotic form once-more filled the shadows.

She inched forward. I could hardly contain myself. I watched, and then she came.

She moved into the light, and I saw her for her horror, a fleshy creature, the skin falling away in great chunks, the eyes nearly gone. The fear raced through me as I waited; but a more potent feeling called, gave me strength and perseverance to wait and find this demon for what it was.

She grabbed the lapels of my shirt and immediately I saw the smoke billow forth from her touch, could feel the acid grip scald me even to the flesh, and with my right hand I reached for my Bible and held it high.

"In the name of the Lord," I called again, my voice resonating and not my own, "What are you? What do you want?"

"Murder," she hissed. "Murder. Avenge. I cannot sleep. I cannot rest." Her voice was like shards of glass, her working throat rotten and forcing the words, her dry tongue flopping out, her tone low and raspy.

She backed away and I thought, for a moment, she was going to dissipate, But she didn't. She raised her hands together, intertwined her fingers, her leaden eyes staring through me. An audible snap filled the silence of the room and her left hand reached out, in its palm the bones of three fingers off her right hand. With much fear I held out my own hand, watched hers turn down and felt the plop of the bones as they fell into my palm.

Only then did she vanish, and I was left alone, clenching the osseous digits. I did not faint this time, but only stared into the darkness. For how long I stood there I am not aware, but presently I left, returned to my car and drove back to my house.

This exodus from the house and return home had all transpired in a manner of a dream for me, for I do not remember the actual drive, or that I laid the bones on my coffee table nor curling up in my bed. I remember being extremely tired, though, and when I awoke the following morning, I felt refreshed, and my mind wiped clear almost of the night's events.

That was only a few hours ago, and all that changed when I walked into the living room. The bones still laid on the table. They caught my attention immediately. Did I lay them as they lay now? —had they moved themselves…I am not sure. But they lay in the formation of the letter B, three digits, two curled at what would have been the knuckles, and one laying straight. I take pause in writing this to you only to stare at them; it seems as though they are beckoning to me.

Yours,
Pastor Wallace

October 20, 2004

Dear Timothy,

We have returned to the house tonight, for the finale, so to speak. The detective and Bufort are with me. Bufort is looking worse than ever, like he is not long for this world. I had gone to the detective first with my story and the evidence. (Logically he would not verbalize that a ghost had handed it to me but felt I had fallen into some form of hypnotic somnolence and discovered the remains while sleepwalking in a trance.) He came with me to confront Bufort, ready to arrest him on the spot, and decided when this course of action was presented, that he would accompany us here.

It was Bufort who suggested we return tonight. At present he is still telling his same story to the detective, unwavering, even as I write all this to you. He wants the detective to see for himself what others have seen here, including me. He has agreed to be taken into custody in the morning, with no fight. But I get the strangest feeling that Bufort doesn't believe he will last till morning, and there is a peace about him, as though he is ready. I have seen such a state amongst the elderly and dying before, but that he is calm in the face of *this* I cannot fathom.

Bufort says that she must have known and reinterpreted the letter for us. He was prepared to marry her, he said, but his old ways had not quieted, and he met a girl that could entertain those fancies one more time, before he took the plunge. The stress of helping her care for her ailing grandmother had gotten to him, he said. The very night the elderly woman passed away, he was in the arms of this other woman.

But he keeps saying over and over again he did not kill her; he doesn't know what she is talking about, and couples it with a strange utterance about her grandmother. All he'll say is, "She weren't right," but he won't give us details, save that it was this period in his life that led him to Christ.

I must go. We've all heard it—even the detective acknowledges those steps are coming from where the cellar is. She's getting closer. I'll write again later.

We have reached a resolution, and yet again I am forced to admit my ignorance. For as that thing once again entered the room—our detective drew his gun, his hands quivering—I saw its true face, and realized what it wanted. It had trapped me into bringing him, and all was clear. She reached for him and I dove, unaware that I had left my Bible on the desk, so that when her fingers clutched about a neck, it was not the intended's but mine.

I screamed in pain as my flesh seared in her grasp. Detective Bullocks holstered his gun and strove to pull her off me. Bufort too had realized what she was, and was screaming at her in defiance, though he could hardly get away.

She had us cornered; the detective's hands were falling through her, unable to grip any part of her, and all the while she was laughing. Then, thinking clearer than I was, Detective Bullocks did something I had yet the opportunity or the foresight to do. Reaching for my Bible that lay upon the desk, he hoisted it above his head and called upon our Lord to deliver us from this demon. He smashed the Bible down in an arcing motion, and unlike his hands—to which she seemed a shadow—the book connected. Her laugh turned to a shriek of pain and she fell away from us, staggering back and gripping her shoulder.

With hatred she looked up at all of us as we hunkered in pain, struggling for breath. She too seemed to be gathering again her strength, frowning at us, a feral growl erupting from somewhere within her. Then her frown twitched and formed into a hideous smile, mirthless, and she began to rise.

"How strong your faith if you require a book to save you?" she asked, and while she looked at all three of us, I felt her gaze steady on me.

It dawned on me then, Timothy—my best friend; she was right. My faith comes not from what I surround myself with, but from my heart and what I know to be the truth. Resolutely I stepped forward, glaring down upon her, intentionally empty of all those icons, including my Bible.

Recognizing the challenge she brought herself higher, her mouth widening even as I hid my revulsion. Fear was creeping back over me, I cannot lie. But I stood motionless, waiting as she squared off with me. Then we reached for each other.

Instantly the grip of her hands began to sizzle and smoke; likewise where I grabbed her, her own flesh and clothing began to sear, and the scream that issued forth was like nothing I've ever heard. Both the detective and Bufort were watching, and both were mistaken as to my own safety and chance at victory.

Afraid I was in trouble Detective Bullocks once more swung the Bible, connecting with her head. She screamed and laughed and she evaporated into a scattering of enflamed cinders, which instantly spread about the room and set walls and furniture and floor ablaze.

We had not grasped this action yet, however. All three of us stood, staring as her body seemed at once to light up then splinter off into those tiny flames. It only dawned on us the real detriment when a laugh issued from the depths of the house and around us, the room alighted and smoke billowed forth. Quickly the detective and I struggled to pull Bufort from his chair and the three of us dodged crumbling wood and burning ash as we made our way to the exit in the kitchen. That we nearly lost our lives in the blaze is proven by the pile of charred wood as the only remains of that once grand edifice. We had just hit the yard when the flames exploded out the windows and the heat stung at us; with a thunderous creak and groan the supports gave and the house collapsed.

We stood in the yard, panting for breath, sweating, watching as the flames leapt to the surrounding foliage and trees and brush began to burn. The pile of wood and stone burned continuously, and presently we heard the wail of sirens in the distance.

"We need to leave," Bullocks suggested, and without further explanation needed, we did. Our culpability would have been in question, I know. Something neither he—a decorated police officer—nor I needed. But more than that we knew that when the county fire department showed up, they would be able to extinguish the trees and brush without difficulty. The house was lost; this was for the best.

We drove back to town, wincing only when the fire trucks passed us. I bit at my knuckle and stared into the darkness, half expecting to see her again, and wondering about that laugh. It was as malicious as her other peals, as violent and triumphant. And I was unnerved that it had resounded after she had apparently burst into flame.

"She weren't right," Bufort said to start. Detective Bullocks and I remained silent. His voice was raspy, his words slow and winded; I could tell it took great effort for him to breathe, much less relate his story.

"Her grandmother had learned her, I'm sure of that. Her grandmother was always trying to talk around me, and Annabelle was always shushing her but her grandmother would always say 'He's gonna know someday, might as well be now.' Annabelle kept it from me for a time, and I guess when I learned about it I ignored the bad feeling in my gut and decided I still wanted to marry her. But maybe it was that, and not just her dying grandmother, that led me to the other woman. Maybe it was seeing her communicate with Lucifer hisself that led to all this, and led me to salvation." He paused, then added reflectively, "Yeah, I'm sure it was."

I'm ready for bed, Timothy. I must end this letter. It was too exhausting a night, and I can only hope this will prove cathartic. Until I began writing this ending here at home, my mind was dancing. There would have been no way I could have slept, despite how physically exhausted I am. But putting pen to paper, maybe some of that is released. Yes, I do feel drowsier now, and I believe that rest will be a welcome friend.

Yours,
Pastor Wallace

October 28, 2004

Dear Timothy,

The morning after my last letter, Bufort passed away. I oversaw the funeral, which was lovely. He seemed at rest. Detective Bullocks and I met just before and after and even today, discussing all that happened. I told him about my letters to you, and he suggested that while those were out of our hands, I should tell no one else what has happened. I ask now—because I agree with him—that you share this story with no one. Just as our reputations and names would have been ruined were we caught at the house, our fates would be just as sealed if the story spread as a rumor. Right now the investigation has been steered toward a gang of teenagers out for a prank, and the detective suggests that we leave it as such.

I know I can trust you with this. I look forward to your return. The solace I have, at least, is that Bufort is resting, and that evil has been quelled by the power of our Father.

Yours,
Pastor Wallace

PS-

Yes, that laughter still bothers me. I wake at night and hear it, and have yet to deduce a logical explanation for it, unless she knew that Bufort was about to pass away. I shall take solace in this conclusion.

 C3&0

October 31, 2004

Dear Timothy,

I gave a sermon this morning, and assured my congregation that for those who wished to take their children trick or treating this evening, there would be nothing wrong with it. I myself have found my adventure not over. You see last night I dreamed all about the laughter, and this morning I woke to find a solemn house. I fixed coffee, unaware of the muddy footprints that stained my linoleum. I walked into the living room and saw, to my astonishment, the front door. I had locked it before bed last night—an old habit. This morning it stood wide open. I stood staring at nothing but the dawn glinting back at me, and in my terror I dropped the cup, shattered it all over the hardwood floor.

I understand all now, Timothy. Your story is more than similar men dating similar women at different times. You were found on the doorstop of the local church in 1965. It is only now that I have put it together; you were found two weeks after thirty-year-old Bufort lost Annabelle. I connected the times of Bufort's story. But there is more, even more than the muddy footprints. The osseous digits of her hand were back on my coffee table, formed into another letter, the capital T.

I must rest.

She'll be back tonight.

Pastor Wallace

INFATUATED

$\mathcal{J}$n a ground floor apartment with only one bedroom, the closet doorknob turned. Patrick was too far gone in sleep to notice. She emerged from the closet, watched him for most of the night. She had dark hair and angular features; her mysterious brown eyes were sunken, her olive skin was pale, her white shorts and t-shirt were stained maroon.

◇◇◇

Patrick straightened his tie and stared into the mirror. He was well-groomed, built. She watched him—unnoticed—as a reflection.

◇◇◇

Denise had a lovely time during her date with Patrick. He took her to dinner at a Thai restaurant and then drinks at a club on the strip, and she loved the idea of going back to his place, until she walked across the threshold. She felt chilled, gooseflesh on her forearms.

Still, she stayed for drinks, the trepidation eased as they sipped and talked. They laughed, flirted. Denise sat her third drink on the coffee table, glanced about, felt jittery all of a sudden. Her own drink jumped, spilled over the carpet, down the table, across her dress.

"I'm so—"

"Don't worry about it. You can freshen up in there." He pointed down the short hall to a door immediately on the left, right across from the washer and dryer.

Denise smiled, walked into the bathroom, flicked on the light. The small room was clean, the wastebasket empty, a fresh hand towel and body towel draped across the two bars. The colors matched, a fresh roll of toilet paper hung on the dispenser, and there was a little clutter around the porcelain sink, which like the tub was mostly clean. She turned on the faucet, a rush of water and steam. Denise looked to examine herself in the mirror…

And screamed—

A little buzzed, Patrick finished his drink as the door closed behind Denise, and then he downed the one he had prepared for her. He went to bed not long after. He was completely unaware of the closet doorknob being turned from the inside. She watched him breathe, his chest rise and fall until early dawn, and then she retreated back into the closet as he rose.

CR℘℘

The first of the month, Patrick answered the door to a bald spot and the smell of cigar smoke, amid a blackout.

"Did you pay your electric bill?" The landlord was a round man with the stub of a cigar tucked permanently between his teeth, his gray wife-beater stained brown with sweat.

"Called an electrician out, said the wiring was faulty."

The landlord grumbled a bit, cursed when his clipboard flew from his hand, the pages spilling and whipping about, sheets tearing, whirling about the two of them as though thrashed by a tornado.

"Has anyone ever died here?"

Gathering his papers, tucking them back into the clipboard, the landlord paused long enough to look up to Patrick from where he knelt. "Yeah, once, a girl."

Patrick handed the landlord the rent check, and the sweaty man snatched it from his hand, papers tucked haphazardly under his greasy arm.

CR℘℘

She had thought it was her boyfriend, that night; that's why she opened the door. The police finally caught the real intruder, but this brought no relief for her. He had violated her in many ways, worse than just killing her. What he did to her both before and after he eviscerated her was unspeakable.

❧

Patrick dropped his bags in front of the closet and crashed into the mattress, the sheets falling about him. He felt himself drift off.

Patrick sat up in bed. Twilight crept in through the blinds, producing shadows only, no real shapes. There was a pounding that would not go away, and a smell—decay. He looked straight ahead, his eyes adjusting to the light. He could see the bags, vibrating off the closet door, and then he saw them fall away. The door blew open.

Patrick screamed.

THE HANGED WOMAN

In a two-story farmhouse atop a hill in the Ozarks, a man sits backward on a plastic armless chair in the attic, his forearms on the back of the chair, his head resting on his arms. His flesh is pallid, sores split his cheeks, his forehead. A brown recluse scurries out of his left ear, down his cheek, and pulls the carcass of its brother from his right nostril before entering his frozen agape mouth.

At night he is joined, though he no longer sees, by the hanged woman. Her eyes bulge, unblinking, focused on the door that no one dares open after dark. The rope that hangs from the rafter, that forms the noose, creaks like a hammock in a summer breeze, and joins the other nightly sounds of the settling house, the pops and creaks and twists and pulls of locked doorknobs.

A few nights ago, the boy forgot about the rule about not going into the attic after dark. He wanted to play with his trainset that had been packed away a few summers ago. When his parents realized where he was headed, his father rushed up the stairs after him.

❦

The boy plays with his trainset in the mornings while his mother knits the shroud. He says, "When Daddy wakes up, maybe he can take me fishing, or maybe he can push me on the tire swing. I like the tire swing."

She does not raise her eyes from the shroud when she responds. "Now you know you have to be good honey, lest the hanged woman comes for you next."

HAUNTED HOUSES

The old Victorian mansion, the only abandoned house on Smith Street, had been passed by the neighborhood kids a hundred times to and from school, had hovered over them as they played street-hockey and stickball on the shared street. One of the few Victorian's left in town, its architecture highlighted the home against its more mundane, modern neighbors. Long-since denied human occupation, the house's windows black like pupils, watched the children and their joy and life, watched with envy and maybe even a bit of contempt.

"We come back after dinner," Terry said, pushing the wire-framed glasses up his nose.

"Do we wear our costumes?" Billy Lancaster asked. Billy was short and pudgy, his blonde hair in a crew cut.

"Of course, we wear our costumes, dick weed," Joey Tanner said. "It's Halloween. That's how we get our parents to let us out." Joey was as tall as Terry, but where Terry was lanky Joey was more athletic. Terry's hair was wispy and a dirty blond and Joey's was jet black.

Terry said: "We wouldn't much convince them that we were going trick or treating if we didn't wear our costumes."

"Sorry," Billy said. Then added under breath: "Geez."

"So what time did we decide on," Joey asked.

"Seven-thirty," Terry said, and looked to the other two boys. They nodded in unison and the three shook an oath, then went their separate ways.

⚜

"Swear to me, Terry," his father had said last Halloween when Terry had stood looking up at that house. "Swear to me you won't go in that house. No matter what."

"I swear," Terry had said.

⚜

Dinner was a quiet, reflexive time. His mom and uncle were good as pretending when other faces were around. When it was just the three of them, a heavy uncomfortable silence hung in the stagnant air of the closed in home. They would attempt civility with any guest, but that guest could still feel the palpable tension. Once he thought Grandma and Grandpa had wanted to talk about his dad, just a month ago when they were visiting, and his mom and uncle were just as polite and chipper. They completely ignored any sentence that contained his father's name.

"You going trick or treating tonight?" his uncle asked.

"Yeah, with Joey and Billy. We're really looking forward to going…"

"Kay," his uncle said, and shoved a forkful of mash potatoes into his mouth.

Terry finished his meatloaf and went upstairs to change into his costume. He was going as a zombie. Joey was going to be the vampire. Billy was going to be the werewolf. Laboriously Terry applied the make-up after dressing in his torn rags. In the old days, his dad would help him. His dad said you should be the monsters in shifts, and you shouldn't be the same monster as one of your friends. The order should go—as per his dad: zombie; witch/warlock/wizard; vampire; werewolf; ghost; Frankenstein's monster; this catalogue just long enough that it avoided any overlap.

Terry stepped back to examine himself in the mirror and was pretty satisfied with what he saw. It wasn't as good as his dad's zombie—that he could remember—or maybe it was just that he was six the last time he put on the costume.

"I know I promised," Terry said into the mirror. He pushed the glasses up his nose. "But I got to do this. And that promise was last year.

Everyone knows promises end at New Year's."

That was his dad's rule, but there were also stipulations. That rule applied unless the promise was really, really important. Then it didn't matter how many times you saw January First.

❧

Terry walked out of the house and down the street and stood in front of the old Victorian mansion. The house looked even worse than last year. There were more windows busted. The black hole in the porch was larger. From either side Billy and Joey walked up. Joey was dressed as his vampire. Billy was dressed as a zombie.

"What the hell?" Terry asked.

"What?" Billy asked. "It was my turn."

"What the hell are you two bitching about?" Joey asked.

"It was my turn," Terry said.

"Bull shit," Billy said.

"Bull true."

"It was my turn," Billy said. "and I got proof."

The sound of the wrought-iron gate swinging open ended the spat. Joey was the first to step into the front yard. Billy followed next. He had rubbed almost all the zombie makeup off his cheeks so that what was left was merely a smudge of green and brown and a few smeared trickles of red.

Terry pushed his glasses up his nose and stepped through the gate. The roots of the old oak broke up through the cement sidewalk. The lawn was bare dirt, some rocks. Terry looked up to the house as the wind picked up, whistling about the eaves, screeching through the broken panes of glass.

"So how come we're standing still? Terry asked.

"You should tell us the story," Joey said.

"I don't know guys," Billy said.

"About the house. Like your dad told it. Then we go in."

"Brian Marsden's parents are letting him throw a party," Billy said.

Terry nodded and cleared his throat. He would do the best he could, but no one could tell the story like his father.

"Dr. Wilhelm Schultz built the house for his wife in 1950. He had been a scientist in Germany during the war, and brought over to the U.S. in what was called Operation: Paperclip. They say during the war, he experimented on the Jewish people in concentration camps. Some were afraid he was continuing his experiments over here. The house was his wedding gift to her. Her gift to him was to have a baby boy. Try as she might, though, she couldn't get pregnant. Dr. Schultz grew desp…despond…*desp…on…dent*. He began drinking. His wife grew depressed.

"He called her sister to come help around the house. Her sister, a nurse, began to care for Dr. Schultz's wife. And that's when the rumors started. The town wasn't as big as it is now, and people were a lot more in each other's business. They saw only the sister and Dr. Schultz come and go. They never saw his wife. Pretty soon, the sister was pregnant, and people began to suspect foul play. When the sheriff got word of this, he decided to pay a visit to the house.

"She was still alive, but she was not the beautiful woman the town had known. She was rail thin with sunken cheeks and eyes, the skin hanging off her bones. Her hair was cracked and dry, and she refused to come out of her bedroom. The doctor had already moved out of the room and in with her sister. When the sheriff tried to talk to her, she talked about a curse on them that her husband had brought from the war. She laughed, and the sheriff would later report that the look on her face was the most horrific thing he had ever seen.

"The night the baby was born was the night of the year's worst thunderstorm. It was spring, 1955, an unusually hot March. Townspeople all up and down the street could hear the screams coming from the house. The screams lasted well into the night, but soon enough the cry of a baby could be heard down the street. As things quieted the street finally slept and nobody suspected anything for a few days.

"People began to realize that no one had seen hide nor hair of the doctor or his wife's sister or even the new baby. More than that, there was a smell coming from the house. The sheriff returned along with a few of his deputies. When no one answered their knocks they forced the door open and went inside."

Billy and Joey stared at Terry wide-eyed, but Terry's eyes hadn't left the house. He pushed the glasses up on his nose and sighed. They knew the story, but still they waited with bated breath for him to finish.

"A few children have gone missing in there, over the years," Terry said. "My dad said one time a homeless man broke into the house when it was storming bad only to run out screaming just before one o'clock."

"What happened to the family?" Joey asked.

"What happened to the baby?" Billy asked. Both knew the answer already, but caught up in the story as they were, it became a sort of rite for Terry to finish, no matter how many times they had heard the story before.

Terry looked away from the house, looked them each in the eye with a little smile. "The baby? Nobody knows. The sheriff couldn't find the baby anywhere in the house. They dug up the yard trying find any evidence of the kid but couldn't find anything. They found the others, though. Dr. Winters was found in the kitchen. The cops believed the butcher knife found in his back was the one used to stab him fifty times. The wife's sister was found in the bed, her stomach torn wide open, blood everywhere. One of the deputies wrote later that it looked like something had clawed its way out. The wife was found in her room, her door locked from the outside. She had hung herself over her four post bed from an exposed beam, using the sheets from her bed. The key to her door was found in her husband's pants pocket. Police could find no evidence of forced entry. But it was her fingerprints on the knife's handle."

❦

The three boys looked up to the black windows. The shadow-veiled secrets in the oblong rooms dared the boys to enter and discover them.

Billy said: "We can tell everyone we did. We can go to Brian Marsden's party and you know Ginny Phillips likes you, right Joey?"

"We're going in," Terry said.

"Yeah…yeah," Joey stammered, his fists clinched. "Right."

"But we can just tell people we did," Billy said.

"We're going in!"

"Why?" Billy asked. His cheeks were red and he looked like he was on the verge of crying.

"Because we have to," Terry said. "I have to. You two queef queens can stay out here if you want." He wiped away a tear that stung his eye and stared at both boys to see which would defy him. When neither did, Terry walked up the porch steps, stepped over the hole in the porch, and tried the front door. It swung open invitingly and Terry took in the first images of the house's interior as his flashlight beam illuminated the front entryway. The crimson wallpaper peeling, in the corner stood a high table, a broken vase, the skeletons of roses and baby's breath that had wilted long ago. He pushed the door wider and stepped into the consuming shadow. There, hung over the mantle and caked in dust, a gold-framed portrait of the doctor and his wife. He turned the flashlight right to a breakfast area, an octagon-shaped room with a great bay window that let in moonlight, casting everything in a pale blue glow. He could make out dark silhouettes of objects, the round table, four chairs, and the tall silhouette of a man in the doorway leading to the kitchen.

Terry shined his light to the doorway. There was no one there. Fingers tapped his shoulders. He spun around to laughter, to two flashlights illuminating the face of a short vampire and a short and pudgy zombie with runny makeup. Anger flashed over Terry's face then faded quickly to laughter and for a moment the only sounds in the house came from the three boys.

Something heavy scooted across the upstairs floor.

The boy's looked up, shined their flashlights to the ceiling as plaster snowed down on them. Terry broke their grip and walked through the front entryway to the sitting room, the cracked chimney with plaster in piles on the hearth, the stuffing torn out of the cushions of the couch and chair, the coffee table lay in two big splintered pieces on the floor. Terry stood at the base of the stairs at the back of the room as Joey and Billy caught up to him. His light did little to pierce the darkness only six steps up. Something heavy scooted again.

"C'mon," Terry said.

Each step creaked as the boys ascended. Pressed together, they moved slowly, their lights dancing on the wall and window just beyond the top riser. The sound came again as they reached the top of the stairs. Louder now, they looked down the hall to the source of the sound. Thin light seeped out from around a door frame at the other end of the hall.

Terry crept down the hall. The light flickered His flashlight illuminated dirty wooden floors, cracks in the paneling, a rat in a far corner whose eyes glowed red. He heard crackling, saw the light dance. He clicked the flashlight off and reached for the doorknob even as it turned and pulled away from him. Terry glanced down the hall to his friends, looked back into the room and entered.

He guessed it had been the sister's room. A fire blazed in the wood-trimmed fireplace, bathing the room in flickering light gold and yellow.

A crimson stain in the center of the large four-post bed still covered the checkered quilt. The door creaked.

"What the hell?" Joey asked.

"I don't know," Terry said.

Billy walked up to the bed, stared at the stain.

"Why is there a fire in this room?" Terry asked. "Why was the front door unlocked?" The boys watched the shadows dance in the firelight as a moan rolled through the house. Just outside the bedroom door, the wooden slat floorboards creaked. As the creaking stopped, the silhouette of someone short appeared in the doorway. Billy and Joey's backs were to the door, but they saw Terry's face and neither wanted to turn around. Billy squeezed his eyes shut. Joey's lower lip quivered in the soft glow.

A giggle wiggled through the halls and abandoned dusty rooms. The silhouette vanished and quick steps could be heard receding down the stairs. There came a creaking, soft and slow from down the hall, like the old rocker Terry's grandmother kept on her porch.

A few rooms down, a door stood partially open and the black room beyond concealed the source of the rhythmic creak . Terry touched the wood paneled door, pushed. The creaking louder, like a rope hammock stretched and swinging in the wind, his hand trembling, Terry shined the light into the room.

The doctor's wife swung from the noose in the darkness, her eyes bulging from their sockets, staring down at the boys. Her once pale face was blue black and swollen, a fat black tongue flopped out from her mouth. The boys screamed and ran down the stairs till they stood, doubled over and huffing in the front room. Using the tail of his shirt, Terry cleaned the fog off his lenses and then walked to the front door. He didn't like that it was closed. He hadn't heard it shut and tried to remember which of them came in last.

"I left it open," Billy said.

Terry tried it. The knob wouldn't even turn.

"We could jump out a window," Joey said.

"There's a back door off the kitchen," Terry said.

Circles of light danced in the darkness, spotlighting a broken vase, the brown and crusted doily on the old table, the corner of a picture frame. Terry shined his light into the kitchen, saw broken tile on the wall, a cracked countertop. The man's face bloody, his eyes open, and as Terry moved the light, he saw the disembodied head floating in the darkness. Only when he tried to find the head again had it disappeared.

"I saw that," Billy said.

"We all did," Joey said.

"The house," Terry said. "Trying to scare us is all."

In the kitchen, their lights illuminated bits of wall and cabinets, cherry doors barely hanging from the hinges, cobwebs and a black widow scurried up a line to her hiding spot. Then Terry's flashlight trained on the back door. He tried the knob but the door wouldn't give. Terry turned his shoulder and slammed into the door only to ricochet off.

"Dammit to hell," Terry said.

"You don't sound any tougher when you cuss," Joey said.

"O yeah, tough guy, why don't you try?"   Joey bounced off also. Even Billy tried. Terry found a rolling pin in a drawer, and each boy tried to smash that against the cracked glass to no avail. Suddenly Billy began to jump up and down and even laughed.

"Why are you playing the 'tard card?" Joey asked.

"Basement," Billy said. "Window. I saw a window when we were coming in. It was a tiny window near the ground. But it was broken some and if you could break the rest out then someone could climb out and get to the front door and open it or go get help. Only…O no…!"

"What?" Terry and Joey asked in unison.

"I won't fit through."

"Then one of us should go," Terry said.

"You're skinnier than me," Joey said. "Quicker too."

"You're stronger than me," Terry said. "You could get the door open better."

"I am stronger than you. That's why I should stay. I can pull from this side while you push from the outside."

"Whatever," Terry said, shined his light around until he found the basement door. It stood open, a cold draft wafted up from the cellar depths. "Pussies," Terry said, pushed his glasses up the bridge of his nose and started down.

There was a smell, wood rot and stale air, a cool dampness all in the darkness. Terry knew he was near something ancient, though his flashlight only showed a regular, run-of-the-mill basement. There were shelves and glass jars filled with murky water and flesh-colored amorphous shapes. In one corner an assortment of stacked white buckets, one inside the other. There were other knickknacks, regular things one would store in a basement, an antique lawnmower and sling-blade, boxes of various sizes. Terry's hopes rose and fell in a single second as he saw the window Billy had mentioned, above a six-foot bookcase, well over his head. That's where most of those glass jars stood, dust-covered and rank. Terry walked up to it, pushed it only to feel it wobble. It wasn't secure against the wall, if he tried to scale it the book case would topple and crush him. But even worse than that, the thought that he would knock the jars over and spill out whatever they contained.

There was another smell, pungent, and the closer he stood to the jars, the stronger it reeked. It smelled like Biology class, like the frogs they had to dissect. It was sweet and noxious and made him gag.

"I do like this house."

The voice came from a dark corner. Terry shined his light to the source but saw nothing, cracked plaster and some empty paint cans. Out of the corner of his eye, he saw a silhouette. Not very tall, and he thought about shining his light that way, then thought better of it. He didn't really want to see what had to hide in the shadows down here.

"What do you want?" Terry asked.

"To make friends. I've been alone so long."

"You killed your family."

Laughter. "You think I'm the child? I am so much older than that. I watched what the doctor did in Europe, then what he did here. I watched the boy birth himself and grow to nine years old. I watched the doctor's wife hang herself the night the child was born. I listened to the rumors that wound through the town. The boy grew despondent. The *family* fell apart. Ever since I've wanted a friend. Boys have come, some vagabonds too. No one stays when I show them the house. Some were swallowed. They still walk these halls, but I can't enjoy them after they succumb. The dead's fear is useless. Most of the living just walk on the other side of the street and watch me, keeping their fear all to themselves when they could so easily share it with me."

"What are you?" Terry asked.

"Shine the light and find out," the simulacrum said.

Terry started to then saw an alien shape. He caught an outline of a segmented body, a thorax tapering to a point and what looked like several skinny legs. He pulled the flashlight away. His breaths came quick and shallow, and he only thought of his father. Oh God why couldn't he still have his father.

"But you aren't terrified, either. You're preoccupied. Here or there, it's all the same to you, isn't it," the voice sounded disappointed. "I don't want anyone here who isn't scared."

"What about my friends?"

"Take them too. I don't care. There are some high school boys coming tomorrow. They thought Halloween would be too obvious. I think we'll have some fun."

Terry wasted no time; he rushed upstairs to the kitchen to find his friends and led them through the breakfast area. The ghosts stood against the walls. The doctor with his stab wounds stood next to his wife with the noose around her neck. On the other side of the doctor stood his wife's sister, her dress bloodstained just below the waist. Next to her stood a nine year old boy, emaciated. The child held his mother's hand.

Terry tried the door and it opened easily. Cold dry air blasted him in the face. The stark night greeted them. The boys rushed into the yard, collapsed in the dirt.

"We get to go home," Billy said.

The boys stood, looked back to the house. It squatted dark and silent on the side of the street. Rust-colored leaves scraped the sidewalk, propelled by an autumn zephyr. Terry saw the faces of the dead in the black windows, longing to come outside.

"Yeah," he said. "We get to go home."

One by one the boys walked through the gate, Joey first and then Billy and Terry trailed. Terry turned back to the house but saw no one in the windows.

☙❧

Terry's home was dark as he approached with no discernible artificial light in the windows. The wrought iron gate squeaked open and dead leaves crunched under foot. He walked up the five wooden steps to the porch and opened the door. Upstairs he greeted his parents' room, dark, the sound of snoring reverberating into the hall. A golden bulb illuminated the carpeted gallery. Terry peeked in and saw his father's side of the bed, a lump still for the moment, its shape masked by bed sheets and a comforter. His mother's side was flat.

He heard a quiet sob. Terry walked around the bannister and down the hall and saw his door open. He peeked around the corner and saw his mother. She laid on his bed, cradling the pillows. Tears flowed mercilessly. She was trying to be silent but was not too successful.

"Mom," Terry said.

He heard a rustle and a creak, looked over to see his uncle out of his parent's bed, leaning on the doorframe, staring at him. His eyelids were heavy, his cheeks puffy.

"Leave her alone," his uncle said.

Terry walked to the guestroom. He didn't turn the light on. He undressed in the dark, but rather than get in the bed he walked to the window and peeled apart the blinds. He couldn't see the house exactly but knew where it should be. He thought about his father again. The accident felt like yesterday. Only when the night caught up to him, with a great yawn Terry crawled under the covers and fell into a dreamless sleep.

PERIWINKLE, PERIWINKLE

Rapps Barren, Arkansas, the 1950's—

Periwinkle Roberts shut her eyes when the slap came. When she opened them she focused outside the window where a chirping blue jay perched on a limb of the maple in bloom. The sky beyond was cloudless. Outside looked warm, safe. She could hear a soft mewling, just under breath, and though the hand hadn't touched her, she felt the sting all the same.

Waiting to turn around until after the door slammed shut, the footsteps faded, Periwinkle turned and faced her younger brother. A red welt already began to rise on his left cheek. His eyes welled with tears, but rather than allowing those tears to fall, he puffed his cheeks out and pouted his lips. She crawled off her bed and slid across the mauve carpet to put her arm around him. He leaned on her shoulder. Presently she felt a teardrop splash on her shoulder.

They lived in a two-story farmhouse with nearly an acre of yard, front and back, and the backyard faced a deep wood. A mile-long country road led from the driveway to the county highway, which in turn meandered lazily toward town some ten more miles away. The nearest neighbor was a half a mile away on either side. They had a pool, a tire swing, and a trail that led into the woods. Outside this particular afternoon their father was roofing a tree house in the old elm by the front drive. Every Saturday from ten till about three, he'd sip his beer and work with Mr. Johnson up in the tree-house.

Their father ran an auto-home-and-life insurance company in town, their mother stayed at home and the family was always well-received at church. They were a typical family of the time and place, WASP's and upper middle-class, the children blonde and blue-eyed and rosy cheeked. They seemed perfect and lived in what looked like a perfect home. But this home held secrets that would change an outsider's view of the Roberts family. Or maybe just expose them for who they truly were. Whenever Periwinkle thought of these secrets—like now, as she held her little brother—she thought of a long time ago, when she was even smaller.

❦

Periwinkle stood outside her parent's door, her ear pressed against the surface, listening. They had been talking for over an hour. Earlier that evening, at dinner, they told Periwinkle that she was going to have a little baby to play with. Periwinkle was excited. But her parents had quickly moved their conversation upstairs. They didn't do that often and this intrigued Peri. She had waited a few minutes before sneaking up the stairs and listening at their door.

"I do love her," said her father.

"You don't spend any time with her!"

"I spend time with her. She knows I love her. I was raised in a house…"

"I know, I know. We've heard it a million times. Your mom raised a bunch of boys. You don't know how to act around girls. Funny, but you didn't have a problem with me in college."

"That was different, Maureen."

"Fine. I hope it's a boy too, if it will get you off my back. But you better not play favorites. You better not neglect Peri anymore, you understand?"

Her father was silent for a time. Periwinkle heard her mother say, "What?" several times, before her father spoke.

"You remember my secretary. The one I fired."

"I remember."

"I had to fire her. She wanted to come to you."

"You bastard," her mother said. Periwinkle clapped a hand to her mouth to muffle the gasp. She could not remember ever hearing her mother curse.

"She didn't understand what I have here," her father said.

"Nothing," Periwinkle's mother said. "Absolutely nothing."

⎄⎅

Not long after Joe's birth, Periwinkle again overheard a conversation. Outside Joe's nursery, little Peri had followed her mother upstairs to ask if she could ride Mr. Johnson's horse—their nearest neighbor and a dear old friend of their father's. But she stopped when she heard her mother address her tiny baby brother.

"You are a bastard child, aren't you? Yes you are. Uh huh." Mingling with her mother's voice came chuckling from an infant boy.

"Your daddy wanted a boy. He doesn't care about his daughter. Did you know that?"

Chuckling.

"He has whored around and he thinks you are the pride of his world. But you know what I think?"

The boy-infant made a gurgling sound.

"I think you are the prize from his whore-mongering."

The infant began to whimper, then cry. Periwinkle saw a little hand reach up through the railing bars. Her mother turned on a heel and Periwinkle swung around the corner and darted down the hall to her own room. Periwinkle leaned against her bedroom door, breathing hard, only sure that her mother had not seen her when she heard footfalls on the stairs.

That was a long time ago. Peri was now nine and Joe was now three, and his left cheek had reddened to a welt. Peri listened to her mother explain away the dark pattern on Joe's cheek as her dad drank a beer with dinner, and after her bath that night, Periwinkle knelt at her bedside and folded her hands together and closed her eyes.

"I don't think I can protect my little brother, so maybe You can protect him. Or even, maybe You can help him protect himself. I know You can, God. I always believed in You. In Christ Jesus name Amen."

The next morning, Periwinkle's father came into her room, asked her to dress quietly and meet him downstairs, in the kitchen. Periwinkle found him sipping a cup of coffee at the kitchen table, rubbing his temple. The light from outside was blue, the chill of the early morning had invited itself into the kitchen. They exited out the back door off the laundry room, cut through the yard, and took the trail that led into the woods. Her sandaled feet fell upon dewy grass that plashed mud on her heels and ankles.

Her father didn't speak as they walked slowly down the dirt path, undergrowth reaching out for their shins. They had walked for a pretty long while when he paused under a cedar, pointing down to a clump of red and white flowers. "You were named after those flowers," he said. Periwinkle knelt, stroked the blossoms before plucking a few and carrying them like a bunch of daisies.

"Periwinkles, Daddy?"

"That's right, sweetheart."

"And what was Joe named after?" she asked.

She caught sight of a frown on her father's face before he looked away.

"Nothing."

After a time they came upon a brook. A family of deer stretched their necks till their lips kissed the water. The doe was almost a solid brown with a white underbelly, the two fawns—twins, it appeared—still fresh with spots. At first they took no notice of either Periwinkle or her father, his hand on her shoulder. When the deer finally noticed, they looked wide-eyed from her to her father, they blinked and turned and scampered into the underbrush.

Further up the stream they found a hollow oak log, bark peeling and worms and maggots and millipedes scurrying underneath. The sky through the canopy of oak leaves and piney tops was whiter now, the air warmer, drawing sweat out of their pores. The dew now burned off, Periwinkle's feet now felt mud-caked in the sunlight, laden by the clinging dew and sweat and dust kicked up by footfalls.

"The deer were neat," Periwinkle said.

"You know I love you, don't you?"

"Yes, Daddy. I know you love me. I love you."

"I would not trade you for anything in this world."

"I know, Daddy." She didn't want to cry right now. He looked away, staring up at the cloudless sky, a warm breeze flowed between the oaks and maples and cedars.

"Your brother isn't as clumsy as all that, is he?"

Periwinkle shook her head.

"You'd tell me, wouldn't you?" her father asked, meeting her eyes. "Big girl promise, now," he added, holding out his fist but with his thumb up. Mimicking his fist, she touched her thumb to his.

"I promise," she said.

> "Periwinkle, Periwinkle
> Where have you gone?
> My Ma killed me and you took away my bones.
> My Pa ate me though he didn't know it
> I really want to sing but my Ma slit my throat."
>
> --Old Ozark folk song

She woke long enough the next morning to hear her father say that the Studebaker needed a tune-up and he'd be a bit late, and then she went back to sleep. When she woke up again she heard her mother shouting foul words that the old ladies at church would say didn't *fit* her mother.

Periwinkle's mother thrashed about the kitchen, tossing pots and pans every which way. Her little brother, eyes wide and unblinking, sat on a stool nearby, nibbling on a cracker, crumbs about his lips.

"You think I can prepare such a dinner in time, you little bastard? His boss is coming over. Did he ask me if that was okay? He just assumes I'll do it. Like he assumed I wouldn't find out about that blonde number in the tight sweater they just hired and I'd forget that your daddy has been coming home later and later."

Joe didn't respond.

Her apron was wrinkled, her flower-patterned dress was wrinkled and faded, the armpits stained with sweat.

"Your father wants a feast for him and his boss," her mother said calmly when Periwinkle walked around the corner. "Go upstairs."

She looked to Joe. He shook his head, but she had no choice. She wanted to run to him, to hug him. In that moment she wanted to show him the periwinkle flowers, the deer.

Periwinkle walked upstairs to her room, her head swooning, and spent the afternoon staring out the window to the treehouse. Forever passed slowly as bluebirds frolicked outside, a couple of squirrels scampered about, until the sound of her mother's calm yet high-pitched voice called her back down to the kitchen.

She noticed the smell, first, something like pork boiling in a large pot on the stove. Steam rolled out from under the lid. Her mother sat at the kitchen table, staring, rocking slowly in a chair. Her skin was oily and sweat-sheened, her hair disheveled. Blood was everywhere on the island bar. The blade of a large meat cleaver had been wedged into the cutting board atop the counter, covered in blood. A wad of clothes, now just crimson dyed rags, were crumpled up in the corner. A burlap sack stained maroon sat at her mother's feet.

Periwinkle said nothing, her mind tried to organize things, but the scene became cartoonish in the eyes of the child, appeared as bright vibrant colors leaping out at her, painted on in a smear.

"Bury this." Her mother pointed to the sack. "I'm going to clean up before your father gets home."

Periwinkle rushed to the back door, pushed it open, just barely making it to the grass before she wretched and heaved, last night's supper spilling out then bile burned her throat and mouth. From behind her the sack rolled into the yard; her mother's shadow loomed over her. A cold sweat broke out over her body, the color gone from her face, Periwinkle trembled, reached out and hoisted the bag up.

She drug the burlap sack across the back yard, leaving a sanguine smear atop the grass blades. Mounting the hill, Periwinkle immediately found relief in the shade, a cool breeze blowing from the east. As she dragged the sack, the burlap fibers cut into her clenched fist. She and Joe should be playing up in the tree house.

Periwinkle released the bag and prostrated on the dirt path by a florid patch underneath a large cedar, her hands covering her face and muffling her sobs.

He needed a proper burial.

She knew where she wanted to bury him: under that clump of periwinkle flowers. He would be shaded easily by the cedar, and have a cool breeze during the warmer months, and a pretty good view. But she had nothing to bury him with, and this thought brought more tears.

She found a rock, just large enough but one she could still handle. Periwinkle wept and her tears dampened the soil, then the jagged edge of the rock tilled the soil loose. The flowers undisturbed, she found she could pull the patch—roots and all—off the soil bed. She laid it aside and continued stabbing at the dirt, crying harder and harder until a modest hole lay in front of her. She picked up the bag, struggling not to simply drop it in the hole, but place it gently.

"I love you, Joe. And Daddy loves you. I'm sorry I couldn't help you. I hope God can protect you now."

Kneeling, she raked the dirt back over the bag and all, finding that she hadn't enough to completely cover the bag. So she walked the area, gathering rocks, the larger the better, and laid them over the bag as well. A cairn just slightly rounded above the surface of the ground was crowned by the jagged rock she had used to dig the hole. Finally she blanketed the grave with the patch of periwinkle flowers. She stepped back to look at her work.

Periwinkle wiped her cheeks, blew a kiss toward the grave, then made her way home. Two hours after she had vomited, Periwinkle approached the house, noticed the black fifty-gallon trash bag just beside the door. The kitchen was immaculate, the smell of bleach overwhelming. Her mother had time enough to even clean herself up. Standing at the stove, stirring the pot, her mother looked over her shoulder and smiled at Periwinkle.

"Did you play well, honey? That bag shouldn't be too heavy. I just did a little lawn care, if you'd take it to the curb for me. Trash comes tomorrow, remember. Joe went over to Mr. Johnson's via the woods. I told him to be back by dinner."

Her father's car pulled into the drive followed by a black Packard as she hoisted the trash-bag to the curb. Periwinkle bounded to him, fresh tears and sobs, clinging to his neck.

"Dear," he said, patting her back, then rubbing just below her shoulders. The driver of the other car exited. A bald man in a suit smiled at her. She sobbed into his nice dress shirt. "It'll be okay," he whispered, and then he said, "Hi, honey?"

Periwinkle froze, held her breath. She stared over her father's shoulder, her lips quivering. Her mother's voice sounded like cracking ice.

"How was your day, dear?"

"Long. You know Mr. Sherman, our District Supervisor," he said as he carried Periwinkle inside. Still rubbing her back, he asked in a slightly softer tone, "What's wrong with her?"

"Poor dear is coming down with something, I think. She's been playing outside all day, and I'm sure she got too hot. Might be a case of spring fever."

He set her down, ruffled her hair. "Where's Joe?"

"He said he was cutting through the woods to go visit Mr. Johnson. Dinner's ready."

"Smells great. I'll be right back." He patted his boss on the shoulder and invited him to tour the house. As the two men headed upstairs, Periwinkle was spun around, her arm tight in her mother's grip, her pasty skin already reddening, her mother knelt to look at her eye level.

"I did this for you, okay. You best straighten up and remember that."

When her father returned, Periwinkle sat at the table, elbows on the doily covered top and hands under her chin. Five place settings were laid out; her father went immediately to the telephone and dialed Mr. Johnson's number.

"Phil? Hey, it's Bill. Would you send Joe back? ... Oh, he isn't. Oh, okay. Well thank you."

"When did he leave?"

"A couple of hours ago," her mother said, stumbling a little across her words. She ushered her husband toward his chair. "Sit. Eat. I'll go look for him. I'm sure he's just out playing in back or in the tree house.

Periwinkle's father stirred the bowl of stew with a spoon. The liquid turbid, the meat gray and chunky, bits of gristle her father spit out fell onto the saucer under the bowl. He slurped the broth from the spoon, sopped up more juice with the crackers.

"This is really good," his boss said.

Periwinkle felt nauseas. Sweat beaded on her forehead. Her father took notice, brushed her matted hair away, felt her clammy forehead.

"Why don't you go to bed," he said, his voice gentle.

"I love you, Daddy," she said. He pulled her close, hugged her as fresh tears moistened her flushed cheeks. The door opened and her mother entered. She fumbled for a chair, put the back of her right hand to her forehead and closed her eyes.

"O dear, I'm so sorry, I couldn't find him, I'm feeling ever so faint, I just can't go on further."

"I can help," his boss said.

"Thank you. I'll get my neighbor, Mr. Johnson. Thank you. I'm sorry." His boss left as her mother made her way to the stairs, and her father patted her head. "You off to bed, sweetie, I'm going to go find your brother."

No, you're not, she thought.

ℂℕℝℤ

She lay in the bed, her face smothered by the pillow, held by her hands. She wished to join her brother rather than carry all of this. Her father would not find her brother, no more a successful search than her mother had attempted.

Now her mother lay in bed asleep. The door had not opened and closed since her father had left. So when Periwinkle felt fingers caress the back of her right hand, she jumped. It couldn't be anyone else. It just couldn't. It had to be her mother, and now it was her turn.

Her eyes tried to adjust to the dark. Periwinkle reached over and turned on her bedside lamp. The pillow that had covered her face now lay in her lap, and covering it a handful of petals, small red and white buds.

A scream filled the house. Frozen, unable to block out the sound, Periwinkle was only able to move when the quiet returned; she shivered as gooseflesh chased up her arms and across the back of her neck.

The door creaked open. Periwinkle stared into her parent's room, afraid to even call out for her mother. What moonlight came through the drawn blinds tiger-striped across the bed and sheets, suggested a lump in the middle. A glint of metal caught her eye, she saw a shadow at the foot of the bed. A black mass no taller than three feet swayed a bit, held up the knife so that the moonlight glinted off the blood-soaked blade. Periwinkle heard it breathing.

Something familiar in the simulacrum, its size, the way it panted, she was on the verge of recognition as the light came on after footsteps from behind, and the horror in the bed, splayed out before her. Periwinkle turned her head away, buried her face in her father's stomach, even as he patted her with his right hand. She noticed how rigid he stood, how his left hand was held up by his chest, clenched into a fist, his knuckles whitening.

Periwinkle peaked around, found no black mass at the base of the bed and no knife. Instead a jagged rock, pointed, with clumps of dirt and blood, lay at the foot of the bed on the comforter.

"How long you been in here?" Periwinkle's dad asked.

"I didn't..." she stammered. He knelt. His right hand caressed her cheek, his left stayed clenched.

"I know, dear. I know just about everything." He held his left fist up for her, opened his fingers, and watched the petals fall to the floor. "I heard a song, and found when it was over that I was laying down, and these were on my chest."

"So now we call the police, Daddy?" because the police were the good guys, and her dad always told her she could trust the police.

"They wouldn't believe that neither one of us did this. They wouldn't believe who did do this."

"Do you think Joe's with God, now, Daddy?"

He nodded, closing the door and pulling her into the hall.

ભજી

The promises from fathers to their little girls after such horrific events are often proven ineffectual once the police are involved. Police would not stay out when such events were revealed, as such events were impossible to keep concealed. There were answers that were needed and Periwinkle often reflected on those answers that he gave, in the years that had passed since that horrible night. Her dad had all the answers. He knew what their mother was doing, how she was treating Joe, but no one would believe that Joe or his ghost had done this. So he offered up another answer, one more believable.

Periwinkle had not spoken since that night to anyone. Her father had visited her twice after that, once to tell her she'd live here a while and another to tell her he had remarried. The second time he came she would have been old enough to get her driver's license, if the circumstances were different. The lights hummed and the doctors gave up talking to her years ago. They learned a long time ago that all she needed was three squares a day and her pot of soil and periwinkle flowers. She could even do without the food, but they learned quickly not to take the flowers away from her, and if the flowers wilted or died then the staff learned to replace them immediately. There wasn't enough Haldol in the hospital to subdue her if she had to go without her red and white flowers. She held them and stared out of the window, and hummed the song she first heard that horrible night so long ago.

About a Girl

ay Nelson liked to keep the office a comfortable seventy-two degrees Fahrenheit, and at this time of day, the rooms primarily stood dark, though one exam lane remained lit. A girl, if you could call her that, sat on the exam table wearing a paper apron that opened in the back. She kicked her legs up and down, watched her knees bend. Her legs and forearms and hands were pale, the cuticles of her fingernails and toenails were purple. Her stringy hair fell in greasy strands to her shoulders. Outside the window, the moon three quarters full and many stars the only natural light.

He still wore his lab coat, his tie, dress shirt and slacks. He stared at her for a time from the doorway and looked down at his clipboard when she glanced up at him. Her eyes on him made him uncomfortable, and as a matter of his discomfort he pushed his glasses up the bridge of his nose.

"I have to wait on some lab work," he said, "but my initial tests are…"

Her thin lips were dry, her eyes glassy, her pupils constricted. She looked like a corpse.

"What's wrong with your initial tests?"

"Your pulse is almost nonexistent and you're registering at room temperature. I can detect no heartbeat or respiratory function, no pupillary reaction to light, nor glandular swelling."

"What do you think it means?"

"Why don't you tell me what you remember?"

"I don't know when it happened, a few nights ago, maybe. I met this john and we went into an alley and the next thing I know I'm really cold. I'm on this metal slab and it's dark and when I get out, I see walls and walls of shelves like the one I just climbed out of."

"I sent off your blood work. I should be getting back the MRI results of your abdominal cavity soon, too."

"You're a terrible liar, Doctor Nelson," she said. When their eyes met, his stomach churned. A noxious smell poured out of every orifice, even the pores of her skin, cool and rancid like old meat, once freezer-burned and now rotting.

⁂

He poured himself a scotch at his townhouse and checked his messages. His father called; it had been late. Ray glanced at the clock by his bed as he undressed and saw that his father hadn't called that long ago. He dialed from his portable as he threw on his robe and downed the last of the scotch. This might be a two glass night, he decided as he thought of that girl. He had taken her call because she sounded frantic and had refused any alternative treatment. The ER was out of the question. She had no other doctor. Left to wonder why she chose him, he was puzzling this out as his father answered and so deep in thought that he forgot to reply.

"Ray, you there?"

"Yeah, Dad," he said. "I just missed your call."

"I've actually called three times tonight, son. Where were you?"

It wasn't his business, for chrissakes. "Working," he said, hoping he came across as curt and short as he felt.

"This late?" His father sounded incredulous. It was hard skirting the truth with a preacher. His father was probably about to say his nightly prayers.

"You coming to church tomorrow?" The age-old Saturday night question, posed every week since Ray had moved back to town, had not diminished in its ability to guilt him and irritate him all at once. While at college and at med school, he had absconded from church till not going became habit, so since his return he felt more comfortable offering up his weekly response.

"I've got rounds."

His father never challenged this. He harrumphed and mumbled a "goodnight, then" and hung up, but his father was no fool. He knew doctors didn't have rounds every weekend. Ray shared the clinic with three other general practitioners, and everyone knew doctors traded on-call shifts like high rollers traded casino chips.

Three other partners, and yet his secretary had been called, and he had been called to the phone, and she asked for him by name. He poured his second glass and paused in the kitchen as he passed by the window. He looked out into the darkness, to nothing. He laughed to himself, tired as he was. He actually thought he saw her outside his window.

ࣘ

"You were supposed to hold off feeding," he said. Three nights had passed and the clinic had again long since closed from the day's normal traffic of physicians and nurses and sick people.

"Do you know what it feels like, to want to feed? Worse than heroine, this hunger, because the high's better. The high is there and always satisfying. All you have to do is feed."

"I can get something from the blood bank, maybe. Find a safer…"

She laughed. "Addicts will tell you that methadone's a poor substitute also."

Dr. Nelson looked at her blood work, then to her MRI. The blood was active, full of nutrients. Corpse blood would not be in this condition. Depending on the level of breakdown, the white blood count would decrease the longer she had been dead. The white blood count now was that of a normal human. As well as her plasma, fine, again something that should be just the opposite. For as long as she's been in this condition, her blood should be a congealed, gelatinous mess. Her veins would lose their elasticity and dry and crack, the thinning blood would seep into the body's cavities.

The MRI showed something else. The scan of her thoracic and abdominal cavities showed weakened but active lungs and a shriveled large intestine. Capillaries, larger than normal, connected the circulatory system to the small intestine, the stomach—capillaries that more close-ly resembled bronchials. Her enlarged heart a bit discolored, a picture began forming that fit the profile of what he knew she was: the digested blood would carry the nutrients she needed, the blood would be ingested and then transmitted through the rest of the body via the digestive tract, more specifically the stomach and the small intestine, the lungs would be of little use until the veins and arteries began pulling the blood through the body and complete pulmonary function would resume only after the heart began pumping again.

"I need to sedate you," he said.

"I don't think that would be a good idea."

"You wanted me to find out what you have become. Sedation will help me to restrain you so that this blood will run its course and I can test you. I can do tests that are impossible on normal people, because you should be resilient."

"I don't believe you," she said. "I don't believe that you believe what you are saying." His hypothesis was based on old movies and old books from dead writers who set the rules, but what if the real rules weren't her rules?

"I can't know what's real and what's pretend unless you allow me to sedate you."

Her dead eyes searched his. He felt embarrassed, then invaded, then violated. There was something beautiful and heretical in her consuming, hypnotic eyes.

"Soon," she said. "But not tonight."

"Tonight's as good a time as any."

"No," she said. "I'm not ready tonight. He turned to grab the anes-thetic and a syringe, and thought of what he could say to convince her. When he turned back around, however, she was gone.

❦

Ray tried to sleep that night, after three scotches and a beer and a melatonin pill. But sleep evaded him. He tossed and turned and thought of this young woman who had sought him out. Her image swam in his mind. Possibly the alcohol aided her in infiltrating his mind, or perhaps she would have been encapsulated by his mind even more if he stayed sober. When sleep finally came, it stole in like a thief and pickpocketed his consciousness. When he slept he dreamed of her, disrobing, lying naked on the exam table. Beckoning him with her dead eyes. When she opened her mouth, he saw a rictus and two pearl incisors impossibly long.

He dressed without realizing he was fully awake and snatched up his keys from the fireplace mantle downstairs and walked out to his BMW and drove through the bleak night, passing slowly the downtown alleys, searching, ever searching. Prostitutes walked downtown, some dressed stereotypically in fur and skirts and fishnet hose, most all of them looking cold, and none of them were her. He drove for nearly two hours up and down the strip, turning down streets and side-streets, doubling back, knowing full well that his black BMW was conspicuous with its MD tag.

It was nearly three o'clock when he saw the gaggle of cop cars blocking off an alley. He pulled up to a strobe of blue, harsh in the night, a blinding and rhythmic flash of light that engendered ghost images in the vacuous alley shadows. He parked and thought he saw the girl in the shadows, then dismissed it as he secured his wool coat and jammed his hands in his pockets and approached the tape.

"All okay?" he asked the officer.

"Should ask you the same, Doc. You've been driving up and down the strip all night. Looking for a piece?" The cop wore a shit-eating grin and offered a wink and a nod.

"Looking for a friend," Ray said and was surprised at the sincerity in his voice.

The cop lifted up the tape and ushered him under and yelled out that a doctor was on site. A detective in a trench coat scoffed. "Fat lot a good it'll do this guy."

A squatting ME's assistant lifted off the canvas covering the upper body.

"What's your medical opinion, doctor?" the ME assistant asked.

Ray audibly gasped. He could taste the scotch and the beer on his own breath and hoped that they didn't notice. He took a step back and woke up fully. Prior to this, he had only thought he was awake, but he must have been moving in a kind of somnolence. A middle-aged, overweight man in a business suit lay on the gurney, the flesh over his neck jagged and pulled back to expose a shattered trachea, a serrated carotid, shredded muscle, and little blood. There should be more blood, he thought. Oh God in heaven there should be more blood.

He looked around the alleyway and the ME's assistant and the detective seemed to understand what he was searching for with futility. They looked at each other and smiled as if sharing an inside joke.

"No capsules or vials," the ME's assistant said. "Patrolmen have checked the whole alley."

"Got anything to add?" the detective asked.

Ray could feel the blood rush from his face. Unable to respond, he shook his head and stared at the dead body. He left a few minutes later, driving straight home. He poured himself another scotch at home and double-checked all the locks in his house. What if he had seen her? He drank the scotch and poured another, his fourth of the night, against better judgment. Better judgment had stepped out for a Caribbean vacation, he realized, and wouldn't be back anytime soon, had opted for a package trip with rationality and sensibility and sanity.

Sufficiently drunk, he noticed only after turning out his bedroom light that someone had called his house. It could be from his dad. He didn't think so. He ran through who all had his unlisted home number. His dad, his sister, his partners at the clinic. More people had his cell. That he gave out if he was on call or treating a particularly pernicious patient who might need him after hours. The girl had his cell. But the voicemail was on his home line.

He shuddered as he listened to the voicemail.

"I've decided, Doctor Nelson, that if you feel it necessary, then you may put me under tomorrow night at your clinic. If you feel it's necessary. I really would like to understand what is happening to me." Then she added unconvincingly: "I'm so scared."

CR&SO

He administered a general anesthetic that took effect quickly, perhaps because her whole system depended on the very blood he neutralized with the administration of this injection. He watched for a slow, rhythmic rise and fall of the chest, till he remembered she no longer needed such a conventional exercise. He pulled leather-bound straps over her biceps first, then tightened two more over her forearms and ribcage. Another large strap held down her thighs. Another pinned down her calves. He started with a scraping, and when that didn't prove adequate, he took a scalpel and dug into the flesh of her right bicep. He didn't dig deep and she didn't bleed. He placed the slice into a slide under a microscope and turned up the power. The cells quickly withered and shriveled.

Dr. Nelson rolled his stool back to her side. She was peaceful in repose. He used his scalpel to trace the line of her cheek, without penetrating her skin. She was beautiful, asleep like this. Natural. A thought came to him: if he could supply her with enough fresh blood and balance that with enough general anesthetic then he could keep her like this indefinitely. He could do all the tests in the world. He could revolutionize science, and medicine, and ideas of death and even religion. How would his dad the Southern Baptist preacher take that?

ॐ

He needed no scotch to fall asleep that night. He awoke just before dawn to a rustle in his bedroom and the fog of extreme exhaustion weighing down his eyelids and his alert mind. He looked around without raising his head from his pillow and, satisfied that his house was empty, he rose and began to ready for work. She had responded with a bit of trepidation when he asked her to return, but he assured her she would be okay. As he readied for work he found he was already counting down the hours and minutes and seconds to sunset.

ॐ

At lunch he met his father, the question on his mind again that had never been answered, that returned whenever he saw his father's face or heard his father's voice. His father looked tired, with dark bags under his eyes and his skin was pale, nearly ashen. There was a chill in the morning that made his father look older. Before—that is the last time he saw his father—Ray had thought the old man wore sixty-nine well, with salt-and-pepper hair and few wrinkles and few crow's feet. Now the skin sagged dryly off his father's bones, dripped off his jowls and bunched up at the line where his scarf and wool coat cinched around his neck. His gloved hand trembled as it struggled to raise a spoonful of soup to his parched cracked lips.

"You look like hell, Dad," Ray said, munching on his grilled cheese. That was all he felt like saying. He had never posed the question to his father, the question that had haunted him nearly as consistently as his patient had of late. *What's haunting you?* Ray really wanted to ask.

"Not sleeping," his dad mumbled. "I woke up," his father said then, "and she was gone. I can't tell you what happened." His gaze was shiftless and Ray could tell this wasn't the whole story on the condition of his father or what happened to his mother, but it was more than he'd gotten in a while. His father always obfuscated any talk concerning the untimely passing of Ray's mother, not committing to undiagnosed illness or accident or anything else. But this admission was the closest to an answer Ray had gotten to the question he'd so desperately wanted to ask. Where had his mother gone so many years ago?

"I'm sorry," Ray said. It was stupid and reactionary and made no sense. It was something acquaintances said to the mourners at funerals. It was a lazy sentiment, but Ray was at a loss for what else to say.

"We took different paths, then. I drug us over to Tulsa and went to seminary."

"I remember, once you were a deacon."

"That was another life. Before your mother died, I sold insurance. When she passed I turned to the Lord and you turned to your god—science. You may not remember this but in the months just after the funeral, you would ask me all the time about your mother. I never knew what to tell a child so young."

"I don't remember that," Ray admitted, but he was sure that birthed the unanswered question, and that explained his selfish reason for wanting to see his patient back. Science and religion could only hypothesize as to what happened after death. This girl knew, and she could tell him.

⌘

He sliced off another ounce of flesh and slid his stool over the UV light, but as he placed the sample under the light, it began to shrivel, smoke, and then blacken. It withered to nothing. His mind raced. He hooked a USB cable to the UV light and connected the other end of the cable to his exam room desktop nearby. He rolled back over to the patient and sliced a piece of flesh just above her breast. He right-clicked on the mouse as he rolled back to the UV light so to start the recording, shoved the sample under the light and watched it deteriorate, like the other.

Only when it was completely gone did he return to the computer and stop the recording, then watched again, slowly. There was something like an allergic reaction that he witnessed. They were allergic to UV light.

He slid his stool over, lifted a nearby handheld mirror off the counter as he rolled. He held the mirror in front of her face, bent his body into a pretzel until his cheek touched hers. Hers was cool, leathery, dry. Hers felt like Play-Dough. He looked up into the mirror and saw—where her face should be—an indented pillow cased in blue, and a hospital bed covered in the sheet of the same color.

Optics suggested this was impossible. He sliced of several layers of epidermal tissue and found success with liquid nitrogen in flash-freezing the cells with little damage. The digital microscope allowed him sufficient time to record the frozen cells to his computer before they dissolved. What he found astounded him. Her epidermal cells contained high amounts of biochromes. Chromatopheres in the cytoplasm of skin cells, Xanthophores and Erythrophores in the upper dermis, Iridophores and Guanophores in the middle, and in the deeper levels, Melanophores. All of these in abundance would give her a chameleon-like ability. One result of this would be the apparent lack of a reflection in the mirror.

He allowed her to wake, done for the night. His questions began to drift to the metaphysical, the gothic. There was no scientific proof for a soul, though he'd read fringe research on the origin of thought at the cellular level, which if isolated and located might mirror the qualities of a soul. He wondered if she hated crosses, holy water.

"We need to hold off for about a week. But there are more tests I'd like to perform."

"But why must we wait?" she asked.

He told her the truth. "Our security company has been noticing the late-night entrance to the building. There's already a question about our first meeting. I shouldn't have brought you in on a Saturday night. I told everyone I hired a cleaning crew but they could all punch a hole in that lie quickly if they chose."

She nodded and dressed slowly, something he had come to realize she didn't have to do. She studied him while he dressed.

"You want to ask me a question, Doctor Nelson, don't you?"

His back was to her. She could not have seen his eyes grow wide, a catch in his throat. His hands, holding the I-pad that revealed her chart, began to tremble.

"I don't know what you mean," he said.

"You want to ask me about what's on the other side. You want to ask me about your mother. I can hear you in your mind, fluttering around like a bat trapped in an attic."

"Where do you go, from here?"

"You can ask me if you like, but you have to promise me something. Or do something for me, I'm not sure which yet. Maybe both." There was a coyness in her voice, but the dead, trying to sound coquettish, only sounded dead.

"Where do you sleep?"

"I find a hole or an unused place, sometimes not particularly warm, but as long as it's dark and un-trafficked, that's all that matters. Permanence, you might be surprised to learn, isn't as important as it was before."

Her language was changing. He turned around. There was a flicker of intelligence in her black pupils, something cunning like a rattler. She was learning. The blood was used by her mind, as well. She was adapting.

Dressed now, she waited, staring at him lasciviously but trying to hide her lust behind innocent flirting. The air was cool in the office and he understood instantly just how vulnerable he was. If she wanted, she could attack and he could not stop her. How he'd never realized this before he could not understand. He was a fool. She began to laugh.

"Doctor, if I wanted you dead I would have killed you by now. I need answers. I need them for myself and I need to give you yours. But I can't until you ask me, those are the rules. You have to ask me."

He opened his mouth but nothing came out, and after a moment she turned slowly and walked away. He went home, nervous, sure she'd pop up in the backseat of his car or sneak into his room. He realized quickly she couldn't, though. That was the rule. She couldn't do anything or go anywhere without first being asked.

He slept fitfully that night. That morning he called into the clinic and cashed in a few vacation days as well as a few of his on-calls. He needed some time off, he said, and luckily he wasn't selfish in the job and luckily he had a good friendship with the other doctors because no one questioned him. He worried briefly that some connection might be made to his absence from work and the security violations late at night, till he realized that he really had nothing to worry about. Nothing was missing and if any security footage was viewed, they'd see a doctor working and running tests in one of the exam rooms. As with the mirror test, he was sure she wouldn't expose herself to a video camera.

☙❧

He spent his nights hunting her down, traveling the streets, parking in a public lot and walking the sidewalks with the druggies and the pimps and the whores and the degenerates. All manner of dregs camped out downtown and he came to know a lot of them. He introduced himself as a doctor and asked about the girl, describing her as best he could.

"Sure, Heather. A john shanked her in that alley," one prostitute named Kiki said.

Ray thanked her and walked toward an alley and ignored Kiki's offerings to please him. He stepped into the alley and noticed the stench of refuge and sewer. A black tomcat screeched and knocked over a garbage can lid. Bags of trash shuffled.

"You shouldn't have come, Dr. Nelson. You shouldn't be searching for me."

"I'm trying to help you," he said, scanning the darkness, turning in place.

"Do you want me to answer the question?"

"Why me?" he asked. "Why did you call my office and why did you pick me, Heather?"

"Sometimes," she said, still keeping herself hidden so that not even her voice gave away her location in the shadows, but seemed to come from all around him, "when a jane-doe or a john-doe is brought into the morgue, sometimes to help put them at rest, one or another of the preachers come in to say a prayer. On the night I was brought in, your father arrived, and through his vocal mumblings and half-assed attempts to get me into heaven, I heard his real prayer. I heard his uncertainty, his lack of faith. He wanted to know what happened to his wife, and he invited me to tell him."

Ray rushed to his BMW and drove straightaway to his father's house, and banged on the door uninterested in the time. His father's heavy padded footfalls could be heard within, and presently the porch light came on, and then his dad stood in the doorway, dressed only in a robe cinched around a tee-shirt and slippers and, in the yellow light of the porch, the marks on his neck a red-orange color and rotten around the edges, two puncture wounds the size of seventeen-gauge needle, scabbed over, tattooing the carotid artery. Ray forced himself into the home before his father could even respond and flicked on the hall light.

"You knew," Ray said, backing his father against the wall. "You sent her to me."

"I know you've wanted to ask me about your mom for some time, Ray, and I knew you could help her understand what she is."

"You know what she is!" He stormed down the hall, flicking on lights, fearful that she was somewhere in the shadows of the house but sure—from the scabs on his father's neck—that she hadn't been there in a while.

"I had to know what happened. I had to know if your mom was alright."

"And is she, Dad? Is she alright? You're a fucking preacher. I thought your beliefs were enough to sustain you."

His father, burying his face in his hands, leaning against the wall, wept silently. He had always presented himself as a strong man in front of his son. Now, the curtain pulled away, the weak and ineffectual man Ray had accused his father of being in the heat of the moment presented as the true man.

"I can't tell you," his father said. "I promised her. She could visit me whenever she wanted and I could not tell anyone about her visits or about what she told me, if she told me what happened to your mother."

෬෩

As she had promised, she showed up for their next meeting, and allowed him to strap her to examination table. He knew he had around thirty to forty-five seconds from the administering of the anesthesia before she lost consciousness, so he wasn't quite finished emptying the syringe's contents into her neck when he finally asked the question. Surprisingly, he realized, it mattered to him little how his mother died, though that had plagued him for many years and that's what drove his interest in science and delivered him to his god Caduceus.

"Is she at peace? Is there life after death?"

"Peace is all there is in the black void, well peace and silence and emptiness. I am life after death in its only incarnation."

He looked over at the PC and thought about all he'd learned of her. He contemplated the presented physio-philosophical quandaries as she rose so silently and swiftly the straps snapped in unison. Only the flash of movement out of the corner of his eye alerted him to her condition, and he spun in place, gripping the desk with his right hand as his left dipped into his lab coat. He had little time to react before her eyes fell upon him. He didn't like the way she looked at him. He pushed his stool back as she pulled her legs from the straps and draped her calves over the exam bed.

"I'm trying to help."

"I can hear you, in here," she said, an index finger pointing toward her temple.

"I was just…"

"You helped."

Ray Nelson closed his eyes, pressed his temples, as though added pressure could alleviate the throbbing behind his eyes. When he blinked he saw the girl still on the slab, strapped down. The exam room silent, dim, the straps all held. Her eyelids fluttered.

"You're awake."

"And still trying to find you in here."

"You're still strapped down."

"Oh."

He reached into a drawer and drew out a sharpened stake carved from ash. In his time away from work he had studied and read, and arrived after the clinic closed but before sunset to deliver his needed tools. From his lab coat he pulled a rosary the local priest had given him once Ray had introduced himself as his father's son.

He examined the point of the ash stake, then her face. He discovered a fresh desire, to lose himself in her gaze. He imagined thrusting into her, her legs spread and wrapped around his hips. He imagined her smiling and clawing at his back.

He imagined fucking her. He imagined her sweaty and cold and clinging to him. Her thighs and her arms snaked around him, pulling him into her. He imagined coming, climaxing with her, her lips on his neck. Kissing. Biting. Gnawing. Now she laid tan and exotic, her thighs supple and her large breasts with erect areolas and he suckled. He came inside her and she recoiled with sighs but she came with him also, kissing him. He rose up on his knees, penetrating her deeper, his arms above his head. Could that be the nesting rooting maggots in her uterus squirming over his rigorist penis? He was naked and she was naked and they were on the table. His body weight rested on his thighs and knees. She reached up and clawed at his chest.

"I love you," he said.

Then he blinked. They were still clothed, the apron crinkled as her writing body struggled under the tight straps. He still stood next to the desk but now, seeing the truth, he walked to the exam table and straddled her.

"Who were you?" he asked. "Can you tell me that? Who were you before this?"

She sighed. She writhed under his weight but the rosary kept her down and she never tore her gaze away from the tip of the ash stake.

"Does it matter? Does it matter if I was a girl fresh off the bus from Ohio looking to make it big in the Windy City or if I was raised by a junkie whore mother on the Southside who taught me what I had to do to make it in life? Would you change your mind on what you are about to do?"

"You've been like this for a while," he said. She was too comfortable in this skin, and at his realization she smiled.

"I promised a woman a long time ago that I'd find out what I was, when she came to me, unsatisfied with her life, searching for excitement. I didn't know back then, though I'd been at this for more years than I could count. The story I told you was true, about me waking up in the morgue, but it happened not a few days ago but years. As she pleaded for her life and for her family, she asked me if I knew what I was and made me promise I'd find out. I thought it befitting, then, that I'd tell her husband what happened to her, and I'd ask her son for help."

He delivered the stake's point to her chest. She was ready to scream but didn't get the chance. The ash wood penetrated her heart and the struggling instantly ceased. Ray leaned over her, his nose nearly touching hers. He stared.

She flailed a bit against the restraints that still held. Nothing violent. Nothing he couldn't control. Her beauty faded fast, the hypnotic allure she exuded with the first illusion evaporated. She sighed something rancid. He recoiled but held the rosary directly over her face.

He noticed no blood spurted out from her chest while he sat, straddling her, waiting for whatever was to happen. He stayed in that position till the sun rose and she began to fade, and he sank lower to his exam table until she was gone. Sadness and anger overcame him as she faded. He prayed that he had given her all the answers she needed, even as he realized what she'd done and what she was and how she deserved worse.

CRSO

He rolled up slowly, just after dawn, to his father's house. It sat quiet on the street like all the other houses. He walked up the drive as the door opened before he even reached the steps. His father now wore a bandage over his neck and didn't wince at the predawn light. He pushed open the screen in time for Ray to catch it and enter. In the kitchen the two men sat at the table in the breakfast nook for some time without speaking, each sipping at a cup of coffee. Finally Ray told his father what he had done.

"She probably would have killed you today."

"What did she tell you about Mom?"

His father looked impossibly old and impossibly tired. "It doesn't matter now. She was a liar. She said things only to either confuse or to rile. The truth was as malleable as the lie, so it doesn't matter what she said. Just why she said it."

Ray sipped his coffee and did not disagree. Outside the sun contin-ued skyward. The day would warm some but not enough, and then cool when the sun set, and tomorrow would bring the same. Still, he could not shake the idea of the power of a truth hidden amidst the lies, like a loan daffodil in a field of heather.

TIME TO KEEP AUNT POLLY

This was not the way to spend Christmas Eve – traveling down two-lane state highways with a thin layer of frost on the roadside grass and icy limbs on the overhanging trees under a gunmetal skies, his girlfriend stewing in the passenger seat – but Bobby Joe could no more help the fact that it was his turn to be called than he could Angelica's displeasure. He was trapped between family and relationship obligations, so the only choice he could make was as much out of control as it was dissatisfying to what he and Angelica had planned. Later, after his world fell apart, he'd remind himself that he was stuck and had no choice.

"The damn tree'll probably catch fire before we get back," Angelica said.

"I unplugged the lights," Bobby Joe said, though he hadn't checked the water level before they left, so it'd probably be dried out.

"You should've known your dad would call you. He's never liked me, Bobby."

"Like your folks approve of me?"

"What the hell is wrong with her, anyway?" Angelica asked. "Your family's being awfully cagey not telling us."

"Dad says she'll tell us," he said with a sigh. He'd been just as put out by their secretiveness. "She's been lonely, Angelica. Since my uncle died."

Angelica looked out the window. "It's been a year since their accident."

"She's in mourning," he said. "Besides, she's giving five-grand to everyone who sits with her."

"It isn't about the money, Bobby Joe," she said and squeezed his right hand as it rested on the console gear shift. The box in his right coat pocket, it's sudden weight tugging at the jacket under the force of gravity, forced him to silently disagree.

"It's my family, Angelica. What do you want from me?"

"This was supposed to be our Christmas," she said, and faced front, folding her arms across her chest.

Ahead of them, a ridge of Ozark mountains stood sentry against them, and the road veered hard to the left to skirt the mountains under a canopy of naked tree limbs. As the road narrowed, the car slowed. Angelica gripped the Oh-Jesus-handle hanging overhead. The narrow two-lane turned to gravel and Bobby Joe slowed again, asked her to read the directions off the cell.

"Two miles after it goes to gravel, you'll see a row of mailboxes on the right, and before that a road. Take that road."

The road they were meant to take was such in name only: a path of gravel to guide them through the brush and across several lower water bridges, with no place to pull the Blazer over if they met an oncoming vehicle.

"Get your camera ready," Bobby Joe said.

"For what?"

"Bigfoot."

Neither laughed. They passed a couple of houses nowhere near in sight of each other as the trail turned and veered and crossed two more bridges. Someone had hung a confederate flag in the loft opening of a barn, the only edifice before they arrived ten minutes later at two corner posts on either side of the trail.

"You made your aunt sound a bit uppity. She came from money. Right?"

"Right?"

"Then why is she living way out here?"

Bobby Joe had no answer.

❧

The path ended at a riverbank across from a steep slope of oak and elm and cedar, the two former naked and the latter still green but frosted over. The trail curled into a semicircular drive in front of a wooden cabin, but neither fully grasped the setting till he parked next to a Jeep.

There was a horse pen and a pen for steers and some goats and a henhouse. This took up the expanse of what otherwise would be yard. There were two cabins and they were connected by a wooden boardwalk, both with tin roofs and walls of thick oak logs. Great stone steps led up to the larger cabin with a heavy front door that flew open as an emaciated woman in thick flannel marched down the steps, her arms swinging.

As Bobby Joe and Angelica both exited, the diminutive woman gave the slightest of pauses, looked from one to the other, a smile frozen on her lips, then took a few more steps and hugged Bobby Joe tight and kissed his cheek. Then she walked over to Angelica. She took a hand in each of her own and smiled and took Angelica all in.

"Aren't you a vision. And who are you, love? A friend of Robert's."

Angelica blushed. "I'm his girlfriend. He didn't tell you I was coming."

Aunt Polly smiled, shifted her eyes to Bobby Joe for a moment before looking back.

"It's usually a family affair, sweetie. My condition is persnickety, and generally requires the attention of one set of particular eyes to overlook me for a few days. Not that I want to be a fussbudget, but with my condition there are certain … necessary precautions." She let her eyes roam over Angelica once more and her smile broadened. "But you are more than welcome, dear. Robert is lucky to have you and so I am lucky to meet you."

"Thank you." Angelica said as she shot Bobby Joe a look, then followed Aunt Polly inside while he tended to the bags.

❧

Dinner was a three-course meal Aunt Polly had been putting the finishing touches on as they arrived. They ate noisily, talking between bites, Polly grilling Angelica good-naturedly on who this woman was who'd stolen her little Robert's heart. Talk then turned to memories, to family, and to times that still played upon their minds.

"You remember my mother? She always had such meals when we came for a visit."

Bobby Joe said, "I remember shelling peas with her in that screened-in patio. The breeze was cool and it was peaceful and I was so restless. I got bored in five minutes, like I had so many other things to do. I rushed out. Ready to explore the world. I should have stayed with her."

They drained the last of their bottles of Ozark stout in silence. Aunt Polly directed Angelica to a bottle of chilled Merlot, pouring a glass for each to start…

☙❧

"You were choking!" Aunt Polly said.

"I was toppling over sideways, giving the Okay Sign!"

They were all laughing. Angelica waved her hands like a baby bird trying to fly too early all while saying, "Stop it! Stop it. I'm going to wet myself."

This sent them all into another fit of uncontrollable laughter, which died down slowly and easily with a few sighs and some contemplation.

"I got to shower and go to bed," Angelica said after a yawn and a glance at the clock in the kitchen.

"Gas log fireplace in the guest cabin," Aunt Polly said. "Piping hot water and it has its own generator."

Angelica kissed Bobby Joe and hugged Aunt Polly, walked through the kitchen and pulled the door to behind her. When they heard her footfalls on the boardwalk, Aunt Polly spoke.

"You got to know some things about my condition. It's why I called you hear."

From his pocket, Bobby Joe produced the box, opened it to reveal the diamond princess cut on 14K gold. "Christmas was supposed to be just the two of us," Bobby Joe said. "I'm asking her…"

Aunt Polly's face lit up. She hugged her nephew and kissed his forehead, took his hand and led him into the living room. She made him sit in the chair and started rummaging around the presents under the tree.

"Robert, this is great. This is what's important now. I'm so sorry they called you."   "My dad—"

"Shush now," she said, and perhaps she knew he was about to admonish his own father for calling him, because she said, "I know my brother and you have to say nothing else. But he won't ruin this special moment for you both.”

She stood and thrust into his hands a small box that was heavier than it looked.

“Well, still we’re here,” he said. “So whatever you need.”

“Open,” she said, smiling, looming over him.

He looked up at her and smiled and looked back at the box, felt the heft in his hands. Slowly he unwrapped the gift, pulling daintily at the taped edges leave as tiny a mess as possible. When he saw a box for shotgun shells, he wondered if she’d run out of gift boxes, but from the heft and the metallic jingle he knew otherwise. Aunt Polly no longer stood over him but had walked into her room and emerged quickly carrying a double-barreled twelve-gauge shotgun.

Bobby stood to protest. “Aunt Polly,” but though he held his hands palm up, she shoved the weapon into his hands. “What’s wrong, Aunt Polly? Why are we here?”

She swallowed hard and stared at him, her dark eyes shadowy and sunken. Her tongue moistened her cracked lips, which she flexed and pursed and flattened. Finally, she said, “Nevermind about that now. You just promise me three things.”

He nodded, but from her icy stare he thought he’d better add, “Anything, Aunt Polly.”

“One, you take that gun. Two, you do exactly what I ask of you tomorrow when I get ill, no matter how it sounds. Three, you go and propose to your girl.”

He nodded.

“Say it.”

“I promise, Aunt Polly.”

ა⁊⁋

Bobby Joe’s footfalls echoed across the planks of the snow-covered boardwalk, placed his bare palms on the rail, and looked up the shadow-soaked hill.

What creatures lurked at this hour? What nocturnal beasts roaming these hills returned his gaze this very instant, espying the chickens in their house or the steers or horses in their pen or the goats continuously trimming the yard? What else did the dark conceal that could necessitate this Christmas gift, the shotgun in his hands and the box of shells that she’d insisted he open.

He jumped when something tugged his arm, spun and saw Angelica smiling up at him. He put an arm around her even as his heart began to calm and he hugged her to him, her hands close to his jacket pocket where he'd folded the check.

"Peaceful," she said.

"Cold," he said. Her body was warm.

"Yes, but peaceful, too."

"What possessed your aunt to move here?" she asked.

"I don't know."

Angelica asked, "Why do you have a gun?"

"It was my Christmas gift. Thank you for allowing us some time to catch up."

She yawned. "I'm tired anyway. Wasn't planning on a trip for Christmas."

"I'm sorry again. My dad said all the family has sat with her."

"Your dad. Okay. She doesn't look sick, Bobby Joe." When he frowned in contemplation, she said, "What?"

"She says she will be."

The words drifted from his lips to her ears and then off into the darkness. She nestled into him, unresponsive to his words because they were just strange enough, too strange to be considered tonight.

"Merry Christmas," he said, and kissed her forehead.

"Merry Christmas. Make love to me?"

�&⋑

Bobby awoke refreshed, the beer a fading ghost on his breath. He sat up in the bed, trying to organize the whole night, but too much pleasure blurred the last. Angelica slept, under the blankets her nude flesh pressed against his, on her finger the engagement ring. He removed the covers and stood, bracing against the windowpane and exposed to the world, the cold seeping in from the outside, a draft threatening to shrivel him. The valley, the vehicles, everything white and glistening. At the steep hill just past the creek, snow covered the slope, the limbs white and brilliant beneath a gunmetal sky, and from above a brightness reflecting off the snow, forcing him to squint.

"Hey cowboy," Angelica said, eyes half open, a drowsy smile on her lips. She held up her left hand and examined again the diamond he'd finally given her after their third collective orgasm.

"You said yes," he said as he slid back under the covers.

"Of course."

"Bobby!"

The voice was faint but loud enough to give them pause.

"Bobby Joe!"

Louder now, but no closer. The valley carried sound.

"Go," she said with a huff.

۞

The kitchen and front room were dark, the dishes and empty beer cans still piled up. He felt like a trespasser, traipsing around the cavernous home. With each step, the boards felt cold like stone under his feet. He glanced to the bedroom door. How could he have heard Polly through all these doors and eight-inch thick walls and a good fifty-foot run of a walkway up to the guest house?

Bobby reached for the knob, but his hand trembled. He squeezed the wrought-iron handle without engaging the trigger latch as Angelica's cool voice caressed his ears.

"It's Christmas. I was being a bitch. Your aunt needs you. I'm sorry."

He nodded without looking at her, engaged the latch, and pushed the door open.

۞

Whatever cloud had settled over the valley seemed to cast its deepest shadow here above Aunt Polly's bed. Bobby's eyes glanced over the lump under the covers to the window with shades drawn, back to the massive quilt, like a patchwork death-shroud, under which there came no movement and no noise or sign of breath.

"Aunt Polly? Merry Christmas, Aunt Polly."

"Bring me a cup of water," came the raspy voice, barely audible. "Cups above the stove."

"Help me up," Aunt Polly said. "We have gifts to unwrap."

He reached for the covers but there came a yelp like he had hurt her, wondered if he had snagged some of her hair in clutching the heavy quilt.

"Don't pull it back. Please."

"Aunt Polly? You just need some aspirin, some water, you'll be fine. I swear." He laughed a little, despite himself. "It's just a bit of the hair of the dog that bit ya."

He grabbed the quilt and pulled but she still clutched the sheet. Her form quivered under the covers; he could see where her hands bunched the sheet above her head, holding tight.

"You want to open gifts, you have to get up." She'd made him swear the night before that no matter how sick she was, he'd make her get up.

"Aunt Polly," Angelica said from behind him, "I got your water and some Tylenol."

"No Tylenol," Bobby said. "With the alcohol it'll kill the liver."

Angelica turned on a heel and walked out.

"Child!" Aunt Polly called, so quickly that the sound and strength in her voice made Bobby jump. Angelica stuck her head around the corner and for a second Bobby caught scent of her perfume before a more rancid smell assailed his nostrils from underneath the sheet.

"Make it hot chocolate instead. We have no Aspirin, the Tylenol will do fine, my liver will stand it."

As Angelica left, Aunt Polly pushed off the covers. Bobby Joe backed away. Her skin ashen, and overnight she had shed fifty pounds, a lithe woman already who couldn't spare ten. The flesh had shriveled and wrinkled, her eyes sunken, her dry hair now thin. She gasped for breath, looked at him, the whites of her eyes jaundiced and veiny, giving them almost an orange color.

"Yes," she said, gasping at every breath. "Hot chocolate will do me some good."

Bobby Joe could only stare and fought not to recoil when she reached for him, a bony, dried hand and fingers warped into claws, her reptilian touch stiffening the hairs on the back of his neck.

"I'm going to come back to bed later. Don't argue. Remember what I want, what I asked of you last night." She said all of this while taking heavy breaths between words, her orange eyes bulging, her cheeks deflating with each intake of air.

"No," Bobby Joe said. "You're going to rest. In fact, you're going to rest until I can get a hold of the nearest hospital and you'll only get up when we get you ready to drive to either meet the ambulance or meet the doctor."

"No!" Bobby couldn't pull away from her if he tried. "The ice is too thick," she said. She let go his arm and he cradled it, rubbing it reflexively, and felt the dimples in his flesh left by her yellow nails. "I'll be okay. I know I look like I'm at death's door now, but this is nothing new. It's why you're here."

"Aunt Polly…?" Angelica stood at the door, her toes unable to break the barrier, she unable to look away. The cup of hot chocolate clanked on the saucer, sloshing mud-colored froth over the sides. Bobby Joe willed her to look at him, to see him nod and to see him offer a smile and assure her that it was okay, but Angelica refused to look.

"I'm thirsty, child. I'm oh so thirsty," Aunt Polly with a lascivious smile on her lips that unnerved her nephew.

Trembling, Angelica crossed the threshold and passed the cup to Aunt Polly's eager hands.

;;;

"She needs a hospital," Angelica said, sitting on the couch. The door to the bedroom was closed and in these tight quarters, they could hear Aunt Polly splashing around the sink in her bathroom.

"When you walked over from the guesthouse, did you happen to notice outside?

This valley is at least ten degrees cooler than the rest of the area, and that's summertime. I bet it gets colder than that in the winter. Those streams and low water bridges are iced over, and this whole trail out here has got to be covered. If we go out now, we could end up in a ditch and…"

She began biting her nails, staring intently out the window. She was trembling, so he put his hand to her back and began to rub. She arched away then stood and moved to the other couch. He knew better than to follow. Aunt Polly, now dressed, inched her way out. Angelica helped the elder woman to her seat.

"Is all okay?" Aunt Polly asked. "I heard yelling."

"Fine," Angelica said.

"Let's open our gifts then," the elderly woman said.

Bobby Joe passed out the gifts and the three eased off wrapping paper. Bobby Joe and Angelica placated her, tried not to make the morning feel rushed, but their goal was not to keep her up any longer than they had to. Still, they did not return to their cabin till she had returned to bed.

;;;

"She's sleeping, finally," Angelica said as he reentered from checking the outside locks on the window. He kicked the snow off his shoes in the doorway and pulled the door closed, then kicked his shoes off and stood by the fire.

"It sounded like she was jumping on the bed," Bobby Joe said.

Angelica looked worn. There were bags under her eyes.

"She was moaning, Bobby. The sounds from in there…"

"Bobby Joe," the voice was barely audible through the thick door.

His left hand on the handle, his right up to the silver deadbolt, but he didn't pull it back.

"I can't come in, Aunt Polly."

"I need a flower, Bobby Joe. I got a patch of 'em growing down by the bank of the creek."

Under the snow--the fever, still unbroken, she must be hallucinating.

"Ac-ac-aconite!" She stuttered. "I got some a few months back. It'll shine yellow on my chin, and if you grind it into a powder, it will slow me down, if I drink it.

" 'No, no, go not to Lethe, neither twist Wolf's bane, tight-rooted, for its poisonous wine…' Keats, such a smart man. I take aconite on this night and die, I take it a week from now and I'm back to what I am tonight. Life's a bitch, isn't it, so get me some of that aconite wine."

She began to laugh, then cackle, then scream, and her screams turned to howls, as though she were being ripped apart. The heavy wooden bed posts thumped against the floorboards. Something slammed against the door, hard enough to explode dust and mortar and knock Bobby Joe back. Sounds like leather shredding intertwined with her screams of pain and ecstasy.

"Aunt Polly!"

Glass was breaking, she was crying, so loud, begging for "that root drink, just bring me that root drink, I beg you, I hate this night."

Bobby shut his eyes, leaned against the door. He remembered how Aunt Polly was when he was a kid: laughing, full of life and spirit, always keeping up with the kids. She'd looked out for them when they were kids.

Aunt Polly shrieked: "Monk's Hood, Wolfsbane, Leopard's Bane, Devil's Helmet—have a taste most nights and feel your blood run cold and howl, three nights have a taste and your fate will be dour, everyone who is pure in heart and says their prayers by night, can fall prey when the Wolfsbane blooms and the full moon's shining bright!"

Still leaning against the door, Bobby Joe wished he could peer between the cracks in the planks. He waited as silence fell again, and the whole house finally settled into a stillness. It wasn't until he reached up for the deadbolt did he hear a weak voice.

"Tonight is the worst, Bobby Joe. Protect the animals. Protect yourselves."

⊂⊃

Angelica grabbed her shoulders and shivered despite the fire in the fireplace and the thermostat that read eighty degrees, and she wore a tweed turtleneck. She wasn't sure why Bobby loaded his shotgun and why he felt he had to go out now and patrol the grounds. She wasn't sure why she felt very afraid looking at that closed door, especially now with Bobby Joe gone.

"Child." A whisper from behind the locked door. "I need you, child. I need you. I'm so cold. Can you come help me?"

You aren't afraid of Aunt Polly, Angelica mouthed, and even allowed an unconvincing scoff, but she dare not take her eyes off that door as it rumbled, and dust flew off the hinges. The lock matched the hinges, the old-fashioned door handle; they all glowed a faint silver, a web of light in front of the door that she, inexplicably, found strength in, as though the ethereal argent dreamcatcher kept the nightmares out and Aunt Polly in. Or what if the nightmare was in there with Aunt Polly, and the dreamcatcher was meant to keep everyone outside that room safe.

"Child?" The voice from the other side of the door was barely a whisper.

"I'm here Aunt Polly."

"I'm thirsty, child. Bring me some water. Child, where's Bobby Joe?"

"Outside."

"Good."

The rules were stupid, and Angelica felt no hesitation fulfilling the sick old woman's request, but as the door opened, the silver web immediately dimmed. A figure stood at the foot of the bed, hidden in shadow. Angelica's breath fogged as it escaped her lips and, as she lifted the glass of water, her stomach began to turn over on itself and any solace she thought she'd find proved a lie as a low growl shook the blackness, and the thing lunged.

⊂⊃

Large flakes fell wet and heavy, obscuring Bobby Joe's view of the pens and the animals. A winter's wind howled deafeningly through the valley, loud but not enough to mask an explosion at the front of the house

He plodded through the snow toward the front steps, his feet heavy in the thick snowpack, the audible crunch under foot with every step, and errant flakes escaping through eyelets and cracks in his canvas and leather boots, chilling his socks and his shin hairs, his feet and calves and knees. He'd nearly reached the porch when he heard a scream from the henhouse like a woman, and then Aunt Polly's voice calling across the frozen valley.

"It's got us here, Bobby Joe. Me and Angelica."

He reached the corner of the chicken coop and pressed his body against the wood slats and listened to the screams of the hens and the rooster. He closed his eyes and pressed the gun barrel to his chest, praying either Aunt Polly or Angelica would say something. Holding a deep cold breath, he peeked around the corner. The entrance ramp was midway down the length of the henhouse with a hole he might just fit through if he crouched, and the chickens were now silent.

He placed a foot upon the ramp and glanced up to the black entrance, a few stray white feathers littered the ramp. He took another step as the clouds dissipated and he crouch-crawled through the rectangular hole.

Moonlight glinted off the scattered, blood-stained feathers and pools of thick crimson, black in the dimness of the interior. The corpses of mangled birds were scattered about. Some legs still twitched. At his foot a dislocated beak soaked in blood.

From behind he heard the cattle. He drew the bead and retreated down the ramp, the noise was disorienting, the cattle … screaming … just like the chickens.

Bobby Joe plodded through the snow with shotgun close, scanning, as the tangled blob became a herd of steers and then a herd of steers standing defensively. His thighs burned from walking in the snow and his lungs burned from breathing in the cold. One steer lay on his side. A dark figure straddled the yearling, its arms flailing on top of the felled beast, claws ripping and tearing at the cow's flesh. A wolf from the shape of the head -- he took aim. It growled, sat straight up, its shoulders square to him, its yellow eyes piercing the night as its claws dug into the cow's chest and spine, ripping both. And then it howled.

Bobby Joe took three deep breaths and, without exhaling, squeezed the trigger. The wolf met the bullet dead on, thumped backward in the snow as the gunshot echoed off the slopes of the surrounding hills.

His gun still raised, his eyes wide and his hands shaking, he neared but didn't see a wolf. He saw nails, not claws, on the fingers, splayed out into the snow. He heard labored breathing.

Aunt Polly's chest had been shattered by the shot, blood caked about her mouth. She wore a half-drowsy smile.

"Thank you," Polly said with the last gasp of steam escaping into the dark winter night.

Her eyes lost focus and her body settled into the snow and as Bobby Joe realized how she must have gotten here, he tossed the gun and bolted up the steps. The ajar door revealed a soft flickering of yellow light, and when he pushed it open, he found the living room and kitchen peaceful. Still. Silent. His gaze fell to the master bedroom, the door open, darkness spilling out. He turned on the light and froze.

Angelica lay beside the bed, ashen and trembling, blood painting her torso, the wall, and underneath her to pool over the wooden floorboards. A deep gash ran from her left shoulder to just above the right false ribs. Cradling her head in his arms, he began rocking her. Outside the animals were starting up again.

"Just hang on," he said.

He laid her gently back on the floor and kissed her forehead, then moved to the bathroom. He tossed open cabinet doors and began rummaging, unsure he'd find what he thought he needed, but when he did he returned to her. He washed her in the alcohol and rubbed the Neosporin into her wounds and then wrapped her in the rest of the bandages. Finally, he lifted her onto the bed, covered her up, and watched as her breathing slowed. He brushed the hair back away from her eyes as she drifted away.

Bobby Joe didn't sleep. Couldn't. He lay at Angelica's side for the rest of the night, his hand gently on her abdomen, staring at her, feeling the soft undulations of her belly as she breathed. At one point around dawn he might have dozed, but when he thought she'd stilled, he awoke instantly. On her hand another scar: a five-pointed star.

Around noon she opened her eyes.

"I'm hungry," she whispered.

"I didn't think we could make it out." Bobby Joe got her some water then fixed some eggs, some bacon. She sat up, devouring her breakfast. He cleaned up the blood and realized that her wounds must have been superficial when he checked her bandages; her wounds were not gashes but mere raised abrasions. But there had been an awful lot of blood. The phone rang then. Angelica kissed him and said she was tired, then wrapped her arms around him and snuggled in, nuzzling his chest. He could reach the landline on the nightstand but chose not to. When his cell rang and he saw it was his dad, he sent the call to voicemail. He'd have to make the call soon enough, he knew, but first he opened Safari and searched Google. "Aconite" "Pentagram" "Wolf's Bane"

He understood what Aunt Polly was and now what Angelica was. But he'd call on no family members to come sit with her next month. He'd be the one to bring her out here and lock her in the room. He accepted all of this as fact and resigned himself quickly to this fate, knowing full well that halfway between the moons he'd face the greatest doubt in what was happening and even supposing that now he was tired and had missed a wolf and hit his aunt instead. But of course, that didn't make sense, and he was sure his father would confirm it. So, he closed his eyes and pulled her tight and fell asleep alongside her.

** The following was published in the Nafallen University Course Catalog 2022-2023 edition by Madness Heart Press

COMMUNICATION
Comm 103: Intro to Mediumship
Prerequisites: None
In this freshman level course, students are taught the basics of *mediumship* (communicating with the dead) in practice, as well as the history of the practice and how its rituals have evolved over the years.

Credit Hours: 3

Comm 203: Advanced Mediumship
Prerequisites: Successful completion of Comm 103 or Instructor Approval
The second course in this sequence focuses more on the specific rituals unique to mediumship, with attention given to the students own successful practice of mediumship as a requirement for successful completion of the course.

Credit Hours: 3

Comm 326: Necromancy
Prerequisites: Junior standing; Successful completion of Comm 103 & 203
In this two-semester course, students will learn the history of the practice as well as the more successful rituals meant to succeed at the practice of *necromancy* (the raising of the dead), will study the biographies of the more successful necromancers throughout history, and will finally complete a necromancy ritual meant to raise the corpse of their choice with instructor approval.

Credit Hours: 6

Comm 388: Psychic Communication + Lab
Prerequisites: Junior standing
This two-semester course with it's accompanying lab will teach students the fundamentals of *telepathy* (speaking only with the mind), *telekinesis* (moving objects with the mind), *astral projection* (moving the consciousness outside of the body), *clairvoyance* (the ability to see visions), *divination* (the practice of gathering evidence from the spiritual world), *precognition* (the ability to predict the future), *scrying* (using mediums like crystals and orbs to obtain information from the spirit world), and *remote viewing* (the ability to receive visions or impressions of distant places). While students

will be given ample time to practice these eight types of communication, they must show mastery of at least three in order to successfully complete this course and qualify for the senior practicum.

Credit Hours: 8

Comm 405: Senior Practicum
Prerequisites: Senior Standing
In this required course, students must successfully demonstrate fundamental principles from each of the previous courses to show that they are prepared to finish matriculation as an undergraduate. This practicum is also a showcase to gauge the students most ready to move on to graduate studies.

Credit Hours: 5

Comm 533: Summoning the Eldritch Gods
Prerequisites: Graduate Standing + Outstanding Practicum Scores
Summoning the Eldritch Gods requires great patience and an understanding that practitioners can't control the gods, but merely beseech them for assistance. This seminar is meant to introduce students to the rituals deemed most successful by practicing sorcerers.

Credit Hours: 3

Comm 603: The Abramelin in Theory and Practice
Prerequisites: Graduate Standing
This graduate level course will examine the various translations of the *Abramelin* as well as show the fallacies in the Thelema translation, discuss the history of the book, and prepare students for successful completion of the ritual so that they might summon their own Eldritch Guide.

Credit Hours: 3

Comm 604: Solomon's Key to Controlling Demonic Entities
Prerequisites: Graduate Standing
Once upon a time, King Solomon controlled the hordes of Hell and forced them to construct the Holy Temple in Jerusalem. While difficult in and of themselves, demons can be controlled where the Eldritch Ones can't be, so students in this course will learn the rituals and practices to call a demon unto th]emselves to do their bidding. Studying ancient texts referencing the Jewish Kabballah, students will be asked to summon their own demon by the end of the semester and show control over said demon by ordering it to fulfill a command. This course has an accompanying lab.

ONE PARTICULAR NIGHT ON HIGHWAY 365

Listless like he's stuck in a fog, perhaps because it feels like years since he was home and perhaps it's because he's been driving so long that the terrain always appears the same, Dillon steers his car onto Arkansas State Highway 365. Above him the pines sway, illuminated by the gibbous moon as wisps of clouds drift slowly across the firmament. He wipes condensation off the windshield and his palm comes back frigid and wet, and from the dash the vents cough out the heat asthmatically, but this is nothing new.

❧

And then he sees her. And the fog lifts.

❧

Dillon's headlights illuminated her back as he crested a hill. Her head down, her thin sundress blew in the wind though her arms were pinned to her side to try and control it. He braked, a loud squeak indicating disuse and he couldn't recall the last time his car had rested; she spun in the light, raising a hand to shield her eyes.

Stepping out of the car Dillon did his best to smile. "Can I offer you a lift?"

She wasn't dressed for the night. Her auburn hair whipped in the wind. She was pale but a pretty kind of pale, like she was studious or a homebody. She looked at him with a raised eyebrow and a focused gaze practiced out of distrust of strange men picking her up on the highway. "I'm fine. I don't have much further."

"Okay. But it's no trouble."

She glanced around again, still hugging her waist. Gooseflesh on her purple-pale arms, her deep-sunk eyes darted around as she hugged herself. Finally, she walked to the car.

The windows fogged then thawed, the outside cold battling the vented heat. She felt the leather, her seat preternaturally cold, the chaffs of rough leather picking at the back of her thighs. She adjusted herself and squeaked, made sure to press herself against the door and hoping that the door would hold. He looked at her a few times and smiled easily. She returned the look appreciatively but timidly.

"So how far are you?" he asked.

"About twenty miles." She stared out the window, biting her nails. The land was relatively flat with only minor curves and hills to break the monotony of the drive. The full moon and star-filled firmament did little to penetrate the thick shadows of the pine forest. She turned and offered him a small grin while her eyes remained downcast, blushing. "I guess a little too far to walk."

"I'm Dillon."

"Ashley. Nice car, what is it?"

" '70 'Cuda—my pride."

"Why are you out so late?"

"Going home too," he said. "Feels like forever since I've been home."

"You don't look old enough for it to have been forever," she said. "And you?"

"My car broke down a ways back so I'm hoofing it."

He frowned but kept his eyes forward. He recalled no car a ways back anywhere, on either side of the road. But he had been driving for so long. He was tired and cold. He might have missed a car on the side of the road.

She shivered. Dillon turned up the heat. He reached for her hands but she jerked away.

"Nice night," he said, returning both hands to the wheel.

"Mmmh. Cold."

She was pretty but quiet. He'd hoped in picking her up that she'd provide a bit of company. The few words he'd said felt raspy; his whole voice felt dry and unused. He coughed to shake out the cobwebs before asking her how far.

"It's ten miles passed the diner." She still focused out the window.

"I haven't seen a diner," he said.

The car topped a steep hill, rounded a bend to a flattened stretch of road, where a diner sat a quarter of a mile away on the right. "Oh," he said.

"You want to pull in? I could buy you a drink or something, repay your kindness."

Dillon parked next to the only other vehicle, a semi-truck with no trailer attached. He shut the car off and looked down to the keys in his hand. It felt wrong. The keys should be in the ignition and he should be driving. Her door creaked open as though that were an unnatural position. He felt her eyes on him and her hand on his shoulder. He looked up to find her halfway in the car, leaning in with one knee on the leather seat. She smiled at him, but he saw also a look of concern on her face. Like maybe she thought he was going to leave her here.

"You okay?"

He nodded and fondled the keys.

"You looked like…"

"Like I was lost?"

"No," she shook her head. "Like you weren't where you were supposed to be."

He climbed out of the car and jammed the keys into jeans pocket. The wind forced a wish that he had something with a little more insulation than the lining-less shell of his black leather jacket.

The door opened to an explosion of glass. Behind the bar an overweight, balding man yelled. A young girl with stringy blonde hair—her nametag read MARIE—stood over a tray of dishes. She stared at Dillon. At the bar sat the trucker. All Dillon could see of him was the back of a jean jacket and scraggily mess of brownish gray hair ruffling out between the collar and his black trucker's cap. His arm raised and lowered a coffee cup to his obscured face. He never turned around.

The lighting was sparse, the darkly trimmed room all the darker. The air reeked of cigarettes and stale beer. Dillon led Ashley to a corner booth and ordered a couple of Cokes. The waitress stammered a yes and walked away even as the bartender asked what she was doing.

"Filling our customers' orders," she said.

The bartender looked at the trucker, then to where the waitress stood, then to them. He blinked at them for a moment, said nothing, and waited to holler at her until she had rounded the corner of the bar, something Dillon couldn't hear. He leaned over to Ashley.

"Well this is an interesting place," he whispered.

"To say the least," she whispered back. She giggled and that brought out a smile in him. "I can't believe this place was reopened," she said.

"What do you mean?" he asked. He leaned in, elbows on the table, eager to engage in gossip and eager more to get her to speak. He was fascinated by her.

She sipped her Coke and looked at the table and shook her head. "No, no." Conspiratorially she leaned in and flashed her green eyes and smiled and whispered, "I'll tell you when we leave."

He sipped at his Coke until it was brown ice and his straw made slurping sounds and he smiled and was delighted to see her gaze warm and her smile seemed genuine. Whatever fear she exhibited toward him now seemed to dissipate.

"Now I've got this," she said.

"I'm a quick-draw with my wallet," he said, grinning.

"You such a chauvinist you can't let a girl pick up a bill?"

"You use a lot of big words."

"For a girl?"

"For anyone."

The waitress walked up to their booth and laid down a bill, face down. She offered them a smile but still seemed shifty. Over her shoulder, the bartender shot their booth the stink eye.

"What if we want another Coke?" Dillon asked.

"Or what if we want something to eat?" Ashley asked.

"Just, we're about to close," the waitress said. "It's on me."

Dillon turned the bill over and saw no charge, as in his periphery the bartender began yelling at the waitress and pointing to them. They climbed back in the car and headed on down Highway 365.

"The diner did close once," Ashley said. "They say once it was run by an old man and his very young wife. He thought she was cheating on him. He beat her often. Most said he was jealous, but as it turns out he was right, though he himself never saw the proof. Her boyfriend, a long-range trucker she only saw twice a year, came calling."

"What happened?"

"He drove his truck through the diner when he heard that the girl had gone missing. Everyone knew the old codger had killed her and stashed the body, but no one could prove it. So the trucker sought justice his own way. The impact killed them both."

"You're suggesting we just visited a haunted diner and saw three ghosts!" he said.

She laughed, a wild raucous thing where she tossed her hair around, and it wasn't till she caught sight of the terrain outside that she settled herself and spoke. "Right, here please."

Dillon did not see a street or a house; he slowed then stopped the car on the shoulder. Through the darkness her hand crept and found his. "Do you believe in ghosts?" she asked.

"I don't know."

"I have a dream all the time that I'm searching for my family and can't ever find them."

"I never saw nothing that suggested we go on."

"So you think this is it? That once we die, we just cease to exist? That all we experienced, all we saw, is just gone."

He could remember spending his life working on cars and teaching himself the guitar. He'd led a perfectly mediocre life, so that all he could see was him driving the Barracuda once it was ready and playing a few songs, Don McClean and the Animals and even some Jim Croce. Talk of the afterlife was reserved for church and ghosts were saved for Hallow-een.

"I guess not," he said finally but not convinced. "I mean, if that's what you believe, that's fine, I suppose. It just seems sad and depressing to me, a bit fatalistic, and could lead to a cynical world view. No account-ability, if this is all there is."

"I suppose you think we get our just desserts when we die. Good people go to heaven and bad folks go to hell."

"It makes more sense to me," she said after a moment of introspec-tion to consider his position.

Dillon just shook his head. "No ma'am, not me. Too much coincidence. But that seems to be the only two choices, doesn't it? Either we die and are judged or we die and nothing."

"You have a third option?"

"What if we die and just keep doing what we're doing, what we know and what we're used to and what we love."

"There'd be an awful lot of ghosts roaming around," she acquiesced. "They'd probably run into each other."

"Not necessarily," he said, really studying his position. "You don't do what I do, so if I'm just doing what I do when I die, then I wouldn't necessarily meet you. Maybe grandma likes watching her shows on the tube. Maybe the old teacher likes to read books in the library. Maybe the housewife from England in the Middle Ages likes to churn butter. If they're all just going on, experiencing their reality, there's no guarantee they'll run into any other soul."

"I like it," she said, matter-of-factly. "We all just go on, doing what we're doing."

"What do you want for?"

She looked longingly up the hill. "To finally make it home. You?"

He gripped the steering wheel and stared at the speedometer, and thought about how much he liked driving it, but said, "Me too," like he were admitting a deep, dark secret.

He put the car in park, but left it running. "I don't see anything near-by."

"I'll be okay. It really isn't far now." And then, almost to herself, "I really miss them."

"You want my jacket?"

"If you want. I'm just over the hill. Give me your address and I'll send it back to you."

"I'd like to see you again," he said. Corny, he hung his head and shut his eyes and laughed at himself. "What I mean is…" he looked up. His passenger seat was empty.

The car door never opened – he never heard it. He looked around for her. He got out. She must have left the car. Walking into the headlights, he searched the darkness, searched for a sign, a rustling of underbrush, the sound of footsteps, laughter, something. All was quiet, a still late-au-tumn night in the middle of nowhere; he was freezing and his jacket was gone.

He drove slowly on up the hill, searching for her, calling her name, and passed a lonely cemetery and then he saw a lone house on the ridge he pulled into the drive and raced up to the porch. He banged on the door till it opened and a middle-aged man walked outside.

"Who's there!" he called.

"Sorry for the lateness sir, but I was just driving…"

"Who's there?!"

From inside a woman: "Who was it?"

"My name is Dillon." He stood right in front of the man who looked through him and all around.

"No one."

The woman appeared at the door.

Dillon said, "Ma'am, I think your daughter…"

"It's cold, Tom," the woman said. "Come back in."

"I heard a car," the man, Tom, said, and looked at Dillon's Barracuda but looked right through it. "I thought it might be another boy."

She hugged her arms. Dillon looked from one to the other, long since tired of trying to communicate. "It's about time for another one, sure enough. They seem to describe Ashley right. You think…?"

Tom scoffed, gave another glance around, then led his wife back inside, slamming the door closed. Dillon leaned against it and found he could hear their conversation still.

"Bunch of assholes all them boys are," Tom was saying.

"But…"

"She's been dead thirty years. Someday, maybe after we're dead and gone, maybe then they'll let it go."

Dillon's mouth hung open. He leaned on the door, clawed at it. She had been his car and she had spoken to him and she had sat with him … and they both acted like he wasn't even there. And they said she'd been dead thirty years, and she'd sat with him…

The 'Cuda's tires spit gravel as he pulled back out onto the highway, and Dillon raced to the one other place he thought he could get answers.

The waitress stood in the middle of the floor, flanked by the trucker and the greasy bartender. Beads of sweat dotted her brow and her hair was soggy and drooping, her eyeliner smeared. Dillon thought he'd feel better getting answers here, but upon entering the diner he felt queasy and stumbled back against the wall.

"Don't you remember," the girl was saying. "He was first. His muscle car wrecked on this highway back in the early seventies. They say he died instantly, but you can still see his car, trying to get home. And she … she's always hitchhiking. People always talk about picking her up and then she vanishes right before they reach her destination. It isn't her home but the cemetery. They found each other this time. Somehow this time they found each other. They were here. I got scared and dropped the tray. That's who I was waiting on."

Dillon shook his head as he backed away through the door. It was all he could do. He could not comprehend what he was hearing, but merely stare at his hands then to the unopened door, his mouth agape, his eyes wide, as he now stood outside looking at diner. He'd passed through the door without even opening it. He returned to his car and revved the engine, tried to scream over the noise of the Barracuda. The tires threw gravel as he peeled from the drive to the paved road, and soon he was back on 365, headed into the night, almost home, still shaking. He just had to make it home.

❦

Listless like he's stuck in a fog, perhaps because it feels like years since he was home and perhaps it's because he's been driving so long that the terrain always appears the same, Dillon steers his car onto Arkansas State Highway 365. Above him the pines sway, illuminated by the gibbous moon as wisps of clouds drift slowly across the firmament. He wipes condensation off the windshield and his palm comes back frigid and wet, and from the dash the vents cough out the heat asthmatically, but this is nothing new…

MY FATHER'S HOME

I stand in front of my father's house on Evers Street, staring at the boards over the front windows like duct tape over the mouth so no one can hear it scream. The street is empty this time of night. Always has been. That's what he loved about this neighborhood: they always rolled up the sidewalks at the same time every night.

If anyone were to see me, they might think I walk aimlessly. My head down, hands tucked in my coat pockets. No on would recognize me. It's been years and I've changed my name, anyways. If I showed them a picture of me when I was thirteen or if I told them my real name, they'd remember. In a heartbeat, they'd remember. No one in this city will ever forget. They'd know who I was and who my father was and they'd fear me, more than likely, imagining that the sins of the father are passed to the son.

A couple jog past me as I cross a neighborhood park. It's cool and the man and woman are dressed in neon spandex that accentuates each muscular curve. I watch her closely much as I imagine my father might have. I feel sick watching her with his eyes and force myself to look away as I walk on. Luckily, they move at a fast pace and are out of view quickly.

The park leads to a pedestrian bridge that rises over an expressway that is still busy enough with cars this time of evening, probably mostly people coming home from work to their families. This was usually when my father would leave the neighborhood to start his other job. Not the one at the electric company, reading meters. The other one. The one that they got him on. He'd have come to this park regularly. There were a few female joggers who weren't as lucky as the one I saw tonight. She gets to go home. She gets to pretend that she's safe, next to her man, and that monsters no longer exist. Still, if she knows anything about this city, she might wonder if the monster still lurks in the shadows. If somehow it weren't slayed. Or maybe it reproduced.

I cross the pedestrian bridge and see the downtown and *smell* downtown and it is the first time I really admonish myself for returning to this city. I shouldn't even go to the job interview tomorrow. I should just go home and tell my wife I didn't get it, and we'll stay far away, and everything will be okay. Though as I think these things, I still cross the bridge and enter the tenements of downtown. I smell the sewer and the disease. Downtown is busier. The sidewalks are still alive, but the alleyways are just as dark. Every manner of humanity exists at all times here. My father wouldn't have seen them as humans. He would have seen them as something else. Something less.

The first time we went to stay with him at his new place after the divorce, I remember asking him about this spot on the wall. It was reddish brown. Just a little spot. He said he'd killed a fly there. He'd been in the home only a few weeks at that point, but the spot still looked fresh. Turns out, he'd "killed that fly" only two days before we arrived. That's how he saw them: as insects.

A dirty man in a ragged dun coat buzzes around me, shoving a flyer in my face. I wave him away and keep walking, head down. I see a beat cop on the other corner talking to a couple of women in fishnets and tight bodices. He eyes me for a second, so I avert my gaze, sure he recognizes me. I wonder if my father did the same thing even as I'm sure the policeman, also thinking about my father, is warning these women against being on the streets. My father proved time and again streets weren't safe.

The building on the corner of Main and 5th looks as though it should be condemned. It's dirty and stained with all manner of filth. I buzz the number (I have memorized the address after so many years of staring at it) and when the voice asks who it is, I proclaim the words I'd prepared so carefully.

"John Silver," I say, a close but not accurate pseudonym for my real name, invoking my born middle name and mother's maiden name. "We had an appointment." I feel a jolt up my spine, tingling and buzzing me, from using a pseudonym that could potentially tie me back to my real identity and, therefore, to my father, and I wonder if he felt the same when he played with the police.

The door unlatches and I pull it open before she can change her mind, then take the stairs to the second floor and find her apartment easily. She stands in front of the door, her hand behind her and on the knob, I think, as I top the last riser, hoping I'm sure to get a good look at me.

She eyes me suspiciously, her left eye squinting from old injuries from which she's never fully recovered. She's impossibly skinny with blotchy skin, her tee stained various shades of dark and her sweatpants baggy, her pale feet bony and flat. I force my eyes up. My father was a foot man. Her cheeks are sunken, her hair stringy and unkempt. There is a greasy quality to her, like she's a silverfish that's been plucked from a mud puddle.

My phone rings as I reach out to shake her hand. I glance to see the number is local and know it's probably one of two people who might call me. She spies my hand and offers it a quick, limp shake before pulling it away and casting her door open for me to enter.

Her apartment is small and smells of old cigarettes and booze. A sulfurous tint hangs over the entirety of the apartment. I find it ironic that having survived my father, she's been reduced to the very thing he saw her as in the first place. Is that survival?

She offers me some coffee and I abstain. I have to sleep, I say.

"So you're writing a book? Why in God's name?"

"The story needs to be told. Your story needs to be told. Of course, I've worked it out with my publisher that you'll get some of the royalties. You deserve it, after all."

This is a lie. There is no book. At least, not from me. Not my line of work. Not even a hobby of mine. But they are the best way to reach such people. Survivors. Stroke the ego.

"What about the families of the other victims?"

"Some didn't have families," I say. "But the one's they found, sure."

She sits across from me and takes a pull at a bottle of Jim Beam that she'd already been working on, as the bottle's half empty. At this range, in this light, I can see her age around her eyes and mouth and in the strands of hair that are no longer as dark as the rest.

"You look familiar," she says, and for a minute I catch my breath as she lets her eyes roam over me.

"I guess I have one of those faces," I say as she takes a drag off her cigarette and raises the bottle to her lips.

"So, what do you want to know?"

"Well, the story really is about you and who you were then and who you are now. I have a lot of research on him, but only what they released about you publicly during the trial."

She shrugs. "My mother was a prostitute and I was her only little girl. I was trying to rise above, you know. I'd just enrolled in the community college. He caught me getting off the train one night."

I nod. This was all in the court transcripts. "That's fine, but I want to humanize you," I say. "I want to know who it was that was able to beat him. How did you do it? What did you feel?"

She shook her head and looked away. I saw her eyes well up, and with the cigarette in her hand, she pointed toward her door.

"Turn around," she says, and I do, and I see a series of locks up the side of the door, like something out of a cartoon. She has deadbolts and chain locks and latch locks and reinforced hinges hidden from the outside. I look to the windows visible from where I sit and see that they've been nailed shut. She follows my gaze for a second before looking at me and nodding.

"Even the one at the fire escape?" I ask, and when she nods and takes a draw on her cigarette, I quip, "Isn't that a safety hazard?" but the joke doesn't go over.

"Does it look like I beat him?" she asks. "People tell me how strong I am. How I won. I beat the monster, but this don't feel like winning. I didn't finish college. I live off my disability that he gave me. I lived because I was scared. I was scared of him, of dying. And secretly, you know, I wanted to die. I wanted it to end right there, but I was scared too of being seen like a failure."

As she speaks, her tears are falling and her voice gets louder and louder like a screeching beetle and I feel the beginnings of a headache coming on, and I remember going to see my dad after he was sentenced and he looked so much different. Like the face I'd known as my father was a mask and this was the real face. There was nothing in his eyes but a dull matte blackness, and his voice was monotone. It was the one and only time I saw him in prison.

"You know you found the right one," he said, "because they sound like razors. Their voices cut into your brain so much it hurts and there is only one way to stop it."

"You alright?" she asks. I look up and nod. Since planning on coming back to this city, this has been happening more and more.

"Have you sought help in the years since—"

"Yes," she says matter-of-factly. "Three therapists over the past ten years. They all try to remind me that I survived. That I beat him. That I accomplished something."

As a response to this, she takes another pull from the bottle and another drag from the smoke before tapping the ash in the glass tray on the table by her chair.

"You sure I can't get you something?" she asks and uncrosses then crosses her legs. I see the bruises on her shins and know those aren't from my father and I realize then how she's subsidized her income over these years. Returned to the family trade.

"I'm fine, really." I say and choke down revulsion like it was the greasy burger I'd eaten earlier at the diner just a mile from my old house.

I get up to leave, turn to face the door and stop, then turn around to see her sitting there, her insect legs rubbing together like she could get them to chirp like a cricket. Her fly-like eyes bulging out of her pale, thin face. Like I can see her skull. A blue vein throbs in her forehead.

"Can I visit you again? Maybe in a few weeks? Like I said, this is your story and I want to get it right. What happened then. How it started. How you beat him. And the ending."

She nods and says sure and rises but I wave her away, open the door and shut it behind me, feeling sick and my head pounding, I make my way to the stairs even as I hear the locks all latch. I know she'll unlatch them when I return.

As I return across the bridge and return through the park, my head clears. I know it would be best not to return those two phone calls, to fly back home and tell my wife I didn't get the job, but still I check my voicemail even as I walk back to my father's house and open the door.

Two messages.

"This is Captain Ross. I'm afraid we need to move your appointment tomorrow to two, if that's alright. I know you flew into town for this, and I apologize. Please rest assured that we are very interested in a cop with your credentials joining our detective's division, and we are looking forward to meeting with you. Still, if this conflicts with your departure flight, let me know and we'll work something out. Looking forward to speaking with you."

"Hi Detective Black. This is Andrea at Midtown Realtors. Yes, the house on Evers Street is available, and with your loan approval you should have more than enough for renovations after purchase price. I still think we can get them down some. Let me know if you're still interested."

I stare up at the house, mentally retracing my steps through all the rooms. I know it's too late to call my wife. I call the captain's number and get a voicemail and say that two o'clock will work fine. I also get the voicemail of the realtor and tell her to see if they'll come down ten thousand and imagine all the things I could do with this house, once its mine. I can get this job and move my family here and once we are back in my house, then I can revisit the one woman who survived and, at some point perhaps, see how many others are out there that my father missed.

TO GO A SOULIN'

ordy shielded himself against the wind as the lawyer unlocked the front door, and they stepped inside to the grand front hall as quickly as possible. Gordy's eyes immediately cut left to the shamble of boards that had been nailed up to block off the east wing. Not as bitterly cold as outside, still there poured a draft from between the boards that smelled of rank dust and claustrophobic air.

"He was afraid," Gordy said.

"Of what?" the attorney asked.

Gordy tried to imagine the house alive with his parents, with his uncle as a young man, of grandparents and cousins and aunts and other uncles and friends of the family, of children and adults and teenagers and fiancés and fiancées. He'd heard stories and was sure the house could accommodate comfortably such a battalion, though he couldn't remember seeing it for himself. For as long as he could remember, it had only been he and his uncle.

"Of Death," Gordy said. "He didn't want to die."

"But he has, and your uncle has left you a number of items to complete before you receive your sum of the inheritance." Still cradling the briefcase against his chest, the attorney was careful to open it and extract a collection of papers stapled together, and managed to hand that paper over before clasping the briefcase without spilling out anything else. The papers contained a catalogue of to-do items and a list of what was to be donated, sold, or destroyed, and if dispersed where and how it should go. Still, there would be plenty left to Gordy even after the funeral costs were covered and the last of the medical bills paid.

"How long have you been coming to this house?" Gordy asked the attorney.

"Your uncle had my father on retainer until he retired back before you were taken in. Law school seemed a reasonable vocation, so I took up my father's client list when he could no longer serve."

"Congratulations, by the way," Gordy said. "I heard your wife is expecting."

They entered the study where Gordy found some of his uncle's port and poured them both a glass. The lawyer thanked him sheepishly, said he didn't know if it was a boy or girl yet, just that the baby appeared to be developing well in the womb. It was Gordy who steered the conversation back on course.

"I really don't like the idea of staying here any longer." He had an apartment back where he went to college, and while his professors understood that this was his only family and gave him as much time as needed to get the affairs in order, he was anxious to get back. He was not his uncle; though this was the only home he could remember and his uncle had been a caring man who had provided for him, this house was too big and too much for a single person.

"That is, unfortunately, a stipulation of the will, and as an agent of the court I am bound by the law and by your uncle's wishes to ensure that you meet that requirement in order to secure your inheritance."

Gordy downed the last of his port and poured another glass. The lawyer, he noticed, had only taken a few sips. "Jesus," he said, another drink washing down his throat, "nobody but lawyers talk like that."

The man smiled as though the stick up his ass was just slightly uncomfortable.

"I'll bring the urn tomorrow, of course. Your uncle wants it placed in his suite. I'll also check on your progress. In the meantime, if there is anything you need, don't hesitate to phone me at any time. I'll have my cell on me always. For what it's worth, Merry Christmas, sir."

"Sure thing," Gordy said as he showed the attorney to the door.

Back in the study, Gordy combined the attorney's undrunk portion with more from the bottle and sipped and rummaged the liquor cabinet for whatever else he might imbibe. He'd made doubly sure that his instructions had not that the alcohol be rationed out to some wine collector or old friend or that the stores were to be sold on EBay. "Waste not, want not," the best mantra Gordy could bring to mind, and his favorite when it came to liquor in general, and he passed the next few hours meandering through the halls of the unsealed section of the old manor and reminiscing about the Christmases long since passed.

As the night waned on, Gordy, lost in drink and memories, buried himself so deeply in the study that he could still here the plaintive wails of his uncle calling him to dinner, echoing through the dark and silent halls, and so engrained in the past that at these times he turned, expecting to find his uncle, catching only the fleeting shadow of movement that he attributed to the drink as the phantom sounds faded to susurrations and then to nothing, not even an echo.

The lawyer found him the next morning slumped in his uncle's chaise lounge in the study, the goblet bone dry and on its side on the floor by the chair. But it wasn't until the attorney cleared his throat for the third time did Gordy stir and peel himself out of the prone position to stagger upright.

"Get much work done," Gordy slurred, unsure if he was asking himself or confessing to the attorney, deciding only that he was still inebriated from the night before.

"I brought the urn, sir," the attorney said, displaying the metal box held in both hands.

Gordy led him from the study and up the stairs to his uncle's suite, and the box found its way to the mantle of the fireplace. Gordy, perhaps due to the draft blasting through the walls that sobered him more, decided to make a fire in the stone firebox. He pulled out logs from the abutting wood box and laid them on the hearth, and he cleaned out the ashes and spread a bit of kindling and lit a starter log he'd found in a box next to the stacks of oak and green pine. Soon the suite warmed and a healthy flame brightened the large room.

"I think I'll sleep in here tonight," Gordy said, feeling the invitation of his uncle's old room.

"I think you should, sir," the attorney agreed.

"Would you like a drink?" Gordy asked, then thought better of it, and added, "Or something to eat? I could go for some lunch."

"I really must be getting back to town, sir," the attorney said.

"It's no trouble," Gordy said, and heard the excitement in his own voice. The whispers and fleeting glances from the night before returned, now less susceptible to the rationale he'd attributed to them, and while the room was inviting, the rest of the house was decidedly cold and dark. He could not ignore what he'd seen, what he'd heard, and the drunk logic he'd used to dismiss the visitations now failed miserably in the light of day.

"Is everything okay?" the attorney asked.

The bedroom window was scarred with iron latticework that formed diamond patterns of glass and played shadows on the far wall, but the window stood where direct sunlight could never reach it, and it struck Gordy for the first time just how resistant to sunlight this house was. Every shudder drawn, every window closed, and not enough windows to provide natural light into this too-large home, as though his uncle were an enemy to the day. So, when the attorney left, Gordy set about the house, opening as many shudders as he could, leaving only those shut where the window was in a state of disrepair or the glass missing, the weather-stripping dry and cracked, the framework rusted or busted. Still, as he stood in the great hall in the middle of the afternoon, the house still succumbed to the darkness, Gordy found his interest peaked at the sealed off portion of the manor from where the cold draft seemed to originate.

With crowbar and hammer procured from the shed in the back yard, he removed the boards that blocked the east wing arch.

The hall yawned, pitch and silent, the draft unabated, a torrent or a gust that blasted him. Had his uncle, in health, driven the nails to secure the boards against this entrance, or had the attorney helped, or had one or the other hired a local handyman for this work? Gordy was sweating, and he knew he was in better shape than his uncle and he was sure he was in better shape than the suit-pressed bespectacled barrister who primly pimped his mannerisms as though he were the better man. Snobby bastard probably would consider getting his hands dirty a debasement.

So why then, he pondered, fetching a flashlight and checking the batteries, did his uncle so completely seal off this section of the house?

Standing at the precipice again, crowbar in one hand and flashlight in the other, the draft ruffling his hair like some great yawn from a slumbering giant, Gordy remembered the sights and sounds from the night before, and he came to the realization that perhaps his uncle hadn't sealed up this portion of the house for frugality. This portion of the house held many old bedrooms, an old sitting room, attic space unconnected to the attic space of the main hall, an old kitchen which led down to the original cellar. He recalled, in fact, that what stood now as a sprawling manor home had once been just this east wing, two stories with a pitched roof. His uncle or his grandfather or someone years ago had, dipping into just a percentage of the family money, built on the addition and changed forever the hall into an estate.

He entered the wing unsure of where he'd go, deciding finally he'd just investigate room by room, mentally cataloging the items he'd see but not spending too much time in any one space. He sneezed upon entering, and continued to sneeze, his footfalls stirring up the dust that carpeted the floor. He found also that as resistant as the rest of the house seemed to be to sunlight, the east wing was utterly defiant. Even where the light tried to snake through the blinds, it was obstructed from bringing any quality of illumination to the rest of the room, so that until the beam of the flashlight swept the various and sundry furnishings and knickknacks did the claw become a candlestick or the hunkered beast become a sofa. Gordy called to mind the creeping things from the night before, and imagined again the settling house moaned to him in his uncle's voice, and the billow of a drape caught in an alien draft was the movement of some visitant to this abandoned abode. He hurried his pace, not satisfied that the house would be secure till he'd seen every room, but he was sure he didn't want to be caught in the east wing after sunset, as unreasonable fears played with his isolated imagination, suggesting danger.

In the east wing parlor, he found a book. The parlor was filled with the normal trappings found in any such room in the country, and came with its own stone fireplace not dissimilar to the one in the master suite or in the study, but the book stood out to him because of where it was placed and because of its cover, which he could see easily enough when the beam of his light fell on it. He stood at the door, hesitant to enter. The book appeared leather-bound, the cover adorned with a goat-like head with furled horns on either side, its title written in embossed gold script in a language he thought was Latin. It rested, closed, on the coffee table, as though someone had been reading it and had left it there with a place holder till they could return to it.

Despite his better judgment, his fear and his curiosity clawing from opposing sides at his intrepidness, but his curiosity winning out with this tug-of-war just barely, Gordy entered the room and approached the book.

He sat on the dust-covered couch with a plop and a plume of dust and coughed then sneezed again, bent and placed the crowbar to his side, and ran his fingers over the letters.

"Mort-i-mag-o-leg-is," he sounded out. He ran the sounds over his tongue a few more times, then said *"Mortimagolegis."*

It was a hefty tome, its gilded-edged pages like something out of an old family Bible, easily torn if not carefully handled. The first letter of each chapter was embossed in gold and twisted into a vine-entwined ani-mal. The thin scrawls were serpents and the fat blocked letters rams—an M more resembled a bat, and a V resembled more a stag's glaring face. He tried it with one hand and found, like a family Bible, it was too heavy. He'd have to make a choice: the crowbar, the flashlight, or the book--two but not all three. He was surprised he was considering bringing the book back at all. That face on the front, goat-like but the furrowed brow, the pupil-less eyes unblinking, and the teeth in the snout more carnivorous than any goat he'd ever seen giving it a demonic appearance, suggested that any trepidation he felt about the east wing could have come directly from this source. Perhaps this was why his uncle had shut up the house, for such a book could contain nothing pure. Gordy rose, even as the front door thundered a knock that echoed through the halls, and in that second he resolved himself to take the flashlight and the crowbar and leave the book, and nearly in a sprint he hurried out of the east wing and back into the great hall as someone rapped at the knockers again.

"Coming!" he called, nearly tripping over the boards, and decided he could easily take the hammer and pound the boards back into place to reseal that section of the house again. He reached the door as another knock rolled through the halls, swung the door open, and stood bemused and on the border of fear.

No one was there.

He stepped out onto the landing to look across the expanse of the yard; dusk would arrive soon, the lengthening shadows and dimming afternoon light a portent of the night to come, but still there was just enough light to reveal he was utterly alone. The only movement came with the gentle breeze rustling the dead leaves over the dry, drab grass.

"That I scarce was sure I'd heard you," he quoted, then, "Only darkness, nothing more." He steeled himself with a great breath that fleeted as a whimpering sigh, shut the door and locked it.

"Not tonight," he said aloud, turned and took the hammer to the nails still in the boards, and in no time the east wing was again sealed. Sweaty, he longed for a shower, but he also longed for a drink, and so returned to his uncle's study where, as he flipped on the lights, a scream welled up in his throat and threatened to erupt from his mouth, and the only reason he didn't cry out was because in a great and exhaustive gasp his breath left him and he collapsed against the wall.

The *Morgimagolegis* lay unopened on the coffee table, the great demon face glaring at him.

Gordy grabbed for the wall, and his mind searched first the fantastic and then the rational for the presence of the book. His uncle's spirit, haunting the halls, must want him to read it; the book itself is possessed; whatever knocked for him at the door must be an omnipresence desiring him to read the book. Or what if…? He brought it with him, in some sort of fugue state brought on by mold or stale air from the boarded section of the house; or he'd misidentified the book's location, and it had been in the den the whole time and he'd only thought he saw it traipsing through the boarded section of the house.

Steadying his breathing, he approached the book like a wary puppy might approach a snake hole. He opened its cover and sat down carefully. He thumbed through the pages, finding incantations, ancient carvings, spells, and rituals. He found a discussion on the soul and another on the transference of energy. He found pages and pages of script written in Latin. And scattered throughout, carvings and drawings of such imagery not unlike the beast on the cover of the book. Images of orgies between man, woman, and things that were neither, mockeries of masses, blood sacrifices.

There came another knock at the door.

Gordy walked back to the front door and opened it, thinking about the images, his only thought about the visitor that no one would be there, like before. So, he jumped when he found a little boy on the stoop, dressed in a black suit, a red rose pinned to his lapel that matched his blood red bow tie. The boy offered a smile that unnerved Gordy, as from the yard a wind assaulted him and just above the tree line, a lightning-flashed squall-line slowly overtook the stars, punctuated by distant rolls of rumbles.

"You better get on home, little boy," Gordy said. "Can I help you with something?" Rogue drops of rain splattered on his neck. There wasn't enough of a cover over the stoop to shield the little boy.

"If you give me a piece of candy," the little boy said, "I'll pray for your soul!" And he let loose a horrible, snaggle toothed laugh and turned and ran into the squall. Gordy took a few steps forward and called for the boy, but the evening and the pressing storm had consumed him and, despite the echoing laughter, would not give him back.

⚭

The soul, the book revealed, could not be destroyed, but it could be relocated. Gordy had nearly finished the bottle of port, but he knew his uncle had more stashed in the cabinet. He could stay drunk for a month here while he rummaged through his uncle's things.

The soul was not superfluous, and it was not mutable. One could not retain the very definition of life without the soul; no matter where or what it inhabited, it never changed. But if the book was suggesting past lives, then it did not suggest that the soul could not forget. In fact, it made the distinction that while a soul may not remember where it was before, this did not mean that the soul had changed. It had merely forgotten.

Outside the storm had overtaken the estate. Rain pelted the roof and windows metronomic and lightning crashed metallically and intermittently. The wind wailed and rallied against the eaves, and throaty thunder rattled the walls and windows of the home. And despite all this, Gordy could still hear the deliberate booming knocks suggesting someone stood at his door.

It was the boy, he was sure, lost in the rain and remorseful for his practical joke. And while he was sure it served the boy right for pulling a prank, he could not in good conscience leave a child out in this weather.

"Coming," he said, and opened the door, but the boy didn't stand on the stoop. This time a teenager stood there, dressed in his red bowtie that matched his red rose and his black suit. He stood bone-dry on the stoop as the storm raged around him, not even a hair out of place though the wind tousled Gordy's hair and blades of rain stabbed at his cheeks and forehead and his left hand bracing him on the door jam.

"If you give me something to eat," the teenager said, "I'll pray for your soul."

Gordy slammed the door and locked it.

He leaned against the door, listening for the young man on the stoop, but only hearing the rain. Maybe he should have let the kid in, but why was he dressed like the little boy, and why was he not wet, and why the hell were they saying the same thing over and over again? As the book appeared, he suddenly feared the boy or the teen would appear as well, and rushed back to the study, but was thankful only to find the book and the rest of the room as he left it.

☙

Shortly after midnight, Gordy had quelled his fears with another two glasses of port and had retired with the book to his uncle's suite, he hoped well out of earshot of the front door. He locked the suite and started a fire and sat with the book closed, drinking and staring at the bed. He'd contemplated not bringing the book but knew his fears would overwhelm him if he left it in the study only for it to resurface here mysteriously. No, don't think about such things. He'd grabbed a few more bottles to keep him company through the rest of the long night, and there was still plenty downstairs he could retrieve once the sun came up.

So why even stay? He stared at the bed, at the spot where his uncle had died, his Cheyne-Stoke death rattle, eyes flitting, skin ashen, finger-tips purpling. This house had become a funerary for him, as dead as his only family.

His uncle praised the isolation and felt like a king when he could survey his land from horizon to horizon. So where had those goddamn kids come from? That's it, then, he thought. Too much to drink. He'd had too much; he always knew he'd had too much when the curse words flowed too easily. His uncle had always said only the ignorant cuss.

He sat down his glass and turned with a new vigor inspired by just enough alcohol and just enough mourning to the collection of boxes in the corner of the room nearest the bookcase. These had been brought down by hired hands from the lawyer (they were too dusty and had too many spider corpses and cobwebs for the lawyer himself, Gordy imagined) and were first on the list to be sorted. The first box, labeled pictures, seemed innocuous enough, so Gordy opened it and began to rummage, and nearly instantly felt his breath leave him again.

It couldn't be. Just couldn't. It was impossible, but there, in his hands, undeniable proof that conjured memories so palpable he could hear his uncle's voice again. "Gordon. In the end, it's the legacy you leave behind for others to sort through, discard, and keep."

"Why don't you have any pictures of you at my age?" Gordy had asked his uncle nearly fifteen years ago, an inquisitive child interested in learning then that his only living relative hadn't always been old. "Because I was born old," his uncle said, and he had laughed good-naturedly, and Gordy had said "No you weren't," and they had laughed together, the young and the old.

Here, framed and sepia-toned, pictures of the little boy from earlier this evening, dressed in a black suit and a bow tie and a rose, and another picture of a boy of around fifteen dressed the same, with the same fur-rowed brow and the same crooked smile that had illuminated his uncle's face in the firelight, that had only vanished as he gasped for breath under the watchful gaze of his nephew, his doctor, his nurse, and his lawyer. Popping the backs off, Gordy's fears were confirmed when he saw the pencil-scrawled date and name. Montague, age 10. Montague, age 15. And the date. The date! By god, the date, impossible as it was—March, 1838 and on the other—September, 1843. The dates—after a quick cal-culation and a double-check given how inebriated he was, suggested his uncle had been almost two-hundred years old! Impossible, Uncle Mon-tague, and he screamed this, and because he wasn't ready for the pictures and rationalizing them with the visitors, he took a good long drink then smashed the glass into the fireplace, then opened the bottle of Pinot and took a long pull from the neck and felt his world swoon. He blinked and imagined his uncle lying in the bed, looking at him with those dead eyes, gasping for breath. What if he had seen with those eyes, Gordy thought? Those horribly lifeless, listless eyes, that should have robbed his vision and his understanding. What if he saw with those eyes? What if he was aware of his breath leaving him by startles and spurts? What if he could feel the life leaving him?

As if to answer, another knock from the door below, the sound climbing up the steps to rap on the chamber door, and Gordy thought of his loving uncle who'd provided for him and given him a good life with good instruction, and sure sometimes they butted heads like families do, but they always came around, especially when they were needed, family always came around. His uncle was coming around now, and he was needed. Gordy threw open the door and bolted down the stairs, one hand on the railing to guide him, taking the stairs by twos and threes until he was at the door and he'd tossed it open and all the sounds of the storm returned and in front of him stood not a child or a teenager but a young man, still dressed in the dark suit with the bow tie that matched the rose in his pocket.

Gordy understood so much now. He was no longer afraid for himself, but worried that his uncle had met something tragic and permanent on the other side. He smiled and held out a hand from which the young man retreated a step, but did not stop smiling.

"Uncle Montague, you should have told me. If I'd known you were in trouble. What do you need from me?"

"Give me something to eat, maybe to drink," the young man said. "And I'll pray for your soul."

Gordy understood.

"Come in," he said and turned to light the path toward the kitchen, and stumbled and caught himself and spun again, only to find he was alone in the front hall.

Gordy turned in place, searching, pleading. His uncle was in trouble and he couldn't help him if his uncle didn't ask, and that's what he was doing. Asking, right? A crash from above drew his attention up the stairs; Gordy could place it instantly. As quickly as he had descended he bounded up the stairs and rushed back into his uncle's empty suite, and found the source of the sound.

The urn had not been precariously placed on the hearth. There had been plenty of room, and it was not in danger of teetering or tottering. Still, it lay on the floor, the lid open, and Gordy approached cautiously, sure he was encroaching on his uncle's last remains. But he noticed something as he approached, and what he saw caused him to hurry across the floor and bend and pick up the urn. The hasp had snapped and the lid dangled on one hinge, but no ash had spilled because no ash filled the interior. The urn's interior was dry and clean, like it had never held a particulate or a cinder.

Gordy thought of the visitors dressed like his uncle in the pictures and asked aloud: "Where are you, Uncle Montague?"

He should have been in the urn. Just what kind of fucked up game was that lawyer playing, anyway? The lawyer. The idea of the attorney behind these shenanigans muddled Gordy's image of the uptight attorney and humanized the barrister all at once. But what could he gain, tormenting the heir like this. Gordy got the bright idea to ask him himself. He set the urn down and picked up the portable and dialed but received no other sound for several seconds, and then a gasp of a breath, and then another, like a rattle, like snoring almost, and then nothing. And just as he was about to speak, another great gasp for air, a few snores, and settling, shallower, shallower, till nothing.

"Uncle?" his voice shook as he spoke into the phone. "Uncle Monty?"

The voice that answered was dry and raspy and filled with those struggling sounds, the gurgling, choking, gasping sounds of a body trying to hang on to…

"Give me something to eat and I'll pray for your soul."

Gordy hung up the phone.

He said to himself--a demon has taken my uncle's form, and something monstrous has infiltrated this house, and realizing he hadn't the strength or the know-how or the power to fight it, he thought: my uncle would want me safe more than he'd want his fortune secure, I'm drunk and I'll probably get stopped by a cop or crash in this storm but the hospital or the drunk tank would be better than here. His keys he found downstairs in the study after he tied his shoes, and he remembered that upon meeting the attorney, he had pulled around and parked in the garage.

Flicking on the garage light, he saw his Prius, and saw his uncle's old Cadillac, and saw the young man still in his suit standing in front of the driver's side door of the Prius. Gordy clenched the keys in his sweaty palms and struggled to find his own breath. When he spoke, his own voice rattled.

"You want me safe, Uncle. You want me safe. You wanted to pray for my soul."

The young man no longer smiled. "It's too late for that."

And then he lunged, and Gordy tried to scream, but he only saw black.

The lawyer hovered over him, examining him, and seemed to be waiting patiently for Gordy's eyes to open. He helped Gordy to his feet and led him back into the kitchen out of the garage, and poured a glass of water with three ice cubes and let Gordy drink it down and fixed him another.

"Am I safe to assume it worked, sir," the attorney asked.

"Just cold enough," Gordy said. His voice different. Older. Raspier. "Three ice cubes."

"That is how you've always taken it. That is how my father said you took it."

To this Gordy let out a chuckle and closed his eyes to the memories fresh to his mind. These were Montague's memories, from Montague's perspective. He downed the last of the water and winced a bit, then began snapping his fingers. Anticipating this, the attorney fished through the drawers till he produced a bottle of aspirin and dumped several into Gordy's hands.

"Jesus," he said, and washed the aspirin down with a fresh cold glass offered by the lawyer, "I didn't want him to drink so much."

"And what now, sir?" the lawyer asked, returning the bottle to the drawer. "Father said you might look for an orphan."

"No, no, too soon," the other said, waving his hands. "Much too soon for that, old chap. We'll find one when the time is right, when we are very old and I have used up this body. And I will love the little street urchin. Love him without boundaries, like he was my own son. He'll never suspect anything else, as long as I love him, once I'm old. Now is the time for revelry, and … do you know what you're having?"

"We are going to the doctor tomorrow, sir."

"Son or daughter," he said with a shrug, "just make sure that the family practice carries on. I can't go to just any lawyer with this."

The two men laughed. The essence wearing Gordy clapped Gordy's arms around the attorney and hugged his shoulders and said, "I'm famished!" like it was an epiphany and the attorney said that there was a diner down the road—Melinda's, he believed the name was—and this new resident in Gordy's skin asked if she was still alive, and the attorney shook his head.

"No sir, you are remembering her grandmother. It seems we have a lot to catch you up on."

"We have time," the man who looked like Gordy said. "We have an eternity."

BROKEN, CHARRED, WINGS OF SOOT

Under a gunmetal sky, Thomas Rockridge leaned on the hood of his silver 3-series while a red Camaro growled and rumbled into the hotel's parking lot, a manila folder tucked under his arm as he sipped his coffee, a grin of victory as a woman wearing a crimson skirt and an untied overcoat slammed the driver's side door and clicked her heels on the pavement – the rhythmic sound like a beating war drum.

"Give it to me," she said.

"Maybe I should call your husband," he said and took another sip.

She reached in and snatched the folder from under his arm, opened it, began thumbing through it. "Go to hell!"

"You get your husband to drop his claim."

"He isn't faking, you son of a bitch! He's hurt, bad. I…"

She was tearing up. "Since the accident, he's been unable to fulfill … we love each other." She pulled a handkerchief from her clutch and dabbed at the corners of her eyes, sniffling gracelessly. "I have needs, Mr. Rockridge. Ours was a passionate relationship. But what he's been through, I've lived it with him. But such passion is hard to give up."

"I understand," Thomas said, but understanding was not what the job called for. "But do you think he would?"

She whimpered a little.

"I've got copies," Thomas said. "You get him to drop the claim, or the next set of photos will be hand-delivered to him."

✿

Thomas poured his third glass of bourbon that night in his apartment, a one-bedroom in a nice set of condos in the gentrified downtown. Pearl Jam's channel still played on the satellite music station on his TV. Having relaxed with his eyes closed as the liquor warmed him for a couple of hours, he was finally ready to open the next casefile on his laptop. They never stopped coming.

He drank a lot to cope with the work, though he wasn't a full-blown alcoholic—a simple career change could sober him up. There were plenty of people out there like the woman he had just met who were just trying to collect what was owed to them so they could live, and what the insurance company was asking him to do was unconscionable. It hadn't been so long ago the recurring nightmare started.

When he passed out from drinking, his nights were generally a dreamless haze, although one dream whispered to him Occasionally, on nights when he would come home from the bar with some pretty little coed, he would sleep without the dream to haunt him; although, he could rarely bring the same girl home twice without invoking the dream, so the idea of a committed relationship did little to assuage his night terrors.

Neither narrative nor still-picture, but rather snippets in time, dark and hot with coal-red embers burning wherever he looked, his red flesh burned and bubbled. Around him only the ripples and wrinkles of heat warped rock with nothing smooth, nothing carved out by water, but stone charred and hot and broken by fire. The denizens crawled in the shadows, claws and nails clicking on hard surfaces, hissing like vented steam and smacking their lips, knowing this place was theirs and they were hungry. Each time they inserted their teeth into his flesh, the pain was fresh and new and scorching no matter how many of them bit. But to suggest it was merely about cannibalism would not do justice to the truth of the nightmare. Never consumed, there was never release with death, only incessant pain. Besides, to suggest cannibalism would be to suggest that the devourers were human. And while they resembled human in the basest of descriptions, there was nothing human in their eyes.

They saw through the darkness; they were charred, they had wings soot-soaked and broken. They might have been perfect, once, and sentient, but that life had been forgotten by them, and the denizens of this pit fought ravenously for scraps and enjoyed the screams of the long-suffering and the tortured.

He understood the metaphor, beyond the abject terror and absolute realism the dream instilled, and questioned the moral compass of his center, a man who hadn't been to church since his formative years.

Thomas opened the file and weighed the reasons for this persistent dream, for the pain he felt when they came for a visit at night. Maybe he had eaten something bad and maybe it was stress from work. But nearly every night? That just told him how imperative it had become that he quit this job.

The diagnosis codes were all there: 300.02; 300.14; 300.6; 295.30; 301.1 and 301.22; 2971—Thomas recognized them as psychiatric codes. He picked up his cell and dialed, glanced over the HCFA CMS-1500 form and sat the folder aside, got up and poured another drink. As he took his first sip, the phone was answered.

"Jesus Tom what time is it?" the man on the other end asked.

"I was just looking over the file you sent Dominick, are you shitting me?"

"That's why I sent it to you, Tom. Your bull-shit-meter is better than anyone."

"The legal ramifications alone make this claim unpayable. A priest can't file a HCFA as a provider."

"Look again, Tom. The priest is listed as a secondary. The girl's pediatrician filed the claim through his office."

"They got the fucking doctor involved?"

"Can you get to the bottom of this?"

Thomas took a slow drink then looked over the file again, and Dominick asked if he were there several times before he said yeah. What a prick. Dom was supposed to be there to answer calls. And Christ it wasn't late, not even ten o'clock.

"I'm not up on my psych codes," he said finally. "But it looks like a collection of schizophrenic codes, personality and anxiety disorders and delusional codes."

"I'll email you a physician's DCM manual tomorrow morning. How did the other thing go this afternoon?"

"I think they'll drop the charges," Thomas said, scrolling through the attachments.

"What's wrong?"

"Are they serious?" Thomas asked.

"Yeah."

"They think the girl is possessed?"

Thomas hung up the phone and dropped the folder on the coffee table. He took another drink and finished off that glass, then poured another.

☙❧

The dream didn't haunt him, this night.

☙❧

He awoke the next morning to dew gathered on the window, scattering the sunlight, and thought he'd been dreaming about an explosion overhead. He made some coffee and nearly slipped on the loose sheet with a letterhead and typed statement, signed by the family attorney. He bent and picked up the sheet; the attorney was ready to draw up legal papers attesting to the fact of the validity of this claim and his present involvement in the case. Thomas stepped around the bar and stopped cold before he could enter the living room. *Un…fucking…believable.* The file's paperwork he'd just printed out before bed had been scattered about the front room. How could this have happened? He didn't think he'd drank that much that he'd trashed his own place; he'd never done such a thing before.

But only the file's papers had been scattered, he noticed. Absolutely nothing else was out of place in the apartment, down to the cockeyed position of the remote and the glass on the table, half-filled now with clear water and shrunken ice cubes, the ambrosia liquid diluted, swirls like cloudy mists trailing off into the clear.

☙❧

The lawyer -- Kel Bryant, a third generation WASP with a carried-over name and clout in Fayetteville, Arkansas -- wore a pin-striped suit, was short and pudgy, his gray hair trimmed conservatively and face clean-shaven. He looked to be in his mid-fifties, a jovial man whose oak desk had been trimmed in leather, everything in his office and on his person suggesting that he was, at the very least, successful at his job. Shelves lined the walls of his office with only two windows on either side of his desk that permitted natural light, stained-glass with the scales of justice in one and Christ the Redeemer in the other.

Thomas sat after the two men shook hands and Southern pleasantries were exchanged.

"Quite the book collection you have," Thomas said.

Kel Bryant chuckled. "My grandpappy was a forward thinker back in his day. He went to church on Sundays and worked hard through the week. He believed God was somehow connected to all this new-fangled science we were discovering."

"And what do you believe, Mr. Bryant?"

"I believe the same. That science is meant to explain what God does. I got the exact same books in this exact same order at my home library."

Motioning to the books, he said, "Some might call that obsessive compulsive."

Kel Bryant did not smile. "I'm showing my hand to the world, Mr. Rockridge, and I'm not afraid to do so. I am a proud Baptist who thinks that scientists are too narrow-minded and too dependent on luck for their answers, and preachers are too narrow-minded and want to believe in magic too much for their answers."

"What do you mean?"

"Both sides are blinded by hubris. If they just opened their minds, they might be surprised by what they see."

"Like what you saw at that farmhouse? Like what you saw with that little girl?"

"I have been a friend of that family for years, sir, and that little girl is not a monster. She is a precious little thing, a wondrous child. She is twelve and I bounced her on my knee when she was an infant."

"Then what about your testimony?"

"Something evil is in there," the lawyer said. His vacant gaze drifted to some nonspecific spot on his desk and his voice trembled. "Something has corrupted that little innocent precious child."

"Then she isn't innocent anymore."

"So because this is hard for you to understand, you are going to fight this claim. There is precedent, Mr. Rockridge."

"I'd say your interpretation of *force majeure* is a bit fluid."

"And I'd say these good Christian people are due the burden of their yoke."

"They're cashing in on their daughter's illness. I thought you people believed that everyone's cross was their own to bear."

"Even Jesus had help."

Thomas shook his head. "Not if I'd been there, sir. Not if I'd been there."

The response didn't come immediately. Thomas glanced up to see the lawyer staring at him. "I got nothing more to say."

☙❧

Thomas poured a drink as the sun set and stared at the file, sure he had gotten into that old lawyer's head. He was a reader of people and he was sure. They were asking for ten million to cover the medical bills and psychiatric trauma and future bills of what hadn't yet accrued. Truth is, the case was quickly drifting from a claim to a lawsuit and Thomas Rockridge had the opportunity to derail that lawsuit.

A few drinks in, but before it was too late, he called the number in the file again. When the voicemail picked up again, he delivered his message, again.

"Mr. and Mrs. Jenkins. I need to speak to you about the claim you had filed on behalf of your daughter, the patient, that landed in our office a few days ago." He felt his words slurring and cut the message off with a brief introduction – he'd given the full title in the earlier messages and so didn't need to fully introduce himself again – and then hung up.

He drank until the Scotch ran out and scratched a note that he'd need to buy more tomorrow before passing out in bed.

☙❧

He awoke at some indeterminable hour to a blanket of darkness and the sound scratches on the plaster overhead. He lifted his eyes to a crone's finger raking at the wall and realized too slowly that it was merely a silhouette. He shifted his gaze to the window where the gnarled limb of an oak rustled in the wind and clawed at the windowpane, the streetlamp behind it shining brightly into his room. Thomas blinked to shake off the drunkenness. The limb stopped and the shadow of the crone's finger stilled also, but the noise continued overhead in the plaster of the wall over his headboard.

Thomas sat up, clutching the sheets to his chin, securely covered by the sheet and the blanket over it, no flesh exposed but his head and the knuckles of his hands, his eyes wide as he stared through the darkness to the oak and the streetlight beyond, wondering how his blinds had raised and his curtains had tied back and trying to fathom how he'd done that drunk and not remembered. He sat like that—frozen, unblinking—for some minutes, until the scratching subsided and his inebriation took over again, and he slid into the mattress and drifted off to a dreamless sleep.

The young pediatrician had proven more patient than the lawyer and Thomas pressed the doctor further.

"Her delivery was normal," the pediatrician said. He leaned in his seat on his desk, fingers meeting in a pyramid over which he looked.

"You'd have a lot of reason to say that, wouldn't you?" From his side of the desk, Thomas mimicked the doctor's actions.

"Because it's true."

"Because if it weren't, you'd be handed a malpractice lawsuit."

"I've had plenty of threats of malpractice lawsuits over the years. As have had most practicing physicians today. That's why we have insurance."

"Thank God," Thomas said. "Insurance is our savior, yours and mine. What I don't understand is why you signed off on this dribble. Why did you associate with all of this? Why did you put your own license at risk? Why did you involve your clinic?"

"I own my clinic, Mr. Rockridge. But we are networked in with other clinics in the area, including over a thousand physicians and specialists in the area. We have privileges in the three major hospitals in Northwest Arkansas."

"Exactly! So you have a lot to lose," Thomas said.

"I have a lot of resources at my disposal, Mr. Rockridge. I have a lot of labs and a lot of equipment. Science could not give the answers she needed. Believe me. We tried."

"Do you believe she was possessed?"

The doctor averted his eyes to the desk calendar that covered most of the surface. "Ouroborus," the doctor said so softly Thomas wondered if he were meant to hear. "I believe she still is."

Thomas flipped over every couch cushion, overturned both pillows on his bed, yanked off the sheets and bedspread, and he rummaged through all his drawers and scattered his own papers, and, yes, the house was in shambles, but it was his own doing this time. He had been drinking again last night, but he was sure he had emptied his pockets at the coffee table in the living room, next to the folder.

His keys weren't the only thing to come up missing. Every day he had to search for a misplaced coffee cup or a pen he needed or once even his briefcase (he found the latter under the sink by the detergent).

He was drinking too much. Each morning he'd tell himself he'd have to slow down, and each night at sundown the resolve would go out the window as he'd pour the first glass of scotch or whiskey or rum & coke. The truth was, he only admitted to himself after the second or third drink, he was scared to be sober.

He hadn't picked up the file in a week; a few other cases took precedent: one was a last-minute ditch to stave off a litigation that could cripple the company. A few of Thomas' midnight photos showed a man physically doing what he shouldn't be able to do, according to the CMS-1500 form filed by his doctor, and a few more photos showed that doctor having a few drinks with the patient, and a few more showed that doctor engaged in a few extracurricular midnight activities with a woman too young and too blonde to be his wife.

Saturday came and Thomas was without a new file, and so begrudgingly he opened up the folder of the possessed little girl. He read the pages and drank a few cups of Irish coffee.

As much as Thomas disdained the work, as soulless as the job of insurance investigator made him feel, Thomas knew the abysmal position offered him a better quality of life than any other he could attain with a B.A. in English.

Still, he didn't like this case. He wasn't a superstitious man, or a particularly religious man, but this case was heading in a direction that would leave him just as uncomfortable as if a couple of smiling Jehovah's Witnesses appeared at his door asking if he had heard the good news. The case was too dark. He liked more the adultery, the fraud. This demon stuff—he wasn't much for horror stories and he didn't believe in any ghosts.

⋐⋑

Thomas looked up to the cross, empty of Christ, outside the church, and he paused at the glass doors, the file tight under his arm, wondering

if his fist would steam when he grabbed the knob. He walked past the
front offices and entered the sanctuary where cedar pews lined the aisles
up to the dais and altar. Marble statues of Mary the mother and Joseph
on either side of Jesus hanging on the Cross, life-sized, as though the
Catholics didn't want him to quit suffering, didn't want him to offer up
his ghost so he could get on with the resurrecting and the saving and
such.

"Can I help you?" came the voice from behind.

Thomas found the priest at his shoulder and turned to shake the hand
of the ephebic man with Japanese features and a touch of gray about the
temples.

"So how are you a Father John Smith?" Thomas asked. He didn't really care how he came off. They were seated in another formal office.

The priest shifted his glasses up his nose. "I was adopted by a won-
derful Little Rock family when I was an infant. God chose this path for
me when the time came."   "And what do you have to say about the
patient, Jennifer Jenkins?"

"She is a sick little girl," the priest said after a brief pause.

"Some of your colleagues feel like she is possessed."

"I'm not a Vatican exorcist."

"Her family's Baptist. The Baptists and Catholics on some kind
of truce lately, sitting down at the table together to break bread and
such?"

"They came to me for help, guided to me by Mr. Bryant. He thought I
could help and he approached me with their Baptist preacher at his side.
So, I guess, Mr. Rockridge, in this instance, yes … we did break bread
together."

Thomas smiled. "Good, good, harmony amongst the religions. Now
let's work on the Jews and the Muslims."

"'Catholic' means universal, Mr. Rockridge. Any Christian who has
accepted Christ and accepts the tenements of the New Testament – I
personally believe – will enter Heaven. We are at such a crossroads now,
that we can no longer nitpick theology. But as I said, it was easier for
me to get involved, because I had known of the family and the little girl
since her birth."

His grin widened. "I bet you have, Father Smith. You don't look that
old yourself."

"I wear my wrinkles well," he said as a few lines creased the sides of his mouth and crow's feet lined the temporal corners of the eyes.

"I want to speak with 'the Exorcist'," Thomas said.

"You can't." Father John looked away and cleaned his glasses with a tissue he drew from under the robe. "He's dead."

Thomas perused the file and then shut it closed on his lap. "How convenient."

All smile and sense of politeness left the priest's face. "Convenience has nothing to do with it, Mr. Rockridge. He walked into that family's home a man filled with faith and died in battle. Tell me, are you at the stage yet where you are misplacing things?" Thomas thought of his keys, his mug, the file. He thought about the last week then about the scratches at the walls and the dreams he'd had, the vivid, realistic dreams. He could only look at the floor and then he shook his head.

"At least the dream hasn't come, yet. It is different for everyone, but it is always recurring, a nightmare, followed quickly by strange sounds at all hours, objects moved, but when you experience it all at once…"

"What is it?" Thomas asked, looking up. He'd snapped at the man, and knew he sounded desperate. He gripped the wooden arms of his chair tightly and had leaned forward so much that he nearly stood now, stretching over the desk toward the priest. "You're infected," Father John said. "I could tell when you walked in. You are going to get worse. You do not have the power to fight it."

"I don't believe. I don't give a shit about what anybody did for me or what I'm supposed to believe. I never felt a soul, Father John."

The priest said, "Doesn't matter. You're about to lose yours. You had a shot at knowledge once." The priest cocked his head, studying him. "What happened? The god Mammon too enticing?"

"This case isn't about me."

"Isn't it?"

✿

Thomas thrashed, disheveling the covers, as the dream returned him to the gnawing and the biting. The scratching on the walls pulled him from his sleep to find the mattress was soaked. He could taste the sweat, but he could also taste the release of his bladder and smell the acidic waste soaking the sheets and his boxers and coating his thighs and the small of his back.

❦

The sun was just beginning to rise as his sheets finished drying and he—having since showered—sat in sweatpants staring at the file.

Of course, it wasn't real. Religion was propaganda used to keep the illiterate and ill-informed from joining any dangerous or progressive cause. There were no demon possessions because there were no demons. There was only man, and right or wrong, Thomas had made—from his bonuses and quarterly reviews and the number of dismissed litigations—a career out of being right.

❦

Google maps and a narrow gravel road built over hard clay led him to the isolated farm. The fence row had rusted barbs and gray wooden posts, rotted and crumbling. A yearling wandered out in front of his car; he wasn't going that fast, dare not go any faster because he didn't want to chance damaging the body. The calf had to be nearly five hundred pounds and mooed obstinately at him. He waited for it to pass and resumed to the drive.

The signs of abandonment carried over from the fence row to the main house and even the yard, the barn. Weeds had been growing unchecked up through the rocks and pebbles and gray dry dirt. The paint peeled off the house's whitewashed wood siding. The pickup under the carport sat on four flat tires and even the bed and the cab had an unused look to them, both filled with cobwebs and tarnished chrome.

Outside wet and damp, overcast, the two oaks that shaded the thin splotches of crabgrass drooped, imitating weeping willows. A heaviness weighed down his chest and stifled the breath, humidity gluing the shirt to his back. Thomas turned his attention to the house, the windows dark. He couldn't rationalize the abandonment of the place with the recent filing of a claim from an address still in residence. Incongruent, like such a case landing in the lap of a staunch agnostic.

Inside, the living room revealed shadows and, upon closer inspection, that the bulbs in the lamps and light fixtures had busted. Windowpanes had been cracked or shattered, cushions shredded, papers scattered. Wooden legs of busted tables had been splintered and tossed. And over everything a layer of dust hinted that things hadn't been disturbed in quite some time.

But the claim was less than two weeks old. People had been here recently -- Thomas had met them, talked to them. Feet had tread through these rooms, but no footfalls disturbed the carpet of dust on the floor. And none of them mentioned this disrepair, which carried over to the den to his left, and beyond to the remnants of a dining room. He'd called numerous times, after all, so surely they expected him, and they had to sell the claim. He found the stairs near the front door and decided that he must investigate the next level after he found nothing on the first. The first riser creaked as Thomas took a step, and when he took the next riser, it creaked also. Gripping the banister, Thomas looked back to daylight entering the dust-caked windows, enough to show that even he left no footprints, and when he removed his hand from the banister, he found his fingers and palm caked in dust, while the rail's dirty vestment appeared undisturbed.

From above a child's whimsical chuckle, loose and out of place like a grin in the dark. Thomas ascended the stairs and found a hall with doors on either side. Where were the parents? He called the names that had been catalogued in the file. The laughter louder now, effeminate, cool, like the air in here; he exhaled, and his breath rose and vanished in the darkness. He coughed out an odor that greeted him with his first draw of breath on the second floor, a smell that blended sex and rot.

Something laughed again, easy and light and cool, and it sent a shiver down Thomas' spine. He opened the second door on the right, to a pink and flowery room with a dollhouse in the corner.

Twelve-year-old Jennifer Jenkins stood by the dollhouse. Her eyes were vacant, pupils like pinpoints and the blue of the irises cloudy with cataracts.

"Jennifer."

A great groan rocked the house, expanded the boards under his feet, and air rushed into the room.

"I dream of you," she said. "You dream of me. I know you do. I walk through your house. I handle your things. We have lived together, you and I."

"Where are your parents?" Thomas asked. She laughed at some inside joke.

"They chained me here."

"So, then you haven't been to my place."

"We have seen where you shit and where you fuck your whores and where you drink, nearly soiling yourself on that same spot on the couch every night, drinking and staring at your files and trying to figure out how to burn another innocent soul. They got me all chained up, Tommy, but you—they got you free-range."

"You don't know me."

She smiled. He felt naked when she smiled, hungered for and tiny and weak. "I know that pride and lust guide all of you. I know there aren't seven deadly sins but two – a great two – and two in you. You can have both with me." She blew him a kiss. "Come show me your pride. Come show me your lust."

Thomas turned his back on her, staring out the broken window, his feet crunching over the pebbles of glass under his soles. The sun had nearly succumbed to the horizon and the shadows stretched across the yard and hills, and Thomas winced, and the mattress squeaked and squeaked and squeaked.

"Shut up!"

"Come," she commanded, no longer by the dollhouse, but vanished into the walls as though consumed into the house itself. "Don't you realize yet who made them file that claim?"

Thomas shut his eyes. The bedsprings creaked louder. He could taste the bourbon and through his silk pants he could feel his cock stiffening. How many nights had exploring the cases led to internet porn or adult videos, his erectness exploding as he discovered the way to win the litigation?

Thomas saw a buxom blonde, tanned, dressed in red lingerie and four-inch heels, in her best come-hither pose on the bed—the woman driving the Camaro. He shut his eyes and felt his pants tighten. He opened them again to see a Latina beauty with similar attributes smiling at him from the mattress.

And then Jennifer, in a blink of an eye, chained to the bed posts, her eyes black and blue and swollen red, her teeth rotting in her wide mouth as she screamed "Unchain Me!" over and over again. A flash of a shadow across a doorway and Thomas glanced from it back to the bed.

Jennifer screamed, shaking her head, horror on her face and fear … real fear in her eyes, for she had seen the shadow in the doorway also and realized it was no longer in her, but searching for a new host.

Thomas straddled her, his hands around her throat, and the shadow filled the doorway as Thomas thought the simulacrum smiled when he squeezed Jennifer's neck. The flesh like clay as her eyes bulged, and she thrashed under his weight, he squeezed more, relishing the coolness of her skin. Her eyes rolled back in her head and finally she stopped thrashing. Only when she stayed still for several minutes did he remove his hands. The shadow at the door flickered and shimmered out of sight.

⌘

Dominique Yarborough drank more since his best investigator had gone missing. The police had come by twice, asking about the mess, a cop or two from the local Little Rock PD to ask general questions, and then earlier today he received a visit from a fellowship from Northwest Arkansas. The men introduced themselves as a pediatrician—a young man—a youngish looking Japanese priest with a Caucasian name, and an older Southern lawyer.

"No," Dom answered them, "I haven't heard from him."

"When was the last time?" the lawyer asked.

Dom talked about the last case, the little girl. As he talked the priest shut off the iPad in his lap and folded his hands over it.

"The little girl was found chained to her bed. She was alive, just barely. Her family not so lucky. Her father was found in the barn, a pitchfork in his chest, the only handprints found on the handle belonged to the little girl. The mother was found out back, her mind gone. She rambled about what her little baby girl did to the livestock, to her own cousin. She said her own daughter tortured her to madness. Showed her things nobody should see."

"Will she be okay?" the lawyer asked.

"No," Dom said. "But that's not what we're concerned about, at this moment. Some of what the mother told us about happened before the girl got chained up. But some of it…according to the testimony of everyone involved, including you three… some of it had to happen after she was chained up."

Dom shifted nervously in his chair and took a healthy drink of scotch.

"When did you send Thomas Rockridge the file?" the lawyer asked.

"He's a good investigator," Dom said. "Damn good. He's looked out for this company more than I have. He has busted several real criminals."

"We got a look at his personnel file," the lawyer said. "His background. Other than some Internet porn we saw nothing to suggest a

~246~

proclivity for the destruction that happened at that farm. So when did you send him the file?"

"Maybe a few weeks ago or so, I don't recall exactly. Hundreds of claims cross our desk every week. It would have been stamped urgent and sent right after filing."

"Okay," the lawyer said, his voice easy. "That's all we wanted to know?"

Dom rose and walked to the mini fridge and pulled out a glass and a bottle of bourbon and added a few ice cubes. He took a long sip and then poured another drink.

"You boys want one?" he asked the men, his back to them.

"Yes." The voice was singular, but he imagined it spoke for the group. He poured three more glasses.

"Was Thomas involved?" Dom asked.

The lawyer didn't answer right away. When Dom faced him, he saw the man take a sip and regard the short glass tumbler, cold in his hand. "Not then."

Dom asked, "Why did you file this claim? You should have known that this would have initiated a response from us, so why…" he stopped and regarded them. He'd answered his own question. "Thomas?"

"My predecessor said she'd call his name during the rites sometimes," the priest said. "He said that the father came to him requesting that they file a claim and would not be dissuaded. We think she told him to say that."

"We think she's known about Thomas for a long time," the doctor said.

They left, the alcohol festering in their bellies. They left not telling Dom about the recent homicide in Texarkana, a massacre really, where the security tape showed only one survivor, one man leaving, a man who looked a lot like Thomas Rockridge, scribbled black marks blotting out his eyes. What these men knew could not help Thomas Rockridge's boss.

Nor Dom would tell these men of the dreams he had been having lately, and how just last night he had heard some scratching in the walls, like the woman next door was trimming her newly pressed nails on the popcorn plaster like a cat at a scratching post.

They shook hands and parted company forever. Dom went home and drank and tried to repress the recurring dream and the sounds, and when little items began to go missing around his place, there was no connection for him to make.

RELATIONSHIPS CULTIVATED ON THE BIKE TRAIL

Time had escaped Clem and Maple as they walked the bike trail this cold, autumn night. The sky had settled darkly, and so they had taken a shortcut across the empty University of Arkansas campus, vacated for fall break and the Halloween weekend because it was better lit than the first section of the bike trail. Dead, dry leaves scuffled behind them like encroaching footsteps. Clem's eyes darted skittishly the darker it got, sure that every sound signaled some shadowy menace. More than once, he said, "I knowed we should have left an hour ago. I just knowed it."

"Just a little ways to the Skull Creek Trail," Maple answered, "and then we'll be home." The bike path was segmented into different trails depending on the part of town through which the asphalt stretch meandered. Running north and south, the trail snaked through woods and abutted parks and apartment complexes and crossed over and alongside a shallow water flow with a name that only heightened Clem's trepidation as he whispered its name: "Skull Creek."

At night, the college campus felt strange and out of touch, like they'd passed into another world full of darkness housing things that gnashed and preyed, existing on the periphery, just waiting for the right moment. The rectangular buildings and the angular shadows, the Senior Walk barely illuminated by a smattering of streetlights, its carved names of graduates in the concrete blurry under any light that wasn't sun.

There was no one on campus to welcome any trick r treaters, though their laughs and sounds of mirth echoed afar off like a requiem, a cry of the wind mourning the past. It had only been a few years since Clem had gone trick or treating. He'd gone with Maple and Maple's father. They had just entered middle school and Maple was already saying he was too old for it, but Clem convinced him to go one more time. The last time, as it were. A piece of youth they'd never get back.

Clem knew normalcy had evanesced from Maple's life over the past few years, beginning with a diagnosis after the last vacation his family had taken, and the last vacation his father would take ever. Maple had been the clown of the two, but he lost any ability to laugh when his parents came home from the doctor's and lost all pretense of a smile when his father and mother sat him down and told him the diagnosis.

There was a mole. The adults tossed around medical terms that drained the color from their faces while Clem and Maple tried to keep up: *metastatic, lymph nodes, melanoma, immune boosters.* Though he had Clem, Maple sank further and further into a humorless, zombified existence. He slept a lot, barely ate, doted on his father, spoke little of himself or what he was thinking. Six months after the initial diagnosis, not even a month ago, Maple lost the opportunity to say goodbye as the cancer spread to his father's brain and robbed him of his last hours of consciousness and senility. Clem didn't know what to say as they watched his father's heart slow, the oxygen levels drop, the respirations crawl shallowly from the chest up to the throat. Maple later had said he felt the depression lift. Replaced by a grim determination to muddle through the rest of his life. Rolling off him, a resolute sadness that had brought him through the valley of his father's death older, wiser about the ways of the world: *it don't have a happy ending.*

Maple's ringtone, a snippet of the Eagles "Hole in the World Tonight," broke the silence of the night, and he stopped just before the Engineering Building to answer.

"Hello?" he clenched and unclenched his fist repetitively.

"On my way home. Yeah, I'll be fine." He met Clem's gaze then mouthed the word "Mom," then shifted to look all around the campus. Clem checked his own phone, but his mother hadn't called.

"I'm fine, Mom."

Clem shivered, the wind cold against his flesh. It was too dark and with every subtle sound from the shadows, he jumped. As Maple had grown stoic, Clem's temerity had remained as thin as the carpet of falling leaves dancing over the college grounds. Over by the library steps, the silhouette of a stranger in a coat and fedora. Was he watching them?

"Good," Maple said but he looked so uninterested in the conversation. Still, Clem knew Maple would never hang up on his mother.

Clem glanced to the left -- something scuttled behind the fountain in front of the student union, the stranger now gone.

"Just saw some friends," Maple said.

Clem could read his buddy. Knew Maple was hurting.

Maple had ended their last deep conversation with, "Loss is inevitable." Clem wasn't sure if it were the words or the tone that had scared him more.

"I'm walking home," Maple said.

Clem was afraid he'd lose his one friend if he pushed too hard, but sadness hung on Maple like an old suit; he could see it now as his friend stood under the streetlight.

"What does that even mean, Mom?"

Clem snapped his head in the direction of the library. A wisp of a shadow. Fleeting. Like a whisper in the air. He felt that old clichéd feeling -- they were being watched. Around them a ground fog rolled in and the temperature dropped another ten degrees. The figure, silhouetted against the dusk now back by the music building. *Fedoradorned.*

"No, Mom. Of course not. Just me and Clem is all."

Maple's father had looked so still and ashen in the coffin. They'd done their best to make him look natural, like he was sleeping. But the skin looked like Play-Doh and the mouth and the corners of the eyes had settled towards the ground. There was an unnatural stillness about the body: no slight rise and fall of the chest, no twitch of a digit or of the lip, no slight breath ruffling a hair of the gray mustache. Even the hair looked plastered on.

"No, ma'am. No homework. Yes ma'am: trash and dishes. Got it."

Clem scanned the darkness. The figure had faded back into the night.

"Yes'um," Maple said. He tucked his phone into his back pocket and asked, "What's up bud?"

"Nothing," Clem said. "Thought I saw something."

Maple stared across the campus but didn't react if he saw anything out of place. "Let's get moving. We aren't far from the bike trail."

They crossed the campus, Clem continuing his darting gaze, jumping at every shadow, until Maple said, "What?"

Clem cinched his coat around his thin form and cast another glance over his right shoulder. "I think we're being followed."

Maple checked. "I don't see anyone."

Clem sighed in disappointment. Of course, there'd be no one there when Maple looked.

"That's always been your problem, buddy," Maple said. "You're too jittery. This world will eat you alive if you don't toughen up."

They pressed on.

"That night, after the funeral," Clem tried. He knew Maple would know he was talking about the only time Maple had opened up to him. Maple needed more of that, or the hardness would spread and kill his friend like those hard tumors had spread and killed his father.

"I said all I want to say about that," Maple said.

The boys crossed the crosswalk, and though there was no car on the street, Clem still looked both ways. It was when he looked back up the hill from where they came that he saw the stranger in the fedora and long coat and he thought he heard whistling. "If you ever wanna talk again…"

As they reached the other side of the street, Maple said, "What good would it do, Clem? I said all I got to say. I mean, why should I rehash it? He's dead. I couldn't do nothing to help him just like the doctors couldn't and just like God wouldn't, so what's the point?"

"I'm sorry, man. I just…"

"Drop it," Maple said. "Don't push it."

They walked on silent for a few minutes, the sound of whistling a distant echo. They descended the slope and crossed the old train tracks then passed under the railroad bridge's wooden structure. Heard the burbling of the small stream that accompanied the trail. They crossed a couple of other streets then made it to the trail itself.

Maple asked what the homework was in Civics class and Clem told him, and Clem asked him what his plans were for Christmas and when

Maple didn't answer, Clem didn't push. When Maple asked him when the SAT's were given, Clem told him and said that he should think about studying for the ACT's also. Maple said, "yeah," and shrugged and Clem realized this was less actual planning for the future and more small talk to pass the time. Lost in his own thoughts, it wasn't until Clem looked up that he saw someone ahead of them. Whistling that same tune. Nearby children screamed out, giggling "...*give us something good to eat*" but they were separated from the bike trail by a row of trees and shrubs.

The stranger whistled while he walked, his fedora-covered head tilted up to the full moon, his hands stuffed in the pockets of his black coat as he meandered toward them, slight and pale with an easy smile and a gait that for some reason unnerved Clem.

He said, "Howdy," as he passed them and Maple said, "Hi," and Clem kept his head down against the wind until he realized that the whistling had stopped abruptly. He looked back then clutched at Maple's collar, stopping his friend.

As Maple turned, Clem stammered: "Where'd he go, Maple? The whistling man?"

The creek stood to one side of them, down a slight gravel embankment. To the other a five-foot high brick retaining wall and above that a six-foot-high shrub and tree-lined chain-link fence that blocked off the property of their apartment complex. The path in either direction was empty.

"Maybe he..." and that was all Maple got out.

"Maybe he," came the voice and the boys turned back the way they'd been going and there he stood, the whistling man in the fine black suit and the black fedora, hands still in the pockets of his dark overcoat. "Sorry! Didn't mean to startle y'all. How you boys doing tonight?"

Instinctively, they both took a step back.

"Where's my manners?" the man asked and drew out his left hand and offered it to them, his fingers long and pale with jaundiced nails gleaming in the soft light of the overhead lamp. Blue veins scarred the back of the hand, and under that light, the man's shadow stretched impossibly long.

Clem grabbed Maple by the arm and yanked him down away from the path to the creek, then hopped the swift, shallow flow to the sandbar in the middle. Surprised, the man skidded down the gravel bank till his toes kissed the water's edge. Here he watched the stream like he was watching a tennis match until he remembered them, looked up and flashed a toothy smile that glistened unnaturally white in the moonlight.

"I'm right glad we met, boys. Right glad. You needed me to come along. Why, I could feel it in my bones. I set out this night to find someone in dire need of my services and I could feel you boys – I say, *feel you boys!* – calling to me, desperate for what I had to give."

His accent sounded forced, like he was trying too hard to mimic them.

"What do we need?" Maple asked.

"Don't listen to him. Why can't you come over here?" Clem thought he had an answer, but if he said, he knew Maple would call him insane.

The man smiled and looked down and resumed the tennis match, then brought his smile back up to them. "Why, for someone to show you that you matter, Maple. You and Clem, y'uns don't have a lot of friends, do you? Just each other? That's fine most days, but don't it ever get lonely? Don't you ever want something more? More than what your mommas give? More than what any of them girls at school would give? I could give you all of that and more. Just help me remove them lodestones from around y'un's necks and give you a new purpose, a new life."

Maple said, "I got friends." His voice trembled.

Clem wanted to cry and never so much just wanted to go home.

"I got an idea," the stranger said, his face lighting on an epiphany that produced a smile more like a gruesome rictus in the moonlight. He waved his hand in a flourish, like a magician, and like that a swirl of leaves and gravel engulfed him in a whirlwind that, when it settled, had consumed him completely.

"He must've followed us," Clem said, trying to reason.

"How the hell did he disappear like that?" Maple asked.

Maple chanced a step or two then hopped to the bank and scampered up to the bike trail, Clem on his heels.

"Followed us?" Maple asked. They each looked one direction down the trail then switched directions. Clem saw only a bare oak limb dancing in the soft glow of a trail light, and then the small tunnel under the Sycamore Street Bridge that divided their apartment parking from the hospital parking lot.

"I think he was back on the campus," Clem said, "but he looks …" His voice faltered with no words to keep his thought going.

A sound. The rustling of leaves or more footsteps. Or a breath.

"Run!" Maple whispered.

Hunkering under the tunnel, Clem and Maple scanned the darkness past the small pool of light that illuminated the bike trail ahead of them. Maple's home was closest, and his mother's car was near the door. Clem was fast. A lot faster than Maple. They heard the trickle of the creek, but there was no sign of the stranger. They had just caught their breaths, but they hadn't yet the opportunity to discuss any kind of plan when the man's voice boomed all around them.

"Why don't you boys come on out here and enjoy the night. Maple, we can say hi to your mom. I think she'd be right proud to see you. I asked her so myself, just now."

"Why's he doing this?" Maple asked.

"Because you boys need me. Especially you, Maple." The stranger reappeared in front of them, grinning under the trail light some fifteen feet away. His eyes, still under the shadow of the fedora's brim, appeared to glow like white stars. Clem forced himself to remember to blink lest he fall under the spell of those stars and begin orbiting them, but when he glanced at Maple, his friend stared dully and swayed just slightly as if a breeze raced through the tunnel.

"I smelled you in the cemetery that day, Maple. The day your father was chucked in the grave, your scent awoke me. You should know that. You should know that I won't let you make it to the car once he's inside. I won't let you make it five feet from this tunnel."

Maple said, "I just want to go home, Mister. Just go home, and you can go on your way and just leave us be."

"It ... I don't work like that."

"I'm just fine, Mister."

"I can be the daddy you lost. I can instruct you and punish you when you're bad and reward you oh so nicely when you're good. But it takes some time. Cultivatin' y'uns and growin' you in the earth, that is. More than just blood rites. It's about nurturing and growth."

"I'll get back to the Baptist church. I'll start saying my prayers. I'll get back to studying and I'll be nice to people and I'll get a job to help my momma."

"You'll grow inside of him," Clem said. "You'll rot him to the core from the inside out."

"Baptists!" the stranger laughed. "Petulant children who watched their elders and mimicked them without understanding what it all means. Evangelicals, ha! Don't have a real understanding of the AGE of it all. You have to have been around to really get it. The Jews and the Catholics and the Muslims, and there's a sect of practicing Sumarians in Iraq I could introduce you to. But don't talk to me about Baptists or Methodists or snake-handling, tongue-speaking Assembly of God."

"If I went to the Catholic church and grabbed me one of their crosses, what would you say to that? If I had some of their holy water would you say those things?"

"You might as well have a Star of David or the Koran."

"And if I did, would you leave us alone."

"You have two choices, Maple. Try to become me … or nourish me."

Clem looked down at his hands, clinched into fists, then looked back up to the stranger. He stepped in front of Maple, breaking his gaze, and stared resolutely into those white eyes.

"There's another choice," Clem said. "You can leave him alone. He's my friend and he's suffered enough, and he ain't gone with you. You wanna try and take someone, you try and take me."

The brim of the hat dipped and the toothy smile fell under the penumbra. "Why my dear Clem, all you'll ever be is food. But he has called to me, ever since his daddy got sick. He's longed for this. He wants the quiet. The darkness is the key, you see, to ever hope to become like me, to survive the cultivation. You have to want it. Despite his protests, Maple knows deep down he wants it."

Clem said, "So why not just come in here and take us? There ain't no running water between us and this ain't no holy site."

"You know the rules," the stranger said. "I can't go where I'm not welcome." He leaned to the side, probably to get a better glimpse of Maple. "You'll have to come out of there at some point. But know that even if you decide to join me, it don't always take, and most just end up in the ground. You know, faced in that moment, how many people realize that this is it? That there ain't no more than this, 'cept for what I offer them, and even as old as I am, I can't always guarantee that they'll get life everlasting. Why, I tried changing a whole host of people over the years, and I can count on one hand how many actually made it through the cultivating."

"I don't believe that," Maple said, his voice wavering. "I don't believe this is it."

"Cause it isn't," Clem said," but Maple stepped around him and once more locked eyes with the stranger.

"Believe it or not, make's no never mind to me. Don't make it no less true. I'm the only chance you got, Maple. I'm you're only hope for survival. Not Clem getting your momma's car and not the sunlight and not the creek and not the Baptists or the Catholics or any whole host of crosses and not just giving up the ghost and dying, cause all those ways are just nothing."

Maple fell against the cool cement of the tunnel wall and closed his eyes and grabbed for his head, and said, "Stop laughing in my brain!" and Clem, hearing nothing, looked from him to the stranger then knelt by his friend.

"Maple," he said, pulling his hands away. "Maple look at me. It's going to be okay. We can be okay."

"I just want to sleep, Clem."

"We can do this. I know it."

"It'll be just blackness," Maple said. "And that awful quiet."

"He'll eat away at you till there's nothing left, Maple. He'll grow inside you till there is just blackness. But if you come with me, we can do this. We can beat him home."

"He said there was no other way," Maple said, and he looked up at Clem and Clem saw, in his friend's eyes, more than just fear. Maple wore the same look his father had right before the end.

"He's a liar," Clem said.

"I don't want to lose me," Maple said, but he sounded as though he'd lost all say in the matter.

When Clem looked back, the stranger was gone, but he could still feel him. Something rotten lingered in the air. Perhaps he really was waiting for them to make a break for it.

"Give me the key," Clem said.

"Why you want my key? Where's yours?"

"I left mine at home this morning," Clem admitted. "Besides, my place is too far. I can make it to your place, get your mom's car, and pull in back there, to the parking lot. You run out and hop in, and I'll get us home and safe."

"What if I can't make it up the hill?" Maple asked.

"What is this?" Clem asked. All the lonely nights, all the times he felt like he couldn't make it through, he'd depended on Maple's strength. Even in the face of those insurmountable odds, with his best friend at his lowest, Clem had relied on the strength Maple exhibited. "I can make it. We can."

"What would stop him from getting in the car?"

"He hasn't come in here because we didn't invite him," Clem said. He took his friend's hand and squeezed it until Maple met his gaze.

"What if he's faster than you?"

"I don't know," Clem said. But he knew there was no other way. He had the legs and Maple had the key, and Clem couldn't part with his legs, but Maple could part with his key. Maple removed the jumbled key ring from his pocket and clenched it tightly in his fist, and stared at their building, impossibly far away. Begrudgingly he held out his fist and dropped the ring in Clem's empty palm. There were so many keys on the small wire band.

"Why you need so many keys anyway, Maple?"

"I got stuff."

"Don't go nowhere."

"You be right back," Maple said.

Clem stood and stretched his calves and thighs, staring all along at the apartment building. "I promise."

The wind to his back, Clem sprinted off the tunnel, the keys tight in his fist, pumping, pumping as he pushed harder. Don't look around. Don't respond to Maple's withering cries. The stranger was out there in the dark. Clem felt his thighs burn. His stride lengthened and once he nearly slipped on the dew-soaked grass. Pulled himself up. Didn't look around. Regained his footing and limped up under the soft hum of the nearest sidewalk fluorescent, and only then glanced back.

Thick shadows gathered around the entrance to the tunnel. That darkness reached up to him as he resumed his sprint up the hill, the soles of his shoes skidding on the moist blades of grass. He reached the door frame, sure he'd be yanked into the dark sky and drift into the oblivion of the outer atmosphere. Then into the emptiness of space, orbiting those stars. He fumbled for the keys. There seemed an impossible number of keys on an impossibly short ring and he was sure he would not find safety, not until the door closed with him inside and locked behind him and he heard the air conditioner kick on. He closed his eyes and rested his head against the door paneling, then reached his free hand up and caressed the door.

In the wicker wastebasket in the bedroom occupied by Maple's mother, Clem saw no liner, but wads of toilet paper, a tampon, and a photo of Maple, his mom, and his dad smiling, arm in arm on the beach. Her keys were on her dresser, next to the wedding ring she hadn't worn since the funeral. She lay on the bed, fully dressed in the red and white striped uniform that she wore to work everyday at the pharmacy on Dickson, a near empty bottle of Xanax on her nightstand. She snored oblivious to the world around her, to the danger her son was in. Clem snatched up the keys.

He bolted from the apartment to the parking lot, turned the key and choked the ignition, pressed the gas and heard the engine sputter to life. Whipping the car around, he thought that it was more than just the fear of total isolation that spurred him on. Maple would never abandon him.

On the radio, the Eagles sang "Hole in the World Tonight." If it was a portent, Clem would give his dying breath to keep it from coming true.

He crossed the two-lane road and barreled into the hospital parking lot, then rolled down his window and called and honked the horn. His neck strained around to see any sign of Maple, but he saw nothing but the bike trail. Ever-reaching shadows and silence, in the distance the trees danced. Clem sensed a trap and knew he wasn't prepared, but he couldn't … wouldn't abandon his friend. So he shut the car off and opened the door.

The wind had picked up, and he heard cars in the distance. Somewhere he couldn't see, the kids sang the Halloween song. Though the bike trail stretched through the middle of town, out here on it he felt isolated. If help came, it would be too late.

"Maple!" he called.

Nothing.

"Maple!"

The zephyr carried a whisper sounding like his name, drawn out and drowsy. Clem bounded down the hill and skidded under the tunnel and searched but saw no one.

"Maple."

"Clem." The voice was in his ear, but when he looked around, he was alone.

⳾

The fedora had been tossed haphazardly on a coffin lid. The stranger's nearly bald head was claylike, the hair on the back of his head flattened and fanning out, the world's worst cowlick. "Cultivating is all about nurturing. It's a sign of true, unyielding love."

Maple stared up at the ceiling of the dank mausoleum, unmoving. He did not blink; he did not stir. His chest neither rose nor fell.

"I hope you survive the cultivating. It's important you know that. I hope I can continue to love you. I heard you that day when you walked through my cemetery, laying your daddy in this very dirt. I heard you from this mausoleum, and I opened the door to hear your heart."

He took fistfuls of dirt and sprinkled it over Maple's bare chest, then his groin. The pebbles and clumps and small stones dimpled his flesh, but Maple could not feel it. He could not feel his inner left thigh being caressed, or the hairs on his left calf stimulated by an index finger or the arch of his bare foot caressed by the supplest and longest of fingers.

"I want you to be happy, Maple. Should you make it through this, perhaps you'll tell me if you were happy in this moment."

Maple could not respond; he could not hear the words or smell the decay of his own flesh or even think of a response.

⳾

Clem shared the bike trail with no one. Walks were long slow treks with only his thoughts to greet the coming dusk. This was how it had been in the months since Maple's disappearance.

That Halloween night felt like a dream. Even the next day, when the search party was formed, and when the cops questioned Clem, all of it like some nightmare.

⳾

The moon was full and the air was warmer, spring in full bloom, the creeks higher thanks to all the rain. It was lighter out longer. It had been almost this hour on Halloween when they'd encountered the whistling stranger, and it was pitch black then. Now, though he couldn't see the sun, he could still see well enough through the dusk to make out the pretty girl jogging from around the bend up ahead, the father riding his bike with his kid who still needed training wheels. The skateboarder. The middle-aged man trucking along jogging and huffing at a pace Clem could powerwalk.

Lost in his thoughts, it wasn't until he heard the whistling that he realized just how quickly the bike trail had emptied out. He wasn't near enough the creeks to make it to them, once he caught sight of the pedestrians to either side of him, smiling, staring.

"God, Maple. Everyone's been so worried." Clem tried to steady his voice.

"I got some answers I needed. How you been, buddy?"

Clem took a step back. "I've been doing good. Made some friends. I have a girlfriend now."

"We've been watching," the stranger said. "I told you it weren't easy to make another'n. It took me a month just to cultivate him."

Clem took another step back and they both took a casual step forward. Clem reached under his shirt and fetched the silver chain around his neck. From it dangled a crucifix. Maple and the stranger instinctively retreated a step or two.

"I've been going to church, too," Clem said. Holding the chain up, showing off the crucifix, Clem found his voice a little less shaky. "I should be getting home. I've got a date tonight. My mom said I can take the car. Hardship license."

They parted and let him through. He paused, but didn't turn back to them, instead gripped the chain tight. "Don't follow me. And you best leave your momma alone too. She's hurt enough." He paused for a breath. "I'm really sorry, Maple."

Only then did he look back. Maple and the man were gone.

HERE IN THE STACKS

ayne Eubanks stepped down off the bus and winced at the pain ripping through his knee. The pain was as familiar to him as the quirks and foibles of the old two-story limestone with iron lattice-work on the windows in front of him. The interior mostly dark now in anticipation of closing, successively dimming lights not a subtle hint for those straggling patrons lost in the pages of some tome who had forgotten such trivialities as the passing of time. The old man cinched his coat tight about his thin frame and noticed a young woman in a white dress staring out of one of the semi-dark third story windows. He regarded her only a moment before ascending the wide stone steps and pulling open one of the two heavy oak doors. In the small foyer, he shed his outer coat, shook off the cold, and hung his navy blazer on the coatrack in the corner before turning to the second set of doors that led into the interior. A young boy no more than six held his father's hand as they pushed the door open for the exit.

The old man said: "How are you boys tonight, Eric, Mr. Missini?"

"Great, Mr. Eubanks," the boy said as the father said, "Hey Layne," and wished him a good night. Layne held the door open for them with a wide, denture-filled smile before shuffling to the front desk. The evening desk girl, barely old enough to drink, her dark hair streaked pink and a sterling silver loop through her upper lip, greeted him with a smile as he walked up. She was a nice girl but hadn't worked there long, yet still the customers responded well to her despite the overall conservativeness of the community given her daily appearance. Tonight, her black leggings stemmed out from under a wide pink tutu, and she wore black lipstick, her short hair spiked.

"Are all the patrons gone?" he asked. The wide desk she manned in the front hall held everything: the computer she used for check-ins and checkouts, a phone connected to a PA system where she made the time known every few minutes for the last stragglers, a locked drawer directly underneath the computer's keyboard holding a till with enough cash and coin to accommodate the meager fines that came with overdue or damaged books. To the right of the monitor a double row of smaller screens, their views focused around the upper two floors, showing the stacks and empty reading areas, tables and microfiche machines. The only cameras downstairs showed the lobby where they stood and the two meeting rooms, one in the east wing and one in the west. The rest of the first floor was filled with private offices where cameras had not been placed. The front desk girl took a cursory glance at the row of screens and nodded.

"I still have to go upstairs and check, though," she said, her eyes wide.

Layne offered her a warm smile. "This is a place for seekers of knowledge, a warm and comforting place."

"They just…they wait, always. Why do they wait till after dark?"

"This place gives them somewhere to belong. They are a family." That wasn't much of an answer, he knew, and thought of the girl he glimpsed in the third-floor window. "I'll go upstairs for you," he said. "Have a good night."

Because of her scare last week, and that he'd only worked with her a few times – her name was Rebecca, but she went by Becca or something like that – she seemed no different from the other girls who'd come and gone, and so he figured she'd turn out the same way. She was a sweet girl, but if she couldn't get a handle on what happened upstairs, she wouldn't last long here in the stacks.

She didn't leap up, however. He tried to meet her eyes, but she focused on the desktop. Usually most desk girls were anxious to leave when he offered to check the upper floors for them, and in fact he'd anticipated such a response from her. But not this acquiescent silence; her dress suggested a character that rebelled against submissiveness.

"Are you okay, dear?" Layne asked.

"I'm fine," Becca said after a deep sigh, and rose and kissed his cheek. She forced a smile with no real power behind the lips. "Thank you, Mr. Eubanks."

Layne locked the door after Becca left and dropped the keys into the breast pocket of his shirt. He adjusted his tie, then walked to the far end of the hall, taking the elevator up to the third floor to begin his rounds.

He hadn't always followed the advice he had offered Becca. Back when he started at the library, just after college, when he was a single young man starting out in the world, there were plenty of times the bumps and shadows and glimpses in the dark had made him question his position as the new night librarian. Back then, his life still before him, his master's in library sciences diploma fresh in frame, he questioned often the position he had been relegated to. Never with bitterness did Layne feel he deserved more; his momma did not permit an entitled outlook from her children. At that point in his career, it was not the hours or the small-town library with little chance for advancement that gave him pause, nor the realization that of all the applications he had sent out and all the interviews he went on, the only job offer he received came from this library. No, what gave him pause, when he was twenty-four, were the after-hour's patrons that frequented the stacks between ten p.m. and seven a.m.

On the third floor in the fiction shelves, Layne found the night's set of stacked books. The first night Layne found the titles, oh so many years ago, he had to restack *The Count of Monte Cristo*, *The Tell-Tale Heart and Other Stories by Edgar Allen Poe*, *A Tale of Two Cities*, *Pride and Prejudice*, and *Robinson Crusoe*. Over the years the stacks of books had different themes, and he'd managed to only memorize the most unique collection of titles. Tonight's stack contained more modern authors: *Hard-boiled Wonderland and the End of the World*, *Libra*, *Red Dragon*, *The Road*, and a thin, little-known work by a regional author, a journalist by trade—John Cross' *Renegade Mustang*.

Layne paused, held the spine of Cross' book up to his lips so that he could breathe in the yellowing, fading paper, that acrid smell common only to old bookstores and the libraries and attics of literature professors. A moldy smell, the fiction stacks of the library were segregated between serious literature and hard Sci-Fi/Fantasy/Horror, Romance, Young-Adult, Westerns, Short Story Collections, and Mysteries. He might have found five Mysteries or five Westerns, but never had the genres been mixed. Even those first books, who the layman might argue came from different genres, were all of the same time-period and all classified by author in General Fiction. While he was not an expert on the paranormal by any means, he had spent enough time with the inhabitants here to know they were all creatures of habit.

He finished his rounds upstairs and found Mr. Lorenson, the head librarian, readying the deposit at the front desk. Mr. Lorenson was balding with some white tufts over his ears and sprouting from the back of his scalp, and he had a gut, but he was probably twenty or thirty years younger than Layne. Layne liked him well enough. By the time the position had come available, and Mr. Lorenson joined the team, Layne had become settled into his nightly routine. He had been offered the job first, of course, by the county, which would have allowed him better hours, a raise, and more responsibility, but Layne politely absconded and said he'd like to stay right where he was. By then the after-hour's patrons here in the stacks were old friends. When Layne had finally learned to accept them, he also learned not to fear getting older.

"You wear the same suit every night, Mr. Eubanks," Mr. Lorenson said.

Layne nodded. "It don't get dirty here in the stacks. I don't sweat much, and I have it dry-cleaned once a week."

"Layne, I been thinking. You, you have a minute?"

"All the time in the world, Mr. Lorenson. What's on your mind?" Concern wrinkled his brow, made thin his pale lips. Layne was no stranger to the conversation that was about to begin. He and Mr. Lorenson had been having one form or another of it on and off over the past few years. At least Lorenson wasn't petulant and at least he wasn't tenacious.

"This work, these hours, they don't bother you? I mean, these aren't the hours of the day mostly frequented by men our age."

Layne smiled. "The work ain't hard, Mr. Lorenson. And if I might admit something to you, I don't think the county would begrudge me a nap for a time after my nightly work is done."

"No, Mr. Eubanks, I'm sure they wouldn't."

The two men shared a chuckle followed by a moment of silence, punctuated with a few quick steps from the floor above. They cast their eyes up as if they could see through the eight-foot ceiling to the second story stacks, then Mr. Lorenson hurried to gather up his paperwork and the rest of the day's deposit. Bustling toward the front doors, he offered Layne several well-wishes and goodbyes and, fumbling with his keys, finally made his way outside. Not many day-employees cared to discuss what happened in the stacks after the library closed.

ㆆㆂ

Around three in the morning, a knock came at the outer double doors, rousing Layne from his short nap behind the front desk. He'd been dreaming of the pretty little girl he'd dated for a time when he first took the job. Once she'd accepted a proposal he'd offered. Then she vanished. He'd been dabbling in poetry at the time and had a few poems published and had tried his hand at a one-act play that he was sure would get published. He'd based their wedding and their futures on such hopes. This wasn't enough, he realized, when she'd sent him a telegram announcing her marriage to a literary critic in St. Louis.

His arms were folded across his chest, crinkling his tie. He smoothed it out as he hobbled to the front doors as on a floor above, he heard the heavy legs of a reading table scoot across the tile.

Persistent rain on a flat roof was always a concern with the library, that the rainwater would collect and soak the plaster and drip into the attic, but weekly diligence on Layne's part had so far dammed nature's efforts. He'd spent many a weekend with a strapping young man tarring the roof, years after he was able to physically patch and tar the flat roof of the library himself. Tonight, with the storm overhead, Layne took some notice of the ceiling tiles as he hobbled toward the front door, where he found a young girl, soaked to the bone and staring up at him, her eyes the color of the jade dragon statue that perched on a pedestal as patrons entered the Asian studies section of the library on the third floor.

"Library's closed, miss," he said, and then recognized her rain-soaked form as the front-desk girl. She'd changed since leaving earlier.

"Please, Mr. Eubanks." Fear swirled in the undercurrent of her green irises, swam and danced as her pupils constricted. She forced a smile but her lips quivered, and the smile looked as though its wearer was without confidence in the smile's authenticity.

"Becca?" the old librarian said and unlocked the deadbolt and let her in before securing the lock once more.

He brought her a few towels hoping she had stayed on the entry-way carpet, a bit disappointed when he found her by his desk, staring anxiously at the front door. He'd have to get out the mop bucket later. Wouldn't do to let the water stand overnight till the janitor came in at five. She thanked him and dried off, never taking her eyes off the door, never losing that worried, furrowed brow. She had removed the wet slick-er and draped it over the desk, which he hurried to remove for fear that rainwater would ruin the monitors.

"Doors are locked," he said, following her gaze.

"He won't care."

Layne asked who but Becca said she didn't want to talk about it. He said he had some books to reshelf on the second floor and she asked desperately if she could come with him, and he wondered what had changed since earlier, or if she had just not wanted to go up alone before.

A second-floor patron delivered a mournful cry and sniffling sobs that gave Becca pause as Layne went about his nightly duties. She crept right behind him through the low-lit stacks, illuminated by the dimmest of county-approved nightlights just bright enough for him to see objects and furniture (he operated the book return with a small flashlight he kept in his right front pocket), and at the sound of the wail he felt her fingers on his elbow and heard her breath catch and suck at the flesh on his neck.

"I wish we were alone in here," she said.

For his part, Layne continued humming a tune he hoped was sooth-ing as he worked. A couple of notes mimicked a yes sound, and the girl's grip relaxed a little. Only when a silhouette passed in front of a lightning brightened window did she squeal and grip his arm so tight he nearly dropped the three books he desired to re-shelve.

"This building is over a hundred years old," he said. "A lot of peo-ple have come here over the years, and this building was not always a library. It started out as a hospital, then was converted to a tuberculosis ward, then an orphanage. But even as a library it has had its history; I've worked here for fifty-six years and have known five people that have passed away on the premises during my employment."

"How can you stand it?"

Ignoring her, Layne continued as though he were giving an historical tour. This he did as he examined the spines of the books he held and delivered them to their proper space on the shelf. "They say the wail you just heard is from a woman who died during childbirth back when this was a hospital. The story goes that she was murdered by her physician because he, a married man, was actually the father of the baby and didn't want to be found out by his wife."

"How many are here?"

He'd always fancied giving a guided tour, but the times he'd had this opportunity were few and far between and didn't seem to warrant his memorization of the history of the place and its patrons. Didn't warrant, but still he'd memorized. "A man suspected of multiple killings around the turn of last century was brought here when, before his trial, he was diagnosed with tuberculosis. In a controversial move, the CEO of the ward opted to stick the man in solitary in a fashioned cell down in the basement. He was neglected, denied visitors, denied treatment, and died screaming in pain."

"Does he ever leave, the…um…?"

He met her eyes in the dim light. Her features were soft, and he felt at that moment what it must be like to be a grandfather, staring at the expected hopeful youthful child wanting to be told everything was going to be okay. When his wife passed ten years ago, he knew it was too late to marry again, to have children, but he had seen so many of his friends look at their grandkids the way he now looked at this young girl.

"No, sweetheart," Layne said. "He doesn't come out of the basement, but we don't go down there, not by ourselves and not after dark." Off in the darkness, another sniffle, another sob. "They were people once, like you and me. Mostly they can't hurt you now. I've gotten to know each of them, in my way, they're like family."

"What about the killer in the basement?"

The library had only been open a year prior to Layne's hiring when his predecessor suffered a mysterious and violent death. During his nightly duties, he found he had business down the in the basement. He had of course been told the history of the library, but he went downstairs alone after dark anyway. Layne was hired before the funeral was even scheduled.

Before he could answer her there came such a pounding on the front door; her eyes grew wide with more fear than any mention of ghosts could conjure. Layne started for the stairs, but she pulled him back.

"He's big," she said. "He could bust down the door. Especially if he sees you."

"Who is he?"

"He won't leave me alone. He doesn't care. He won't obey the restraining order."

"I'll be okay. They'll make sure of it." Layne smiled then walked down to the lobby, leaving her on the first floor.

Between the thin panes of front door glass came the heated conversation.

"Bitch in there?"

"I truly don't know what you are talking about, sir, and I don't appreciate the language."

"She ran this way man and I ain't stupid. You let me in right now and let me take what's mine."

Layne unlocked the door and stepped aside. "You may go upstairs or down each wing, but I must say you should stay out of the basement."

"Basement, huh," said the hulking man. "Which way is the goddamn basement?"

"Sir, the basement is off limits."

He pulled Layne up by the collar till the tips of the old man's loafers barely scraped the tile. His breath smelled like alcohol. His face was pockmarked and ruddy, his nose fat, his eyes black and soulless.

"Where the fuck is she, you old codger?"

Layne merely lifted a hand, pointing a finger aiming down the ground floor wing to the left, where the stairs to the basement stood behind a closed door.

"Take me!" the bull snapped.

"Okay," Layne nodded. "Just let me fetch my keys." He backed away from the behemoth slowly. The man had such hate in his eyes, Layne dare not anger him. Still, what if he opened the basement door and the man descended and nothing happened? Then this night, Layne realized, glancing up the stairs to make sure the coast was clear, might be the night he joined the family he'd acquired here in the stacks.

He walked with the man, removing his large ring of keys and un-locked the basement door. Only the first few steps could be seen from the hall, and then only darkness. But a shuffling from below helped convince the brute that his destination was downstairs, so with a triumphant *Hmph!* he stormed down to the basement and after fumbling for a light switch, he called Becca's name in a tone with as many flourishes of filth as he could muster.

Calmly Layne shut the door and looked back down the hall. Becca had ventured nearly to the bottom of the steps and peeked over the railing down the hall to watch Layne, who only smiled at her and gave her a nod. The residents would not disappoint. They hadn't yet, tonight, and he was sure the basement's visitant would deliver the same.

Sure enough, a scream, followed by the thud of steps, and Becca hurried up the stairs. The door flew open and out ran the hulking man, his rain-soaked shirt and jacket slashed across the torso, blood around the edges. Layne judged the wound superficial, but the man didn't stop to give him a better look. He sprinted down the hall and out the front door. Layne locked the basement door first then raced to lock the front doors again, smiling to himself. When he turned, he jumped a little; Becca stood at the base of the stairs, a smile unpunctuated by her sad eyes.

"Thank you," she said and when he approached, she hugged him.

"He won't come back here, and he shouldn't bother you again."

"No," she said, and hung her head. "He'll find me once I leave. He always does."

"Don't you have any family? Anywhere to go?"

She shook her head then looked around. "I could come here."

"You have no one to care for you?"

She laughed—a snort or a chuckle, something selfish. "I work at the shirt factory part time when I'm not here. I sew pockets on men's shirts. I'm one of twenty women in my department who sew hundreds of pockets on hundreds of men's shirts each day. I barely scrape by with the two jobs."

"I guess I could watch you here," he said. "There is no going back. Once your mind is made up…"

"I understand," she said, and hung her head like she was being scolded. Then she bit her lip and regarded a thought briefly. "But the others have interesting stories. They sound so memorable."

"I think this night would be memorable," he said.

Layne took her by the hand and led her up the stairs. They sat at the top of the wide spiral case, and he spent the rest of the night telling her about all the ghosts in building--how they died, how they revealed themselves from time to time. At a quarter of five she yawned and stood and leaned against the rail.

He stood. "Are you ready?"

"Yes," she said. Her voice was a singsong. Her eyelids drooped as if she'd already slipped into a dream. He hugged her, kissed her cheek and felt her kiss his cheek in turn. Layne smiled at her as warmly as possible, staring into her eyes. He did care for Becca, but he'd known this, that she'd turn out like the others.

"I'll care for you, like I care for the others."

She nodded, seemed to consider something. When she looked back up into his eyes, there was an assuredness. "Thank you for tonight."

"You're welcome," he said. And then he pushed.

◈

There is a story at the Region Hills Public Library, about a girl on the main staircase, her neck broke. She appears most frequently of all the spirits at the century old building. Some people say that she is the newest spirit, so that's why more people claim to see her. Others suggest she is searching for her murderer, or regrets committing suicide (depending on whether you believe she was murdered or killed herself). The official report listed suicide—Layne told the police most of what happened that night, told them about her boyfriend coming, about how sad and afraid she was, and this meshed with what others who knew Becca told the police.

If you go to the library and meet old Layne Eubanks, still the night librarian, he'll tell you about the ghosts of the building. But of Becca, the former night clerk, he will only say this: When she came to him that night she was in search of a home, a family. And now she has one.

IN VIEW OF THE MOONS OF JUPITER

It was her first shuttle ride since she was eleven, but the ridges of the craters of the moon were just as she'd remembered. The New System Base – now twenty years old and no longer new – rose over the horizon, a series of rectangular shapes on the horizon, the same color as the landscape because this was the material at hand to build. Shuttles launched every ten seconds in this direction or that, commanded by a moon-white tower that loomed in the distance, the rocket fuel expended in the thin atmosphere against the glare of the sun causing a false borealis above.

Overhead, she heard the automated words of the flight attendant.

"For Saturn, go to Gate 7B. Saturn's rings are best viewed by shuttle at 7p Earth time. For Mars's New Texas Settlement, go to Gate 10A. For Jupiter and moons, go to the east wing."

She fought her way off shuttle amidst a rabble of tourists and lolly-gaggers and elbowed her way down the terminal toward the east wing, pausing only at the arrivals/departures screen long enough to see she had about an hour till boarding, then turned to the nearby bar and sank onto a stool, ordering a beer. It should still be daylight when she arrived at the station, after all.

Overhead, the terminal announcer intermingled facts with flight details.

"Pluto flight: cancelled."

I got this assignment.

"With nearly eighty moons circling Jupiter, observers will see a full moon every night circumnavigating the globe."

A full moon every night.

"The last warp flight to Uranus leaves in ten minutes. Will the Brading Family report to Gate 10."

Oh, Ben. I need you now. I'm sorry.

"Titan Zoo is ready and has repaired the Nitrogen masks."

I could really use you now, Ben.

She sipped her Miller Lite and stared straight ahead. ESPN was on, the commentators going on and on about the Patriots 50th Superbowl win aided by a cybernetic Tom Brady (the league went to hell when it allowed artificial enhancements).

She drank a second and a third while she waited for her flight. When it was called, she staggered off her stool and made her way to the gate and flashed her badge and sank into her cushioned window seat.

She saw the moon's craters fade quickly and the distant stars brighten, and she closed her eyes at the thrust. The pilot announced that the passengers on the other side of the shuttle could see the Martian landscape and the rumored "face," and while many passengers flocked to that side and while she'd never seen Mars, she sat in her seat and stared out to the endless void.

She closed her eyes a few times. Once she felt a tap on her sleeve. It wasn't anything intrusive. She merely raised an eyebrow and peered out from under her sleepy lids and a single strand of auburn hair that never wanted to cooperate.

There stood a boy maybe five years old, frowning at her.

"You a cop?" he asked.

"Where's your parents?" but that question didn't dissuade him and didn't draw anyone else, so she lifted her lapel to reveal her badge.

"Detective," she said.

He pointed. "What's wrong with your neck?"

She felt herself blush and she hiked up her collar too late hide the scars. Her fingers brushed one of the three abrasions that scarred the left side of her neck and torso.

"Someone scratched me."

"Who?"

"I'm on my way to find out."

His mother appeared and yanked his arm. She apologized.

"Fine," the detective said.

The woman's eyes dropped to her neck and she winced. She led her child away as if she'd found a freak.

She was allowed to sleep, then.

She dreamed of the recent past, just forty-eight hours earlier, when she sat packing her suitcase as her best friend, Ben, rummaged through her cabinets. Outside a waning gibbous moon highlighted the limestone construction of the city. She sighed, worried she'd forget something. There must have been something audible because her friend entered and sat on the mattress, and he offered her one of the wine glasses and held the other.

"Don't even try."

"I'm worried," he said.

"It's my only option. If I have a positive lead —"

He draped a hand over hers and took a sip of his glass.

"The legends…"

He balked and slammed the last of his wine and stood and paced, and she watched him worried that he was shutting her out or ignoring her physical cries, which he couldn't do, because he'd been there through it all.

He had cradled her that night she came home from the hospital, still weak. He had taken her keys and locked her doors and held her on the couch till she fell asleep, and he had curled up on the couch until the morning where she found him.

"We have to deal with the now," he said, staring down at her open suitcase.

But there was only one thing in the now. She scrunched her eyes and huffed. "You're my best friend."

"I can't let you do this. It's suicide."

"I can find him!" She slammed her wine glass down on her dresser.

"But at what cost? I can't lose you, Red. You're all I got." He sighed, dropped his gaze, and clenched her hand. She saw he was defeated and was relinquishing himself. With her free hand she reached out and ran her fingers through his pale hair.

"If it works, I lose him and I lose this … curse. If it doesn't …"

She smiled and cocked her head and pouted her lips. Gay or not, he couldn't resist this look on her. She knew he saw her as vulnerable, and he smiled in response and cocked his head and wrapped his arms around her.

"Will you promise me you'll be careful?" he asked.

"I'll try," she said. But she knew even this was a lie.

⊗⊗⊗

As they docked, she checked her watch and saw that Jupiter still had two hours of sunlight. That was good. The station smelled of ammonia and sulfur. She was greeted by the head foreman and given an oxygen mask and ushered through doors off limits to the tourists, who departed through another entry with no masks.

"Two filtration systems run the oxygen systems," he was saying, leading her through a series of passages filled with metal piping, their boots clinking on the steel grates. "The tourists get the purist air. Ours is less filtered. Breathable, but the mask helps."

She took another breath. "Not much."

Overhead there came a squeal of the loudspeaker that muted the constant hiss of steam and grinding of gears.

"Welcome tourists. Here you'll see the mining efforts of the Sol Corporation. From the Skydeck tonight you'll be able to witness real time footage of explorers sending automated divers beneath Euorpa's icy surface, and tomorrow be sure to catch the symposium on the rich gasses and diamonds we can mine from the planet to help fuel further exploration in our solar system."

Another squeal.

"Foreman Jones, please report to HR."

They entered though another passage and found a series of offices partitioned off by glass and framed in steel. Fluorescent lights flickered and hummed.

"They don't spend a lot on upgrades for you guys," she said, following his lead to remove the mask as they entered an unassuming office with an unassuming desk.

He shook his head and slid a packet across to her. "Fucking internet is always down up here."

She opened it and began to scan.

"Why'd a bit of a thing like you request this detail anyway?"

She glanced up to see him grinning and figured he'd been up here so long, he'd forgotten how to flirt, forgotten what was appropriate, forgotten what was sleazy, and she remembered that other than tourists, women didn't come to this mine.

"A murder a night since you had shift change a hundred nights ago?"

He nodded and remembered to speak when she looked up at him. He'd been too encapsulated by this file. "This crew has two weeks to go, and we'll swap them out again."

"Anyone return from furlough acting funny?"

"How do you mean?"

"Sick. Sweaty. Jittery. You know. Funny."

"Not to my knowledge, but I can ask around. Each crew is 1500 men. We swap them out regularly because the fumes up here can get to them."

"Any new hires this last round."

"We always have new hires."

"Can you get me a list?"

He picked up a desk phone and called out, cursing the damn antique with buttons. The Sol Corporation must have spent all their money on the tourist trap above, given what she heard about the budget for this operation.

"I also wanna see the bodies," she added.

They walked to the infirmary three decks down, past more steaming grates and steel gratings and steps and were met by a slovenly man in dirty white scrubs with disheveled hair and three-day growth on his jowls.

"Detective Rachel Pendergrass, this is Doctor Howell."

She shook the gloved hand as he offered up some pleasantry in a cockney accent.

"I'll get right to it, doctor. I would like to examine the bodies you have in cold storage."

He huffed something about her being American and turned and said, "Body," as he walked to the cooler.

"I'm limited in space here, Detective. So, I've taken to documenting the evidence as best I can and disposing of the rest.

She looked at her watch. One hour to sundown. "Where are those names?" she asked the foreman and saw from the look they both gave her that she must have snapped at him without intending to. He dismissed himself and she followed the doctor into the cooler.

"I finished with the post, ma'am," he said.

"You fool! You disposed of bodies without prior approval. Those were evidence in an ongoing murder investigation."

He pulled out a cube and met her stare without wavering. "All requisite photos, videos, and files on the victims have been recorded here." He lifted his hand. "I told you that I ain't got the room. Look around, chirpy. This is it."

He pulled the sheet back and gauged her response. Perhaps he was searching for an expression of shock, but he got nothing but stoicism as she knelt close, eyes squinting, nostrils flaring. She pulled out her smart phone and began speaking.

"I have the cube that should detail a similar condition of the bodies as to the most recent victim. His throat has been slashed and there are claw marks on his torso. No sign of a struggle, suggesting the attacker either used speed or enormous strength to overpower this …"

He was a big man, this miner. Broad-shouldered. In the prime of his life. For something to overpower him like this seemed impossible. She frowned. She was on the right track.

❦

She had insisted on a private room, sheltered off from others. She said it was so she could think. She told the foreman and the doctor that she had to formulate a list of questions for the men and she had to go over the case files, and for that she needed to be isolated. They found her an unused office without windows or glass partitions far away from any other bodies. They brought in an old cot and mattress. When they left she locked the door. She slid the metal desk in front of the door. As the sun disappeared behind Jupiter's substantial girth of a horizon, she fell into deep sweats and studied her hands. How they shook. How pale they were. Her last thought, before passing out, was a wish that she'd have been able to solve this case before sundown.

She awoke with a start.

Her eyes darted to the desk, but it still held fast against the locked door. She rose slowly, surveying the wood paneled walls, fresh with deep scratches that penetrated the maple stain. In some places the wood splintered, but it had held. That was what was important. The walls had held.

She found the electronics basically untouched, flicked on the system news via satellite and prepared a cup of coffee. Her shower still intact, she bathed in lukewarm water and stepped out feeling fresh and clean. She dialed the operator on the landline and asked for poached eggs and toast and oatmeal. Yes, copious amounts of butter. Jam? Two strawberry, one grape. When the operator asked if she wanted sausage and bacon, she thought she was salivating and said yes and doubled the rations of each and ordered a few more eggs.

It wasn't until she was nearly finished with breakfast that the little girl appeared. She'd rotted some since the last time; her cheeks were now hollow and the jawline was visible. Either gum or cartilage dripped in great goopy blobs from the mandible.

Rachel pushed her breakfast away and tried not to vomit.

"You have good intentions," the little girl said.

"Go away!"

Though she averted her eyes, the little girl didn't budge.

"If you're worried, don't be. I know you didn't mean to."

"Leave me be," the detective said.

"He's here, you know. Of course, you know. It's why you're here."

"I'm sorry." Rachel bowed her head in supplication to the bowl of oatmeal with not much left. A mound of butter and a mound of granules of sugar slowly melted into the oats.

"We don't haunt to condemn. We know you aren't in control of the wolf. We return to remind the human that they can still be in control. You can still be in control of this."

The little girl smiled. She winked.

The knock at the door drew her attention and vanished her ghost. Rachel slid the breakfast tray off her lap, and opened the door a crack to the doctor and the foreman. While each tried to peek inside, she shut the door long enough to finish dressing then inched herself out. They didn't need to see what she'd done to her room.

"There's been another murder," the foreman said. Both men wore a haggard look. She followed them through the miner's barracks, up two levels to the rec room, across the port that opened to the tourist's view bridge. During this time, they talked hurriedly of the death, to her but also over her. They threw out names and the doctor confirmed the cause of death, the mortal wounds of the body. Finally, she asked them to start at the beginning.

"It happened last night around eleven," the foreman said, the doctor nodding. "It was a three-man crew down by the fuel stores for the orbiting thrusters."

"Three men murdered?" she said.

"No, just one," the doctor said, as though he couldn't imagine trying to create space for three bodies. "One was wounded though. I patched him up as best I could. He should live."

The foreman said, "One got away. They said it came for them quickly, and that it howled. They had no early warning."

"How many crews were working down there last night?" she asked.

"They were the overnight engineering crew in charge of the fuel systems for the thrusters. There was a janitorial staff of two a couple of decks up and a maintenance crew working on the stabilizers two rooms over."

"Any access tunnels leading to the level?"

"One," the foreman said, "but you need a passkey." They walked across the skybar and approached an elevator with a sign that said employees only. The foreman produced a passkey and swiped it so the doors would open.

She said, "Does the access tunnel lead up to where the janitors were?" and when he said it did, she asked to stop there first. The tunnel itself required a key fob like what the foreman had. She inspected it thoroughly and had them open the portal, but there was no sign of tampering nor damage. They headed on down to the crime scene's level, but again found the access point intact. They led her to the scene itself. Puddles and smears of blood were drying. With a gloved hand she touched a smear on the wall and found it tacky.

"How many people were on the maintenance crew?" she asked as she kneeled over the puddle.

"Two," the foreman said. We've got security running them down now."

"And the third man," she said. "The one who got away. And I'll need to speak to the wounded man also. Do you have a map of the station?"

He pulled out his organizer and produced a hologram of the station's layout and floorplans. After studying it, she pointed to a section that looked isolated and said, "Bring everyone there when you've found them."

The foreman nodded and left, and she stood and faced the foreman. "Doc, will you take me there?"

"Of course," he said, "but why did you want to meet there?"

"Just take me," she said."

It took them thirty minutes to reach the space port, one of six engineering ports scattered about the stations. The room was spacious enough, filled with storage lockers that held all sorts of tools and equipment. A closet of space suits hung without an empty hangar.

As she guessed, she and the doctor were the first to arrive. She inspected the airlocked transition area (ATA) and found it functional. Good. She didn't need any more surprises. The doctor asked her several times what she was thinking to which she only answered partially.

"There are six spacewalk ports around the station. Two are being used today for regular maintenance, a third is down for repairs, one faces the tourist section of the station and one is right by the shuttle hangar. This is the only secluded one that is currently completely private."

"What does that matter?" the doctor asked, but then they were joined by the foreman, a six-man security detail, and four other men, one with his torso and head bandaged.

"I am Detective Rachel Pendergrass," she announced to the room. She examined the four men. "I've been sent here to investigate the string of murders that has plagued this station for months now. It has been a tricky thing, keeping such information from the tourists so as to not jeopardize business while trying to ensure the safety of everyone possible. My bosses have been keeping your foreman here up to speed as to what is happening and real danger of the situation. He is aware that this is why they sent me, and why the culprit can't be sent back to earth for a trial."

"What do you mean, no trial?" the doctor asked, taken aback. "I can't, as an officer of this station and one who has sworn no harm to fellow man…"

"Doctor please," she said. "Mr. Foreman, are your men ready and willing the comply with my commands?"

The security detail all nodded in unison. She walked up to the wounded man. He was tall, his eyes blackened and puffy, and she had to stand at his chest and look up to see his face. She tried to show empathy.

"I am so sorry you were hurt," she said. "But in truth, it would have been better if you were killed. Guards, please lead him to the airlock."

Again the doctor broke in. "The spacewalk suits are in that closet…"

"He won't be needing one," she said.

The truth settled on the small group then, one she already knew and one she'd hoped her superiors had imparted on the foreman. There was only one solution to all of this.

The bandaged man hadn't the strength to fight against the three security officers who led him to the airlock, so he screamed and struggled as best he could. They closed the door on him. One arm was in a sling, but with his free arm he beat on the door and cried and pleaded. He blubbered about his family and the doctor began yelling at the foreman and the security detail averted their eyes as they surrounded the three remaining men, whom she focused on intently.

"I will have your job if you—" the doctor was saying, but the foreman hit the button anyway. The outside door opened with what sounded like a sucking of air, and the wounded man was pulled into the vacuum of space. Floating, they could see him freeze, his mouth frozen mid-scream, and slowly he drifted away from the station. One of the security men raced to the wall and puked. The surviving crewman began to cry at the loss of another friend. Of the two maintenance workers, one looked at the floating corpse while the other looked desperately between the foreman and the doctor.

"What the hell," that man was saying. "What in fucking hell. This bitch is crazy, man. You can't do this to us. You can't…"

"What'll happen to him?" the surviving crewman said.

The doctor had been unable to tear his eyes from the scene, even after the outside portal closed. When he answered, it was almost to himself. "He'll slow his orbiting speed till Jupiter's gravity pulls him down to the planet. As there is no hard surface, he'll be crushed in the density as he's pulled toward the center and boiled in the extreme temperatures until there is nothing left."

She walked up to the one engineer who stayed quiet. He still stared to the airlock, a tear in his eye. Only when she closed in and stared hard enough did he look at her.

"You thought you could run, didn't you? You thought," she said, searching his eyes, "that if you left the planet's surface, you'd be free of the curse. Why didn't you leave when you learned what was happening here?"

He swallowed hard. He was pale and sweat beaded on his forehead. "When I ran, I thought I could outrun the ghosts. I thought, this is only about the earth's moon, but as I stayed here, the wolf got stronger, and I knew I should leave. Oh God! Every night they come to me, and all day long too! I see them, even now. Like you see…" he studied her for a moment, cocking his head this way and that, ears perked. "Like you see that little girl."

She nodded. "It happened two nights after you scratched me," she said. "Since then, I've locked myself in my apartment as I've looked for you."

"Even if you kill me," he said, "it won't end for you."

"I know," she said, and drew her gun. She ushered him toward the airlock, led him inside, then ordered the foreman to close it on the two of them.

"No," said the doctor. Again, to no avail. Only when the lock was secure did she holster her weapon and look at this man whose name she did not know but with whom she felt an undeniable connection. The familiar scent rose off his shoulders and neck, something she'd whiffed for many nights now, as his smell had comingled with hers, especially on the nights when she changed.

"Whatever he's done," the doctor said, "we can fix it. We can help you both."

"Mr. Foreman," the detective said. "Please, do it now."

There was a momentary pause with his hand raised. She looked him in the eye and said, "Please," and his hand came down. There was a whoosh of air and then blackness.

ACKNOWLEDGMENTS

I'm never any good at this. Talking about myself or my craft choices. So, maybe I'll tell you a little about me.

I was born in Mountain Home, Arkansas, but I lived in other parts of the state, as well as Mississippi, Louisiana, and Texas. From an early age, I was indoctrinated into the culture of the South. This is all well and good if you're talking about fishing, handling cattle, and chicken spaghetti, and I am, for a large part. If you're talking about the Southern Baptist church I was raised in, especially within the context of its eventual evolution to Evangelical Conservatism, then not so much. If you're talking the casual racism that existed even in the most progressive of older Southerners during my childhood, people who would serve as role models to my generation, then no, not good at all.

There is a fine, thin line between Southern realist literature and the Southern Gothic. In this collection, I straddle that distinction as carefully as I straddled the barbed wire fence my granddad built to keep the cows in their pens.

From afar off, you can't really see the barbs, you just get a hint of the fence, and one pen looks no different from another to an outsider. That's the way I feel about this distinction, so let's just call it all Southern Gothic and be done with it. The line between this, then, and horror, is only a little more defined. The truth is, both genres compliment each other, like peanut butter and chocolate.

You can't really have one without the other. You can't just divide the culture and cull out the horror. Horror is ingrained in the Southern Gothic. In assembling this collection, I considered just mixing up the stories and letting the reader choose into which genre each fell, until I realized it didn't matter. Horror shadows the more realistic fiction in this collection and no story is untouched by the South.

The choice was then made to keep them divided, as the SG stories, all centered around a particular family, were ordered chronologically, so we can see family members born, grow, change, and die.

Is there some great message here, then? Some wisdom I feel I'm imparting to the reader? No. These are a collection of observations and nightmares that have both shaped and have been shaped from my imagination and my life experiences.

I want to thank all the publications that took a chance with my fiction over the years. I want to thank the high school teacher who saw promise in an early story I did for senior year AP English. To that end, I should also thank authors Barry Hannah, Ellen Gilchrist, Victoria Nelson, and Aimee Liu for serving as inspiration and as my writing professors as an undergraduate and later a graduate student.

But I was also shaped by my grandfathers. They weren't perfect. They saw the world as their minds had been shaped, but always with kind hearts and strong work ethic. I lost them both, one year after another, less than ten years ago, and I still miss them both to this day. A year before that, my stepfather passed away. Barry and Ellen are both gone. I guess, if this collection is dedicated to anyone, it would be to the people no longer with us.

But I should also acknowledge my wife, Kerri. She's the reason Sley House is possible. She helped name it and she's been my staunchest supporter. I should also acknowledge my parents, my grandmothers, my siblings. But Sley House wouldn't exist if not for Trevor and Kate Williamson, who have brought respectability and insight to our podcast, *Sley House Presents*, and Lillian Erhart and K.A. Hough have devoted their talents as editors to bring quality to the stories we publish.

To everyone I've mentioned here and to everyone I didn't, I just want to say thank you. I hope we can continue to entertain for years to come. And I hope you enjoy this collection.